The MONSTROUS MISSES MAI

A Novel

VAN HOANG

47NORTH

Published by 47North, Seattle

www.apub.com

Amazon, the Amazon logo, and 47North are trademarks of Amazon.com, Inc., or its affiliates.

ISBN-13: 9781662517846 (paperback)
ISBN-13: 9781662517839 (digital)

Cover design by Kimberly Glyder
Cover image: © lambada / Getty Images; © Stephanie Frey, © tangerinestudio / Shutterstock

Printed in the United States of America

The
MONSTROUS
MISSES
MAI

ALSO BY VAN HOANG

Girl Giant and the Monkey King

Girl Giant and the Jade War

For Lety

Chapter One

Los Angeles, 1959

Cordelia Mai Yin was accustomed to her family disowning her periodically, but as she stood in front of the redbrick apartment building on Third Street and Grand Avenue, holding the newspaper advertising an available room, she knew that this time, it was for good.

There was no way they would take her back, and she needed to find a place to stay, something cheap, until she found a real job. At this point, anything would be better than the hostel where she was currently staying, sharing a room with four other girls.

Around her, the noise of Los Angeles thrummed—people shouted at one another, and a mint-colored car whooshed past, sunlight glinting off the metal trim of the bumper. A Red Car rattled down its tracks in the distance, punctuated by the clack of a woman's heels like a never-ending ellipsis. Construction seemed constant, filling the air with the persistent drone of machinery, dust adding to the smog that forever clouded the atmosphere. The smell of exhaust mixed with the aroma of fried chicken from a restaurant around the corner.

At least, despite the blazing-hot August day, the tall buildings shaded her from the sun, reminding her of how small, how utterly insignificant, she was in the grand scheme of things. As a little girl, the buildings had seemed large to Cordi, the way everything feels vast and infinite to children, though in Los Angeles, the city seemed to grow with her, buildings gaining height with each year, more skyscrapers popping up, announcing themselves as landmarks to attract tourists and make money.

Cordi knew she was blocking the steps, but for some reason, she stood frozen in place, dizzy with the temptation to turn around and leave. The thought of walking through one more roach-infested hallway while the landlord named an exorbitant price she couldn't afford made her want to scream.

"Hi," a friendly voice said behind her, and Cordi jerked around, so on edge from her sleepless night that she didn't answer right away. A man approached the steps, pausing with one foot on the bottom stair. He had his hands in the pockets of his charcoal slacks and wore a sweater that matched his shockingly blue eyes. With his wavy blond hair gleaming in the sunlight, he looked like he had just stepped out of a meticulously illustrated advertisement, at odds with the grimy dirt on the buildings and street surrounding him.

She swayed a bit on her feet. She hadn't slept much the night before because one of the girls at the hostel snored, and another had grumbled in frustration every few seconds. The noise of the city outside had never dissipated—cars honking, men's booming laughter, a woman drunk and giggling and shouting "Darling!" loud enough for the entire neighborhood to hear, and then at three in the morning, a man had started calling, "Oscar! Oscar!"—until Cordi finally gave up and got out of bed at six. Cordi suspected Oscar was a cat, but she couldn't be sure.

"Can I help you?" the man asked, smiling so wide that crinkles appeared at the corners of his eyes. He spoke with a slightly foreign accent, barely noticeable except for the roughness around the consonants. It sounded Russian, though Cordi really had no idea, and it gave him the sophisticated and intimidating air of someone who had traveled well. She'd heard a lot of talk among customers at her parents' shop about Russians and some sort of party years ago, but Cordi had never paid much attention to it, and now she wished she had.

"Yes," she blurted out, realizing she had been staring rudely. "I mean, maybe. I'm here to answer an ad." She held up her newspaper. "For a room. Are you—do you live here?"

"No." His smile seemed to hold a number of secrets. "But maybe I can help. Which apartment is it?" He stepped closer to peer over her shoulder at the listing. "Ah, 4C. Mikhail is the landlord. If you want, I can show you."

He led her inside the building, holding open the dilapidated door, which creaked on its hinges. Oddly, he wore gloves despite the heat. They looked like driving gloves, black and decorative, with geometric designs embroidered on the cuffs. Cordi had always wanted gloves like that, gloves that sophisticated people wore not because they needed to, but for the pure luxury of it. As was her habit, she mentally deconstructed them, picturing how she would cut a square of fabric to fit her fingers, sew tiny darts at the curve of each tip, and carefully hand stitch the embellishments.

She followed him down a dim hallway, their shoes leaving imprints on the ugly brown carpet that might have featured a colorful pattern at one point. The low ceilings made her want to stoop, even though she wasn't particularly tall, as the man led her to a set of stairs. A metal-gated elevator next to it looked like it hadn't been used in years.

Her head throbbed along with each step as she fought to keep up with his long strides. It wasn't just that she was much shorter than the man; her feet ached from running around the city. This was the fourth place she'd toured that day. The previous unit had been a literal closet, and at the apartment before that, she was pretty sure something was growing in the bathtub—what looked like some unknown species of fungus.

She paused hopefully by the elevator. "It's better if you don't get on that thing," the man said over his shoulder. He headed up the stairs. "I'm sure Misha is planning to get it fixed at some point. The apartment is on the fourth floor."

"Right," Cordi said, trying to sound cheerful.

"The name's Callum, by the way," he added. "Callum Domina."

"Cordi," she replied, a bit out of breath as they reached the second floor. "Short for Cordelia."

"Lovely."

They didn't talk as they trudged up the stairs, for which Cordi was grateful because she was breathing too hard to manage any polite conversation. She tried to hide it by keeping her breath even, used to not drawing any attention to herself, but that brought spots to her vision.

"This is it," Callum said, showing her to a door at the end of the hall next to the fire escape, which let in bright sun like the beam of a spotlight. He knocked loudly, then stood back and smiled at her.

"Thank you so much for helping me," Cordi said, aware that the man had no reason to walk her all the way up the stairs, or to even wait with her, not when he didn't live in the building. "Are you a friend of . . . Mikhail?"

He made a line with his mouth and shrugged an answer that could have been taken in any way. "Don't mention it—I was in the area."

The door swung open, and a short, slim man filled the entrance. His hair was parted down the side and combed so meticulously, the lines from the teeth still defined the strands, his face covered in a stubble.

"Misha!" Callum held out his arms, but the other man didn't respond as warmly.

"What do you want?" he grunted in an accent similar to Callum's, though much thicker, then noticed Cordi. "Not another one of your stupid liaisons—" He broke off into a foreign language, interspersed with the random English word. Cordi thought she heard "Your voodoo witchcraft," but that couldn't be right. "I don't have any spare rooms for you to come and go as you please, practicing your stupid rit—"

"Don't flip a lid. She's answering your ad," Callum interrupted. He winked at Cordi, then stepped into the apartment. The other man had no choice but to move aside. He met Cordi's gaze, and she tried to affect the most innocent, apologetic expression she could muster. It must have worked because Mikhail sighed and nodded his head for her to follow them in.

If Cordi hadn't still been panting from the walk up the stairs, she might have gasped. The apartment wasn't large, but it was absolutely adorable. The open living room was spacious, with a large rug dominating the center of the floor, and furnished with plush sofas and armchairs arranged in a communal square. Bold, colorful throw pillows and blankets were piled on top of every piece of furniture. Nothing separated the living room from the kitchen, which looked clean and uncluttered, tucked in the corner of the apartment. Opposite the entrance, huge windows looked out on the street below, the rest of the walls papered with pretty lilac flowers.

"Wow," she breathed.

"I told you," the other man said to Callum as he glanced at her with a frown. "No more rooms. I rented them this morning. She's too late."

"I know, I'm sorry," Cordi said. "I was looking at some other places before this." She regretted the choice to save this one for last, but it had seemed sensible at the time since she had bought an all-day pass on the Red Car.

"Come on, Mikhail," Callum said. "Have a heart. What about the loft?"

"That's not a room," Mikhail replied.

"There's a loft?" She spotted a ladder on the wall adjacent to the window, leading up to a platform overlooking the living room. A curtain had been strung up and was pushed to the side to reveal a boxy corner secluded from the rest of the apartment.

Mikhail let out an exhale. "It's not legal."

"Since when have you cared about that?" Callum asked. "You had ten people living here just a month ago."

"Different thing." Mikhail waved his hand.

"You can't send her away, Misha. Think about where she could end up." Callum lowered his voice and said something Cordi couldn't understand.

"What?" Cordi interrupted. "Where would I end up?"

"He is superstitious," Mikhail said.

"There are bad people in this city," Callum said, ignoring him. "You don't want to end up with them."

"Bad people?" Cordi sucked in a breath. Was Callum just trying to scare her? Did he think she was some innocent, gullible little girl he could easily prank? She realized how foolish she'd been, trusting a complete stranger and following him to the apartment.

"He thinks all the buildings are owned by witches," Mikhail said. "Nonsense."

Callum laughed. "Not witches, no." He noticed the skeptical look on Cordi's face. "Never mind. He's right, it's all superstition."

"Um." Cordi didn't know what to think, but this was the first place she'd seen all day that didn't make her want to gag as soon as she stepped through the door. "Can I look at it? The loft?" She was so desperate, she would have slept in the living room on the couch if he offered it to her. That faded pink sofa that dominated the square of seating in the middle looked more comfortable than the bunk bed at the hostel, its mattress so thin and lumpy she could feel the slats beneath her.

Callum raised his brows at Mikhail. "Come on, Misha, help the girl out. She looks terrible," he added with a whisper. "She's obviously been through something."

Cordi almost scoffed, but Callum gave her a conspiratorial look, so she turned away and pretended not to listen to them arguing. They whispered furiously to each other, and then finally, Mikhail broke away from Callum.

"You can look at it," he said. "But no promise."

Cordi smiled gratefully at him and started up the ladder, hopeful as she pulled herself up by its rungs, careful not to trip over her skirt. When she reached the top, it took her eyes a moment to adjust.

The corner was dark, and not all that big, just enough room to fit a full-size mattress shoved against the wall, a small bedside table, and a chest of drawers, leaving a narrow walkway between the bed and the railing. At least there *was* a railing to keep her from plummeting off the side. It wasn't much. It was a box in the wall. A mattress on the floor. But it was beautiful, and her heart ached with longing. This could be hers.

She climbed back down the ladder and stood, twisting her fingers together. The two men were still arguing in their language but stopped when she approached. Callum smiled. Mikhail scowled.

"It's lovely. I'll . . . I'll take it—I would like to." Nervousness filled her—she wasn't used to making such impulsive decisions, but she couldn't let this place go. "How much is it?"

"Sixty," Mikhail said at the same time Callum said, "Fifty." They looked at each other.

"It's a box in the wall," Callum said.

"I don't even want to rent it," Mikhail snapped.

"She doesn't have a door, Misha."

"She has curtain, what more?"

"My friend—"

"Do you have job?" Mikhail asked Cordi.

"Oh. Um." Cordi shifted uneasily.

"You don't," Callum deduced, smile disappearing. Mikhail harrumphed, full of vindication. "Well, ain't that a bite."

"No—I mean, yes. I—I just left my job, so I have money saved up. I can pay the rent." It wasn't a complete lie. She had worked at her parents' alterations shop until very recently, and she had enough for three months' rent if she didn't eat much or buy anything unnecessary. "And I have a job interview tomorrow," she added. "At a hair salon. As a receptionist."

"A hair salon, huh?" A teasing lilt lifted Callum's voice. He nudged Mikhail in the side. "See? Rent *and* free haircuts. What a deal, huh?"

Mikhail didn't look convinced, but then again his expression hadn't changed much since she'd met him, so perhaps his face was just stuck that way.

"I can't rent to someone without a job. What will I do? I have bills too. The three girls who came today—they all have jobs. You? No job. No job? No apartment." He slashed the air outward with both hands, putting an end to the discussion.

Cordi wanted to protest, but she knew he was right. It would be silly to rent to her and he had already been rather nice, letting her see the loft when he hadn't even planned on renting it.

"Why don't you come back tomorrow after your interview?" Callum continued as if Mikhail hadn't spoken. The other man made a grunt of anger, laced with amusement, as if he were used to Callum's antics and couldn't help but wonder what he would do next.

"You can meet your roommates—potential roommates—see if you even want to live with them. You never know. Girls can be . . ." Callum cocked his head back and forth but didn't finish the sentiment. "And if you get the job, it's yours."

"Oh, thank you," Cordi gushed, unable to help herself. She almost burst into tears, so relieved that they hadn't said no, not yet anyway. She still had a chance. "Yes, I'll come back. Of course, thank you. Thank you, Mikhail." She nodded to the other man, who still hadn't agreed to this arrangement, but hadn't argued against it either.

Callum laughed. "Don't worry," he muttered as he walked her to the door. "I'll work my magic with Mikhail."

"How?" Cordi asked, even as hope blossomed within her, a longing for someone to help. She wished that some higher power really did exist, some higher power that could grant her all her wishes, or at least lift her out of the trouble she was in. It warred with the part of herself that wanted to take charge, to control her own destiny, now that she was free of obligation to her parents, and especially after the fight she'd had with them that had set all this in motion. But she was also so tired and beginning to understand how little control she had.

"Oh, I have my ways," Callum said. "He wouldn't have this building if it wasn't for my help. Trust me, I'll get you in."

Cordi felt her lower lip trembling as it occurred to her again that Callum had no reason to help her. They didn't know each other, and it didn't even seem like the landlord liked him very much.

"Thank you, Callum," she said.

"Hang tough, darling," he said with a laugh as he held open the door. "You have to do your part as well and get your job at the salon."

Chapter Two

She didn't know where to go after she left Mikhail and Callum, emotions vacillating between hopeful excitement that she had finally found a place to live and utter despair that it wouldn't be hers after all, and that she was destined to live out her life in broken-down hovels with filthy bathrooms, surrounded by mean people, completely alone and friendless. Or even worse, what if she never found a place she could afford? What if no one would rent to her?

As she rambled aimlessly, the city was going to sleep and yet coming to life at the same time. Offices closed and businesses turned off their lights, while clubs and bars opened. She passed an open door, her mood temporarily lifted by the music—jazzy notes from saxophones, the clang of cymbals, and the beat of drums.

Cordi found herself back in downtown LA, in an area that looked dirty in the daylight, its streets pockmarked with old, spit-out chewing gum, its corners stinking of urine. But now, with the sun going down, it began to sparkle. People dressed for a night out crowded the sidewalks. Girls in glittery wiggle dresses, their heels clacking on the pavement, men in silk shirts and vests. The sky had darkened, a black canvas upon which the city painted its bright lights, flickering from neon signs and advertising boards like temporary ink. A reminder that the night was short and shouldn't be wasted.

As she rounded a corner, she almost crashed into a man holding a poster.

"I'm so sorry," she said, stumbling backward, but the man hardly noticed her. He held a megaphone up to his mouth and shouted into it, and Cordi had to cover her ears, ducking as she backed away.

"Repent of your evil ways!" the man called, his voice amplified to catch the attention of everyone walking nearby. He wore black slacks and a white button-down shirt with a red tie, clean and well fitting, and yet he smelled badly of body odor. "Do not let the evil mongers lure you onto the crooked path." He met Cordi's eyes and focused on her. "You, girl, you are vulnerable! Do not let them fool you with their promises."

People turned to stare at them, and Cordi moved past the man with hurried strides, but he kept shouting after her.

"Do not let the lurasts win!" he implored her, but his words were drowned out by another man across the street laughing hysterically as he threw an amber bottle at the preaching man. It landed in the street, almost hitting a car, whose driver cursed out the window at both of them.

Cordi breathed hard and hurried away from the corner. It wasn't the first time she'd been yelled at by some overzealous preacher, and everyone knew they liked to frequent that block due to the high foot traffic from the nearby business offices. Usually she ignored their warnings about lura, a type of witchcraft she'd heard about vaguely from her mom, who only admonished her to stay away. Today, though, Cordi couldn't help looking over her shoulder as the man remained intensely fixated on her.

She felt so tired, and not just from walking, but from a life that never gave her a chance to simply enjoy existing. Tomorrow . . . things would get better then. She had found an apartment . . . almost. The idea of having someplace to settle calmed her nerves a bit, and she kept walking, weaving between groups of people crowded around the tall buildings of the city. Everything was going to be fine.

But first, she needed to find a job.

The next day, Cordi put on her best dress and made her way to her job interview. The hair salon wasn't far from Mikhail's apartment, on Ninth and Olympic between a liquor store and a tall office building still under construction, new metal beams adding height to the growing number of floors. Smog clouded the air, cars lining up as traffic thickened, blotting the asphalt streets in mint and pink pastels. Beyond the smoky haze, the faint outline of mountains faded into the clear sky.

Inside the salon, her nostrils stung with the smells of ammonia, bleach, and hair spray, mixed with the heady perfume of the many beauticians and customers. Women sat in chairs while stylists fussed around them, their hair drying under bulbous metal helmets. Cordi waited on a vinyl-covered chair by the reception area, her back stiff, her shoulders tense, unable to shake the sensation that she was being watched. And judged.

The customers glanced at her from the corners of their eyes. The stylists scrutinized her in the way she often picked apart people's clothes to figure out how the fit could be improved. She couldn't help it. Working for so long at her parents' alterations shop had instilled the habit in her.

Not many Vietnamese Americans lived in California, and their shop was located outside Chinatown, where they might have blended in better with the rest of their neighbors. Cordi was used to being either gawked at or ignored completely, but with the war in Vietnam in the headlines lately, it felt like people did more double takes than before, and she couldn't tell if they were hostile or curious, or if she was simply being paranoid.

Other than her own family and one quiet couple at her parents' church, she didn't know many other Asian people. At her school there were a few Chinese and Japanese students, but even though they were nicer than her white classmates, she'd never truly felt like she belonged. The owners at the other shops she'd applied to in the past few days had turned her away as soon as they saw her, all except one man in a corner convenience store, who had leered at her until Cordi made an excuse to leave.

Now, enduring the sly looks, she wished she'd picked a different dress, one not so long, and that she hadn't worn a jacket. The jacket was gorgeous, a full-length brocade that was as long as the dress, just past her knees, but the fabric was far too heavy for the hot day, and her armpits were already drenched underneath. Yet she couldn't bring herself to take it off, didn't think she could withstand the scrutiny and attention the movement would draw if she did.

She must have waited for at least twenty minutes—how much longer would this take? The smell, the heat . . . it all added up to one throbbing headache. Maybe she should just leave. Did she even want to work at a hair salon? Did she have any other choice?

She didn't have any work experience other than altering clothes at her parents' shop, and after the past few days searching for jobs and places to live, she was starting to realize that very few people wanted a young, inexperienced Asian girl who looked so different from what Los Angeles in 1959 was used to.

Cordi knew what she wanted to do, of a sort. She was good at making clothes. Sewing, altering, fixing. It was a skill she'd developed out of necessity, though she had grown to love it. When you're poor and can't afford new things, you learn how to fix what other people cast aside, and when the world is designed for people who are different from you, you learn how to alter yourself and the things around you to fit.

An older woman in a casual but comfortable-looking business suit hurried to the front. Her shiny brown hair was curled, hitting her shoulders with a bounce.

"Are you Cordelia?" the woman asked in an assertive tone with a sense of urgency that made Cordi spring up from her seat.

"Yes, I am."

"I'm Jeanine." The woman looked her up and down, her gaze lingering rather long on Cordi's shoes. "Aren't you hot?" she asked, turning around and waving at Cordi to follow.

"Yes, but—"

"This can be a physically demanding job. You're on your feet a lot and you're expected to still look good. Customers judge our talents based on our appearance. Even if you're just the receptionist, you'll need to look presentable." She led Cordi to the back of the shop and into a small, dimly lit office. The woman took a seat at a desk and gestured for Cordi to sit opposite her.

"Yes, ma—" Cordi was about to call the woman "madam," then thought better of it, and instead cut herself off at an unfortunate spot. She cringed.

Jeanine didn't notice. "Why do you want to work here?"

Cordi had practiced and prepared and rehearsed so many answers, but this question caught her off guard, and she couldn't conjure a response except that she really needed the money. But that wouldn't be appropriate.

"I think I can really make a difference," she managed. "I'm a hard worker, and I'd do a good job."

"Hmm." Jeanine looked at a piece of paper on her desk, which Cordi recognized as her application. "I have to be honest, I'm undecided between you and another girl. You do have quite a lot of experience working at a shop. You've been at Luca Alterations for ten years?"

"Yes." Of course, Cordi didn't mention that it was her parents' alterations shop. They'd kept the name when they bought it, thinking a non-Asian name would attract more customers.

"And excuse me for assuming, but you are Chinese, correct?"

Not knowing exactly what that had to do with the job, Cordi nodded out of habit, then shook her head. "No, I'm Vietnamese. I was born and raised in Chinatown. In LA."

Jeanine scribbled something on Cordi's application. "Vietnam? Didn't I read something about the war happening there? Is that why you moved here?"

"Um, well, no. I was born here."

"Hmm." Jeanine looked displeased with the answer, and Cordi wondered if she should have just lied about it to make the lady feel better. "Thank you. You should expect an answer soon. Is the number here still a good one to call?"

It was the number for the pay phone at the hostel where Cordi was staying. She nodded, saddened at the idea of being there any longer.

Jeanine gave her a tight smile. "Then thank you for your time, Cornelia."

Chapter Three

Cordi had hoped to have better news when she went back to Mikhail's apartment later that afternoon. She almost didn't go, almost barricaded herself in the tiny room at the hostel. But then one of her four roommates had screamed from the coveted top bunk when a roach the size of her thumb crawled across her face, so Cordi had grabbed most of her things in a panic and left as fast as she could.

Now she felt awkward, holding her weekend bag as she passed the boutique on the corner of Grand Avenue and Third Street, glancing in through the window at the pillbox hat, silk gloves, and white-and-black oxford shoes displayed. The smell of meatloaf from the diner across the street made her stomach twist with hunger. She ignored the sensation and continued to the redbrick apartment building from yesterday, climbed the stairs to the fourth floor, and stopped in front of Mikhail's door. Would it look presumptuous, like she was ready to move in? She *was*, but she didn't want to look desperate.

The door stood slightly ajar when she arrived, the sound of conversation and laughter floating into the hallway. She knocked gently, but whoever was inside must not have heard, so she pushed the door open.

Callum stood by the square of couches in the middle of the living room, leaning casually against the back of the pink sofa with his arms crossed loosely. Mikhail stood facing him, his back to the door, and they were talking to the most striking girl Cordi had ever seen. Her shiny, dark hair draped down her back, her cheekbones well defined, and the edges of her large eyes kissed at the corners in a way that made Cordi wonder if she was of Asian descent, though there was something about her other features that indicated a different ethnicity. She looked around Cordi's age, somewhere in her early twenties, though she was much taller—even taller than Callum by a few inches—and dressed in a sophisticated dress cinched at the waist with a tapered skirt that hit her long legs right below the knees. She had taken off her shoes, and the sight of her bare toes made Cordi feel a bit less intimidated, which wasn't to say that she wasn't still very intimidated.

"Hi," Cordi said, because it felt rude to eavesdrop on their conversation when they hadn't noticed her yet.

Mikhail spun around, his frown gone, his face looking much younger, though his smile faded when he saw that it was her.

Callum beamed while the young woman studied Cordi with quick yet thorough interest, her gaze lingering on Cordi's floral skirt, which she'd paired with a simple white, collarless shirt.

"Cordelia," Callum said with a clap, then held out his hands in welcome.

Cordi wasn't sure if she was supposed to hug him or take his hands, but he remained leaning against the couch, so she stopped a few feet away, her hands clasped in front of her.

"The girl with no job," Mikhail said, crossing his arms.

"Hi," the other girl said, surprising Cordi with her friendliness. "I'm Tessa."

"I'm Cordelia Mai Yin," Cordi said, not knowing why she gave her full name and trying not to wince.

Tessa smiled, her eyes squinching charmingly. "That's so strange. My middle name is Mai too. Tessa Mai Hong."

"Oh, you *are* Asian," Cordi said. "I couldn't tell." Immediately, she wanted to kick herself. She hated how strangers often went straight to asking where she was from, annoyed when she answered "LA" because they'd expected somewhere exotic and exciting, like Hong Kong or Tokyo. And here she was doing it to some girl she'd just met. "I'm sorry," she added hastily. "That's so rude—you must get that all the time."

"Oh, I'm used to it." Tessa smoothed a strand of hair over her shoulder. "My mom is Chinese. My father is white. Are we to be roomies then?" She clapped her hands like it was the most delightful news she'd heard all day.

"I hope so," Cordi said, glancing at Mikhail, who'd been watching their exchange in silence. "I—I was hoping to rent the loft."

"Oh, it's so charming!" Tessa squealed. "That's wonderful! Apparently this place is furnished because the last family had to leave in something of a hurry. Isn't it lovely?"

"How was your job interview?" Mikhail asked roughly.

"Splendid, I'm sure," Callum said.

"I ask the girl, not you."

"It went really well, I think," Cordi said, trying to sound bright and happy and not at all uncertain. Her stomach tensed, but the more time passed, the more she convinced herself that she might get the job after all.

"Cordi here plans to work at a hair salon," Callum explained to Tessa.

"Oh my, isn't that a kick? I hope we all get discounts." Tessa had a twinkle in her eyes as she held Cordi's gaze.

"That's exactly what I said." Callum chuckled.

Tessa giggled and nudged him playfully.

Mikhail crossed his arms tighter and scowled deeper. Apparently Cordi's answer hadn't convinced him.

Luckily someone else stepped through the apartment door just then, another girl their age carrying a large brown suitcase. She was of medium height and build, wearing black overalls splattered with splotches of paint. She wore her wavy black hair piled high on her head, and it made her features appear tight, her brown eyes piercing. She also looked Asian, but unlike with Tessa, Cordi sensed an undeniable unfriendliness in her gaze.

"This must be Audrey Wo," Callum said.

Audrey blinked at all of them but didn't say anything. An awkward tension permeated the air.

"Is your middle name Mai too?" Tessa asked, clearly trying to lighten the mood.

Audrey frowned, thick brows pulling together. "How'd you know?"

"Is it really?" Tessa laughed. "So are ours. This is Cordelia. I'm Tessa."

"Cordi for short," Cordi added.

Audrey glanced at the doors to the left. "Which one's mine?"

Mikhail grunted. "The one in the middle."

Audrey nodded, carried her suitcase to the bedroom, then shut the door behind her.

Cordi looked at Tessa, wondering if she thought the exchange had been weird or if it was just in Cordi's head. Tessa pinched her lips as if trying not to laugh, and in that moment, Cordi wanted more than anything to be her friend, to live here and get to see her every day, talk to her, joke and laugh and do things together. She'd never really had friends before—she'd always been too busy with school and helping her parents at their shop. She'd told herself it was fine, she had better things to do, but really she knew that was a lie.

If she moved into the apartment, she was sure things would be different, because *she* could be different.

Though, of course, it wasn't up to her.

After Tessa went to her own room—the one on the end closest to the loft—Callum sat down on the sofa, gesturing for Cordi to join him. Mikhail remained standing, looking down at them with disapproval. She sank into the cushions facing the window at the end of the apartment, which looked directly across the street at another building shaded with spiked palm tree leaves. Balconies revealed glimpses into the residents' lives, housing rusted metal furniture or acting as storage for dusty, overflowing boxes.

"So you think you got the job?" Callum asked.

"Yes," Cordi lied. "The interview went well. The owner said she really liked me, and that it was between me and another girl." That part wasn't a lie, at least.

Callum grinned over his shoulder at Mikhail. "Hear that, Misha? Good news, huh?"

"Other girl might get the job," Mikhail said.

"I have plenty in savings," Cordi promised eagerly. "I can afford the rent, and I *will* get a job, even if this one doesn't work out. I have a lot of experience." She couldn't seem to stop talking, especially because Callum actually listened instead of interrupting like other people tended to do, and Mikhail was not really the talking type to begin with. "I worked at my parents' alterations shop for years. I can mend clothes and work a register and—"

"You know how to sew?" Tessa had come out of her room carrying a couple of glasses, presumably headed to the kitchen. Mikhail's frown eased from his face, and he stepped back to let her join their little circle.

"Yes," Cordi said. "Ever since I was little." It used to be a skill she'd loathed, forced to learn so she could help with the simpler projects at her parents' shop. Instead of playing with any friends she might have made at school, she had spent hours during afternoons and on weekends hunched over her mom's spare Singer beneath fluorescent lights until her back ached and her vision blurred.

"How good are you?" Tessa asked.

"Pretty good," Cordi said slowly, wondering where she was headed with her questions.

"Can you make this?" Tessa gestured down at her dress, a deceptively simple cut tailored perfectly to her body. Like most expensive clothing, its secret was in the fact that it fit well.

"Yes," Cordi said, though she didn't go into details about how the fabric would have been impossible to find and how much interfacing she'd need and all the ironing necessary to make the pieces fit together. It wouldn't be much cheaper than buying the dress at a store.

Tessa turned her full attention on Mikhail, who stood taller. "You have to rent the loft to her, Misha. Think of all the money we'd save on clothes."

"How would that benefit me?" he said.

"We'd have more money to pay the rent." Tessa raised her brows, challenging him to argue.

Mikhail huffed.

Callum leaned over the back of the couch to look at him. "Come, Misha," he said, and Cordi detected a strange quality to his voice that made her turn sharply to him. She couldn't see his face, just the profile, but he had an intensity about him that he directed at Mikhail. "Give her a chance."

There was an unbearably long, stretched moment when no one said anything. In fact, no one moved. Mikhail's frown was fixed, his mouth bracketed by tense muscles. Tessa's face was frozen in its delightful smile, and Callum's expression was darkened with harsh shadows, the light from the window glaring into the room in sharp angles.

Mikhail sucked in a breath, and Cordi did as well, feeling as if someone had just flicked water in her face. She glanced around, but the others didn't seem to notice, focused on Mikhail's answer.

"Fine," he said. "The girl with no job can stay."

Tessa squealed, then leaned over to hug Cordi as if they'd been friends forever. "That's wonderful, darling. We're going to have an absolute gas."

She hurried off so quickly, Cordi didn't have a chance to respond, but she wouldn't have known what to say to begin with. She still couldn't quite believe what had just happened. It couldn't be that easy, could it?

"So that's it?" she asked. "I can move in?"

Mikhail already looked like he regretted his decision, blinking and frowning in befuddlement. He opened his mouth as if to argue, but Callum slapped his hands on his legs and then stood, cutting him off.

"Yes! The place is yours," Callum said.

Mikhail shook his head, though it looked more like he was trying to shake water from his ears than to refuse.

Callum clapped him on the back. "Fifty a month, like we talked about, right, Misha?" He squeezed Mikhail's shoulder.

Mikhail glared at Cordi. "Under condition that you get job as soon as possible. And pay rent on time."

Callum grinned at Cordi's shocked face.

"Of course." Fifty. That was less than half the rent of any place she'd seen since leaving home. "You're sure?"

"Is there reason I shouldn't be?" Mikhail demanded.

"No—no. I'll get a job, I won't be late with the rent. I promise. Thank you. Thanks so much."

Callum let go of Mikhail and stretched his arms dramatically. "Well, my work here is done. I'll be seeing you, Misha."

"Stop bringing your girls around here—this isn't a hotel," Mikhail said as way of goodbye. "And you—" he added to Cordelia. "You need to fill out application with first month rent."

"Okay," Cordi said. She stood and followed Callum to the door. "Thanks so much for all your help. Really, Callum, thank you. It's been . . . such a tough . . ." Her words clogged in her throat.

Callum paused, one hand on the doorknob. He cupped her chin gently with the other, and Cordi stood very still. No one had ever touched her that way, and she wasn't sure if she liked it, and yet she couldn't bring herself to pull back when he had been so nice.

"Don't mention it, sweetheart." His eyes crinkled at the corners, and then he was gone.

"I don't got all day," Mikhail snapped. He was waiting at the table in front of the window, sheets of paper ready for her to sign.

After filling out the paperwork, Cordi handed over a handful of bills, and panicked at how little she had left. But it didn't matter. She had bought herself some time. Mikhail slipped it into his pocket casually, as if it were just change to him, which perhaps it was.

"I'll come back next month," he said. "Every month, you understand? On the first. You can't be late. If you're late, I'll kick you out. Understand?"

"Yes. I won't be late. I promise."

"I don't need your promise. Just the rent."

Once Mikhail had left, she leaned against the door, so relieved that she started shaking. It seemed impossible. But it was real. She had somewhere to go home to now.

Chapter Four

Cordi made her way back to Fifth Street, avoiding the broken chunk of sidewalk that had tripped her when she'd first found the hostel, a gray building that looked like it had once been white, paint peeling off to reveal the dark wood underneath. A car passed from behind her, the turquoise finish reflecting a beam of sunlight in her eye, leaving behind the smell of exhaust to mix with the other odors—rancid trash, urine seeping into the cement, the sourness of days-old vomit, and the stink of unbathed armpits.

Cordi didn't even care, eager to get in the hostel so that she could get back out. Elation buoyed her steps as she rushed down the thick, mustard-brown carpet to grab the rest of her belongings. She passed a girl in her underthings, a flimsy camisole slip under a loosely tied bustier, smoking a cigarette, her hair in rollers.

"Hey, you Cornelia?" the girl asked after blowing out a lungful of smoke.

Cordi resisted the urge to cough. "Yes. I mean, it's Cordelia—Cordi—yes, that's me."

"Lady called for you earlier."

"Oh. What did she say?"

"What am I, your secretary?" The girl flicked ash straight onto the patterned carpet. "I left her number on the pad."

Cordi moved toward the communal phone at the end of the hall-way, but a man shouted on it in a foreign language. He waved his arms animatedly, almost hitting Cordi as she ducked to grab the notepad on the little stand.

It was the hair salon. Jeanine. Maybe Cordi had gotten the job after all. She would have some exciting news to tell Tessa and Callum and Mikhail . . . and maybe even Audrey. The last girl hadn't shown up yet before she left.

She still couldn't quite believe it. The apartment was hers. She had somewhere to go, and roommates—possibly even friends. She couldn't fight back the smile, and she looked up as the man slammed the phone down, then turned to her.

"What are you looking at?" he growled.

Cordi took a step back, palms starting to sweat. Would he attack her? Grab her? Hit her?

But the man just grumbled and walked away.

Cordi took his place and dialed the number carefully. The rotary got stuck on the three, so she had to try a few times before the call went through.

"Stylebox Hair," a girl answered, her voice chirpy and high. "How can I help you?"

Cordi imagined that she would be that girl, or at least be in her position, answering the phones. She could do the job. She might even like it. "Oh, hi. I'm returning Jeanine's call. My name is Cordi."

"One second, please."

The girl put the receiver down, and Cordi could hear the salon in the background—the chatter of customers and stylists and the whir of a blow-dryer. Someone screamed behind her in the hostel, a couple shouted at each other, a child ran down the hallway. Cordi covered the ear not pressed to the phone and closed her eyes. She would be out of this nightmare soon.

"Yes, hi," Jeanine's voice finally boomed, almost blasting her eardrum.

"Hello, Jeanine," Cordi said. She waited awkwardly for Jeanine to speak, but several moments passed. "I'm calling you back—this is Cordi. I interviewed with you yesterday?"

"Oh right, right. It's been a madhouse—is someone crying?"

"Oh, um." The child had tripped just a few feet away. Cordi reached to help her up, but the phone cord didn't extend very far, and anyway, an older woman who must have been the child's grandmother ran over, back stooped, to pick her up. "Yes, but they're all right."

"You didn't tell me you had an ankle biter."

"I don't—"

"Never mind, it doesn't matter. Look, darling, we're going with the other girl."

For a second, Cordi's body went numb. It lasted for only a flash, and then blood rushed through her veins, both cold and hot at the same time.

"You were great and all, but we just have a certain . . . appearance to upkeep, you know, for our clientele, and . . ."

Cordi had trouble comprehending what any of it meant. Appearance? Clientele?

"Our other candidate was just stellar. She really fit the mold, if you know what I'm saying," Jeanine kept going.

"Is there anything I can do?" Cordi asked.

That seemed to take the woman off guard. "Do?"

"I mean, was it something I did or said or—"

"Oh, honey. Listen, doll," she said. "You were great. Excellent. Overqualified, even. Just not the right fit. Nothing that was your fault, honestly. You've got a great future and all. Good luck now."

The phone clicked and then went dead.

Cordi held the receiver against her chest, not understanding exactly what had just happened. If she was as wonderful as Jeanine implied, then why hadn't she gotten the job?

Cordi had grown up at the edge of Chinatown, a neighborhood in Los Angeles marked by templelike buildings with curving red roofs, golden lion statues guarding entryways, and shops and restaurants that sold delicacies like chicken feet and jellied pig's blood. At night, the streets came to life, lights outlining the storefront roofs chasing any lingering gloom from the day, the aroma of chop suey and noodles thickening the air.

The area around North Bunker Hill Avenue and Alpine Street was known for dusty cafés smelling of jasmine tea, its mom-and-pop shops that sold everything from small worship altars to lucky prayer flags to blessed charms for warding off hungry ghosts and unwanted spirits. Small restaurants sold grilled-pork skewers and dried squid, breaded chicken topped with chili powder and basil leaves, and thick-sliced, chewy, savory intestines dipped in lime salt.

Her parents' alterations shop was tucked in a small shopping center next to a grocery store selling outdated soybean milk and stale rice cakes. Just off the corner of a busy main street, the block was untouched by the neighborhood's recent renovations, the black asphalt of the parking lot jagged and broken, the sidewalks cracked, and the dumpster rarely emptied.

Cordi stopped by the grocery store because it was unlucky to show up empty-handed, especially now that she didn't technically work at the shop anymore, and she hoped a gift of some sort would soften her sister Trina's mood, whatever it turned out to be. The orange, square price tag stickers were coated with dust and peeling at the corners, but tea leaves didn't *really* go bad, so Cordi grabbed a tin can of jasmine tea, knowing that she was stalling and yet unable to force herself to hurry.

Finally, she hesitated outside the alterations shop. The blinds were already drawn, even though the neon OPEN sign remained on and the shop wouldn't close for another thirty minutes. It was always slow in the evenings.

She closed her eyes and took a deep breath before she reached for the door. It swung open as soon as her hand skimmed the handle.

"Come in already," Trina snapped, not looking at her. "Stop scaring the customers away with that depressing face. No one's died yet." She disappeared back into the store.

Cordi felt an overwhelming urge to turn around and run away. That was exactly what she'd done when she'd left home a couple of weeks ago, ashamed and wondering if she'd done the right thing, regretting everything she'd said, yet unsure who had been wrong—her or her parents or both—and unable to bring herself to turn back and apologize. The thought of seeing her family again filled her with equal amounts fear, dread, and anger. But her parents wouldn't be at the shop, not on a Wednesday night. They had a standing weekly meeting with their church group, and usually left the shop under Cordi's care. And now Trina's, apparently.

Cordi forced herself to follow her older sister inside. The familiar smell of fabric and steam hit her, nostalgia seeping under her skin and rising like bile in her throat.

Behind the counter was the stool she used to perch on every day after school and on weekends, doing her homework between helping customers. The run-down cash register her mother had found at the flea market and Father had fixed as best he could sat next to a tray of dusty pennies and the box of carelessly organized receipts where they kept track of orders. A notepad with the logo of some obscure company a salesman had dropped off lay next to their grimy beige rotary telephone and their fifteen-inch black-and-white TV.

Trina folded her arms, usually a sign of respect in their culture, but in this case there was nothing respectful about it. She glared at Cordi and raised her thick eyebrows, which she'd darkened with makeup. They were arched too high and made her look perpetually angry, which she often was. Trina was always irritated with her—Cordi was too loud, Cordi was too quiet, Cordi spent too much time in the sun, Cordi read too much when she should be working, Cordi didn't study enough. It seemed as if Trina had never experienced one happy moment in her life.

Though there must have been some warmth in her past. Their past. Trina had taken care of Cordi when Mother and Father were busy, had walked her to school, cooked her meals, helped her with homework. Even though she'd never said as much, Cordi knew that Trina loved her . . . didn't she? They were sisters. Was such a thing even up for debate?

"Well?" Trina demanded.

"I . . ." And even though Trina had always been mean and bossy and scary, Cordi wished that her older sister would forgive her. Or show that she cared about her in some small way. Growing up, their parents had worked constantly just to make enough to pay rent and buy the cheapest but longest-lasting groceries. Trina, ten years older than Cordi, had been forced to take care of her, and made it clear she resented her for it.

Cordi couldn't help scanning Trina's face for any kind of emotion. Any regret or indication that she missed her. Of course, it wasn't Trina who had kicked Cordi out, disowned her, told her to never come home. But she hadn't tried to stop their parents either. She'd watched it happen with blank coldness, and probably agreed with their parents that Cordi was a dishonorable, disrespectful, unfilial daughter.

"Well, spit it out," Trina said. "I have to close up soon. You should know that. This was *your* shift. You know I had to quit one of my classes so I could do your job?"

Guilt flushed through Cordi at that. Trina had finally gone back to college when Cordi was old enough to take care of herself. She'd taken a part-time job at a nail salon because she made more money than working at the shop, leaving Cordi to help her parents. She must have had to quit her job to take over Cordi's duties.

"I'm sorry," Cordi said, even though she'd told herself time and again that she had nothing to apologize for, yet guilt weighed her down like always. "Did you have to quit your other job?"

Trina's lips thinned, turning near white. "What do you want?"

Cordi focused on the clothes hanging on the rack ready for customers to pick up. There weren't many items, five or six geometric shift dresses fluttered in the small breeze of the oscillating fan in the corner of the store. It clicked ominously every time it had to reverse.

"I found a place to live," Cordi said. She found it easier to talk when she didn't have to look Trina in the eye.

Trina made a sound of annoyance. "All right? Congratulations?"

Cordi's heart seized for a moment, and she forced herself to breathe as her body heated with anger and fear—that Trina sided with Mother and Father, that none of them loved her after all. Perhaps never did.

"Could you bring me my things?" she choked out. "Or just leave them outside when Mother and Father aren't home so I can come get them."

Trina didn't say anything, the tension stretching along with the silence, growing tighter and tighter. She started tinkering instead, punching the familiar closing sequence into the cash register.

"Fine," Trina said finally. "Just give me your new address."

Cordi tried to control her shaking hands as she scribbled the address down on the notepad. It felt so strange that she had a new home, hopefully permanent, with girls who seemed nice and friendly. Well, one girl—Tessa. Hopefully she'd get along well with the others too.

"This is downtown," Trina commented, studying the scrap of paper. The neighborhood was more expensive than any of the other boroughs. "You have enough to cover the rent?"

"Yeah, I have money saved up." Mother and Father hadn't paid her much, but they'd still given her a small salary for running the shop, and she didn't have anything to spend it on. She sewed her own clothes, never went out, and had been too busy with work to indulge in any hobbies. "Enough for at least a few months."

Trina hadn't looked at Cordi for more than the brief seconds when she'd arrived. "Okay. I'll try to get your things. It might be a while. Don't want them to suspect anything."

And maybe their parents would change their minds. Neither of them spoke those words, but Cordi secretly hoped it would happen. It could happen. Mother had a temper. Maybe after she calmed down, she'd regret disowning Cordi, like the times she'd thrown Cordi out in the past, only to take her back a few hours later. Maybe Cordi could move back home. Things could be how they had been, and Cordi wouldn't have to worry about not finding a job and possibly ending up on the streets.

"Thank you." Cordi waited for a sign, anything, that showed Trina cared. But Trina turned away, pretending to tidy up the counter, though they both knew it was impossible. Stores like theirs would always look dusty and cluttered.

Without saying goodbye, Cordi left the shop, the bell tinkling above the door.

Chapter Five

Cordi stepped quietly into the new apartment, just as Tessa burst out from her bedroom.

"Oh, you're here—nifty!" Tessa threw her arms up and pulled Cordi into a hug so surprising and brief, Cordi barely had time to react. "What's wrong?" she asked when she pulled back and saw Cordi's face.

Cordi had waited until her eyes weren't as red and swollen before she came inside, but it seemed that Tessa wasn't fooled. Cordi ducked her head. "Nothing . . . I—"

"It's okay. Tell me." Tessa pulled Cordi down to the sofa, her long, slender arm draped easily over Cordi's shorter frame. "Was it your old roommates? They didn't want to lose you, huh? Breakups are so hard, but hey, now you live with us—with me—and we're gonna have a ball. I can already tell that we're going to be the bestest friends."

"No, it . . . I mean, I guess technically. I lived with my family and . . . things didn't end well. They disowned me. I mean, they disown me a lot, but this time, I think they really mean it."

Tessa made a noise of comfort, her hand rubbing Cordi's shoulder in a surprisingly soothing motion. Surprising because Cordi wasn't used to being touched, at least not affectionately. If Mother and Father touched her, it was only to slap or pinch, rare though that was, and usually only if Cordi dared to talk back, something practically sacrilegious in their household.

"I'm fine, I just . . ." Cordi took a deep breath. "I went to ask my sister if she could pack up my things since I'm not allowed home anymore and . . ." To her embarrassment, her chest hitched involuntarily, the way it often did after she'd been crying.

"Hey," Tessa said, with her arm still draped across Cordi's shoulder. "They sound horrible. Whatever they disowned you for, you're better off now."

Cordi wanted to tell her what had happened, but she didn't know if Tessa would understand, and shame washed over her so heavily that she bowed her head, the same way she had when Mother and Father had yelled and scolded and lectured, until finally, they'd shoved her out the door. Before the shame had set in, she'd been argumentative and disobedient, which was unimaginable in their family, in their culture, and everything had been simply blown out of proportion, and . . . well . . . anyway, it didn't matter now. Cordi was here, not at home.

"You know what will make you feel better?" Tessa asked cheerfully. "A mimosa. You want a mimosa?"

"Um, sure, I think."

"Do you like mimosas? We can mix margaritas instead."

"I don't know. I've never had either."

Tessa gave her a horrified look just as a knock came at the door, which then opened slowly.

A girl peeked in, looking nervous. Wiry, curly hair sprouted from her head in an ashy-brown color. She gave Cordi the impression of a frightened mouse.

"Hi!" Tessa said. "You must be our last roommate."

"Hi." The girl waved and smiled at both of them.

"Well, come in," Tessa said. "This is your home now too."

The new girl pushed the door open farther and dragged in a heavy canvas bag. "It was a nightmare getting here. I tried to get on the elevator, and it got stuck."

"You actually got on that thing?" Tessa asked.

The girl was still struggling with her bag, so Cordi rushed forward to help her drag it in.

"Thanks," she said. She was shorter than Cordi, which was rare, and sweetly plump, wearing a baggy, cable-knit sweater and tweed skirt, which Cordi would have hemmed several inches shorter if she had sewn it herself. At that length, it made the girl appear small and frumpy. She looked to be a few years younger than Cordi, but it could have been her slight frame and her round cheeks. "Well, I *really* didn't want to lug this thing up the stairs, and when I got here, I was so relieved, like, *Wow, an elevator, I live in a building with an elevator now.* I lived with my grandma before this, see, and her house is tiny and old but it was only one level. Anyway, the elevator got stuck between the first and second floor, and I was about to panic, but luckily the doors opened enough that I could get out." She sighed. "I'm just happy to be here."

Cordi smiled at her. "I'm glad you made it," she said, proud that she had said something nice and socially acceptable to a stranger, which was admittedly not her strongest skill. Especially when it came to girls her own age. At school the girls had always been mean and intimidating and had instilled in her a fear of saying anything that could be laughed at or corrected or rejected.

"I'm Silly, by the way. Short for Priscilla. Trinidad. Priscilla Trinidad. But Priscilla sounds so 'old aunt,' doesn't it? And it's also my grandma's name, which . . . well . . . Silly will do." She twisted a strand of curly hair round and round a finger.

"I'm Tessa. This is Cordi." Tessa smiled, close-lipped like she was about to tell them something scandalous. Cordi and Silly both leaned toward her, an instinctive move. "So, Silly . . . tell me . . ."

Silly straightened, pushing her shoulders back, and Cordi got the sense that she would jump if Tessa asked her to.

"Is your middle name," Tessa said, and Cordi grinned, realizing where this was going and feeling like she was part of an inner crowd, "Mai?"

Silly's mouth opened into a little O. "But how did you know?"

Tessa clapped and squealed. "Oh, that's absolutely delightful."

The door to the middle bedroom opened and Audrey stepped out, having changed into a black shirt and black pants. "What is it?" she asked in her monotonous tone. Cordi was surprised she was interested at all, and from the bored look on her face, she probably wasn't.

"All our middle names are Mai!" Tessa practically shouted. "Isn't that remarkable?"

Audrey mulled over the question. "Big deal? I mean, it's a pretty common name for Asians. Which we all are, right?"

"Oh, shut up. I think it's marvelous. Like destiny. We were all meant to be together." Tessa swung out her arms, taking Cordi's hand in one and Silly's in the other. Cordi felt a warm tingle travel up her arm and into her chest.

Audrey looked briefly shocked at being told to shut up, but then she came closer. She didn't take anyone's hand, but simply asked, "Did I hear someone say 'margarita'?"

Cordi didn't have many things to unpack since most of her belongings were still at home. She needed to stop thinking of her parents' house as home. *This* was her home now, and even though she knew it wasn't a real room, she climbed up to her loft with an excitement she hadn't felt in a long time.

She had the space all to herself. It was small, but the room that she and Trina had shared hadn't been much bigger. The loft felt luxurious in comparison. Quiet and peaceful. Hers.

While the others were busy unpacking, Cordi worked hard to make her corner more livable, more . . . lively. The furniture was adequate, she had plenty of space for her things, and the bed was fine, but it was dark, as the light from the living room window didn't quite reach its corners.

Cordi hadn't expected to fall asleep so fast when she collapsed on her mattress, sure that being so high on the loft would feel strange and exposed, especially because she didn't have a door. But the apartment was quiet after the girls went to bed, and perhaps it was exhaustion from her nights at the crowded hostel, but she passed out almost within seconds, falling into the deepest dreamless sleep she'd had in months.

———— ∞ ⌇ ⌇ ∞ ————

"You should get a brighter lamp," Tessa suggested the next day as she was on the way out. Cordi sat at the table, drinking tea. Tessa looked lovely in a gray dress with a fitted bodice and flared skirt, her hair pinned back into a sophisticated chignon, silver studs sparkling on her earlobes.

"I don't have any money," Cordi said with embarrassment. It was rude to talk about money, even worse to admit you didn't have any.

"I'll buy one for you," Tessa said. "It'll be a gift, as my new roommate."

"But I can't afford one for you."

Tessa made a noise of amusement. "If I expected something in return, then it wouldn't be a gift, would it?" She adjusted her earrings. "Don't worry about it, trust me. I'll pick something up from Lacy's after my shift."

"You work at Lacy's?" Cordi's eyes widened. She couldn't afford to shop at that department store, but she often stared longingly at the giant sign on the tall building she could see from her parents' shop. It looked especially beautiful at sunset, when the light cast golden beams on the letters and made them shine.

"Yeah, at the Petite counter."

"Petite Beauty?" Cordi practically shrieked. She could never dream of affording makeup from that expensive brand. Once, she'd saved and saved and talked herself into splurging on a lipstick for her birthday. But when she'd finally gone through with the purchase, Trina had found out and told their mother.

"If you can afford a frivolous lipstick, then you can use that money to help us pay the rent this month," Mother had said, and even though it was just an empty, angry threat, Cordi had felt so guilty that she'd returned the lipstick and given her parents the money to help with the shop's bills. Mother hadn't looked less disappointed, but that evening she cooked Cordi's favorite three-string meat with spicy salad.

Tessa smiled. "I know, right? I would consider myself lucky, except it's not exactly my dream to be a shopgirl. I'd much rather be a model. Actually, I'm on the casting call for the next catalog."

"That's great!" Cordi said. "You're so pretty, I thought you already were one."

"I've been on the list for a few months now, but I keep getting passed up. It's just up to Mr. Sinclair. He's the buyer for the store and gets a big say in who they choose, but he keeps making excuses." Tessa sighed, then shook off her frown. "Well, how do I look?"

Cordi was flattered that Tessa had asked her opinion. "You look great! Perfect."

"I know," Tessa replied, and it was such a conceited thing to say, but she was too nice for Cordi to find it unlikable. "It's almost a waste to go to work like this. What have you got planned? Did you hear back from the hair salon?"

Cordi tried not to sound so forlorn as she answered. "They decided to go with someone else. It's just as well—it was on the corner where that preaching man likes to shout about how we shouldn't fall vulnerable to lura and evil or whatnot. I wouldn't want to walk by that every day." Though in all honesty, she would have put up with almost anything for an income.

Tessa slipped into her heels. "Ugh, I hate those zealots. They're so loud. As if they're going to change anything, because, trust me, if lura was real, I'd be the first in line. I'd do anything to have everything I want." She sighed dramatically.

"But isn't it like . . ." For some reason, Cordi felt the need to lower her voice. "Like witchcraft?" She had only the vaguest idea of what lura was: a form of magic that couldn't possibly be real. Teachers always hushed anyone who mentioned it, and once when she and Mother had walked through downtown and been accosted by a preaching man, Mother had lit incense as soon as she came home to ward off any lingering bad luck. Cordi didn't know much about lura, just that she should be afraid of it, like it was a dangerous, addictive yet unattainable drug she was unlikely to ever encounter.

"It's all superstition," Tessa said, smoothing her hands down her skirt. "But wouldn't it be a gas if we could have everything we wanted just by doing a bit of magic?"

Cordi smiled indulgently. Of course magic wasn't real. The only way to get what you wanted was by working hard. That's what she'd been taught. No one was about to simply hand her what she wanted.

"I'll see you tonight, darling." Tessa blew her a kiss and sailed out the door, leaving Cordi smiling for all of two seconds before the quietness of the apartment settled in.

Audrey hadn't stepped out of her room again after discovering last night that they didn't, in fact, have any margaritas, or groceries at all. They hardly had anything—the apartment was furnished, but they lacked dishes or cups and other small necessities Cordi had taken for granted at home. Silly had left her door open while she unpacked, but eventually they'd all gone to bed, and neither girl had woken yet.

Cordi was used to getting up early to cook breakfast for her family, then head to the shop. Now she didn't have much to do or anywhere to go. For a second, she stood in front of the window with her mug of tea—she'd borrowed the mug from Tessa, who was the only one who had brought anything besides clothes—and watched the city come to life. Sunlight cut diagonally across the building across the street, casting the gray paint in a cheerier blue hue. Below, cars carted people to work, mostly men in suits, maneuvering around the streetcars and stopping for pedestrians. Cordi liked mornings best, because the smog that clouded the city wasn't so thick, and she could see the Red Car trolleys still running in the distance. They broke down more often these days—she'd heard talk that the city planned to shut them down altogether since gas was technically cheaper than the fare—and though Cordi didn't have anywhere to be, exactly, she depended on them to get around.

She finished her tea, then took a short walk to the convenience store on the corner to buy the newspaper, dodging foot traffic as people rushed around her to get to their stops in time. Cars honked as the streetcars rattled, people jabbered to each other and stared as she passed, counting how many pennies she still had on her way back to the apartment. She sat at the kitchen table circling every job listing she might be remotely qualified for—could she greet customers at a mechanic shop? How hard could it be?—when Silly came out of her bedroom wearing a frilly cotton nightgown and rubbing her eyes.

"Morning," she said through a yawn.

"Hi," Cordi said.

"Is there any coffee?"

"No, but Tessa has a kettle, and there's some tea."

Silly blinked but went to the kitchen. "I should get us a percolator, but I only have a small budget. Kind of."

Audrey came out of her bedroom then, her face both blank and yet unpleasantly surprised at the sight of Cordi and Silly at the table. She wore her paint-splattered overalls with a black shirt underneath.

"Good morning!" Silly sang out, one arm propped on the back of her chair.

Audrey winced, and it seemed like she was about to retreat to her room. "Coffee?" she croaked.

"No, but there's tea!" Silly replied.

Audrey screwed her eyes closed and took a deep breath. "No thanks." She headed out the front door without another word.

Silly turned back to Cordi with a frown. "Was it something I said?"

"No, I think she's just like that."

Silly looked even more confused. "Are people allowed to be?"

"I don't know." Cordi laughed. "I guess so."

"It's just, I was always taught to be cheerful and kind and friendly. Especially if we're going to be living together."

"Well." Cordi circled another listing in the newspaper. "We're adults now. I guess we're allowed to be whatever we want."

Chapter Six

Cordi was surprised by how quickly she fell into the rhythms of her new home. On her first few mornings, she woke up confused, then sighed when she remembered where she was. Her relief was followed quickly by guilt that she felt so happy when she should have been sad, when she should have been using her time to reflect upon the error of her ways and figure out how to get back in her parents' good graces. And yet, she couldn't help feeling a profound sense of liberation, of lightness, knowing that she wouldn't have to face their disappointment.

She had to keep reminding herself that she had a new home now. This quiet corner in a cozy apartment, which was much brighter and cheerier with the new desk lamp Tessa had bought for her. Tessa had gotten gifts for all the girls—a scarf for Silly and a six-cup percolator for Audrey that rattled on the stovetop and filled the apartment with the deep, rich smell of coffee. Audrey had looked stupefyingly repulsed, then smiled stiffly when she opened the box and inspected the blue starburst painted on the white lacquer. But she seemed pleased when she made her first pot and drank an entire mug standing in the kitchen.

Now Cordi enjoyed the quiet hours of the morning, often the first person to wake. Sunlight would just be breaking across the high-rises of their downtown neighborhood to cast long, sharp shadows of the sidewalk palm trees through the windows. Tessa's plants, which she had placed along the windowsill, shaded the living room with stretches of round and irregularly shaped leaves. Cordi would put the water on, gaze out the window, then turn off the burner right before the kettle started whistling so it wouldn't wake the others, and brew a pot of tea.

And they had a lot of tea. They'd all put their few boxes on the bookcase they used as a pantry, and then more and more accumulated until boxes and jars of different varieties in loose leaf, bagged, and instant cluttered the shelf. Any variety in any flavor. After she had tried all the ones she knew she liked—lychee and vanilla chai and chocolate mint—she began picking them at random.

By the time she finished her first mug, sitting at the kitchen table and perusing the Help Wanted ads, one of the girls would usually be up. Tessa worked different shifts at Lacy's, so it depended on her schedule. Silly talked little in the mornings, instead smiling a groggy greeting, joining Cordi at the table, and quietly sipping her tea while reading a book. When Audrey woke, Cordi knew not to say anything, not even a simple greeting, because Audrey would grumble while fumbling in the kitchen to make her coffee.

Tessa was the only one who had energy first thing in the morning, filling the apartment with her cheerful chatter as she flitted around, watering her plants or getting ready in the bathroom, keeping the door open as she talked. If it was just the two of them, she would sometimes turn the radio on and dance around the apartment.

Cordi had assumed she'd miss her home, her family, but the truth was, there was nothing to really miss. In her parents' house, it had always felt as if she had intruded on someone else's territory, conscious that nothing she touched was hers, afraid to leave a mark or disturb the air in some way that would upset someone. Unhappiness festered in their home, a rancid feeling that permeated the air and lingered, creeping into the walls like mold. It wasn't until she'd moved into this new home that she realized that perhaps, maybe, life . . . wasn't supposed to be like that.

Things would have been perfect, except that Mikhail called often, and when Cordi picked up the phone, he grunted and demanded to know why she wasn't working instead.

Cordi scoured all the classifieds she could find, called every place hiring for a job she thought she qualified for, and went out at least once or twice a day on interviews if she was lucky. Audrey borrowed the paper afterward to snicker over the personals.

"Listen to this," she said one morning as she joined Cordi at the kitchen table and sipped her coffee. "'My one true love, please respond to this ad. I've been waiting for you my whole life. Whoever answers first.'"

Cordi chuckled politely as she crossed out a section on a separate page of the paper. It was an ad for a position that she'd interviewed for last week.

Audrey flipped the page. "I swear, these missed connections get worse every day. Who even pays for them?"

"People who need love, I guess," Cordi said.

"Who has time for that? Don't these people work? Imagine being that rich and desperate."

Cordi took the paper back, skimming the blocks of text. One stood out at her in bold, ancient-looking script: "BEWARE EVIL," it read. "Stay away from luracal offerings. Come to Sunday service to learn more. Free coffee. Jesus is the way." It was followed by an address on Vermont Avenue, but she crossed it out, focusing on the listings for jobs she might qualify for.

"Any luck?" Tessa asked when Cordi returned home one day and let out a heavy sigh as soon as she stepped into the apartment. Tessa sat on the sofa, hair wrapped in a towel with some green paste on her face.

Cordi shook her head. "They told me on the spot that they'd hired the girl before me."

Tessa made a sympathetic noise. "What job was it?"

"Shopgirl at a cigarette shop. I probably don't have the right 'appearance.' Again." Cordi slumped onto the cushion next to her. "What's that on your face?"

"It's this new mask, supposed to soothe my pores. Too bad about the job—free cigarettes would have been nice."

"I just need *a* job." Two weeks had passed, and she was starting to panic. She applied for the most menial of jobs, and still, she hadn't found anything. She had experience and skills and spoke English. What else was missing? Was something wrong with her?

"Too bad you can't work with me at Lacy's," Tessa said, her lips moving stiffly so as not to disturb her mask. "It would be pretty neat to walk together and take our breaks together."

"I would kill to work at the Petite counter." Cordi leaned her head back.

"It's not as glamorous as you think. Customers come in all the time expecting to be transformed if they put on a dash of lipstick, like they'll instantly look like the model on the billboards. Then they're disappointed when they look the same, just . . . glossier. Today, a lady accused me of hiding the *real* lipstick because the one she asked for made her skin look sallow. She said I was *jealous* of her and didn't want her to upstage me. Can you believe it?"

"What? That's ridiculous."

"I know!" She touched the side of her nose. "Great, I'm getting all sweaty and worked up. I need to wash this off. Don't go anywhere. I'm going to fix us a drink."

Cordi stayed on the sofa, pleased that Tessa wanted to keep talking. She was always rushing off to work or to "go out." Cordi had never "gone out" before, an exclusive activity for sophisticated women with friends and places to be, not for someone like her, a shy, awkward, quiet type who couldn't even get a job. Usually she came straight home to crawl into her loft and hope that tomorrow would be different. Audrey was either not home or shut up in her bedroom. Cordi had no idea what she did all day, but she must have a job or else Mikhail wouldn't have rented a room to her. Silly was apparently waiting to hear from some internship but preferred to spend her free time at the public library, something Cordi couldn't quite fathom. What did people actually *do* there?

Tessa came out of the bathroom, her face freshly scrubbed. Without makeup, she looked much younger, and Cordi felt herself relax a bit knowing that they had some time to chat, that Tessa wasn't about to rush off and leave her to stew in the aftermath of rejection from her fruitless job hunt.

"What will it be?" Tessa muttered to herself as she peered into the fridge. "We really need to buy groceries. There's one orange, wonder whose it is. Ooh, grapefruit. I bet I can whip something up with this." She started slicing, then pulled the ice tray out of the freezer. The cubes clinked into a metal pitcher as Tessa continued to do very complicated things at the counter.

"Do you need help?" Cordi asked.

"No, doll. Let the master do her work."

Cordi rose halfway from the couch, but Tessa was already on her way over with two glasses filled with a foamy, iced, pink concoction.

"Try it. You won't even taste the alcohol." Tessa handed her a glass.

"What's the point if you can't taste it?"

"To get drunk, silly." She clinked her glass to Cordi's, then took a gulp and closed her eyes.

Cordi tasted her own drink, mouth flooding with the sweet tang of citrus, a pleasantly bitter undertone, and the tingly mix of something that infused her belly with warmth. "Wow," she said.

"Yeah." Tessa pulled the elastic band from her hair, letting the loose, dark strands unravel in rivulets down her shoulders. "So, Cordi . . . tell me about yourself."

Cordi almost choked, a sour aftertaste lingering at the back of her throat. *Quick, say something witty, or clever, or funny, or . . . well, anything.* "What—what do you want to know?"

Tessa laughed. "Relax. This isn't an interview. I just thought we could be . . . you know, friends. Since we'll be living together and stuff."

"If I can get a job."

"You will. You just need to cut your hair and maybe put on some lipstick. Not the balm you usually wear, but try a deeper color that will . . . brighten up your face. Why don't you visit me at work sometime? I can help you pick out some things."

Cordi's ears and cheeks grew hot, but she wasn't sure if it was the drink or if it was because Tessa had very subtly insulted her. Should she be insulted? Tessa hadn't actually said anything about her was wrong, just how she could improve. Was that the same thing?

"Oh, don't be offended." Tessa must have read something on Cordi's face because she reached for her hands. "Darn it, I've done it again. I always talk too much. But I promise I'm only trying to help."

"It's okay," Cordi said. "You really think I need lipstick?"

"Think of it like wearing your best clothes to an interview. But for your face."

Cordi swallowed. "Uh-huh."

The front door opened and Silly stepped in, speaking over her shoulder to Audrey and, to Cordi's surprise, Callum. "It just seemed like a better idea to move here now, so that I'd be ready to start my internship right away instead of worrying about moving. *If* I get my internship. I was supposed to hear back this week, but I haven't. I even called to give them my new number here." She shut the door behind Audrey, who looked like she had no idea how to respond, or more likely that was just the way her face always looked. Callum grinned at Tessa and Cordi as he walked in, holding a gift bag.

"Hi!" Tessa called to him. "What a nice surprise. What are you doing here?"

Cordi sat up straight. Had he come to collect the rent? Was he spying on them for Mikhail?

"Thought you might like a housewarming gift," he said. "How are you doing?" he asked Cordi when she couldn't stop staring.

"Fine," she said. She didn't mean to sound so short, so she added in an overly friendly tone, "I didn't know you knew the others."

"Why, of course," Callum said. "Who do you think told them about the apartment?"

"I assumed everyone saw the ad for it."

"Callum helped me get the room," Silly said. "My grandmother knew someone who knew someone who knew of a room for rent, and it turned out to be Callum."

"I heard about it from Callum as well," Tessa said. "Through a friend."

"And the world goes on," Callum quipped.

"*I* answered an ad," Audrey said.

"But I was here when you looked at it," Callum pointed out.

"Why?" Audrey asked him almost rudely, though Cordi was also curious. "You don't own the building."

"Mikhail's a friend. He was busy that day. He owns lots of buildings, you know, and I gave him the money to get started, so I feel a certain responsibility to helping him thrive."

"Wow." Audrey sounded skeptical. "How nice of you."

Tessa held up her glass. "Join us for a drink, Callum? I made a pitcher—in the kitchen," she added to the girls.

"Oh, I don't think I should," Silly said while Audrey made a beeline for the alcohol. Callum set the bag on the side table by the couch, as Silly sat on the love seat next to Cordi.

"Any luck today?" Silly asked.

Cordi shook her head, glancing at Callum. "I still haven't found a job."

Callum moved closer, standing behind the couch. "That's because you don't have . . . what is it . . ." His accent sometimes sounded stronger when he searched for the right word. "That quality . . . that magic. Power." He grinned, delighted he had found it.

Tessa laughed. "Power?"

He snapped his fingers. "Um . . . privilege. That's better."

"A little on the nose," Audrey said dryly. She stood just outside the square of couches, hovering near the kitchen table, already half-done with the drink she'd poured herself.

"No, it's true. You're at a disadvantage, being . . ." He waved a hand in the general vicinity of Cordi's face. "I'm an immigrant myself, you know."

None of the girls responded, looking at each other uncomfortably. Cordi hadn't asked any of them, but she assumed that they'd all been born here, like she had.

"Anyway, you need some sort of advantage," Callum continued.

"What, like magic?" Audrey said, snorting into her cup.

"Ooh, let's go grab a lurast from off the street," Tessa said. "Those loudmouth preachers are always shouting about how we could be tricked at any second, since apparently lurasts are everywhere."

"Yes!" Callum responded cheerfully. "That's exactly what you need. Lura. A spell. To make all your dreams come true. Let's do one now!"

"I was just joking, darling," Tessa said with a silly smile. Her cheeks were tinged pink. "Magic isn't real."

"But it is." He held out his hands. "It just needs to come from the right person."

"Are you telling us that you're, what, some sort of witch?"

"Yes. And I can make all your dreams come true."

They fell silent. Then Tessa burst into laughter, which was rather contagious, making Callum laugh too. Cordi couldn't help chuckling along with them.

"Think about it," Callum said, reaching into his gift bag to pull out a box. "It would be a simple spell. Just something to help, huh?"

"What is that?" Tessa asked, distracted by the gift.

"A candle." He flashed them a dimpled smile.

"Thank you," Cordi said when no one else said anything. "You're not going to tell Mikhail, are you? About the job." Or lack thereof. "I promise I've been looking. I even interviewed at a mechanic shop next to that ancient church on Wilshire, and the priest was outside as I walked past and kept trying to get me to confess."

Tessa snickered. "About what?"

"I don't know. Said I was in Satan's path or something." Cordi was sure that religious zealots said that to lots of people, but the encounter had seemed aggressively personal, like the man truly feared whatever future awaited her.

"He probably just wanted your money," Tessa said.

"Maybe he can see how powerful you are," Callum teased. "You're a special one, I can tell. He's just trying to exorcise you before it's too late."

"God." Tessa winced. "Don't even joke about that."

Cordi gave Callum a pleading look, and he made a gesture of sealing his lips. "I'm not Mikhail's spy," he said. "Just a friend."

"Then pour yourself a drink, friend," Tessa said.

Callum glanced at his watch. "I actually stopped by here to meet someone, so I'll take a rain check on that drink."

One of the dalliances that Mikhail had mentioned, probably. Cordi took a sip of her drink, trying not to grimace at the bitter aftertaste.

"Don't forget about the offer," he said as he left.

The girls sat quietly for a moment. Cordi picked up the candle Callum had brought and studied the packaging for lack of anything to say.

"What do you do, Audrey?" Tessa asked. No one had had a chance to ask her since she was usually out or shut in her room.

"I work at an art gallery," Audrey said.

"Oh—are you an artist?"

"Yes, but I only work there as a receptionist. They let me use the storage space when I'm not working, though."

"Do you like it?" Tessa asked.

Audrey lifted one shoulder, then dropped it heavily.

"You're all so lucky you have jobs," Cordi said.

"Not me," Silly said. "Mikhail only rented to me on the condition that I get the internship. If I don't, then it's back to my grandma's." The cushions seemed to swallow her whole as she sank into herself.

"He told me that all three of you had jobs," Cordi said. "He made me feel terrible for letting me stay here even though I don't have one yet."

"Callum convinced him," Silly said. "Said a smart girl like me is sure to get the internship. But . . . I don't know."

"And we're so lucky you're here." Tessa gave Silly's shoulders a squeeze, and Cordi felt something inside her clench as she watched them.

"Callum is so nice," Cordi said, pushing down the feeling. "I've never met anyone as nice as him."

"I know," Silly said with a sigh. "And a dreamboat."

"He creeps me out," Audrey said.

They all fell quiet, waiting for her to elaborate.

"Why was he so eager to help you?" Audrey continued, looking at each of them. "And that stuff with the magic. He wants something. There's a strange aura about him."

"Do you believe in that stuff?" Tessa asked. "Auras and witchcraft?"

Audrey downed the rest of her drink. "Does it matter?"

"Well, if you believed in it, why didn't you take him up on his offer? Get yourself a better job, become successful, achieve your dream? You don't want to be a receptionist for the rest of your life, do you? Don't you want to sell your art and become famous?"

"No," Audrey said.

Tessa hesitated, then laughed, as if she weren't sure whether Audrey was joking. "But . . . of course you do. We all do. Everyone has dreams."

"Are you saying you would take Callum up on his offer?"

Tessa smoothed her hair off her shoulder and over her back. "Well, yeah. If what he's saying is real, then why not? I would kill to be famous."

"Even if all that stuff is real, it doesn't mean we need to dabble in it," Audrey said. "Look—cars are obviously real, but I can't afford one, and I'm not going to put myself in debt just to own one. Magic is the same—trust me, whatever the price is, we don't want to pay it."

"What are you all talking about?" Silly asked, looking at Cordi as if she had all the answers, but Cordi was just as lost. She heard street preachers shouting about lurasts and witchcraft all the time. It seemed as if they singled her out, as if she had some sort of magnetism that drew proselytizers to her, but she always ignored them.

"Maybe Callum *is* a witch," Tessa said.

Cordi felt a bit lightheaded, the drink doing warm, tingly things to her belly. She had a vague sense that she'd forgotten something.

"Men like Callum are never nice for no reason," Tessa said. "He's going to want something down the line."

"Do you think he's spying on us for Mikhail?" Cordi asked. "What if he tells him I still haven't found a job?"

"Don't worry so much." Tessa inspected her nails. "Mikhail won't kick you out. Either of you."

"How do you know?" Silly asked.

"He's a softy."

Cordi wondered whether they were talking about the same person.

"Oh, I know he's all grunts, but trust me. A wink here, a touch there, a giggle at one of his jokes. He won't even consider kicking you out. Let me talk to him." Tessa sipped her drink and smiled secretively.

"You're so sure," Audrey said dryly.

"I just know men like him, that's all."

Audrey looked skeptical, but Cordi remembered the way Mikhail had smiled every time Tessa was near him, the way he'd agreed to rent to Cordi as soon as Tessa urged him to, even knowing she didn't have a job lined up. It had almost been too easy, but Cordi hadn't cared—she was just relieved that she had a place to live.

"I wish I could do that," Silly said. "Then I'd probably have that internship."

"Oh, I'll teach you!" Tessa set her glass down on the coffee table. "First things first, you have to make sure your eyes are wide and innocent, but not too much or they'll know it's fake."

Silly's eyes widened as if she'd just heard terrible news. "Like this?"

"Close," Tessa said. "Like this."

Audrey didn't stay for the impromptu lesson in manipulation, rinsing her glass in the kitchen sink before heading once again to her room.

"What, you don't want to learn how to make men do your bidding?" Tessa asked in her sweet voice, as if she were asking whether Audrey would like a slice of cake.

"I don't need men," Audrey said, acid in her voice. "I can succeed on my own."

Chapter Seven

That weekend, Cordi realized that she had nothing to do. She could go out, like she'd always longed to do, but she had no friends and no place she wanted to go, not when the threat of starvation and homelessness loomed ahead. She could visit Elysian Park—that was free, and she'd always liked the hidden lake on top of the hill there, but she would still have to pay for a streetcar, and even that seemed too frivolous when she should save the fare to get to interviews. Downtown Los Angeles had a number of things to do within walking distance, but the dinners and stand-up and nightclubs she always heard about cost money. She didn't know quite what to do with herself.

Tessa also had the morning off, lounging on the sofa in a pink chiffon nightgown, her hair pulled up in a messy bun as she drank her tea slowly. Silly and Audrey must have still been asleep.

"Why are you up so early?" Tessa asked. "And dressed already?" She studied Cordi's white blouse and sensible midi skirt, her usual outfit for job hunting. "Don't tell me you're going to go looking for more jobs. It's the weekend."

Cordi put her purse on the coffee table and sat down. Rejection would still be waiting for her no matter how early she set out, so what did it matter?

"There are places open on the weekend," she said. "Maybe I'll get lucky."

"Pshh. You need to relax. You've been working so hard. You said you had enough saved for a few months, right?"

"Well, more like two. If I don't eat. If I do eat, I might have enough for one more month." She had no idea what would happen if she couldn't find a job by then.

"Who needs to eat? I hardly do." Tessa laughed. "Come on, stay and hang loose with me today. I don't have anything planned. We can go shopping!"

"But . . . I don't have any money for food. I definitely don't have money for . . . anything else."

"Window-shopping, then. It'll be fun. Please? Say yes?"

It was hard to refuse when Tessa had her hands clasped and her eyes all big. Was she doing that manipulation technique she had tried to teach Silly? Did it matter? Someone wanted Cordi's company, something that didn't happen . . . ever. She'd spent a lot of time alone at her parents' shop. And at home, everyone kept to themselves. Even though she had shared a room with her sister, they hadn't talked about anything except what needed to get done, sticking to their own corners and staying busy.

"What do you want to do?" Cordi asked.

Tessa grinned, knowing she'd won. "There are these shops on Olympic Boulevard that I've heard are all the rage. They have the latest fashions at a fraction of the cost. I've been dying to go."

"I know what you're talking about," Cordi said. She had often gone to the alley, which had sprung up almost overnight a few years ago, its market stands and stores overflowing with rolls and yards of fabric. One time, she'd visited a store that simply had a mountain of fabric in the middle of its floor, and she and Mother had stood at the side watching as women climbed the mound, digging around for heavily discounted scraps. The alley was the one place where she and Mother had gone together that wasn't just work or church, where she had fond memories of searching for zippers or buttons and other notions they needed for the shop.

"Then let's go!" Tessa jumped up from the sofa. "I'll let Silly know."

A bit of Cordi's excitement died. She'd hoped to spend time with Tessa on her own, to become better friends. Not that she didn't like Silly, but now she'd have to share Tessa's attention; she had no idea why she craved it so much, but she did. There was just something about Tessa, a glow she had, an energy that drew people to her. Cordi wanted to be her friend, her confidant, or at least be close to her somehow.

When Silly came out of her room, though, in her dowdy white cotton nightdress, Cordi instantly regretted her disappointment. Silly was so earnest and young and endearing. Who wouldn't want her along?

"You want me to come?" she asked, eyes wide. "I'd love to! Although I don't have much money."

Cordi smiled. "Everything is really cheap, and we're just going to go look more than anything. I'm broke too."

Silly sighed in companionable misery and went back to her room to change.

A few minutes later, the three of them met by the front door. Tessa checked her appearance in the mirror on the wall.

"Should we invite Audrey?" Cordi asked.

"No," Tessa said. She added quickly, "It might be more polite to let her sleep in. I mean, she does work during the week and . . ."

Silly nodded. "Yes, much more polite."

Audrey's door opened and all three of them jumped. Her hair was a frizzy mess, standing up in the back, and the bags under her eyes seemed more prominent than usual.

Cordi felt the need to explain. "We're going to the garment district."

Tessa shook her head at Cordi, a small movement that Audrey hopefully didn't notice.

"Want to come?" Cordi asked, unable to stop herself.

Tessa rolled her eyes and opened the door, Silly close on her heels.

"You're going shopping?" Audrey asked.

"Well, just looking around."

From the hallway Tessa tapped her wrist, even though she didn't wear a watch and it wasn't like they had an appointment.

Audrey gave a tight smile. "Have fun," she said, heading to the kitchen for the coffee percolator.

They took two Red Cars to get to Olympic Boulevard, and by the time they stepped onto the dirty pavement, the morning had heated up so that Cordi started sweating as soon as the trolley clanked away. The tall buildings around them did nothing to provide shade, the sun beating down straight above them, casting the sign for Dy-Rect Furniture in a yellow glow and reflecting off a lime-green Cadillac with winged tails that reminded her of a space rocket. Traffic was already heavy, cars inching down the street as the three of them made their way to the alley. Cordi admired the darts of a woman's cinched-waist dress in front of her, and how her pink flats coordinated with the handle of her bag.

Tessa didn't seem to notice the heat, but she had dressed more sensibly in a light, sleeveless dress, her fingers wrapped around a boxy wicker purse, whereas Silly was already red-faced and panting in her slacks and sweater.

"It's about three blocks that way," Cordi said, pointing southbound and glancing down at Tessa's shoes—strappy high-heeled sandals. She had no idea how anyone could walk in those. Cordi had chosen her comfortable pair of oxfords. Silly wore flats, but Cordi wondered whether either of them would make it to the alley without having to stop.

"Great," Tessa said breezily, and forged ahead.

"Maybe we can get some sort of ice treat," Silly suggested. The sun beamed down without mercy.

"I don't know if there's anything like that around here," Cordi said. Silly didn't say anything, but she looked utterly miserable.

"You poor thing," Tessa said, pulling out a pamphlet from her purse to wave in front of Silly like a fan. Cordi found the gesture oddly affectionate yet mildly annoying for reasons she couldn't explain.

The alley stretched several blocks with warehouses open to the public, overflowing with fabric and notions and counterfeit merchandise. The road itself was closed to cars, lined with stalls selling various knickknacks, clothes, shoes, tools, and anything else a person could possibly want or need.

The voices of customers and shop owners haggling formed a low buzz, interrupted with the shouts of a man advertising his wares— "Purses! Brand name, for your mother or sister. Hey there, beautiful, I'll give you a discount." He snapped his fingers at Tessa, who didn't acknowledge him.

They passed through an alley, the walls covered with posters, corners peeling to reveal layers of outdated ads beneath them. One was full of black lines in an almost indecipherable script. A word jumped out at her: *Lura.* She squinted to make out an image underneath, the shadowy, scratchy illustration of some sort of monster with long, spindly limbs and sharp, extended claws. It was almost comically horrifying, but the longer she stared at it, the more a dreadful sensation formed in her chest, compounded when she read the script under the drawing: "Beware the promises—" The rest of the text was covered by a fresh poster for the movie *Anatomy of a Murder.*

She walked away, brushing aside her fear. She had never liked scary movies and didn't want to look at the image too long in case it gave her nightmares later.

The alley was bustling by this time, people bumping shoulders as they perused the wares. It was too late in the day for any good deals— most people in the garment business would have arrived unimaginably early to snag the best fabrics and rare items before the amateurs set out. Cordi and her mother often woke up at dawn to get there and stand in line before the stores opened.

Cordi glanced back to make sure that Silly was still with them. Surprisingly, Tessa didn't seem bothered by the heat or the walk, making a beeline for a store that specialized in dresses and coats copied straight from the fashion magazines.

"This is divine," Tessa said, running a hand down the length of a wool burgundy coat in a cape-like style displayed on a mannequin in front of the store. Inside, two Korean women argued loudly with the lady at the register over a huge mound of dresses. Cordi didn't speak the language, but she knew they were haggling over the price.

"Goodness, they're buying a lot of dresses," Silly said as Tessa glanced at the price tag of the coat.

"I think they probably resell them at their own stores," Cordi said. "They come here to buy them for cheap, and then they mark up the price for a profit."

Tessa fingered the coat with a sad longing. "There's no way I can afford this, even if it's a knockoff."

Cordi studied the piece. It was a boxy style, its value lying in the quality of fabric rather than the difficulty of its construction, though sewing the type of wool and matching it to a silky lining could be tricky.

"I bet I could re-create it," she said.

"Really?" Tessa clasped her hands in glee. "Do you think so? Would it be cheaper to buy the fabric?"

"Maybe." Cordi tapped her chin and glanced around the alley. "There's another store that usually has coating fabric for a decent price, though we might be too late. We can come back next weekend." Then her heart sank heavily. "But I don't have a sewing machine anymore." She had always used the spare one in her parents' shop, a bulky, industrial model they'd bought from a factory that had updated their equipment. Even then, it had been hugely expensive, but Mother had convinced Father it would be worth the investment since it meant Cordi could double their workload. There was no way she could afford a machine of her own.

"You want to buy?" a lady's voice asked them. She must have been the owner and stood at the entrance of the shop wearing an apron with scissors and a measuring tape sticking out from the top of the pockets. The two women she'd been arguing with had concluded their business and walked down the alley carrying huge bags filled with clothes.

"Oh no," Cordi said. "Just looking."

"How much is this?" Tessa asked innocently, fingering the lapels of the coat.

The lady stepped closer and flicked the price tag. "Ten dollars."

Cordi winced.

"Ten?" Tessa shook her head. "No, more like five, don't you think?"

The lady tsked. "This is premium wool. Look at lining—pure silk."

"This doesn't feel real to me," Cordi said, rubbing the fabric between her fingers. The rough fibers couldn't be as pure as the lady claimed.

The lady frowned at her. "Seven," she said to Tessa.

"And the wool . . . looks more like a felt," Cordi said. "I mean, it's good-quality felt, but not really premium wool, is it?"

The woman looked at the coat, then back at Cordi. "You know about clothes, huh?" she asked.

Cordi realized that she might sound rather conceited and snobby when she hadn't intended to—she just didn't want the woman to take advantage of her friend. "Just a little," she said, her voice growing smaller.

Tessa laughed haughtily. "A little? My friend is an expert. She's worked for all the best designers."

"Really?" The woman raised her brows. "Which ones?"

Cordi stared at Tessa, begging her silently to just move on. But Tessa had a steely look about her.

"George Laurent," Tessa said.

Cordi had no idea who that was, and she doubted the woman did either. In fact, she was pretty sure Tessa had made it up and just spouted out the most European name she could think of.

"Hmm," the woman said. She didn't look at all convinced, scrutinizing Cordi skeptically. "I go six dollar, no less."

"Done," Tessa said, unsnapping the clasp of her purse.

They spent the rest of the day perusing the other stores, though shopping was arguably less fun without any money, and it only made Cordi sad. Not just because she didn't have the money but because even if she could afford the fabric, she no longer had a sewing machine.

Later, as they started toward home, Tessa's new coat draped over one arm, Cordi glanced back at the woman's shop. It reminded her so much of her parents' business, the dim lighting, the mess of fabrics. She could tell at a glance that most, if not all, expenses had been spared, money spent only when absolutely necessary.

Her throat itched, heat blooming behind her eyes. She'd often resented working for her parents, but she had done her best. That's all she ever did, in school, in work, even at home, trying to live up to her parents' expectations. But still, nothing ever came of it. Just like her job search.

Her fingers curled into fists. She was a hard worker, and she could do anything, learn anything. She just needed the chance.

"Wait, I'll be right back," she said to the others, cutting Tessa off midsentence.

She left the girls at a shaded spot around the corner and shouldered her way back to the woman's shop.

"Hi," she said, breathless. The woman stood at the entrance, not saying anything. "My friend was lying earlier. I've never worked for any designers." She trembled slightly, her heart racing, though it was too late to turn back now.

"Hmm," the woman mumbled.

"But I do know a lot about fabric and clothes and sewing. I used to work at an alterations shop."

The woman still didn't say anything, waiting for Cordi to get to her point.

"I was just wondering—" And here, Cordi lost a bit of her nerve. "If you're hiring?"

The woman's stony silence reminded her of Trina. "What language you speak?" she asked finally.

"Um, well, English and Vietnamese."

"We do have some Vietnamese customer—come in and buy bulk." She seemed to think about it for a moment. "Leave your number. I consider."

Cordi let out a breath, all the energy leaving her body, her legs threatening to give out. It was better than nothing.

Chapter Eight

The apartment was blessedly cool when they got home that afternoon, the plants at the window blocking the sunlight. Cordi's face and arms were inflamed from being in the sun all day, the skin already two shades darker.

A heaviness weighed her down, making the climb up the rungs to her loft feel as if she were slogging through water. As she sank into her mattress, she felt something hot and painful swell in her chest and threaten to burst. It had been the sight of all those stores, all that fabric, and nostalgia flooded her, followed by the sickening dread that her old life was truly gone, that she had no idea what awaited her.

Cordi used to go to the alley with Mother at least once a month. Mother never bought any pretty fabrics, of course, nothing frivolous for her. She went for the cheap essential supplies for the shop—zippers, an endless supply of thread, bobbins, and needles for the machines. The alley was the one place where she never criticized Cordi's choices because at least Cordi was spending her money and time wisely by making her clothing instead of wasting it all on overpriced store-ready pieces.

It was the only time Mother spent with Cordi when she didn't scold her or tell her what to do, and even though the outings were technically for the shop, Cordi still cherished them.

Now she had no idea when or if she would see Mother again. It hit her almost out of the blue, even though she'd had weeks to come to terms with it, that part of her life was really over. She couldn't go back. And she wasn't sure that she even wanted to.

With that realization came another one: she was free. She didn't have to return to a cold, unloving home. She could do whatever she wanted with her life. Make whatever she wanted of herself. Get whatever job—well, whichever one hired her anyway. She didn't have to ask for permission to do anything anymore. The only person whose permission she needed was her own.

Cordi sat up, imbued with a sense of urgency, a desire to *do* something.

She pulled out her sketchbook. Quickly, she outlined the pieces that would make up Tessa's wool coat, as well as several other items she'd seen at the alley. She would get a sewing machine as soon as possible. Once she found a job, that would be the first thing she'd buy. Because now that she could be anything, she knew there was only one thing she wanted to be. Only one thing she loved doing more than anything else.

Cordi went back down to the living room, hurrying to the coffee table to dig through Tessa's pile of magazines and catalogs.

She turned to see Audrey in the kitchen and jumped.

"Goodness, I didn't even realize you were home," Cordi said, hand over her thumping heart.

"I've been home all day," Audrey said. She scooped rice out of a bowl with a pair of chopsticks. "How was the garment district?"

Cordi bit back a small trace of guilt for ditching Audrey that morning. "It wasn't very fun since no one has any money, except Tessa."

"I painted a mural there once," Audrey said, sitting at the kitchen table.

"A mural. You mean, like . . . graffiti?"

"I mean a mural."

"Oh." Cordi wished she could retreat to her bed. Tessa's bedroom door was open, so she must have left, and Silly's door was closed, so she was probably gone too.

"Haven't been back in a while, though," Audrey continued. "So don't know if it's still there."

"What's it of?"

"These two women. They're sad and crying. You know, the usual stuff."

"Oh. Oh! Actually, I have seen it." The mural was rather beautiful, though yes, the subjects did look sad. Cordi had never noticed that before, usually distracted by the quality of light that infused the painting, as if the wall itself glowed. "That was you? You're very talented."

Audrey shrugged. "It took a lot of practice runs. Kept getting interrupted."

"Aren't you scared you'll get in trouble?"

"No." Audrey rested her chopsticks across the top of the bowl. "What's the point of that?"

Cordi didn't understand Audrey's way of thinking. All her life, she'd been afraid. Afraid of her parents, afraid of failing, afraid of her sister, afraid of her teachers, afraid of getting in trouble. And here Audrey didn't seem like she was scared of anything.

A knock came at the door, and she breathed out a sigh of relief for not having to think of anything to say in response and went to answer it.

"Callum, hi!" She opened the door wide to let him in, thoughts racing as to why he was there. Had Mikhail somehow known she'd spent all day shopping, even if she hadn't spent any money, instead of hunting for a job? Had he sent Callum to remind her how tenuous her living situation was?

Callum was dressed nicely, like he was on his way to a fancy party. His jacket was perfectly tailored, though unbuttoned, and he had loosened his bow tie. As usual, he wore intricately detailed gloves over his long fingers, one hand wrapped around the neck of a wine bottle, and Cordi eyed the gloves with envy. She wanted a pair like that—though pink, perhaps, with a matching pillbox hat. She always eyed the gloves in the window display at the boutique around the corner on her way home. But they would be a frivolous purchase, and every time she thought about splurging with her limited budget, she remembered once again Mother's fury over the Petite lipstick.

"Hello," he said, stepping inside. He nodded at Audrey. "I was in the neighborhood and thought I'd stop by. I stole this from the dinner party I was at." He handed her the bottle of wine. "Just for you."

"Oh." Cordi laughed. "Thanks, I think."

"What is it?" Audrey asked, still sitting at the table.

"Some sort of red." Cordi didn't know anything about wine.

"Let's open it." Audrey went to the kitchen and came back with a corkscrew. "Want a glass?" she asked Callum.

"Why not?" Callum said. He started pacing the living room.

Cordi fetched some glasses while Audrey twisted the corkscrew into the bottle opening. The cork popped just as Tessa burst through the front door, Silly following behind her.

"Guess what? We got sandwiches from Dipped!" Tessa held up a white paper bag smelling of garlic and butter and chicken and melted cheese. Cordi had known Tessa was gone but hadn't realized she and Silly had left together . . . without her. She found it difficult to return Silly's smile, and then of course she felt ridiculous for resenting the girl and her innocent, baby-plump cheeks. "Hi, Callum! If I'd known you were coming over, I would have gotten you one too."

Callum leaned against the table, hands in his pockets. "Don't worry about it. I just had dinner. But I'll stay for the wine."

"Wine?" Tessa brightened when Audrey sloshed the red liquid into the mismatched glasses.

She and Silly set the bag on the kitchen table and pulled out sandwiches wrapped in white paper and secured with rubber bands. Cordi got two more glasses, and Audrey poured equal amounts into all of them. The rich and dark red pooled at the bottoms of the glasses.

"Thanks for the food," Cordi said, her stomach growling. She'd been scrimping that week on groceries—they all had, judging from the almost-empty shelves of their refrigerator—and the smell of the sandwiches made her mouth water.

Callum took the seat at the head of the table as the others all sat—Audrey surprising Cordi yet again by sitting next to her, Tessa directly in front at Callum's other side, Silly next to Tessa—and Cordi realized it was the first time all of them had eaten together. It felt quite nice, almost like a real family.

Callum picked up his glass and raised it, and they all copied him. "To these lovely ladies who I have the absolute pleasure of befriending," he proclaimed.

Tessa grinned. "To the Mais!"

Callum smiled and clinked Cordi's glass. Silly gave a little giggle, covering her mouth with her hand as she met Cordi's eyes, as if it were also her first time being included in an intimate group of friends. Cordi tried not to show it, but a pleasant warmth swelled in her chest.

They all took a sip, though Cordi tried not to make a face as the dry liquid hit her tongue in a tart, smoky flood of flavor she was pretty sure she hated. It didn't take long for a tingle to spread in her lower belly, her empty stomach absorbing the wine to make her cheeks flare with heat.

"So?" Callum asked, swishing his wineglass around expertly. "Any problems with the place Mikhail should know about?"

"My, how attentive," Tessa cooed as she grabbed a sandwich. Her manicured fingernails pulled back the rubber band slowly. "I've never had a manager who cared so much about his tenants."

"Oh, I'm not a manager." Callum smiled. "Just a . . . caring friend."

"Of ours?" Tessa asked. "Or Mikhail's?"

"Why not both?"

Cordi unwrapped her own sandwich and bit into it, her mouth filling with the savory taste of garlic chicken and some sort of gooey cheese, all sitting on a rich, buttery bread and complemented with creamy sauce oozing between the layers of lettuce and tomato.

"Everything is great—nothing has broken yet," Tessa answered for all of them.

"I still haven't heard from my internship," Silly blurted out. She had her elbows propped on the table, holding her sandwich up as if to hide her face. Tessa reached over to pat her shoulder and coo like a mother hen into her ear, and Cordi's annoyance flared—she hadn't found a job either, but she wasn't making such a fuss about it.

"That's all right," Callum said, surprisingly reassuring. "You've still got time. I don't see Cordi here worrying too much about it." He flashed her a grin to show he was only joking.

Still, Cordi felt her blood run cold, even though she'd just been thinking the same thing. "I've been looking, I promise." She took a gulp of her wine, almost choking.

"Relax. I'm not here as some spy." He chuckled. "Don't forget who convinced Mikhail to rent to you in the first place—and at a cheaper price too! Please, enjoy your night." He held up his hands. "Or should I leave?"

"Nonsense." Tessa reached out, placing her fingers on his forearm. "They're good girls. They just haven't learned how to break the rules yet," she whispered loudly, then winked across the table at Cordi.

Like usual, Cordi had no idea how to navigate the conversational maze. She kept eating, hoping that the food would instill in her some magical talent to help her play along.

"And I suppose you know how to break the rules," Callum said to Tessa, his voice low.

"Do you two want us to leave the room?" Audrey asked in her flat voice.

Tessa took her hand back and resumed eating. "Nope, I do so love an audience."

Audrey let out a loud exhale.

"I applied for a job at a fabric store today," Cordi told Callum, still feeling the need to explain herself. "I have a good feeling about it."

"Sounds dreadfully boring," he mused, but he said everything with a casual, cheerful tone, so Cordi wasn't sure if he really meant it or if it was just the way rich people prattled. Callum struck her as rich—the cut of his suit, the expensive tailoring as well as the silk of his tie, indicating that he could afford to dress well.

"I think I would enjoy it," she said. "I know I will. I love that kind of stuff. Clothes and . . . you know . . . clothes."

Tessa smiled at her. "You should be a fashion designer."

"That's impossible," Cordi said, though it was exactly what she wanted, a dream she hardly dared to admit to herself. It was just a fantasy, not something attainable, and she waited for several long seconds for Callum to laugh in her face.

But he didn't.

"I've wondered to myself if you were a designer," he said. "You're always wearing the most unique threads whenever I see you."

"I like . . . pockets," Cordi said for some reason even she couldn't fathom. Perhaps it was the wine. She drank some more just to be safe. "Not all the dresses in stores have them, so I sew them myself."

"Pockets are rather useful."

"But no one's ever heard of an Asian designer before," Cordi said. She regretted it, because the statement was rather sad, and there was really no way to respond to it, so she didn't blame any of them when the heavy words drooped in the air, abandoned and unclaimed.

Callum grinned at her. He had one dimple on his left cheek, and Cordi found it impossible not to smile back like a lovesick idiot. "I bet we can make that happen," he said. "Have you given any thought to what I proposed last time?"

Cordi met Tessa's eyes.

"About magic?" Tessa asked.

"Yes." He leaned in close. So did the others. "After all, I am a witch."

Cordi giggled. She was starting to feel a bit lightheaded, the room taking on a blurry effect, the lights fuzzy around the edges, and when she met Tessa's eyes across the table, the other girl mouthed, *I knew it*. Cordi took another sip from her glass, surprised to find it almost empty.

"Men can't be witches," she said, cocking her head to one side. The room spun a bit, and when she blinked, she had the sensation that she'd skipped forward in time by a few seconds, and that everyone was staring at her, wondering where she'd just been.

"How do you know? Have you met many witches?" Callum asked.

"No, but . . ." Cordi reached out, her index finger landing on the tip of his nose. "You don't have a wart."

Callum laughed and wrapped his fist around her finger. "Lurasts aren't typical witches, and besides, warts on witches are just a myth. Most witches can only do small magic, like a little love potion that doesn't last."

"*Witches* are a myth." Her tongue felt thick and heavy, and it took more effort to enunciate her words. "They're not real. Neither are lurasts."

"Oh, but I am real." His wide grin made those crinkles appear at the corners of his eyes. "How do you think I'm this handsome? You should see when a spell goes wrong."

He still had hold of her finger, and she pulled it back, her skin sliding along his.

"Lura is real," Audrey surprised them all by saying. "Lura is a type of witchcraft. My aunt used to tell me stories. But it's dangerous—we shouldn't be playing around with that stuff."

"Nonsense," Callum said. "I'm a professional."

"So what, are you going to make our wishes come true?" Audrey asked.

"It depends on what you want."

"At what cost?" Audrey asked.

Callum laughed. "Why is it always about money with you girls?"

"Maybe because we don't have any," Audrey said coldly.

"It's true, Callum, we're flat broke," Tessa said.

Callum grinned at her. "But isn't your dad that rich politician? I just assumed he paid the bills."

"Not *our* bills," Audrey mumbled.

Tessa crossed her arms. "If you're going to be granting wishes, you should know it's gotta be for free."

"Nothing good comes for free," Audrey announced in a voice so full of doom, they all turned and stared at her. "What? It's true."

"On the contrary," Callum said, "all the best things in life are free." Tessa snorted.

"You don't believe me?" Callum stood up. "All right, it's time to show you ladies that I mean business. Come on. We need"—he looked around the apartment—"candles. A bowl. Some of your most senti-mental items."

Cordi finished the last of her sandwich, wishing she had more.

"Come on, chop-chop." Callum clapped twice, and despite her-self, she got up from the table. The others did as well, looking mildly amused. Callum rubbed his hands together. "Let's make some magic."

Chapter Nine

Cordi buzzed with nervous excitement as Callum led them to the square of couches.

"Where's the bowl?" he asked, and Silly handed him a large metal punch bowl. "And candles?"

Tessa came back from her room with a handful of tea light candles and a gold lighter.

"This is nice," Callum said, flicking it open.

"It was a gift," she said.

"Now, you all need to go get a sentimental object," he instructed.

"What kind of sentimental object?" Audrey asked. She looked skeptical but hadn't disappeared to her bedroom yet, standing there stiffly in her paint-splattered overalls and black turtleneck.

"Anything that means something to you."

Audrey stuck a hand deep into a pocket. "Like this?" She held up a small hammer.

"Perfect." Callum took it and dropped it in the punch bowl.

"Why do you carry . . ." Tessa started to ask, then shook her head. "I don't care."

"Are you going to keep it?" Cordi asked. "Like a payment?"

He smiled. "No, that's not the kind of payment I'm looking for."

"I thought you said this was free," Audrey said.

"I consider it an investment," he said. "Once you've all got your wishes, you can pay me back in kind."

Cordi giggled. "You're really going to grant us all our wishes?"

"Just one wish each." The dimple reappeared in his cheek.

"I've got it!" Silly disappeared into her room and came back out with a flimsy piece of metal. "This is a bookmark my dad gave me. Right before he died."

"Aw, Silly," Tessa said. "That's just the most precious thing. All right, fine." She dug through her purse and pulled out a small black compact mirror. "From my mom."

Most of Cordi's things were still at her parents' house. She climbed up to her loft and dug through her bag until her fingers wrapped around an empty thread spool, the first one she'd used completely on her own when she learned how to sew. At first, she'd hated working at the alterations shop, forced to give up any friendships she might have had because she had to work. But then Mother had praised her for the first time ever for sewing the perfect invisible hem. And that was when she realized that sewing was the only way to earn approval from Mother and Father, and she'd started to value her work and actually enjoy it.

She'd used this particular spool of thread to sew one of her first pieces for herself. She had bent over the sewing machine for hours to make the dress she'd hoped to wear to her first school dance. When she'd shown the dress to Mother, for the first time her mom hadn't scolded or criticized any part of the project. They'd even cooked a special dinner that night to celebrate that Cordi could officially work full-time at the shop and take over the more complicated jobs, though she hadn't managed to eat much, her throat clogging each time she saw the proud look on her parents' faces, so rare and fleeting. Even Trina had been nice to her that evening, probably relieved that Cordi could take over her shifts.

Cordi never had the chance to go to the school dance after all. But she'd still cherished the dress. She hoped Trina would remember to pack it with the rest of her things.

Clutching the empty spool, she climbed down and rejoined the others at the coffee table. Audrey's small hammer sat inside the bowl, along with Tessa's compact mirror and Silly's metal bookmark.

The others knelt on the floor around the coffee table while Callum stood over the bowl, and Cordi crouched down next to Tessa.

"Do you really think this is going to work?" Cordi asked.

Tessa giggled. "Oh, who knows. It's like reading cards. One of my friends used to read our fortunes all the time. Nothing she said ever came true, but we had such a ball. As long as it's fun, right?"

"I sure hope it's real," Silly said, staring wistfully into the bowl. "I really, really want that internship."

"So that's your wish, then?" Callum asked. He pulled a small glass vial from the inside pocket of his jacket. It was filled with white crystals and looked like a fancy saltshaker.

"Yes," Silly said. "That's literally all I want. If I can just have that, I'd be so happy."

Callum smiled, turning to Audrey. "And you?"

Audrey debated that for a while. "I don't know. I guess, I don't want to lose what I already have."

"That's it?" Tessa asked.

Audrey ignored her, still looking at Callum, who nodded.

"Done. And what about you?" Callum asked Tessa.

She leaned forward. "I want to be the most beautiful, the most famous model there ever was."

Callum laughed. "I'll see what I can do."

"If I could just get noticed, you know, *discovered*, that would be great. Or a raise would be nice. Even if it's a small gig, like for Lacy's catalog. I'm already on the list, so how hard can it be?"

Callum uncorked the vial and shook a bit of the white crystals into the bowl. "Noted. And you, Cordelia? What do you want?"

"A job," she said immediately.

"That's it? No fame, no fortune?"

She shook her head. "I mean, it would be nice if it was a good job, with a nice boss. At that fabric store, maybe. As long as it pays enough for me to live here." She looked around the circle at the girls. It had been only a month since they'd moved in, but they had been the best weeks of her life. It wasn't just the sudden freedom from the overbearing coldness and expectations of her family—it was *them*. The Mais. Tessa and her warm energy, Silly with her sweet innocence, and even Audrey with her brutal honesty. Cordi didn't think she could start all over again somewhere else, alone. She wanted to stay there.

The other girls returned her gaze as if they knew exactly what she was thinking. Silly's lower lip started to quiver. Like Cordi, she was the only one in any real danger of having to leave.

"Okay, okay, ladies, let's not waste all our emotions just yet," Callum said. "We need them for the spell."

Callum lit the candles and arranged them around the bowl so that a ring of fire burned into Cordi's vision, flickering and reflecting off the surface of the metal. They'd dimmed the apartment lights, so the flames created flickering shadows around them, like demons rising from the dark.

Callum began taking off his gloves slowly, tugging each finger one by one. When his hands emerged, Cordi saw markings on them, almost like tattoos, winding from his wrists, around his fingers, and bleeding like black ink into his fingernails. She wondered if the candlelight was playing tricks on her eyes, and she had to admit that she'd become quite tipsy.

"Beautiful ladies gathered here tonight," he said, which made Tessa giggle, which made Cordi giggle, which prompted Silly to burst into uproarious laughter. Audrey's mouth twitched. "I am here to grant you your most cherished wishes of fame and beauty and . . . an internship . . . a job." He smiled at Cordi. "But before we begin, we must establish something." He gave them all very serious looks, which made the giggles harder to suppress. "You must want this," he whispered, "more than anything in the world."

Tessa covered her mouth with a hand, hiding a grin. "Oh God."

"That's the only way this will work," he continued. "You must be willing to do anything to get it. Anything."

The girls all looked at each other with nervous smiles.

"I don't . . . want this," Audrey said, starting to get up.

"I don't believe you," Callum said with a soft smile.

"Come on, Audrey, don't be such a wet rag," Tessa said.

Audrey shook her head. "This is too dangerous."

"It's not real," Tessa said. "We're just having a gas. Calm down—do you want another drink?"

"No." Audrey looked at Cordi, half kneeling. "Cordi, let's go."

Cordi's gaze ping-ponged between Audrey and Tessa, who pouted. Why didn't Audrey ask the others to get up too? Why just Cordi? Was it so obvious that Cordi was different from everyone around her? Was Cordi that much of a loser that even Audrey thought she didn't belong?

Or was it just that Audrey thought the two of them were the same? Cordi didn't have anything against Audrey, who hadn't been mean to her, but she wasn't exactly friendly either. She wasn't Tessa.

"It's just a game," Cordi said softly.

Audrey let out a sigh and, to Cordi's surprise, sat back down. "Fine."

Callum had waited patiently, and once again flashed his dimpled grin. "Is everyone sure? Do you want this?" When the girls all nodded, he added, "You must say it."

"We want it," Tessa said.

"We want it," Cordi, Silly, and Audrey echoed, voices overlapping and out of cadence.

Callum smiled. He clapped his hands and rubbed them together. "Okay, now we must join hands."

He spread his arms. Everyone took each other's hands, grinning, except Audrey, who looked uncertain. Cordi felt a pleasant lightheadedness as she closed her eyes briefly, breathing in the jasmine-scented candles surrounding the bowl.

"Now, repeat after me," Callum said.

When she opened her eyes, she could see the other girls waiting in anticipation of the magical words that would open doors to a world where all their dreams would come true.

Then Callum opened his mouth. "Mr. Lura," he sang. "Bum, bum, bum, bum." It was to the tune of a catchy doo-wop number, though he'd changed the name of the "mister" in the song.

Tessa laughed. "Oh, come on. I thought you were being serious."

"I am," Callum said, though his crinkly-eyed smile suggested otherwise. "Repeat after me. And don't forget to want. Hold on to your desire, keep it in the front of your mind, and really feel it. Feel how much you want it, and everything you'd be willing to give up to get it. I mean it."

And so, feeling incredibly silly but also enjoying herself through the haze of drunkenness, Cordi sang along.

"Mr. Lura, grant me a wish, give me the good things on my list," she repeated, off-key and a few beats behind the others because she didn't quite know all the lyrics to the song. Their voices overlapped, interrupted here and there with giggles, and their words slurred as they got near the end of the song so that it sounded almost like "Master Lura" instead of "Mr. Lura," but she couldn't be sure. "Master Lura, don't leave me alone, don't turn your back, just take me home, I just want your magic gift, Master Lura, don't cast me adrift." Her eyelids grew heavy, her vision blurring, until all she could see were the dots of flames from the candles. "Master Lura, please, please, please," they sang, their voices reaching a crescendo, "taaaake meeee—"

The metal bowl suddenly burst into flames. The fire from the candles flared into one big ball of blinding light.

The girls screamed. Cordi let go of their hands and threw her arms over her head.

But just as quickly as the fire had flamed, it went out. In fact, all the lights did. The apartment went completely dark, filled only with the sounds of their panicked breathing.

And then the light flickered back on, brighter than before. The refrigerator started humming.

Callum sat up straight. His hair was rumpled and his eyes were wide. The girls all clutched each other. Even Tessa looked less than perfect, face stretched with fright.

And then Callum started laughing. Cordi had no idea what that meant. Had the spell worked? Or was it all just one big joke? The girls looked at each other, and then Tessa smiled, which infused Cordi with a sense of relief that spread like the warmth from a sip of tea. Tessa giggled too, and Cordi couldn't help making a small sound of amusement in return, which prompted Silly to laugh. Audrey breathed easier, but her expression remained slack.

Tessa extracted herself from the rest of them. Cordi got to her feet as well, and then all four girls peered down into the bowl. Their items remained, intact and undamaged in any way despite the fire that had flamed shockingly high from inside and all around the bowl.

The candles, though, were completely gone. Only the glass shells remained, and even those looked pristine, free of any scorch marks.

"Looks like you'll be on your way to beauty and riches any day now," Callum said, tugging his gloves back on.

Cordi picked up her thread spool, Tessa her compact mirror, Audrey her tiny hammer, and Silly her metal bookmark. Everything looked brand new, as if the fire had cleaned and polished the objects.

Tessa opened the compact with a snap and studied herself. "I look the same." She turned this way and that.

Cordi wasn't sure what to expect, but she was equally relieved and yet somewhat disappointed to see that Tessa was right. Tessa still looked like herself—straight black hair, tan skin, hooded eyes. She was, of course, still very beautiful, but she was far from being the most gorgeous model in the world.

"It takes a while to go into effect," Callum said when Cordi turned to him.

"Right." Tessa closed her mirror. "Well then." She turned to the others. "Drink?"

Chapter Ten

Cordi woke up with the most painful headache she had ever had in her life. Her mouth felt like she'd tried to eat a spoonful of flour, and when she sat up, her stomach rolled, along with the rest of the apartment. She had to lie back down and breathe through the worst of it.

Thankfully everything was quiet, so the others must still be asleep. She would have stayed in bed except her throat was so dry that when she tried to swallow, she gagged.

Water. Kitchen. She couldn't process much else beyond that.

She almost died climbing down from the loft, her grip so weak that her fingers slipped off the rungs. Luckily, she made it down to the main floor, her head spinning. Her stomach heaved, and she ran to the bathroom, but by the time she made it, she no longer felt the need to be sick.

Instead, she splashed her face with water, cupping some in her hand to drink.

When she looked at herself in the mirror, she had to blink. Blink again.

She looked . . . different. There was something off about her face, like maybe her nose had grown slimmer . . . but that was odd. And her eyes . . . She stared but her vision began to cross. No, there was nothing wrong. She looked the same.

Could it be the side effects of a bad hangover? Cordi had never had one before—she'd never drunk as much as she had last night.

She scrubbed her face with soap. She couldn't remember much after Callum's magic trick. There had been more drinking, of course, and she vaguely recalled music and . . . dancing? Had she climbed onto the kitchen counter at one point?

She rubbed her eyes and walked back to the living room. Evidence of their evening lay strewn across the sofa and table—the metal bowl, now empty. Their sentimental tokens scattered on the floor between drained glasses and bottles. A dried-out lemon wedge curled on the rug.

Cordi attempted to clean up, but the moment she bent down to retrieve her threadless spool, her head spun, and she pitched forward onto the sofa, swallowing bile. She clutched the spool and clenched her eyes shut and had no idea how long she stayed like that before she felt someone else approach.

"Ugh, you too?" It was Audrey, thankfully blocking out the blinding light from the window. Her face was shadowed as she leaned down to put something in Cordi's hand. "Here. You look like you need this more than me."

It was a couple of painkillers. Cordi stuffed them down her throat as Audrey came back with glasses of water for both of them. She slumped into the love seat next to the sofa and curled into a ball.

They must have dozed off because the next thing Cordi knew, she was blinking at the sight of Tessa standing over them.

"What?" Audrey demanded.

Tessa stared, eyes wide in disbelief.

Cordi stared back. Because Tessa looked different too. Oh, she was still gorgeous, but there was something different about her face, the same thing Cordi had seen in her own reflection. Some sort of . . . filter, like she was looking at Tessa's face through a lens . . . a beauty lens.

"Oh my God," Tessa whispered as she scrutinized Cordi, then Audrey. "You look . . ." She trailed off.

"You too," Cordi said.

Tessa touched her face.

"What?" Audrey got up. "We look what?"

She ran to the bathroom. Tessa glanced at Cordi, then followed Audrey.

"What's going on?" Silly asked, coming out of her bedroom. She stared at Cordi, who stared back. "What . . ."

They both rushed to the bathroom without another word, joining the other two at the sink. Their four reflections barely fit in the mirror, but squeezing their faces next to each other, Cordi could no longer deny the truth. They all looked odd.

"We're beautiful!" Silly gasped. "We look . . ."

"My eyes are definitely bigger, aren't they? Look at us." Tessa stepped back. "You're all taller too."

It was true. Usually, Tessa towered over them, but now Cordi didn't have to look up to meet her eyes. And the sleeves of her sweater, which usually hung off her fingertips, now ended at her wrists.

"There's no way this can be real," Silly said. "Ow!" Audrey had pinched her. "Why'd you do that?"

"I thought that's what people did when they start to question reality," Audrey said. She had changed too, the lashes framing her eyes thick and dark, making them appear larger, and her skin taking on a milky complexion that gave her a young, practically innocent look that was at odds with her personality.

Silly rubbed her arm. "But why did you pinch me? You could have pinched yourself."

"Why would I do that?"

"Ladies!" Tessa swiped her hands outward. "Bigger issues." She gestured at the mirror.

They stood crowded in the bathroom. No one seemed to know what to do or say. Had the spell worked last night? Was Callum really a witch?

"But why do we look like this?" Audrey mumbled. She poked at her cheek. "Only Tessa asked for beauty."

"Well, obviously," Tessa said with a side-eye at Audrey. "You all asked for success, and prettier people tend to be . . ." She chose her next words with care as Audrey's gaze narrowed. "Better . . . perceived by . . . you know . . . other people."

Audrey's mouth opened in consternation. Silly nodded vigorously, though she didn't provide any supporting arguments.

"Does anyone have Callum's phone number?" Cordi asked. "Or address or any way to reach him?"

"Honestly, I don't remember anything after the thing he did with the fire and the lights going out," Audrey said.

"You did drink a lot," Silly said, still rubbing her arm where Audrey had pinched her.

"We all did," Audrey said defensively.

"Yeah, I blacked out after the dancing," Tessa said.

"I thought I imagined that," Cordi said.

Tessa sat down on the toilet seat lid, grabbed a pack of cigarettes off the windowsill, and was about to light one when she stopped. "Where's my lighter?"

No one knew the answer.

"Okay, come on, I love that thing. My favorite boyfriend gave it to me."

"Was it the gold one?" Cordi asked. Tessa nodded. "I think Callum used it for his spell yesterday."

They went back to the coffee table in the living room and dug through the mess. No one could find the lighter.

"Do you think he took it?" Cordi asked.

"That bastard," Tessa said, slapping a hand on the coffee table to push herself off the floor where she'd crouched. "If we see him, I'll make sure he gets smacked in the face."

"Do you think that's what he meant by payment?" Silly asked. "You know. For this." She gestured at herself and then at the three of them, reminding them that the spell had worked and that they all looked, on some level . . . not themselves.

Cordi closed her eyes as it hit her. She had no idea how to feel. She hadn't actually thought the spell would work, had she? They'd all thought it was a game, a fun, drunken night with a handsome man who wanted to impress them. So why not play along?

And yet, she didn't just look different. She *felt* different. Taller, leaner, prettier. It wasn't an unpleasant sensation. But it wasn't what she'd asked for. All she'd wanted was a job.

The phone rang, jolting them out of their thoughts. Tessa answered.

"Misses Mai residence," she said in a breezy voice. "Um. Sure. Hold on." She held the receiver against her chest. "It's for you, Cordi."

Cordi took the phone, her heart racing, hoping it was a potential employer. "Hi, this is Cordelia Yin," she said in as pleasant a voice as she could muster.

"Are you the girl who left her number here?" a lady asked in a Korean accent. Cordi recognized her voice from the fabric store at the garment district alley.

"Yes," she said, hope blossoming in her belly.

"You still want job?"

Though hundreds of people worked at the shops and market stalls in the garment district, it was not, strictly, legal. It didn't matter, though, because no one cared. The customers didn't pay attention, too distracted by the fact that they'd found a designer bag for a fraction of the cost of an authentic one. The cops were paid off, the cash flow was heavy, and the streets were so crowded that it would have been impossible for the authorities to put a stop to it all.

Cordi arrived at the metal gate of the fabric shop just as it rolled up, the woman she'd met a few days ago pressing a button next to the door.

"Oh, you're on time," she said.

"Hi," Cordi said, stepping into the shop. The smell of new fabric flooded her nostrils. "Thanks again for this opportunity. I'm so grateful—"

"You work hard, that's all I ask," the woman interrupted her. "My name is Ms. Ran. What I call you?"

"My name is Cordi."

Ms. Ran gave her a hard look. "I can't pronounce that."

"Um." The woman stared at her, waiting for some sort of solution. "My mother calls me Li-Ah." It was Vietnamese tradition to be called the last syllables of your full name. Her parents had chosen the most American-sounding name they could come up with, but they'd never been able to pronounce it correctly either. So being called Li-Ah was nothing new, although it would feel odd to have a stranger use a name that only her family ever used.

"Better," Ms. Ran said. She looked Cordi up and down. Cordi wore a simple shift dress she'd made that was comfortable to work in but was still rather cute. She had worried it wouldn't fit her changed body, and had been relieved when it did, though it hung off her differently and ended higher above her knees than she would have liked.

"You buy that fabric from Ms. Kim, huh?" Ms. Ran said, jerking her chin to a shop a block down the alley.

"Oh, I think so?" Cordi smoothed a hand down her skirt.

"I recognize, from last fall line. We sold out and she beat us by buying stock before we could." She shook her head and tsked.

"What do you need me to do?" Cordi asked.

"Come, I show you." Ms. Ran led Cordi through the overflowing rows of fabric bolts to the back of the store, where fabric covered a large worktable. "You cut the yards. Scissors." She handed Cordi a heavy metal pair—the good kind. As Cordi measured their weight and gave a few test snips, her respect for Ms. Ran grew. "You cut. Take money. Price here." The woman pulled a bolt of fabric over to show the price tag hidden inside the round cardboard roll. "If they want to buy whole thing, they talk to me."

"Right." Cordi nodded, ready to start working.

"I pay you ten dollars for the week. You come in at five, you leave at five. You get Wednesday and Thursday off. Tuesday, not so busy, so

I call you. Weekends are busiest. Have to work all the weekends, no exceptions. Good?"

Cordi mentally calculated the salary. It was much more than what her parents had given her, but back then she hadn't had any bills, at least not officially. She realized with dull disappointment that it wouldn't be enough, just short of the rent.

"Oh fine, fifteen dollars," Ms. Ran said, waving a hand and looking away. "But I can't afford higher. It's a good deal—no tax, cash only."

"That's great," Cordi said, though her throat started to prickle. It would be just barely enough, and not much left over for food. She'd have to keep looking for another position that paid more or find a second job.

Ms. Ran nodded. "Here." She handed Cordi an apron that tied at the waist, with deep pockets that Cordi immediately stuffed her hands into. "Keep money here. Be prepared—we get early rush soon."

Cordi didn't have time to think about her new predicament, because after Ms. Ran went back to the front counter—so deeply buried in fabric that Cordi hadn't noticed it—the shop filled with customers. Cordi cut yard after yard—knits and wovens in fun, bold colors and patterns, chiffon that she had to rip to prevent fraying, a thick fur trim that left her covered in hair as if a dog had shed all over her. No sooner had she folded a piece of fabric for one customer than another handed her a different bolt to cut.

She didn't realize that most of the morning had passed until the afternoon sun beamed into the shop and sweat soaked her underarms. Her stomach growled loudly just as the crowd of customers started to thin. Across the alley, some warehouse fronts had already rolled down their metal doors, having concluded most of their business in the morning. Now the tourists, window-shoppers, and hagglers would show up, bent on lowering the prices even more.

Ms. Ran appeared behind her. "Go eat, I take over. Fifteen minutes. Hurry. Shop around the corner has good rice bowl."

Cordi wiped the back of her hand over her forehead. "Would you like anything?"

Ms. Ran took the bolt of fabric from a waiting customer without any sort of greeting. She nodded appreciatively. "Something simple, not picky. Go, not much time."

Cordi hurried off, shouldering her way through the crowd to reach the corner. She was sweating and her shoulders ached from taking bolts of fabric from customers to lay them on the table, then stretching the yards out to cut. Her hand felt sore when she pulled a dollar from her pocket, fatigued from cutting for so long, the handles of the scissors leaving bruises around her thumb and index finger.

But in a way, she found it gratifying to work again. The rush exhilarated her, and by the time she came back with their rice bowls, she was eager to keep going.

She and Ms. Ran took turns wolfing down their meals, and then it was back to work. The rush of customers died down a little after three. During the lulls, she and Ms. Ran took the opportunity to tidy their stations. They placed bolts back against the walls, tossed scraps in a pile, and pulled remnants off rolls to put in the sales bin. Now Cordi understood why every shop in the alley was so disorganized. There was simply no time to keep things neat.

By the end of the day, her dress was soaked in sweat. As Ms. Ran closed the store, she turned to give Cordi an impressed look. "I see you in the morning."

Cordi didn't say much as they walked in the same direction toward Olympic, massaging the sore spot between her thumb and index finger where the scissor handle had dug in.

"What's the matter?" Ms. Ran demanded. "I thought a girl like you could handle hard work."

"It's not that—I loved it. I enjoyed working with fabric again."

"Then what is it?"

"I . . ." She should have asked Ms. Ran for a higher salary, but she didn't think the lady was trying to swindle her. If she said she couldn't afford it, it was probably true. And besides, she had been generous enough to offer Cordi the job when most places had turned her away practically at first glance. "I think I have to find a second job. Maybe I can work at a sewing factory." She hated the idea, having heard horror stories from her parents about the terrible working conditions, but without a sewing machine and with no prospects, she didn't see what choice she had.

"Tsk tsk tsk." Ms. Ran shook her head. "You don't want that kind of job. They work you to the bone and pay pennies. Not worth it."

"Maybe I can find some work I can take home? I heard that some shops hire seamstresses—" But she cut herself off, remembering that she still didn't have a sewing machine.

Ms. Ran looked at her sympathetically. "You don't have anyone to take care of you? What about your parents?"

Cordi shook her head.

The lady exhaled, though it was not an exasperated sound. "Why? What happened? You look like a good girl."

"I am," Cordi insisted. "I was. I worked for them, at their alterations shop. I helped them."

"But?"

Cordi hadn't talked about what had happened with anyone, but for some reason, she suddenly felt compelled to. She looked at Ms. Ran's face; her sharp cheekbones, long nose, and thin lips were nothing like Mother's, whose round face and flat nose Cordi had inherited. Maybe that's why she felt a strange sense of companionship. If anyone might understand her, perhaps it was Ms. Ran, the not-unkind, but not-quite-motherly type. Perhaps a motherly type wasn't what Cordi needed.

"We had an argument," she said. "A stupid one." About the shop too, of all the things they could have fought about. They hadn't made a profit for months, barely taking in enough to pay the rent and bills, until eventually her parents had to borrow money just to keep the shop open. So Cordi had suggested a change—selling clothes instead of just fixing them. She had even made some samples of dresses they could

display in the window—nothing she'd designed herself, but styles copied from popular magazines and catalogs, dresses she knew would sell.

Mother had exploded with inexplicable rage when she'd seen the
dresses, pieces that Cordi was proud of. The skirt was too short, Mother
had said. They were all too tight, not sensible for ladies. What was Cordi
thinking? What would their customers say, what would their church
friends think, that they were cheapening themselves for a few dollars?

Shame flooded her when she thought back to the argument. For
most of her life, she'd simply nodded and swallowed her parents' words,
no matter what, like the filial, obedient daughter they'd raised her to be.
But something felt different that day. Maybe she just hadn't slept well,
staying up late to make those dresses, or maybe she'd just been hungry—
they'd eaten nothing except rice and fish sauce that week, having used up
their frozen meats so they could turn down the power on the freezer and
save on their electric bill. Or maybe it had all built up—the things she
didn't say, the emotions she wasn't allowed to feel—finally spilling out of
her like scum on top of an overflowing pot of soup.

"I shouted at them," Cordi said softly. They had reached the streetcar stop, where only one old man waited, and Ms. Ran tsked and shook
her head and reached into her purse to pull out a pack of cigarettes.

Cordi went on, unable to stop. She had shouted back at her parents, words of rage and fear and pent-up resentment, and they had
stood there, their faces slack with shock until they hardened with anger,
and then the shouting really started, and Mother, who rarely raised a
hand, had grabbed the bamboo broom from behind the refrigerator and
held it up with both arms. Cordi didn't duck because, for some reason,
she was transfixed by the skin on her mother's arms, loose and papery
and wrinkled, as Mother brought the thick handle of the broom down
on her head.

When Cordi got to this part of the story, she flinched, even though
the pain was long gone. For days, she had run her fingers over the bump
on her scalp as if testing to see if it still hurt, pressing harder to punish
herself when the pain started to fade. She knew she shouldn't have

talked back to her parents. Good girls did not talk back. Those who did, apparently, got disowned from their homes.

She finished her story just as the trolley clattered down the street, and for a second, they simply watched it approach, the wire cables above them swaying ominously.

"She shouldn't have hit you," Ms. Ran said. "But you shouldn't have talked back."

"I know." Cordi bowed her head.

"It's in the past now. No time for tears, you understand? Only hard work will get you through now. If you have to find second job, then you find second job. Nothing else to do about it." Ms. Ran looked pointedly at Cordi. "When I first saw you, I thought you were just like your friends. Spoiled princess and lazy baby."

"What?" Cordi started to defend Tessa and Silly, but Ms. Ran waved her unlit cigarette in her face.

"No, no. I didn't want to hire you, but then something told me, maybe I was wrong. Not often I feel this way. And today, you showed me that you are a hard worker. You're different. Life is uncertain now, and that's a bad feeling, but get used to it. Always, life will be uncertain. But you can change only one thing, and that's you. Only you. No matter what you decide."

Cordi nodded, but her brain was still playing catch-up on everything Ms. Ran had said.

Ms. Ran gave a stiff nod back, and then she turned and walked away, leaving Cordi feeling more confused. She had thought Ms. Ran was also taking the streetcar home, but all this time she'd just been walking with Cordi to hear the rest of her tale.

Chapter Eleven

Cordi was desperate for a bath, but when she got to the apartment, she found all three girls sitting at the kitchen table, talking animatedly, and Tessa insisted she join them.

"Come on, I made iced tea. Just hang loose for a bit," Tessa said, getting up and pulling Cordi into the chair that faced the window. Cordi didn't particularly enjoy the vines and plants that clawed the glass, especially in the dark of night, when the reflection made it feel as if they lived in some sort of jungle. Traffic whooshed and cars honked, the noise constant.

"Is it just iced tea?" Cordi asked, relenting. She couldn't resist Tessa when she wanted something. "Or did you add something else?" After the night they'd had with Callum, Cordi planned to swear off all alcohol for a while.

"It's just tea, promise." Tessa took the seat at the head of the table, closest to the kitchen.

"I got a second interview!" Silly burst out, practically bouncing in her seat. She must have been dying to tell Cordi the news.

"That's great, Silly," Cordi said, pouring herself a glass.

Audrey had a bowl of pistachios in front of her, and she popped open a shell with her thumbnail.

"It must have been Callum's spell," Silly said. "Look what it did for all of us. For you, Cordi, getting your job, and Audrey . . ." Silly trailed off, looking a bit frightened when Audrey focused her intense gaze on her.

"What happened with you, Audrey?" Cordi asked.

Audrey cracked open another pistachio shell. "Some people came and cleared out the storage closet at the gallery where I work. That's all."

"That's all?" Tessa said with a scoff. "They gave you your own little studio to work in. You can say you're a real artist now."

"I've always been an artist," Audrey said. "I never needed a space to prove it."

"Oh, just be grateful," Tessa snapped.

Audrey met Cordi's eyes as if seeking some sort of allegiance. Not wanting to choose sides, Cordi smiled, hoping to alleviate the tension between Audrey and Tessa, which seemed to grow worse every day.

"That is pretty neat," Cordi said. "They're taking you seriously."

"And look at us," Tessa said, fluttering her eyelashes. "We're also absolutely gorgeous."

Cordi had barely glanced in a mirror all day, and from the way people had stared on the bus ride home, she was pretty sure that Tessa's statement was far from the truth. But the other girls still looked slightly different, features more defined, skin glowing. Even Silly, who had always struck Cordi as a timid, mousy sort of girl, exuded more confidence. Then again, it could have been the fact that she'd received the good news about the internship.

"Aren't you going to ask me for *my* good news?" Tessa asked, one shoulder jutted slightly forward flirtatiously.

Cordi smiled. "What's your good news?"

"I sold a ton of makeup today and made a hundred bucks on my commission," Tessa said.

"A hundred?" Cordi repeated, not sure she'd heard right. That was more than she'd make in two months at Ms. Ran's shop.

Tessa beamed at her. "I know! The only time I've ever come close to making that much was when we had a huge sale."

"But wasn't your wish to be the most famous, most beautiful model there ever was?" Cordi asked. "That hasn't come true yet."

"I heard Mr. Sinclair's picking the models for the catalog on Tuesday. Maybe that's when it will happen for me. Besides, my dream seems to be a lot bigger than all of yours, so maybe it takes more time. Maybe this is just the first step to getting what I want."

"Well, whatever the reason," Silly said, "I'm going to find out how we can make the spell last."

"You're going to become a lurast?" Audrey asked.

"I'm just going to research it. Maybe the library has books that will tell us more."

Tessa reached out and grabbed Silly's hand, beaming at the younger girl, who couldn't have looked more pleased.

Cordi should have been tired of sewing after working at her parents' shop for so long, but truthfully, she missed it. She had taken having access to her mother's spare machine for granted. But a few days later, as she studied the ripped hem of her slacks, which had gotten caught on a loose nail on the ride home from the fabric shop, she breathed out in annoyance. It would have taken her two seconds to fix the hem with a sewing machine.

If she didn't eat out at all over the next year, she might be able to save up for the cheapest model. And once she had the machine, she'd need to save for at least a month to buy fabric.

Cordi sighed, tempted to throw her pen across the room. She sat on her bed—or rather, the mattress on the floor—using a breakfast tray table as a desk while she calculated her budget with her new salary. It was clear that the job wouldn't cover much other than the rent. Part of her had secretly dreamed the spell would fix everything, but it wasn't enough.

An idea wriggled into her thoughts. Had she asked for the wrong thing? For some reason she had gotten the good looks that Tessa had asked for, but perhaps that was what she needed to get the job? Although Ms. Ran didn't seem the type to care about how Cordi looked. Had something gone wrong? Could she perform another spell? Should she ask for something different? Maybe Callum could help her again.

The phone rang in the living room, and Cordi scrambled down the ladder to reach it.

"Misses Mai residence," she said, out of breath. Tessa had come up with the greeting, and Cordi loved answering the phone with it.

"What?" a familiar voice snapped into the phone. "The what?"

"Trina," Cordi said, heart hammering at the sound of her sister's angry voice. "Hi. What are you—is something wrong? Did something happen?"

"Mother and Father will be gone at the end of the month for their annual prayer retreat. It'd be a good time for you to pick up your things then. I've been packing when they're not paying attention."

"Oh," Cordi said in surprise. "Thank you, that's great!" She winced at her cheerfulness, though she couldn't help how excited she'd be to have her clothes back. "How are you doing? How are they?"

Trina's breath turned to static through the phone. "Well enough. What about you? Have you found a job yet?"

"Yes, actually." But she couldn't tell Trina how it wouldn't be enough to survive on. How her funds depleted by the day as she tried to decide whether to eat dinner or buy toothpaste and soap.

"Good. How will you move your stuff? You have a lot of clothes, Cordi. Your stuff takes up more than half the closet."

"I'm sorry." Cordi didn't know what else to say.

"Are you going to carry everything on the streetcar? You'll have to make several trips."

"I can ask one of my friends to help."

At that, there was a tense silence. Had Cordi said the wrong thing? What was on Trina's mind? What demeaning thing would she say next?

"Well, figure it out," Trina said finally, and hung up.

Chapter Twelve

After the busy weekend working at the alley, Cordi was relieved when she called the shop on Tuesday as instructed and Ms. Ran told her she didn't need her to come in. She massaged her wrist where the scissor handles pressed into her flesh and went to the kitchen to rummage scraps for breakfast.

The fridge shelves looked a bit fuller than they used to, but her choices were limited to a wilted head of lettuce and a few strips of cheese. She closed the door, the options depressing her, and went to make tea instead.

"Oh, darn it, I'm late, I'm late," Tessa said, coming out from her room and hopping on one foot as she finished buckling the strap of her other heel. "Sinclair's working on the winter mock-up today. I bet he's going to choose the models." She hurried to the mirror.

"Here." Cordi handed her the mug she'd brewed for herself. "I'm not working today."

"Oh, you're a doll." Tessa took a sip. "You're off today?"

"Ms. Ran said it was too slow for me to come in."

"Lucky." Tessa brightened suddenly. "Say, why don't you visit me at the store? You can pretend to be a customer and maybe compliment me in front of Sinclair, convince him that I would make the perfect model for the winter launch."

Cordi grimaced. "That's . . . not . . ."

"What? Something a *good girl* would do?"

Cordi's mouth dropped open. Tessa said "good girl" as if the words were actually rather bad.

"That's lying," Cordi corrected.

Tessa scoffed, a hand over her chest. "Excuse me? You don't think I'm pretty enough?"

"Of course that's not—Tessa, look at yourself. It's . . . Well, if anything, I'd just make things worse." She imagined stumbling over her words in front of this intimidating man as she did around anyone with any amount of authority. Her face flushed at the thought, and her palms grew sweaty.

"Oh, please, you're the perfect girl for the job. You have this, like, innocent, demure, perfect-daughter look about you."

As usual with Tessa's compliments, Cordi wasn't sure whether she should be offended or flattered, especially after the way she'd been kicked out of her family.

"Please?" Tessa clasped her hands together. "I just really need something good to happen today. This could be the *moment* the lura spell works. Plus, I'll give you the perfect makeover. Not that you need it."

Cordi let out a sigh and smiled. "Fine." But only because she wanted to browse the store, and perhaps look at their sewing machines, even though she knew she couldn't afford any of the models they sold.

Tessa grinned and hugged her so quickly, Cordi didn't have time to hug her back. Then she ran out the door, leaving Cordi alone to reconsider what she'd just agreed to do.

Lacy's was a six-block walk from the apartment, on Eighth and Broadway, but it was much easier to take the streetcar, merely to avoid the pedestrian traffic. Cordi had been to the department store only a few times, and each time she stepped foot inside its sparkly doors and entered the building, with its high ceilings and bright lights, she had the prickling sense that she didn't belong.

She wore an orange-and-white fitted dress made of a thick woven material, shirred at the back of the bodice, with a full pleated skirt that accentuated her figure. It was shorter than she remembered it being, which was probably why so many people turned to stare at her as she stepped into the store.

An overwhelming amount of detail hit her all at once—the reflective floors, the skinny mannequins with their hips thrust forward, the directory that she couldn't for the life of her decipher, as if her brain had decided to stop working. Even the racks from which the clothes hung shone like they'd been lovingly polished.

"May I help you?" a posh girl asked, speaking slowly, enunciating her words like Cordi might not understand the language. She wore a gray frock similar to the one Tessa wore to work and approached with her hands clasped in front. Cordi practically jumped, not used to store associates being so helpful. Usually they ignored her or looked down their noses if she asked for help. But this girl smiled, her expression showing admiration as she took in Cordi's appearance.

"I'm looking for the Petite counter," Cordi said, her voice sounding tiny even to her own ears.

"It's on the second floor, miss," the salesgirl said, speaking much more quickly after a moment of brief surprise. "Would you like me to show you there?"

"No," Cordi said. Perhaps that was rude. She smiled. "Sorry. It's fine, I can—is that the elevator? Okay, thanks." She rushed away, cringing. Why did she have to make even the simplest conversation with a shopgirl so awkward? Her fingers shook as she pressed the button for the elevator, glancing over her shoulder as the salesgirl walked off, probably knowing that Cordi couldn't afford to buy anything anyway.

The elevator gleamed, and the doors closed automatically behind her. Inside, she found the mirrored walls somewhat disconcerting. She tried not to admire her reflection, but she couldn't help it, not because she thought she looked particularly pretty, but because she looked so strangely different. Even more so than before, as if her face had continued to transform. Her eyes appeared wider, lashes longer, jawline tapered. She frowned, and even that looked flattering. This was so . . . creepy. Was it the mirror? Was it the spell? Was it real?

She stared at the floor instead.

The doors dinged as they slid open and deposited her into paradise. Everything was so *bright* and *sparkly*, even the gold mannequins, all dressed in minimalistic designs that looked deceptively simple.

Out of habit, Cordi studied a sheath dress, taking note of the seams and memorizing how the pieces came together so she could reconstruct it later. She fingered the hem of the dress. It was soft, but firm. An expensive knit that felt more like a woven—it wouldn't be much cheaper to re-create it, but it would be *fun*, which would make up for the cost.

Her heart sank. She still didn't have a sewing machine.

"Is there something the matter, miss?"

Cordi let go of the dress, but it was only Tessa. With her dainty name tag pinned on the left side of her chest, she looked like the perfect, professional shopgirl.

"You came!" Tessa beamed. "I knew I could count on you." She moved closer, eyes flickering left and right. "I saw Sinclair here somewhere. He usually checks on the mannequins to make sure they're up to par." They both gazed at the dress Cordi had been admiring. "This is one of my favorites." Tessa touched the hem and sighed. "So cute. So out of my budget."

"I was thinking I could make this myself, but I'd need a sewing machine."

"Oh no." Tessa pouted at the dress. "I'm sure Lacy's sells sewing machines. They sell pretty much everything else. Want to go find them?" She looped her arm through Cordi's and turned around, but then yanked Cordi to a sudden stop as a man walked past them.

He almost kept going, but he must have sensed their attention because he paused and glanced their way. His tailored suit fit him perfectly, his starched shirt skimming his firm chest and broad shoulders and tapering down to his waist. Cordi swallowed as she admired the knot of his tie right below his tanned neck. If it weren't for the dis-tracted tension on his face, she would have found him attractive, with his wavy dark hair just barely tamed and swept back with pomade and his eyes unmarred by smile lines.

Something sharp poked Cordi in the ribs, and she bit back a yelp. Tessa's elbow dug into her side, so bony that it felt like she'd stabbed her.

"Oh, wow," Cordi said, turning to Tessa with what she hoped looked like genuine awe. "You're so beautiful. You must be one of the store's models!"

Redness blossomed under Tessa's complexion as her mouth pinched.

The man—Mr. Sinclair—turned more fully in their direction with a bemused expression. He couldn't have been much older than Cordi, and though he was tall, it wasn't a scary, towering tall. He was rather handsome, with a strong nose and chin, defined brow, and deeply set, almost shadowed eyes. He even smelled . . . pleasant. Soap and expen-sive cologne. And as he looked at her, she felt a startling jolt.

Tessa laughed. "Oh, you flatter me, Miss Yin. But I'm sure Mr. Sinclair has all the models picked out for the upcoming season." She widened her eyes, urging Cordi to speak. Cordi wished she'd gotten a script for this ruse.

"How . . . sad," Cordi said, cringing at herself immediately.

Mr. Sinclair, to his credit, frowned in confusion. "Are you finding everything all right?" he asked her, his voice deep, his tone professional.

"Oh yes." Cordi's head bobbed. "I'm a, uh, a—"

"Miss Yin is a fashion designer," Tessa said.

"A-aspiring—" Cordi stammered, remembering how Tessa had embellished the truth with Ms. Ran at the alley.

"She's looking to upgrade her sewing machine," Tessa added, "aren't you, darling?"

"Um."

"She was telling me about how she's looking for the perfect model for her new line," Tessa said to Mr. Sinclair. Her elbow hovered threat-eningly near Cordi's ribs.

"Tessa—Miss Hong," Cordi said, "would be . . . absolutely divine in my designs."

He paused, looking between the two of them with an unreadable expression, and then smiled politely. "I wish you every success."

Cordi's temperature rose by about two degrees. He must have seen right through their act.

"Well," Tessa said when Mr. Sinclair turned away. "This way to the sewing machines. We've got the perfect selection for you."

As she pulled Cordi away, she kept up a steady string of sales talk. "Our jewel-toned collection is perfect for fall and is all the rage this season. I know just the right dress for that cocktail party you were talking about—quick, laugh." She stabbed Cordi with her elbow.

Cordi gave her most obnoxious, high-pitched giggle.

"A little much," Tessa said, through grinning teeth and her own twinkling laugh.

When they were out of earshot, Tessa glanced back to make sure he was gone. Her shoulders loosened and she let out a sigh. "Great."

"I'm sorry," Cordi said. "I told you I'd be terrible at this."

Tessa's disappointment smoothed into a reassuring smile. "Oh, don't worry. I'm sure there was no harm done. Other than Sinclair thinking I'm an utter miscreant."

"Well, are you?" Cordi joked, hoping Tessa wasn't too angry that she'd botched the plan.

Tessa smiled, close-lipped. "Of *course* I am, haven't you been paying attention? Anyway, let's go look at the sewing machines, and after a few minutes, perhaps you can look for him and just tell him that you decided not to hire me and suggest I'd be perfect for the catalog instead. But don't go too wild, not like with your fake laugh. Be genuine . . . be natural. Now, let's practice the exact words you're going to say."

They went up to the fifth floor to look at the sewing machines. Cordi had suspected correctly—all the models were entirely out of her budget, even the cheapest one, even with Tessa's employee discount. She'd have to go to a secondhand shop. Or perhaps just not buy one at all. What did she need with a sewing machine anyway? Her hands lingered sadly on the Singer that claimed to have a slant needle and featured several fancy stitches, including buttonholes. God, how she wanted it.

Cordi's feet dragged as she left the store. She made a halfhearted attempt to look for Mr. Sinclair, nervous as that made her, but she didn't see him again.

In the elevator, she tried not to look at herself in the mirrors, but as she met the stranger's eyes in the reflection, it hit her that perhaps this was all . . . real. Callum's spell had worked. They had all thought it was a game, a silly, drunken game, but there was no denying it now. She looked different. People treated her differently. And she had gotten what she'd wished for—a job.

Could it all be this easy?

She could ask Callum for another spell—just a small one. Because she *needed* a sewing machine. It wasn't some silly, frivolous purchase. It was a practical investment. She could start making clothes again, come up with new designs like she had planned. Perhaps she could even sell them at the alley, set up her own stall, build a name for herself. Just to pay off the rest of her expenses each month, and then . . . perhaps . . . something bigger down the line. Maybe it wouldn't be such an impossible dream after all.

She was so intent on getting in touch with Callum again that she must have conjured him from her own thoughts, because she practically ran into him in their apartment building. He was walking down the stairs as he gazed admiringly at the girl on his arm. She was pretty, her hair curled and dyed an auburn so rich, the strands appeared to catch fire in the hallway light, and she seemed just as enthralled with him as he was with her—that was, until Cordi interrupted them.

"Callum!" she said. "I was just thinking about you."

"Oh . . . hello," he said. His tone seemed odd, as if he didn't recognize her.

"It's me—Cordelia." When he blinked, she added, "You helped me with Mikhail's apartment. I'm one of the Mais?"

"Oh . . . oh!" His eyes showed instant recognition. Then he looked her up and down. *"Oh,"* he said, this time with awe. His date crossed her arms and glared at Cordi. "Excuse me, Rachel, sweetheart, while I talk to my friend for just a few minutes. Why don't you wait for me downstairs. I'll be right back, Cordelia."

He led the girl down to the next floor, while Cordi debated whether she should wait for him in her apartment or linger awkwardly on the stairs. Before she could decide, he was back.

"Cordelia, my dear, you look . . . absolutely beautiful." He held out his hands, gloved as usual, the embroidered detail rubbing Cordi's fingers as she took them. "I barely recognized you."

"Thanks?" she said.

Callum smiled sheepishly. "How are you? How has Mikhail been treating you?"

"Great, now that I have a job." Mikhail had come to collect the rent and had seemed, if not happy, then at least not as grumpy when he'd learned about her employment. "Listen, Callum. The spell you gave us."

"It's marvelous, isn't it?"

"Yes. It . . . it worked. You're actually a . . . you know?" For some reason, saying it out loud seemed too ridiculous, even despite all the things that had happened.

"A lurast. A type of witch. Yes. It's all very real. Just look at you." He still held her hands, and now he stretched out his arms to get a better look. "I've never seen it work so fast on someone. Or so well. You must be very special."

"How does it work?" she asked.

"It's quite simple. All it required was for you to want something and be willing to sacrifice anything to have it."

Her blood went cold. "Sacrifice?"

"All things come at a price." Callum lifted a shoulder in a shrug. "But as long as you're willing to pay that price, you can have whatever you want. Everything your heart desires. All your wishes—"

"How hard would it be to perform another spell?"

Callum chuckled. "Hooked already, are you?" He let go of her hands to reach inside his jacket pocket and pull out a small notebook and a pen. "I'm a bit busy at the moment, but here." He scribbled something down, then ripped off the sheet and handed it to her. "Why don't you give it a try."

Cordi read the brief instructions. They were very simple—a short incantation around some candles, similar to the one he had performed for them, along with the offer of some sentimental object. "That's it?"

He clicked his pen and tucked it away. "Simple enough. I don't even need to be there."

"Can't you help us again?"

"You can do this, Cordelia. You're powerful enough. Stronger than the others, even. I bet that the magic has worked better for you."

"It has, a bit, I think. But I'm not a lurast."

"Yes, you are. You've been initiated."

"You mean we're . . ."

"You're all lurasts now," Callum said, the corners of his eyes crinkling in his signature smile. "Though spells can only be passed down from one lurast to another, so if you ever need anything else, you can always come to me." He chucked her chin affectionately. "I better run before my date gets impatient. Listen, tell me how it goes, will you?" He disappeared down the stairs, and Cordi clutched the little spell in her fist.

Chapter Thirteen

They had their first official meeting of the Mais when everyone came home that night. Silly wore a dress suit that didn't fit her quite right, and Cordi planned to take it in for her as soon as she got her sewing machine. Audrey wore a sweater covered in paint splatter. Tessa wore her gray frock, but she kicked off her heels at the door and padded barefoot to join them at the kitchen table, though no one sat, as if what they planned to do was too momentous and they needed to be prepared in case something happened.

Cordi had placed the little spell in the middle of the table so they could all stare at it.

"This is the stupidest idea ever," Audrey said. Her arms hung at her sides. Of all of them, she looked like she had changed the least, just a slight difference in her complexion now. Or perhaps the change had worn off her the fastest.

"How was your interview, Silly?" Tessa asked.

Cordi felt a bit guilty. She'd forgotten that Silly had gone in for the second round for her internship today, still in limbo as to whether she'd have a job.

"It was okay," Silly said, and they didn't have to ask further after hearing her sad tone. "I kept saying the word 'basically' and I knew I was saying it a lot, but that only made me say it even more, like I couldn't get it out of my head." She rubbed the bridge of her nose.

"I'm sure it was fine," Audrey said. "They want someone smart, not . . . articulate."

Cordi couldn't stop looking at the spell. "Callum said we needed a sacrifice."

"But we gave a sacrifice, didn't we?" Tessa asked. "Last time. Those things we put in the bowl."

"This is dumb," Audrey said. But she didn't leave.

"You didn't think so last time," Tessa snapped at her.

"I was drunk last time."

"From one glass of wine?"

Audrey took a deep breath. "My aunt told me to never dabble with this sort of stuff. Only bad things will come of it. Didn't you read about that in the books you found?" she asked Silly.

Silly and Tessa exchanged a look. "The books were all very old, the language outdated," Silly said.

"But what did they say?" Cordi asked, hating that Tessa and Silly hadn't shared this with her to begin with. "Tessa?"

"I didn't read them," Tessa said, nudging Silly to speak up.

"I swear I barely found anything," Silly said. "Just that we have to sacrifice something we love, and the stronger that love is, the more powerful the spell."

"What if it's not something we love?" Tessa asked. "But still valuable. Like a ring or something."

"Well, lura values the sacrifice more than money?" Silly squinched her face. "So you still have to love the thing. Or, I don't know. The spell might backfire in some way."

"But you don't *know*, right?" Tessa said. "I mean, as long as the sacrifice is valuable, it still works."

Silly seemed to shrink lower the more Tessa stared at her, challenging her to refute the logic. "I think so."

"Can we see these books?" Cordi asked.

"You can only view them in the research center," Silly said. "I lied and said I worked at the mayor's office, and they let me in for an afternoon, but then they said I need to show my badge next time, so I can't go back. Not until I get the internship, at least."

Cordi wasn't sure what to do now. She studied Callum's note again, as if the instructions would magically change and give her a different answer.

"Cordi, stop this," Audrey said. "It's not a good idea."

"Why?" Tessa asked, moving closer to Cordi as if shielding her. "How do you know only bad things will happen? So far, only good things have happened to us. To you all anyway. I'm still waiting. I want good things too."

Audrey scowled but didn't answer.

"How did it go with Mr. Sinclair?" Cordi asked Tessa. "I couldn't find him before I left, but did you get a chance to talk to him?"

Tessa waved a hand. "He's a lost cause. Said they already picked the models they needed and that I wouldn't be able to handle the long hours. All because my supervisor told him I had left early a few times for very good reasons—once because I didn't feel good, but she didn't believe me." She crossed her arms and tried to look nonchalant, but her nose flared.

"I'm sorry, Tess," Cordi said.

Tessa blinked rapidly, tilting her head back to stop the onslaught of tears. "So you see? I need this. You all got what you wished for. What about me?" She used a long fingernail to gently scrape a tear from the corner of her eye.

"Let's try it," Silly said.

Cordi had been going back and forth about the spell. On the one hand, she agreed with Audrey. Nothing good ever came for free, and Callum had said himself that everything had a price. But Tessa had a point too. Cordi had become very lucky since the first spell, and this was a small thing, really, what she wanted. It wasn't like she was asking for fortune or success—just a sewing machine so she could work harder. What was wrong with that?

"What do you want so badly?" Audrey asked. She directed the question at all three of them, but she looked at Cordi.

"A sewing machine," Cordi said, realizing that it sounded really stupid now that she said it.

"You're going to sell your soul for a sewing machine?" Audrey asked.

"Who said anything about selling our souls?" Tessa asked. "It's just a simple spell. We just chant this line"—she tapped the piece of paper on the table—"and that's it."

"And we offer a small token of sacrifice," Silly added, reading the paper. "Sort of like last time."

Audrey shook her head. "There's no such thing as a small sacrifice, not with lura."

"It's not just that I want a sewing machine." Cordi felt the need to clarify. "I need it. I need to make more money—I barely make enough for rent—and sewing is the only thing I know how to do. And it's more of a symbol. For my bigger dream. Of becoming a designer." She spoke in guttural stops because it still felt silly to say what she wanted out loud. She worried everyone would laugh at how ridiculous it sounded.

"I want what's supposed to be coming to me," Tessa said. "Success and fame and beauty. Silly still needs her internship. It's almost like the only person it's really worked for is Cordi."

"Then the two of you should perform the spell," Cordi said.

"Nuh-uh. We need you too. If you're the only one it worked for, maybe you're the key or something."

"Plus, Callum gave you the spell," Silly said. "Didn't he say it has to be passed from lurast to lurast? So you have to be part of it."

"I'm out," Audrey said, throwing up her hands. She stepped back, but didn't go to her room, instead observing them from the sidelines.

Tessa stared at Cordi imploringly. "So?"

Cordi looked at Silly, whose eyes were pleadingly large. "Are we all sure?"

"Yes," Tessa and Silly both said without hesitating.

Cordi glanced once at Audrey, who shook her head. She'd stepped back from the kitchen light, the rest of the apartment dim.

"All right," Cordi said, turning back to the other two. "Let's do it."

They sat in the middle of the rug in between the couches. Something about performing the luracal spell felt like it should take place on the intimate setting of the floor, barefoot, legs crossed. They set the metal bowl in the middle, along with the few candles they could find.

"As a gift, I offer my reading glasses," Silly said, dropping in a cheap pair of plastic-framed spectacles.

"As a gift, I offer my spare sewing kit," Cordi said, placing a metal tin filled with threads and needles and safety pins in the bowl.

"As a gift, I offer my hairbrush," Tessa said, dropping in the fancy, antique-looking thing with a jade handle.

Audrey stood just outside the circle, arms crossed.

"Now we hold hands," Cordi instructed, reaching for Tessa to her right and Silly to her left. "And say the words 'Lura, take this gift and grant me my wish' seven times."

They all breathed in, and a second passed before they started. This was it. Last time, they had all been tipsy, not quite believing lura was real. But this time, they knew what they were doing. Cordi had deliberately sought Callum out for a spell. They were making their own choice to go through with it.

"Lura, take this gift and grant me my wish," they all started in unison.

Nothing happened.

"Lura, take this gift and grant me my wish."

Something twisted in Cordi's gut.

The other girls' expressions didn't change, focused intently on the bowl.

"Lura, take this gift and grant me my wish."

A presence entered the circle. Cordi couldn't see it, but she could feel it, the way you knew if a television set was on in the next room. The hairs on the back of her neck rose, and her breath caught. She looked at the other girls but no one reacted, still staring at the middle of the circle and repeating the words. She tried to look beyond to see if Audrey had noticed the presence. But it was dark behind Tessa and Silly, and her eyes refused to focus.

"Lura, take this gift and grant me my wish."

As the presence took shape, Cordi could make out that it was small, the size of a cat, and it started moving with fluidity around the circle, scrutinizing them all.

"Lura, take this gift and grant me my wish."

It paused when it got to Cordi. A shadowy shape with no distinguishable outline, she imagined the spots where its eyes would be as hollow sockets. They fixed on hers, and a numb tingle spread over her skin. Her mouth stretched back as if into a scream, but she couldn't find the breath to do it.

"Lura, take this gift and grant me my wish," the other girls continued chanting.

It moved toward her.

"LURA, TAKE THIS GIFT AND GRANT ME MY WISH." Their voices were so loud, they roared in Cordi's ears.

And then all was quiet. Cordi released Tessa's and Silly's hands, then clutched her heart, which was beating too fast. Whatever that presence . . . whatever that thing had been, it was gone now. Had it gone into her? Surely she would have felt something.

"Oh my," Tessa said. She reached into the bowl and pulled out her hairbrush. It was blackened and charred, warped backward into an unrecognizable, cursed object. Cordi picked up her sewing kit, which also looked burned. Inside, the contents had turned to ash, only a single needle remaining intact. Silly's glasses had cracked, the frame melted.

"Did you all feel that?" Cordi asked.

"Feel what?" Tessa asked.

"There was something . . . something with us." She had no idea how else to describe it.

The others all looked skeptical.

"I didn't see anything," Silly said.

"Me neither," Tessa said.

"I didn't see it. I felt it," Cordi said.

Audrey's voice came from outside the circle, sounding distant. "I told you this was a dumb idea."

Tessa shrieked and jumped. "Oh my Goddess, I forgot you were there."

Silly looked at Cordi with a worried expression. "Maybe you were just . . . a bit scared."

Cordi scoffed. She was *not* scared.

"Well, anyway, it must have worked because something happened here," Tessa said, brandishing the burned hairbrush. "Let's hope Silly and I will see success soon! And you too, Cordi. More success, I mean."

Cordi still felt uneasy as the others got up off the floor. Tessa and Silly were in much better moods now, but Cordi moved slowly, unable to shake the unsettling sensation of ants crawling all over her skin.

Chapter Fourteen

"You look different," Ms. Ran said when Cordi showed up at the fabric shop that Friday.

Cordi kept her head down, not wanting the woman to study her too much. The day after the lura spell she, Tessa, and Silly had performed together, they had all woken up with stronger changes to their appearance than before. They looked . . . enhanced. Their lashes thicker, their cheekbones more defined. Their skin lightened yet glowing, like they had put on the most expensive foundation sold at Lacy's.

"Even Petite doesn't sell makeup this good," Tessa had said, turning her face this way and that in the mirror.

And then the phone rang for Silly. "I got the internship!" she screamed as soon as she hung up.

Cordi watched as Tessa hugged and danced along with her until Audrey came out of her room. She stopped dead when she saw their faces.

"You are all in trouble now," she muttered, before going straight for the coffee. No one talked to her after that.

Cordi turned her face away and busied herself preparing her worktable for the flood of customers.

"No, really, is it a new cream?" Ms. Ran asked. "Your skin so supple."

"Yes," Cordi said. "My friend works at the Petite Beauty counter. I'll bring you a sample." That wasn't a lie, at least.

Ms. Ran seemed satisfied, and they didn't have much time to chat before the early rush. Cordi savored the morning hours before the sun heated the store to unbearable levels, when they helped customers who knew exactly what they wanted. In the afternoons, the wanderers showed up, the tourists who had heard of the alley and wanted to see for themselves, the window-shoppers wasting time, not serious about business.

Sometimes in the slow afternoons, Ms. Ran left the shop to wander down the alley. Cordi would have been flattered that she trusted her enough to leave her alone in the shop, but she noticed Ms. Ran was careful never to say when she'd be back, as if she expected to catch Cordi red-handed. Cordi was embarrassed that she'd revealed so much of her past to Ms. Ran, but she remained as aloof as ever, as if nothing had passed between them, which wasn't to say that she wasn't kind in her own way. She often encouraged Cordi to walk around when things were slow and gave her money to buy them both lunch during their breaks, always adding a few extra dollars in the envelope she gave Cordi for the meal without asking for change.

While Ms. Ran was out, Cordi sat down and let out a sigh. It was easier to cut fabric at the workstation standing up, but her back muscles ached from stooping over. She had only a second to take a sip of water before another customer came in, and Cordi stood up, surprised to see someone who looked so out of place at the alley.

She was a young lady about Cordi's age, different from any girls Cordi knew, dressed in a white-and-pink tweed dress suit more appropriate to someone her mother's age. Somehow, she made the outfit look trendy, matching it with flat white loafers. The pink threads of the textured fabric complemented her icy-blonde hair, and as she blocked the light from the door behind her, the sun set her in a white-flamed glow.

Cordi was so blinded that it took her a moment to realize the girl wasn't alone. A man stepped into the shop, looking just as out of place in his perfectly cut suit and pinned tie. He hunched stiffly, even though the ceiling was quite high, and leaned close to the girl as if shielding her from the dirt and grime of their surroundings, one hand reaching up occasionally as if to grip her elbow and pull her away.

"I doubt we'll find what we're looking for here," he said, and the deep grittiness of his voice jerked Cordi upright.

It was Mr. Sinclair. The man who worked at Lacy's Department Store. At the sight of him, Cordi's body flushed hot and cold at the same time, and her heart began racing. After the embarrassing encounter she'd had with him, she never thought she'd see him again, nor did she feel particularly fond of the way he'd turned down Tessa for the catalog. She flicked pieces of thread off her skirt and touched her hair, even though it was too late to do anything about it.

What was he doing at the alley, in this discount shop? Surely he could afford fancier places, and Cordi had no doubt that Lacy's didn't do business with any of the suppliers in the alley.

She started to shrink down in her seat, but she couldn't ignore them with Ms. Ran out of the shop. Perhaps she could pretend she hadn't seen them. Maybe they would leave before they noticed her. Judging from the tense muscles bracketing his mouth, Mr. Sinclair didn't want to be at the shop any more than she wanted him to turn and notice her.

It was too late. The girl had moved farther into the store, and as Mr. Sinclair shadowed her, he ducked beneath a bolt of fabric propped awkwardly against a pillar. When he looked up, their eyes met, and heat pooled at the bottom of her stomach.

He frowned, as if trying to figure out where he knew her from—they had met for only a few brief seconds, after all, and she had pretended to be a sophisticated customer, someone completely different from the poor shopgirl he saw now, dusty and sweaty, hair messily pulled back with a clip. She pushed a loose strand behind her ear, wishing she'd had time to spruce herself up, then berating herself for caring.

"Oh my, look at this," the girl said, holding up a piece of scrap lace fabric she'd found in a box. She looked at Cordi with an expectant expression, and Cordi got the sense that she was used to having her needs met whether she expressed them or not.

"Those are our remnants," Cordi said. "They're . . . half off." Actually, they were priced depending on how polite the customer was to Ms. Ran, but she didn't know how to explain that.

"Remnants," the girl repeated. "Meaning, there are no more?"

"Yes. I mean—" Cordi shook her head, uncomfortably aware that Mr. Sinclair hadn't stopped studying her face, which grew warmer the longer he watched her. "No, there aren't any more of that one. But if you're looking for lace, I can show you others like it." Cordi shouldered her way between the large bolts against the wall, fingering the textures of the fabric to find the delicate material she had in mind.

The girl pulled off her silk gloves, revealing shockingly beautiful hands, the skin so smooth, it looked almost painted, untouched by hard work.

"We've met before," Mr. Sinclair said, making Cordi jump.

Why was she so nervous? He wasn't her boss, and even if he had figured out that Tessa had tricked him by now, they hadn't done any harm.

"Really?" Cordi asked. "Perhaps—maybe—"

"Gabe, for goodness' sake," the other girl said, then smiled at Cordi. "Excuse him, he's clearly forgotten how to have fun or be a normal person. I'm Cressida Thompson," she announced and paused, as if waiting for some sort of reaction.

"Nice to meet you," Cordi said, and introduced herself as well.

Cressida blinked, then her smile widened, and she straightened even taller. "Are you new around here?"

"I just started at this shop a few weeks ago."

"No, I meant LA."

"Oh—I've lived here all my life."

"Have you?" Cressida's gaze flicked over Cordi's features. "Fascinating. People have been transplanting here in droves, especially with everything going on in your part of the world. I don't blame them—the weather, the opportunities—it's all quite magical here, isn't it?"

"Uh." Cordi willed her brain to come up with a clever response.

"But us Californians, we need to stick together, don't we?"

"We do know each other," Mr. Sinclair said. He snapped his fingers, his hand suspended awkwardly, his index finger pointing accusingly at Cordi.

"Honestly, Gabe, you should see yourself," Cressida said, inspecting the first bolt of lace. "You look like a stern schoolteacher."

"You're Ms. Hong's friend," Mr. Sinclair continued. He dropped his hand, then stuffed it in his pants pocket. "The aspiring designer."

"Yes, well." Cordi wiped her sweaty palms against her skirt. "I was . . . was looking for a sewing machine. She was helping me. The store is so large."

Cressida's eyes sparked with interest. "But of course, it makes sense. Here, you get access to all the best underground material."

"Underground . . ." Cordi repeated.

"I'm looking for something special," Cressida continued. "A . . . trousseau, of sorts. I'm thinking about getting married."

Thinking about it? Cordi had always assumed it was a question with a yes or no answer.

Mr. Sinclair looked both exasperated and impatient. "I told you, we won't find anything for you here." He eyed the pile of fabric next to him, his jawline tensing with distaste.

That rankled. Ms. Ran's shop was disorganized, but not any more or less than the rest of the businesses in the alley, and besides that, appearances were deceiving. Cordi had been shopping at these stalls for years and had always been able to find the most valuable gems at discounted prices, so long as she knew where and how to search. And for some reason she couldn't explain, she wanted to impress Mr. Sinclair—it was ridiculous, really, when she hardly knew him—and his derision sent her down a foreboding spiral of disappointment and shame, which turned into anger. She was determined not to care one more second about what he thought.

"Then you'll need more than lace," she said, focusing on Cressida and ignoring Mr. Sinclair. Yet she was more aware of him than ever as she showed Cressida around the store. "What about silks? We also have the best cotton, in different weights. What sort of gowns are you looking to have made?"

"What silhouette would look best on me?" Cressida held out her arms, her dainty purse hanging from the crook of her elbow.

Taken off guard, Cordi answered quickly, having developed a skill for knowing what would be flattering on different shapes after years of working at her parents' alterations shop. "A sweetheart bodice and a flared skirt. To accentuate the, um . . ." She trailed off, not wanting to point out that Cressida, who was tall and coltish, didn't have any curves to, well, accentuate. "Appearance of curves," she finished lamely.

Cressida beamed. "I was right." She lifted her chin in Mr. Sinclair's direction. "You owe me."

"I never agreed to anything," he said.

"Can I see an example?" Cressida asked Cordi sweetly. "Of what you were thinking?"

"Oh, um." She glanced at Mr. Sinclair. In spite of her earlier conviction not to care, annoyance surged at his utter snobbishness. How did he know she wasn't what Cressida claimed to be so sure of—that she was talented, that she could design a gown just as well as any other designers outside the alley? He didn't know her at all, had barely met her and already dismissed her.

Cordi pulled out her sketchbook and flipped through some of her favorite dresses. "These are ones I've done in the past." Cressida oohed and aahed over the designs, which emboldened Cordi to sketch a new one. They were crude drawings of basic shapes, but everything seemed to impress the girl, and by the end, she grabbed Cordi's forearm in a grip so hard, Cordi was afraid she might not let go.

"Yes, this is it, I know it is," Cressida said. "I can feel it." She pulled a small leather notebook from her purse, which turned out to be a checkbook. She held a pen above the blank lines. "How much do you charge?"

Cordi stared at the shiny black metal of the pen, the clip finished with gold. "For what?"

"For designing my gowns, darling," Cressida said with a laugh. "We're here in search of a designer. A new one. I don't want any old name—I want to discover someone new. Someone like you . . . Miss Cordelia . . . Yin . . . you said?" She scribbled Cordi's name down, and didn't even get it wrong, like most people did. Then she waited for Cordi to name a price.

"I don't . . . I—" Cordi shook her head. Then blurted out, "I don't own a sewing machine anymore. That's why I was . . . I was at Lacy's." She glanced at Mr. Sinclair's scowling face, then looked away. "I couldn't . . . afford it." Heat filled her cheeks.

"Of course, of course." Cressida waved pink-painted fingers in the air. "How silly of me. We'll have one delivered to you, right away. What's the address?"

"But—what? Are you—" Her head spun. Was this really happening?

This must be thanks to the lura spell they'd performed. What else could bring this good fortune?

Still, it was absurd.

"I've never done a project this big before," Cordi said.

"But I'm sure that you're more than capable of it." Cressida must have gotten tired of waiting for Cordi to name a price, because she scribbled something down, and then ripped out the check. "A retainer, for your services. Half now, half when you finish the job."

Cordi stared at the check. She counted the zeroes again, sure she was mistaken. It was more than what she'd make in years working for Ms. Ran. She'd have enough for the rent, and to pay Tessa back for covering the groceries.

"I can't . . . This isn't . . . You don't . . ." Her thoughts were just as incoherent, for some reason, flashing to the time in grade ten when she hadn't studied for an exam—too busy working at the shop—but had miraculously passed anyway. She hadn't believed the score, had blinked and read it over and over, and even talked to the teacher after class to make sure it hadn't been a mistake, though a more confident person would have just accepted it and moved on.

But it hadn't been a mistake. She had been lucky, like now. The number Cressida had written was real, the check a solid thing between her fingers.

Cressida seemed to think nothing of it. If she noticed Cordi's shock, she didn't care. It was probably a small amount to her. Luck and wealth came so easily to the fortunate few. But to Cordi, this opportunity could be life changing.

"Wh—which dress?" Cordi asked, still in shock.

"These," Cressida said, flipping through the sketchbook. "This and this."

"That's five," Cordi said stupidly.

"Perhaps just the gowns for now. We'll find a different designer for the wedding dress—or who knows. We might love your work so much, you can make that too. With additional pay, of course. What do you need to get started?"

"Um . . . measurements," Cordi said. "And fabric—which . . ."

"You choose, I can tell you have taste. As for the measurements, shall we?" Cressida snapped her purse closed.

"Cressida," Mr. Sinclair said. "Perhaps you should take some time, interview other designers."

Cordi's heart sank. She had hoped she could prove him wrong, although she felt silly for thinking he would be convinced so easily. He blinked and looked away, and she tried not to look so hurt.

"Gabriel," Cressida said, already shrugging out of her tweed jacket to reveal a thin camisole underneath. "If you insist on being a grouch, then please kindly do so outside."

Who was Cressida Thompson anyway? She carried herself as someone important, and she seemed to expect that Cordi had heard of her. But even if she was famous, Cordi hardly had time to read gossip columns or pay attention to what rich people got up to.

Whoever she was, Cressida Thompson was ridiculous. Or Cordi had gone mad. These sorts of things didn't happen, not to girls like her.

But they had performed that second lura spell Callum gave them, and then she and Tessa and Silly had all looked even more different, and Silly had gotten that internship. Cordi had wanted a sewing machine and a chance to prove herself worthy as a designer. This must be the lura granting her wish.

She was dying to tell the girls about what had happened. When she stepped into the apartment, she found them standing at the window, where a giant box sat proudly, filling the corner.

"Something arrived for you," Tessa said, bounding over and taking Cordi's hand. "Is it that sewing machine you were looking at?"

"No," Cordi said. She had only ever dreamed of owning cheap, ugly, beige-painted things. A high-end, cast-iron machine with its own built-in desk was pictured on the side of the box. She touched it, then pulled her hand back. What if it wasn't real? What if it was some trick, some conjuring?

Audrey leaned against the couch, arms crossed. "How did you afford it so soon?"

"That's the funny thing." Cordi told them about the strange girl who had commissioned her to make five whole elegant ball gowns. "When she found out I didn't have a sewing machine, she said she'd have one delivered. I didn't think she actually would. And the weird thing was, Mr. Sinclair was with her," Cordi added, gauging Tessa's reaction.

Tessa snorted. "Sinclair was at the alley? Did his suit get dirty? Oh, please tell me he ripped a seam or something."

Cordi smiled. "I wouldn't have agreed to design the dresses, but he was so snobby, I'm determined to prove him wrong. Though now I've got a bad case of the gringles. I'm not sure I have the skill to make five ball gowns."

"What? Of course you do," Tessa said.

"And if you don't, the lura will help you," Silly said. "It gave me my internship. Now it's making your dreams come true too."

They both glanced at Tessa, who watched them with a crestfallen expression. She straightened. "Exactly. You're so smart, Silly! I'm sure my time will come any day now. But come on, Cordi, open it." She urged Cordi toward the box. "Think of all the dresses she can make for us," she said to Silly, looping their arms together.

It took all their help to pull the heavy machine out of the box, then place the metal contraption onto the desk it came with. For a second, they stood there, admiring the different parts. Cordi kept rubbing her eyes to make sure this was really happening—they had performed the spell and she had gotten exactly what she'd asked for. Was it really that simple?

Possibilities flashed before her. They could have whatever they wanted. Do anything they wanted. All it took was a small sacrifice, and she could come up with many more. It might be possible—her dreams, Tessa's and Silly's, and even Audrey's if she'd stop being so supercilious about it.

Audrey went to her room and came back with some tools and started screwing things and hammering, her look of concentration telling them all to back off because she knew what she was doing. They watched until she finally stepped back to admire her work.

The sun had set at just the right moment so that a beam of light fell on the machine, and it sparkled. Cordi breathed out in awe. They all did.

"It's beautiful," she said.

Tessa and Silly smiled at her. Audrey started putting her tools back in her heavy-looking metal box.

"I'm so happy for you," Tessa said, dabbing at a corner of her eye. They stood admiring the machine for another moment.

"I'm starving," Tessa said, heading to the kitchen. Silly followed her. "We should probably use this before it goes bad." She pulled out the head of wilting lettuce. "Anyone else want anything to eat?"

"Sure," Cordi said.

"Audrey?"

Audrey frowned. Despite her help with assembling the machine, she stared at it with an air of caution. "This isn't right, you know," she said quietly to Cordi. "It doesn't feel good."

Cordi didn't know what to say in response. Perhaps she should give the machine back. She'd done nothing to deserve it.

But at the thought, her hand went out to touch it. The cold surface seemed to hum under her fingers, even though they hadn't plugged it in yet.

"It'll be fine," Cordi said. "I'm going to use it to do good, you'll see."

"What, are you planning to save the world, one stitch at a time?" Audrey closed her toolbox. The sharp sound echoed in the apartment, and Cordi's unease grew.

"Do you want dinner or not?" Tessa asked Audrey with an exasperated blink.

Audrey let out a breath. "Fine," she said.

Chapter Fifteen

The next week passed in a feverish blur of work. Cordi knew that she could have quit working at Ms. Ran's fabric shop, but she couldn't bring herself to do it, imagining Ms. Ran's disappointed voice, especially because she hadn't really wanted to hire Cordi in the first place. Every day, Cordi made her way to the alley, telling herself that she would tell her in person, only to lose her nerve as soon as the morning rush started and Ms. Ran became too busy for Cordi to contemplate abandoning her.

Her panic grew when the apartment phone rang in the middle of the week, and Cordi answered, surprised to hear Cressida Thompson's voice.

"I wanted to check on your progress." Cressida's voice sounded twinkly over the phone. "Do you have anything to show me?"

"No—almost—"

"Not even a muslin? My last seamstress would whip up a quick mock-up for me to try. Just to make sure everything fit."

"I don't . . . Well, I didn't start with a muslin."

"So you've started? How far along are you? Can I see it?"

"Not yet." Cordi eyed the pile of fabrics lying on top of the sewing machine. She had only started cutting out pieces, too tired to do much more after a day at Ms. Ran's shop.

"How about this weekend? Why don't you meet me? There's this club. Come join me for drinks—it will be a night out."

A night out? Cordi gripped the phone.

"It's quite exclusive, but don't be intimidated. I'll leave your name at the door."

She gave Cordi the address, then hung up before Cordi could protest that she didn't have anything to wear, that she would look rather odd carrying a ball gown into a nightclub.

So after her shift at the fabric shop—which, like most stalls at the alley, didn't have an official name—Cordi would return to the apartment and hunch over her new sewing machine late into the night to make the first gown, desperate to meet the looming deadline. She'd never attempted anything so complicated, and half the time, she had no idea what she was doing. She brought home yards and yards of fabric and cut into it with the perpetual fear that she'd ruin it, and she'd have nothing to show for her work but a pile of scraps.

And yet, her fingers knew what to do, as if her body were possessed by the spirit of some talented designer, and by the end of the week, she held up a stunning piece and couldn't quite remember how she'd made it. It was constructed of several layers of different blue fabrics, with a sweetheart neckline and boning sewn into the fitted bodice. The skirt bloomed with layers of tulle and lace begging to be twirled, and out of habit, she had added pockets hidden from view but sturdy enough to hold all a lady's essentials.

"Whoa," Tessa said when she came home on Friday evening and saw the dress. Audrey and Silly were both still at work.

Cordi put her things away. She liked to keep her workspace tidy— and she felt a bit guilty for taking up an area of the living room when all the girls generally kept their things in their own space. She'd laid the gown out across the sofa because she had nowhere else to put it.

"You made that?" Tessa asked. She dropped her purse and coat on the entrance side table and rushed to the dress. "It's gorgeous. Cordi, I would buy this myself if I saw it in a store—and if I had a bash to wear it to."

"Really?" Cordi folded the sewing machine inside the hinged surface so that it resembled any normal desk. "You think so?"

"Cordi, it's divine. I didn't know you were this good."

"I didn't either." Cordi joined Tessa in the square to stare down at the dress. The stitching was perfect, the different cuts of fabric lining together so that even the rows of threads matched. She ran her hands over the hem, which had always been her least favorite part to finish, and a sharp pain lanced through her fingers. "Ow." She inspected her hands, but she didn't see any small cuts or scratches. And yet an undeniable ache lay just beneath her skin.

"You okay?"

"Yeah, maybe I cut my nails too short." But the white crescents peeking over her fingers looked fine. The pain felt deeper, as if she had cut into the bones instead.

"Oh, this dress makes me want to dance." Tessa took Cordi's elbow and leaned her head on Cordi's shoulder. "I could fall in love in this dress." She looked at Cordi suddenly. "Let's go. Why not?"

"Dancing?" Cordi had never gone dancing before. She'd never even gone out, though she watched Tessa get ready all the time with no small amount of jealousy, shamefully wishing that Tessa would invite her, but fearful of what she might actually say or do if it happened.

"Yeah, I'm dying to do something fun. It's been ages."

"I can't," Cordi said, remembering why she had rushed to get the dress done. "I have to meet Cressida."

Tessa froze, then turned slowly like Cordi was a wild animal that might bolt. "Cressida . . . Thompson?" she repeated.

"Yeah." Cordi stretched her hands behind her back.

"You made this dress for Cressida Thompson," Tessa said slowly.

"Yes." Cordi frowned. "I told you all about it."

Tessa squealed, flailing her hands and feet.

Cordi stepped back. "Goodness, what's gotten into you?"

"You never said it was for *Cressida Thompson*."

"I did—" She was sure she had mentioned it.

"No, you said a strange girl came to the alley with Sinclair. You never once said Cressida. I would have remembered. Oh my lord." Tessa began pacing, fanning her face with both hands. "Oh goodness. What does this mean? How? You've been discovered by Cressida Thompson. This is . . . this is *everything*."

"Tessa," Cordi said. "What are you talking about? I don't understand."

"No, you're right. You don't. This is Cressida! Thompson! Her family practically owns the city!"

"But . . ." What did that have to do with anything?

"Where are you meeting her tonight?"

"Some club called the Society."

Tessa clenched her eyes shut, her face twisted either in agony or excitement, Cordi couldn't tell. "The Society?!" she nearly shouted.

"Is it . . . a nice place?"

Tessa sucked in a deep breath, her face relaxing into a dreamy expression. "It's this absolutely famous nightclub. It's incredibly exclusive. Only the richest families have memberships there. It's owned by the Thompsons. Practically everything is. Come on, Cordi. You must have seen their names everywhere. On all the signs and billboards and buildings."

Come to think of it, she had. She could see their little logo now, the name written in cursive with a swirly underline.

"I met Cressida Thompson once, at a dinner party—she's practically royalty, and she was so friendly, but I didn't get a chance to talk to her much. I bet we could be best friends if I got the chance."

Cordi massaged her fingers, the pain distracting her from the confusing resentment she felt at Tessa's enthusiasm. Tessa's eagerness to be friends with some other girl when she had . . . well, Cordi.

"I," she said, craving Tessa's attention, wanting to claim her own spot as Tessa's best friend, "can get you in."

Tessa smiled, fixing Cordi with renewed interest. "Are you sure?"

"I'm meeting Cressida there tonight. She said she'd give my name to the doorman. I just need to find something to wear—I don't know if I own anything suitable."

"Wear that." Tessa pointed to the blue ball gown that Cordi had just made.

"What? No, I made that for Cressida, and it won't fit me. And it's not something you wear to a nightclub." Then again, she had no idea. She'd never been to a nightclub, and this Society place sounded very fancy.

"Then perhaps . . . I can wear it?" Tessa asked.

Cordi looked at her, then at the dress. "No. I'm bringing it to Cressida. It's her dress. That's the only reason we're meeting."

"I mean, it's not finished, is it? You're taking it to her to see if she'll like it. Well, what better way than to have a model show her how beautiful it is? How beautiful it will look on her? It's not any different than how stores display designs on their mannequins. I'll stick with you the whole time, so she knows I only came for her. For you."

Cordi's heart thudded. This was not a good idea. But she had no idea how to say no without hurting Tessa's feelings, without losing her place on Tessa's ladder of friendships.

"I promise not to get it dirty," Tessa added. "I'll be very careful. How else are you going to get it there? You'll look so silly trying to carry it on the streetcar."

"I don't know . . ."

But as always, Tessa's eyes did that pleading thing, and she clasped her hands against her chest. "Please, Cordi. There's something magical about this dress. I can feel it. What if this is the lura giving me my chance? What if it happens tonight? You and Silly got what you wished for. What about me? I'm still waiting."

Cordi considered for a second longer, but she already knew the answer was yes. No one could resist Tessa—it was as if she were imbued with magic and could coerce anyone into giving her exactly what she wanted.

"You can't do anything to jeopardize this."

Tessa grinned, knowing she had won. "I promise."

Cordi picked out a simple piece to wear, though she didn't have many choices. It wasn't as if she had lived a glamorous life, so all her clothes were functional, cute but built for work. The one dress she had that was even slightly appropriate for a night out was a shift dress she'd made on a whim because she couldn't resist the black, shimmery fabric. She had known Mother wouldn't approve, so she'd hidden it at the back of her closet. This would be her first opportunity to wear it.

When Tessa emerged in her gown, Cordi couldn't stop staring at her. Tessa was beautiful, sure—she had done that magical thing she did with her face that highlighted the right parts and deepened and shaped others. But it was the dress that Cordi admired indulgently, her chest swelling with pride at the way it fit. It hugged in all the right places, and the skirt swirled as if the top layers of the skirt floated, the fabric undulating like the serene surface of a crystalline lake.

"Wow, Tess," Cordi said. "That looks like I made it for you."

"I *know*." Tessa sighed. "Too bad I can't keep it."

Cordi's stomach twisted at the thought that Tessa would beg her to do so, and she desperately tried to think of a way to refuse, but Tessa squealed and grabbed Cordi's arm.

"Come on, let's go," Tessa said. The two of them practically tripped over the layers of skirt as they made their way down the stairs.

Tessa wore the dress as if she were used to wearing such a bold, eye-catching designer piece, the skirt a foot wide on either side. As they walked down the sidewalk and caught stares, she smiled and carried on with the air of someone who couldn't be bothered.

Cordi was so enthralled with her own handiwork and the fact that she had Tessa to herself—no Silly to interrupt their conversations or interject her own insecurities—that she barely noticed that the night had transformed the neighborhood. Dirty and grimy during the day, the streets had become a thriving, crowded space brightened by the flashing signs of restaurants and bars and the blinding lights of cars, the sounds of passengers laughing and shouting floating through the windows like a drunken, already forgotten memory. They passed under the scaffolding of a building under construction, dodging around a person wearing five layers of coats, followed by a group of middle-aged men in suits and fedoras and too much cologne who stopped and eyed Tessa openly. Someone whistled at them. Tessa deliberately didn't respond, but Cordi couldn't help whipping around to see a boy no older than sixteen poking his head out of a window of a passing car. He made a lewd gesture with his tongue, and she looked away quickly, her face flooding inexplicably with heated shame, the aftertaste of bitter coffee filling her mouth.

"It's best to ignore those kinds of things," Tessa said. "Look, the nightclub is just up there."

The building she pointed at had no sign, and nothing set it apart from the rest of the dark high-rises that surrounded them. The only thing distinguishing it was the long line of people that wrapped around the front and into the alley. Everyone wore fancy outfits—the women in sequined and glittery frocks with stubby-looking heels, and the men in tailored three-piece suits and silky shirts and ties.

Even among the elegantly dressed club goers, Tessa stood out in her gown, and as they approached, the buzz of conversation quieted. One by one, the people in line turned and stared.

All eyes were on her friend, the dress catching their attention, but their gazes eventually fixated on her face. Cordi was glad she had made the skirt so full, because she could maneuver herself slightly behind Tessa and hide from view.

Tessa beamed at the crowd and headed straight to the entrance, where a large bulldozer of a man stood next to a stanchion. Cordi fought back her anxiety. What if Cressida forgot to put her name on the list? They'd have to go to the back of the line, and considering how long the queue was, they'd never get into the nightclub before it closed.

But then the man made a strange blubbering sound, not even bothering to check his clipboard. His fingers scrabbled at the rope as he pulled it aside and stepped back to let them through. He barely noticed Cordi, so bewitched by Tessa's beauty.

They stepped into a blackened entryway, their eyes taking several seconds to adjust to darkness. There was another door at the end of the small space, barely concealing the sound of thumping drums and cymbals overlaid with the swingy tunes of a saxophone. A sultry female voice crooned invitingly.

Tessa gave Cordi a conspiratorial smile before opening the door. As they entered the club, the song ended, and a momentary hush fell across the crowd. Cordi and Tessa stood on a platform on the upper level, looking down at the dance floor beneath. Stairs on either side led to the crowd, where tables reserved for exclusive members bordered the perimeter of the large room. On the upper level, the platform wrapped around the wall, the area furnished with daybeds enclosed by canopies strung with white gossamer curtains. With the dim lighting, the whole place had a heavenly, foggy sort of atmosphere.

Tessa paused on the platform overlooking the crowd. The lights spinning around the dance floor suddenly paused, and a beam froze on Tessa like a spotlight. On the stage at the other end of the club, the band looked up at Tessa as if she were a performer. Cordi stood one step behind her, frozen in place, not wanting to draw attention to herself.

Even if she did, she doubted anyone could have looked away from Tessa at the moment. The spotlight cast a dark filter over the dress, making Tessa appear even more ethereal with her pale skin and sharp bone structure. She had curled her hair into a faux bob, and her dark-red lipstick looked like blood in the eerie light, which only added to her mysterious appeal.

When Tessa moved to walk down the stairs to the dance floor, it was as if she broke the trance. The band continued playing, the spotlight continued moving, and the crowd blinked and resumed dancing, seemingly not sure why they'd stopped at all.

Cordi followed after Tessa, cursing her heels. They weren't as high as her friend's, but she was convinced she'd fall and make a fool of herself at any moment. She had no clue how to act or where to go next, but Tessa walked with purpose across the dance floor until someone stopped them. An important-looking man in a black suit with a bright pink silk handkerchief neatly peeking out from his pocket said, "Ladies, allow me to introduce myself. Charles Lavender, manager of the Society."

Tessa towered over him. "Tessa Hong." She didn't hold out a hand. "My friend, Miss Cordelia Yin."

"Lovely," he said, bowing slightly. "I would love to offer a complimentary table, if you are so inclined."

"We're here to meet with Cress—Miss Cressida Thompson," Cordi squeaked, not sure the man could hear her over the music.

But he nodded. "Miss Thompson is expecting you. Right this way."

Mr. Lavender led them up a few steps to a raised area not far from the stage. Everyone on the dance floor could see them, though Cordi tried her best not to think about that as she sat on the elegant, white leather daybed full of matching pillows. White lilies sat on the glass coffee table at the center of their dais—difficult not to think of it as such—and the scent enveloped them. Mr. Lavender filled their glasses with bubbly water.

"Please enjoy our premium mineral water while I notify Miss Thompson of your arrival," he said. His voice was soothing yet still loud enough to be heard over the music. "You'll see some menus on the table, but we can whip up anything else you may prefer."

"I'll have a vodka gimlet," Tessa said without even looking at the cocktail menu.

"I'll have the same," Cordi said, because she had no idea what she wanted and it had sounded so chic and sophisticated when Tessa said it.

Mr. Lavender bowed again and left their table, retreating down the steps. The sheer drapes of their canopy had been tied back, but Tessa got up and released them. The fabric fluttered and created a transparent screen that concealed them from view but through which they could still see the stage.

"There," Tessa said, grabbing a glass of water. "Now everyone will be dying for a glimpse of us."

"This is so fancy," Cordi said. She sat stiffly, unable to relax, afraid that if she moved, she might fall apart or do something embarrassing.

Tessa perched at the end of the sectional, looking like a queen on her throne as she surveyed her subjects. The skirt of her gown flared around her and trailed down to the floor. "Tonight is the night. I can feel it."

Cordi could feel it too, a slight tingling at the back of her neck, the general sense that she wasn't alone. Not just because she was in a night-club surrounded by people, but because she felt something or someone there, close, watching. Familiar but not quite. She resisted the urge to look to the right, knowing the seat was empty, but unable to shake the feeling that someone sat right beside her.

When Mr. Lavender came back with their drinks, he brought Cressida with him. She wore a silvery shift dress, beautifully fitted to her body, her blonde hair smooth like a cascade of snow down her back, her neck adorned with simple diamonds.

Cordi saw Tessa stiffen just a little. Her fingers grasped Cordi's hand.

"Cordelia, hello!" Cressida said, and leaned down to kiss Cordi on both cheeks as if they were long-lost friends.

"Cressida," Cordi said, wanting to explain why Tessa wore the dress. She'd been fretting about it, going over exactly what to say. "This is my friend Tessa—she wanted to model—"

"Of course, Tessa Hong! I thought that was you," Cressida said, and leaned down to hug and kiss Tessa as well.

"Cressida!" Tessa pulled their new companion down onto the seat next to her. "I wasn't sure you'd remember me."

"Of course I do. Our fathers are at the same club, aren't they?"

Tessa's smile froze, but she nodded brightly.

"But how do you two know each other?" Cressida asked.

"Cordi is my friend and house companion," Tessa said, as if they lived in a mansion on a hill and not a cramped apartment. "When she told me that you were meeting her here to see the gown she made for you, I thought how awkward it would be for her to carry it on the streetcar, and how you wouldn't be able to see how beautiful it is, just laid out. I begged her to let me model it for you."

Cordi held her breath, twisting her fingers anxiously as she watched Cressida.

"Is that so?" Cressida fixed her ice-blue eyes on Cordi. In fact, she looked like she was made entirely of ice, from her snowy hair to her pale skin to the silver sequined dress she wore with matching strappy pewter sandals to the glittering jewels on her neck.

"I-I hope—" Cordi stammered, breathing so fast, she couldn't squeeze any more words out.

Cressida took a deep breath. And then she beamed. "I absolutely adore it."

Cordi nearly fainted, she was so relieved.

"It's gorgeous," Cressida went on. "I admired it the moment you stepped into the club. And it looks stunning on you, Tess, almost as if it were made for you."

Tessa smoothed her hair back from her shoulders and smiled.

"But it wasn't," Cordi jumped in. "I made it for you—with your measurements. Tessa just happened to be the perfect model."

"We must be the same size," Tessa said with a laugh, then shot a look at Cordi as if to say, *Get it together*, when Cressida looked away.

"How did you come up with the design?" Cressida asked Cordi.

"I . . ." Cordi had no idea. Every time she thought about the dress, from the sketching to the cutting and sewing, her mind grew fuzzy, and a ticklish numbness spread over her fingers.

"She's a genius," Tessa answered for her. "She can't explain her methods. You should have seen her working, Cressida. Practically possessed."

"Was I really?" Cordi asked, startled at the word. *Possessed.* Not a term she associated with herself with on a regular basis.

Tessa smiled at her and winked.

"And where did you get *your* dress?" Cressida asked Cordi, admiring her knee-length, short-sleeved, shimmery frock.

"I made this a while back," Cordi said, surprised that she sounded so confident despite the turmoil churning inside her. The loud music, the watchful gaze of the crowd, and this intimidating woman now talking to them overwhelmed her. She took a long pull of her drink and tried not to gag as the cloying taste burned down her throat and hit her belly with a searing sensation.

"My, my," Cressida said. "You must come with me, darlings. I want to show you both off to my friends. And win a bet with Gabe." She winked at Cordi, who remained on the sofa, too petrified to move. Tessa was already up, standing next to Cressida, both waiting for Cordi expectantly.

She gulped the rest of her drink down and stood. The world tilted and righted itself with a jerk as she followed the other two, feeling very much like a little girl tagging after her much older sisters. Cressida led them around the daybeds and through a walkway, empty except for a security guard in a suit.

At her table the curtains swayed ever so slightly, stirred by the movement of the guests seated on the tufted leather chairs. Two women and three men were talking, all stunning in glittery wiggle dresses and pressed suits. They stopped and looked up as Cressida approached, like subjects awaiting her majesty. Cressida pulled Tessa in front of her like an offering.

"I found her," she announced.

Tessa didn't miss a beat, unfazed by the attention, or rather, basking in it as she propped one hand against her side, letting the other hang casually. Cressida's friends gazed up at her with open admiration.

"Gabe, are you taking notes?" Cressida demanded.

Cordi snapped to attention. Of course Gabe Sinclair was there—he had, after all, been with Cressida at the fabric store, but Cordi was shocked nonetheless. He seemed too serious to go to a club, a place where people went to have fun, a term that didn't seem to apply to him.

"It *is* a beautiful dress." Mr. Sinclair stood, and seeing Cordi, his face flashed with recognition.

"Miss Yin," he said.

"Mr. Sinclair, hi," Cordi sputtered.

He looked between her and Tessa. "I'm glad you found the modeling work you were looking for," he said to Tessa, who lifted her chin smugly.

"Well, it's no Lacy's catalog, but isn't Cordi talented?" Tessa swished the skirt. Cordi couldn't tell if he liked the dress. It was her best work, but now she saw all the minor flaws—an excess thread she forgot to snip, the one stitch out of line that she had ignored, eager to finish hemming the skirt, the curve in the shoulder seam that wasn't quite perfect.

"It's beautiful," he said. He didn't smile, exactly, but at least he didn't frown, and he gave her an approving nod. "Splendid work," he said, although it seemed the words nearly choked him on the way out.

Heat moved through her veins, and she had no idea where to look or what to say. So she dipped her head, hoping he read it as acknowledgment of his praise, though part of her was loath to accept it from someone who'd been so quick to dismiss her from the start.

"I didn't know you wanted to model, Tessa," Cressida said.

"Oh yes, it's my dream," Tessa said. "Not that I don't love my job at the Petite counter, of course."

"John." Cressida spoke to a man with curly black hair sitting on the tufted leather sofa, who was paying rapt attention. "This is Tessa. She's gorgeous. She shouldn't be selling Petite Beauty; she should be the face of Petite Beauty. Do something about it."

John leaned over, holding a glass of some amber-colored liquid. "Do you have a manager, doll?" he asked Tessa.

Tessa sauntered over to him, the width of the skirt making her hips sway from side to side with dramatic flair. "I've been waiting for the perfect one to come around."

Cressida turned to Cordi, grabbing her by the shoulders, then spinning her around so fast that Cordi found herself inches from Mr. Sinclair.

"And this dress, Gabe," Cressida said. "Isn't it divine? She designed and sewed it herself! I didn't even give her the inspiration." She presented Cordi like a prize.

"It is very well made," Mr. Sinclair said as he studied her. The dress. Not *her*. Cordi's face burned, and she was grateful for the dim lighting. "Have you made many others?"

"Oh yes." She cringed at how earnest she sounded. "I worked at my parents' alterations shop growing up and made my own clothes."

Mr. Sinclair's expression knotted in concentration. "Perhaps you should stop by the store and bring your best designs. We can discuss business then."

Cordi couldn't believe what she'd heard. The loud music and the buzz of conversation must have warped her understanding.

But then Mr. Sinclair looked at her directly and raised his brows as if expecting some sort of response, and she knew it hadn't been a mistake. Her body grew warm all over, and a bit tingly, though perhaps it was from her drink. She shifted as he continued studying her, reminding herself that his attention meant nothing—he was there with Cressida after all, and couldn't possibly have any interest in her beyond professional.

"Yes, of course," she said.

"Next week?" he asked.

Cordi nodded, stunned. On the sofa, Tessa was speaking intimately with the man named John, leaning close, her hair brushing his cheek. She caught Cordi observing them and winked.

"Enough shop talk," the other man sitting on the couch said. He was boyishly handsome, his face clean-shaven, his tie loosened and the top button of his shirt undone. He smiled and fixed his gaze on Cordi as he stood. "Didn't you come here to dance?"

"Oh, I—" Cordi had never danced before, and the thought of embarrassing herself made her want to run back home, but she couldn't think of an excuse.

"Cordelia, this is my brother, Sam," Cressida said. "Sam works in finance. Sam, Cordelia."

"Dress designer, so I heard." Sam's smile crinkled the corners of his eyes.

"Well, not yet," Cordi said.

Mr. Sinclair scowled as Sam stepped between them, but when their eyes met, he looked away quickly and cast his disapproval across the crowd on the dance floor instead.

Sam took her hand, sending soft warmth up her arm as he guided her fingers to loop around his elbow. "Trust me, from the way Sinclair eyed that dress, it won't be long before your designs are all over the city."

As they moved down the steps to the main dance floor, Cordi glanced back to see Cressida lean her head against Gabriel Sinclair's shoulder. He turned to whisper something to her. Cordi looked away, embarrassed to witness such an intimate moment when she hardly knew them. A terrible feeling grew in the pit of her stomach, though she had no idea why she felt so disappointed—Mr. Sinclair and Cressida had come to the fabric shop together. They must be engaged—why else would Cressida be shopping for a trousseau?

But she didn't have time to dwell on it because the band struck up a bouncy tune, and Sam Thompson spun her to face him. Cordi had no idea what to do—were there steps she was supposed to know? She watched Sam sway to the music and followed his lead. Good thing the club was dark. If he noticed how stiff and unsure she felt, he didn't let on, instead taking her hand and spinning her gently. Soon, she fell easily into the rhythm of the music, moving her feet, swaying her hips, never looking away from Sam's smiling, welcoming face.

By the time the song ended, her face was flushed, her breathing fast. Sam laughed as he spun her one last time, then pulled her up against him.

"Beautiful Cordelia," he whispered. His hand smoothed a stray hair out of her eyes. He stood so close, his chest flat under her hands while he held her arms as if afraid she might slip away. "Can I call you sometime?"

Cordi stammered something unintelligible. A phone call. He wanted her number. Maybe other things.

He led her away from the dance floor to an abandoned table, its glasses full of melting ice. He grabbed a napkin and brandished a pen, and somehow, Cordi found herself jotting down the number to the Mais' apartment, hoping that, in the dark, she managed to scribble the right one.

Chapter Sixteen

Her fingers ached the next morning, the pain a dull throb. Her whole body hurt, actually, especially her head. She recognized the telltale signs of a hangover, something that was becoming more and more frequent since she'd moved in with the Mais.

Cordi rubbed her eyes, and the soreness in her fingertips heightened, as if she had clipped her nails too short, only she hadn't. They were actually longer than she normally kept them. She inspected her fingers, finally focusing on the black, bruised tips of her nails. She had once slammed a thumb in a door. The nail had turned purple, then black, before it fell off completely, and her nails looked like that now, like she had slammed all ten fingers in a door.

She hadn't drunk *that* much last night, had she? She remembered finishing the first drink, and then Cressida had ordered more, and then someone else had gotten another round, and another, and another. But she'd spent most of the night with Sam Thompson. She recalled the blurry dance floor spinning behind his charming face. The hint of his expensive cologne still lingered in her nostrils, and now her feet ached as evidence. Why the hell had she worn heels?

During a brief moment when she had returned to the table, thirsty and out of breath, Tessa had pulled her aside to whisper excitedly that John Lenore—the man Cressida had introduced her to—*owned* Petite Beauty.

"Well, not all of it," Tessa added. "His parents technically own it. He just has a huge stake and runs the marketing department. But isn't that great? He's not a model scout, but he'll do."

"Does everyone here own everything?" Cordi asked, aware that her words were a little slurred and not sure that she made much sense. "Are they all rich or something?"

"Shh, it's coarse to talk about it. But yes. Especially the Thompsons, they practically run downtown—all the posh businesses, the restaurants and bars and this whole club. They probably own some of Lacy's too, but I know for a fact the majority shares belong to Ms. Lacy over there." Tessa nodded across the club, but Cordi's vision was too blurry by then to attempt to look. "She controls so much of what people wear and buy. Imagine all that power. And the Vandersons own the theaters and some of the movie studios, and all the real estate north of Spring Street."

"Wow." Cordi hiccuped. For some reason, a memory came to her. She was five and starting school, and her parents didn't know she was supposed to bring her own school supplies, and she had sat at her empty desk watching the other kids with their nice pens and pencils. She didn't remember much about the other students except that they were taller than her, and white, and generally scary to be around simply because she wasn't one of them. She knew even at that young age that she could never have what they had.

"What does Mr. Sinclair own?" she asked, only because she happened to catch his eye at that moment. He hadn't left the safety of the leather seats, not even when Cressida went off to dance. He just sat there studying everyone with what looked like a subtle air of superiority. Why had he even come?

Tessa made a noise of annoyance. "Nothing. He *works*." As if that were the worst thing she could think of.

"So . . . sad," Cordi said. "Why can't everyone just share?"

Tessa smiled and pulled her in for a hug, right before Sam whisked Cordi back to the dance floor. All in all, it had turned out to be a wonderful evening, even if she had to deal with the consequences the morning after.

Lying in bed now, Cordi flexed and clenched her fingers. Despite how bruised the nails looked, they didn't hurt that much. In fact, they felt sort of numb, like if she'd tied a rubber band around each of them. That horrible sensation was back too, the feeling like someone was there, watching her, breathing down her neck.

Cordi climbed down from her loft to put the kettle on. While she waited, she went to Tessa's plants growing by the window and breathed them in, even though they kind of scared her, especially the vine that climbed up to the ceiling and attached its roots to the wall like claws. She couldn't shake the urge to look over her shoulder, but she knew no one was there.

She jumped when the kettle whistled, thankful not to be alone as Silly came out of the room, dressed in a loose pantsuit, her hair a curly mess she was trying unsuccessfully to pin up.

"Are you working today?" Cordi asked, hoping Silly would stick around and rid her of the unease she couldn't shake. "It's Saturday. Isn't the mayor's office closed?" Silly had spoken of nothing except her internship lately, and though Cordi tried really hard to be interested and happy for her, she found Silly's description of the work so incredibly boring that she hardly listened to a word. It was the only time Cordi felt glad that Tessa showed such nurturing interest in Silly. The girl was sweet, but she didn't strike Cordi as someone Tessa would be friends with. Then again, Cordi hadn't thought she would be either, yet Tessa was always kind to her. Look at the night they had had together.

She resolved to be nicer to Silly.

"Yes, but I have so much to do," Silly said, "and I really need to prove myself. There are five other interns. Five! And only one of us will get hired full-time at the end of the internship." She rubbed her temples. "I've got the worst headache."

"I'm sorry," Cordi said with an expression of sympathy. "Would you like some tea before you go?"

"Oh, I can't. I don't want to be late."

Tessa's door opened. She came out in a rush, dashing to put on her shoes by the front door. For once, she looked disheveled, her dress unbelted, bags showing beneath her eyes, and her hair bedraggled.

"I'm having the worst morning," she moaned. "Look at this mess." She held up the limp strands of her hair, then attempted to pull it back into the low bun she usually wore to work. Instead of a sleek chignon, today it looked flat and dead. A far cry from the beauty she had been last night. "I can't go to work looking like this. I'm supposed to meet John to discuss our future partnership."

"Who?" Silly asked.

"My God, Silly, keep up. John Lenore. He wants me to be the new face of Petite Beauty," Tessa snapped with an annoyed huff, turning away to stomp her feet into her shoes.

"What?" Silly's eyes grew moist, and she looked at Cordi for reassurance. Tessa was usually so nice to her, and even Cordi was surprised at her dismissive tone.

"We'll talk later," Tessa said, then sighed at Silly's expression. "Come here, doll, I didn't mean to snap." She pulled Silly in for a brief hug. "I'm going to be late. I'll have to fix my hair on the streetcar or something."

"I can help you," Silly said, her voice nasally.

Tessa patted Silly's cheek, then gave Cordi a companionably annoyed look, as if she could count on Cordi to understand her, and Cordi smiled to herself as the two rushed out the door. After the night at the club, she and Tessa shared a bond, their friendship cemented, no longer just roommates. And though she had no reason to dislike Silly, Cordi was inexplicably satisfied that Tessa seemed to prefer her over Silly.

The phone rang, and Cordi answered it before it could wake Audrey, who was always cranky in the morning.

"Misses Mai residence," she said.

"Cordelia, I was hoping to catch you," Cressida Thompson said, her voice sending a jolt of energy through Cordi stronger than any cup of tea.

"Cressida—hi, how are you? Last night was—"

"It was wonderful, wasn't it? I hope my brother didn't bore you to death with his talk of financial reports. Half the time, I have no idea what he's talking about."

"Oh no, he didn't—we had a great time."

"Splendid! I'll tell him to call you."

"Well, that's not—only if he wants to, really—"

"I called to talk about the dress, darling."

"Right." Cordi spun around, scanning the living room. The gown must be in Tessa's room. "I promise I'll have it dry-cleaned. I shouldn't have let Tessa wear it, but she insisted and I didn't know how to say no, and she was really only supposed to model it. And I didn't know how else to get it to the club. I hope you weren't offended."

"Of course not. She was an excellent model. I should have sent a car—how thoughtless of me. But anyway, I'm calling to ask if you've seen the locals this morning."

"The locals . . ." Cordi felt two steps behind, her brain refusing to catch up.

"The papers. You do subscribe to the dailies? Never mind, you can buy one off the stand later. She was in it."

"She was?" Cordi scrambled to their seating square, where stacks of magazines littered the coffee table. Tessa read all sorts of gossip columns, but of course none of them were recent.

"Yes, but the focus was solely on your dress. Listen to this: 'The skirt seemed made of a mile's worth of spun sugar, the waist cinching the model in elegant beauty.' You're going to be quite famous, you know. And I get to lord it over Gabe that I discovered you." Cressida's laugh twinkled.

Cordi exhaled, relieved that Cressida truly wasn't angry. "I'll have it sent to you right away."

"Don't—Tessa can keep it."

"But it's yours. You've already paid for it."

"Why don't you replace it with the wedding dress we discussed instead? Now that I know you're fully capable of creating such elegant pieces, I want to see what you come up with."

"Oh." Cordi gulped, but then excitement stole her away as she imagined the other four dresses she would make for Cressida, as well as the wedding gown. She had so many ideas and couldn't wait to get right to sketching.

"Perhaps I can come over to discuss more ideas?"

The thought of Cressida in their cramped apartment made Cordi's palms sweat. She switched the phone receiver to her other hand.

"I would love that, but I have to go to work today."

"That dusty place where I found you?"

"Uh, the fabric shop—yes."

"You haven't quit? Was my check not enough? I can write another one, if you'd like."

"No—I mean, yes, it was enough—I just, I tried—Ms. Ran was so nice, is so nice, I can't abandon her when she has so much work."

"Darling," Cressida said in a slightly distracted tone, as if she had already ended the conversation. "You can't have it all, you know. You have to give up something. That's just how it is."

Chapter Seventeen

Tessa was thrilled when Cordi told her she could keep Cressida's gown, hanging it up on one wall of her room like it was a tapestry. She pinned the skirt so that it flared out, the fabric fluttering when she walked by.

"It's the most beautiful thing I've ever been given," she said.

Cordi stood in the doorway of Tessa's bedroom, which was surprisingly neat and organized, the pink bedspread tucked in at the corners, the vanity by the window covered in jars and creams, necklaces sparkling in the jewelry case. She beamed with pride as they both admired the dress pinned to the wall.

The front door opened and closed.

"Who is it?" Tessa asked.

"Silly," Cordi said, smiling and waving as the younger girl slipped off her shoes by the door, looking tired. Her gray skirt sagged down past her knees, the matching jacket draped over her arm, her blouse wrinkled and stained with sweat.

"Silly, come here!" Tessa called out, and Cordi felt an inexplicable surge of annoyance. She'd had Tessa to herself since they'd both gotten home from work, and after the night they'd had at the Society, she didn't feel like she should have to share. But she tamped down her thoughts when Silly put her palms to her cheeks and squealed with delight.

"Oh my goodness, Cordi," Silly said. "It's beautiful! You made that?"

"And I get to keep it!" Tessa grabbed Silly's hands and the two of them bounced up and down. Cordi couldn't decide whether to join them or retreat to process why she suddenly wanted to give Silly a not-too-gentle shove.

Tessa turned her attention to Cordi again, melting away the icy block that had formed in her chest. "We should do something," Tessa said.

"Go out?" Silly asked.

Cordi wanted to say no, just out of spite. She wanted it to be just her and Tessa again. She didn't want to share Tessa with Silly, who claimed all the attention whenever she had the moment.

"We could go to the theater," Tessa suggested. "They're playing some foreign film in 3D."

"3D?" Silly repeated, and it grated Cordi how she repeated and followed everything Tessa did. Was that how Cordi looked to other people?

Audrey arrived home then too, pausing to look at Cordi, who still hovered just outside Tessa's room.

"Tessa's telling us about 3D movies," Cordi explained.

"Yeah, it's supposed to be like real life," Tessa said.

"What's the point of that?" Audrey asked. "Just step outside."

"You're no fun!" Tessa called as she pulled Silly down to the edge of her bed to braid her hair, a casual act of affection that Cordi found baffling.

"How does it work?" Cordi asked.

"Well, you wear these special glasses with these special lenses and everything looks . . . dimensional!" Tessa beamed. "Imagine—if I become a movie star, audiences will see me in 3D!"

"By the time that happens, the technology might improve so much that you could be four-dimensional!" Audrey squealed with mock excitement.

Tessa rolled her eyes at Cordi. "Goodness, if you hate the idea so much, then don't come with us."

Audrey snorted. "Who said I wanted to?"

Tessa's nostrils flared, but then she fixed her expression into a friendlier one. "What about you?" she asked Cordi.

Audrey paused at her bedroom doorway, met Cordi's eyes, and looked pointedly at the sewing machine.

"I'd love to, but I really should get started on the rest of Cressida's dresses," Cordi said. After Audrey closed her door, Cordi felt the need to assure Tessa she wasn't choosing Audrey over her. "I have a lot of ideas—can I show them to you?" She added the last out of impulse, overcome with nervousness that Tessa might not be remotely interested.

"Of course, I want to see them." Tessa finished with Silly's hair and patted her on the top of her head.

Tessa followed Cordi to her sewing machine, where she kept her sketchbook, and Cordi picked it up excitedly. To her disappointment, Silly followed hot on their heels.

"I want to go to the movies," Silly said, her voice almost whiny.

"Right-o, we'll go after this." Tessa threw an arm around Silly's shoulders as she leaned over Cordi to look at the new designs. "Ooh, these are wonderful, Cor!"

But any excitement she'd felt about Tessa's awed reaction fizzled out at the thought of Tessa and Silly going out together, without her. She couldn't change her mind now—it would seem childish—and she really did want to work on the dresses, her fingers itching to get started.

She could only watch enviously as Tessa and Silly got ready while she laid out yards of silk for the work ahead.

After they left, Audrey came out of her room to make a sandwich. She sat at the kitchen table and ate quietly while Cordi's sewing machine purred through layers of fabric. Neither said much at first, and Cordi found her company surprisingly soothing, unencumbered by expectations to make small talk.

It was also a welcome distraction from the distress she felt that Tessa and Silly had gone to the movies without her after all, and even though Cordi didn't like to admit it, lately she hated being alone. It was always when no one was around that she got that disturbing sense that something else lived in the apartment with them, a preposterous notion she knew not to share with the others. She didn't want them to think she was going mad.

Instead of returning to her room after she finished eating, Audrey moved to the couch with a sketchbook of her own. Cordi couldn't see what she worked on, and her curiosity got the better of her.

"Is that for the gallery?" she asked.

Audrey didn't seem bothered by the interruption. "No, just for me."

"Is it sad?"

Audrey chuckled. "A little." She held up the beginnings of a portrait of an older woman, her expression somber, a teardrop on the cheek shaded so well it seemed to pop off the page.

"It's beautiful." Cordi removed the pins from a seam. "Do you ever draw anything happy?"

"Nah. Artists like you and me aren't destined for happiness."

"That's not true." Cordi felt slightly offended to be included in this damaged description, though pleased that Audrey considered her an artist. "Do you really believe that?"

Audrey bent over her sketch. "I recognize a broken soul when I see one."

Cordi tried to laugh this off, but it came out fake and high-pitched.

"I mean," Audrey said, "why else would you be living with three other girls you don't know? Something happened with your family, didn't it?"

Cordi hadn't told anyone but Ms. Ran about her parents or Trina, and neither Tessa nor Silly had asked, probably because they had their own troubled pasts to think about. Tessa always became quiet when someone mentioned her father, and Silly spoke about her grandmother with a panicked glint in her eye.

"They kicked me out," Cordi said. "We had a huge argument." Audrey put her sketchbook on her lap and looked at Cordi patiently, and even though she always felt like Audrey didn't care to listen to any of them, the story spilled out of her. This time, she found it much easier, maybe because it wasn't her first time telling it, or maybe because Audrey seemed more understanding than Ms. Ran. Audrey didn't interrupt, just nodded in the right moments.

"It's always people who are supposed to love you that end up hurting you the most," Audrey said when Cordi told her about how Trina seemed to side with her parents.

"Who was it for you?" Cordi asked.

"My aunt," Audrey said, picking her pencil up to bend over her sketchbook. "My mom died when I was a baby and my dad wasn't around. There was no one else to take me in, so I was left with her. She always threatened to put me in the system, though. Beat me so much, I don't think there was a day when I wasn't bruised or banged up in some way. Even if she wasn't hitting me, she was always so angry, and I was always so scared that I wished she would put me in the system. When I was eight, I almost just turned us both in like she kept threatening. But I was too scared, in the end. Until she abandoned me for weeks. No food, no money for anything. I couldn't take it anymore. So I left and found a youth shelter and got a job and managed to work my way out of that life. Away from her."

Cordi took her foot off the pedal of the sewing machine. "I'm so sorry, Aud." No matter how bad things had been in her family, she had to admit they weren't as bad as that.

"It's fine." Audrey's hands scribbled furiously over her sketch. "It made me strong. At least I'm not like . . . other people we know."

Cordi thought she saw her head flick to Silly's door.

"Look," Audrey continued, not looking up from her notebook. "I know I'm not all breezy and beautiful like Tessa—"

"Audrey, that's not—" Cordi started to reassure her.

"But if you need anything, like . . . we can be friends too." She got up abruptly. "All right?" She didn't look at Cordi, pretending to put the finishing touches on her work, but her lashes fluttered like she was trying to blink away tears.

"Of course, Audrey," Cordi said quickly. "You too." She wished she were more eloquent and sounded as genuine as she felt, but she could also see that Audrey was dying to escape and didn't want to prolong her torture.

"Okay, good." Audrey took a deep breath and went back to her room before Cordi could think of more to say.

Over the next few days, Cordi threw herself into the fervor of making Cressida's dresses. Strangely, her nails had grown dark and brittle, like some sort of fungus had infected them, and her fingers stung as she worked. She fought against the pain, even wrapping her fingertips in gauze as she struggled to piece fabric together. She would get them checked by the doctor later, when she had time and after she found out where to even go.

Halfway through the next dress, a piercing pain ripped through her thumb, and she had to stop sewing, clutching it and biting her lip so as not to cry. It was Thursday afternoon, and she had worked frantically all through the previous day as well, taking advantage of her time off from the alley. No one else was home.

Cordi waited for the pain to subside, but instead her thumb throbbed along to the rhythm of her pulse. Breathing deeply, she pulled back the gauze wrapped around it, squealing in disgust when her thumbnail ripped off along with the bandage, leaving behind a blackened, puckered, bleeding stump.

She stared at it, panicked. What was happening to her? Had she worked too hard, too much?

But that couldn't be it. She'd worked just as hard at her parents' alteration shop and this had never happened. Perhaps all she needed was a break. She looked at the dress longingly. There wasn't much left to do—she just needed to attach the sleeves and add the trim and finish the hemming. She was so close. She wanted to see the final product, revel in how much her talent had grown.

Reluctantly, Cordi tucked her sewing machine into its desk, and then slumped in her seat. Only then did she feel the tightness in her shoulders and back. When she straightened, a few of her joints popped.

With extreme care, she peeled back the rest of the bandages on her fingers. None were as bad as her thumb, but they all looked terrible, blackened and bruised. The tips of her fingers had turned purple.

She should see a doctor, though that would be expensive, and a tad dramatic if all she needed was rest.

Not knowing what else to do, she carefully washed her hands and then applied more gauze, taking extra time with her exposed thumb, which had finally stopped bleeding. Then she climbed up to her loft and lay on her bed, staring into space, dazed and traumatized. She tried not to think of the pain, but she couldn't ignore it when it felt like her heart was threatening to escape through her fingers and every beat caused her skin to swell.

Even worse than the pain was her fear that she'd never be able to sew again. What if this was it? What if her fingers were permanently damaged? The thought brought tears to her eyes. She was still young, her dreams of being a designer dead before they ever had a chance to live.

But she couldn't lie there forever feeling sorry for herself. So what if she couldn't sew right now? It wasn't like the pain would last for all eternity. Maybe it would take a bit of time for her fingers to heal, but as soon as they did, she'd pick up where she had left off.

And anyway, she was supposed to go to her family's house that afternoon to pick up the rest of her things while her parents were off on their church retreat. There was no way she could put it off now, not when she needed to pick out her best designs to bring to her meeting with Mr. Sinclair. Trina said she'd leave a spare key in their usual spot so that Cordi could let herself in. She'd never gotten around to asking one of the Mais to help her, so she had no choice but to make multiple trips.

Cordi inspected her fingers after she made sure she had enough money for the streetcar, but as she stuffed her coin purse back into her bag, the phone rang.

"Misses Mai residence," she said.

"You *are* home," a familiar-sounding man practically shouted. "I thought you'd be at work at this hour."

"Um. Sorry? Who is this?"

"You don't recognize my voice? I'm heartbroken. We danced the whole night together. It's Sam Thompson."

A burst of warmth and giddiness went through her, threatening to erupt into giggles.

"Sam, hi," she said. "It's been so long, I'd forgotten all about you." She was surprised by how calm and even flirtatious she sounded, especially when she really wanted to jump up and down and squeal over the fact that a boy—a handsome, rich boy—had called her.

"I am truly, deeply hurt," Sam said with exaggeration.

Cordi grinned so hard, her cheeks hurt.

Luckily, she was saved from having to come up with a clever reply when Sam kept talking.

"I'll have to rectify that immediately. What are your plans for the day?"

"I was about to leave, actually. I need to go to my parents' house in Chinatown to pick up some clothes." She stopped herself from getting into why she had moved out of her parents' house in the first place. "I want to pick out some designs to show Mr. Sinclair."

"Well, it just so happens that I was planning to go for a drive today, with a loss as to where, and you've just solved my problem. Chinatown it is."

Cordi did giggle this time, but it came out as a breezy chuckle instead of her usual embarrassing, naive laugh. "You'd drive me? The traffic will be terrible." She stopped talking, hoping that he would insist so she wouldn't have to take the streetcar with her things after all.

But then he would see the house, the dilapidated room she used to share with Trina, the poor neighborhood that smelled of fish sauce and garlic.

And then there were her fingers. The bandages covered the damage, but how would she explain it?

She could wear gloves. Callum did it all the time, and no one ever remarked on it. And Cressida had worn an elegant pair when she'd visited the fabric store. She could run down to the boutique around the corner to buy the pair in the window display she'd been eyeing. It was the perfect excuse to allow herself what would otherwise be a foolish purchase.

"Fantastic," Sam said. "I always said there's no better place to get to know someone than when you're stuck in traffic." She could hear the smile in his voice, and it was infectious.

"Okay, then. I suppose I'll let you have the honor of driving me." Where did all this flirty sophistication come from? She'd never been so bold before. It must be the lura improving her personality as well as her outward appearance.

A small twinge of apprehension throbbed at that thought. Cordi had always felt shy and reserved around others and envied how they seemed to know what to say or do, as if everyone had been given a script for life except her. But she'd never hated who she was. What if the lura changed so much about her that she was no longer herself, but just a shell for the magic to work itself through? Could the lura be alive? Controlling her?

She didn't have time to think about that, though. Because Sam laughed sultrily in her ear.

"I'll pick you up in half an hour," he said.

And now she had to decide what to wear.

Chapter Eighteen

Cordi had barely enough time to race to the boutique around the corner. The black lace gloves were far more expensive than she expected. In her panic, she handed off a few bills, then rushed back home to hastily change, with only a spare minute to run down to the front of the building before Sam's car pulled up.

Sam drove a classic black sedan, shiny and sleek, and he wore a casual outfit of black slacks, starched white shirt, and a bold, rust-orange blazer that flattered his pale skin tone. She'd chosen a pinafore dress herself, a summery fabric cinched at her waist over a white shirt. It made her look younger, so she'd paired it with strappy high sandals to balance the look, regretting it immediately as she wobbled down the front steps of her building.

Sam whistled appreciatively when she reached his car. He was double-parked, so they didn't waste time on pleasantries. He ushered Cordi into the passenger seat like a gentleman, then jogged around to the driver's side.

"Where to, my lady?" he asked, starting the engine.

Cordi gave him the address and added, "Just take the 101 to the first Chinatown exit."

"You got it." He busied himself navigating back into traffic, then glanced at her. "You look beautiful, by the way."

There was no dark dance club to hide Cordi's blush today, which made her blush even more. She smoothed a hand over the skirt of her dress. "I made this when I was sixteen. I saw a similar dress in a Lacy's catalog, but there was no way I could have afforded it—" Oh no, she wasn't supposed to allude to money, especially not the fact that she had none. "Or at least, no way I would have wanted to," she added with what she hoped was a casual laugh. "So I learned to make it myself."

"Well, it's absolutely nifty," Sam said. "Why don't you show Gabe that one?"

"It's hardly my best work. I want to show him some of my original designs."

"The ones we're going to pick up?"

"Yes. There's this dress I made. For a school dance, a long time ago." She hadn't bought many ready-to-wear pieces growing up. For one thing, she couldn't afford it, and for another, most clothes sold in stores didn't fit her well. They were cut for taller, leaner frames rather than her shorter, stockier one. She'd made most of her clothes from scratch, carefully cut, measured, basted, taken apart, reassembled, and tailored again and again to fit. At first, Mother had supervised, and those items—the first dress Cordi had made, copied from an ad she'd seen in a magazine, a simple blouse, a color-blocked frock—carried the painful memories of Mother's scoldings and lectures. Mother didn't do things in half measures, especially scolding. It was never a "wrong stitch"; it was "you never listen or pay attention, you'll never find a husband that way."

Most of her early designs had started as castaways from secondhand shops that she'd buy at a discount and alter into something new. She'd known kids who liked to take apart old radio sets to figure out how everything worked. So she'd done the same to her favorite outfits, painstakingly cutting the seams with a sharp blade to separate the small pieces, then duplicating the patterns to sew everything back together. Once she'd learned how garments were constructed—even the most expensive designer pieces—she'd learned how to design original items herself.

Sam had been distracted navigating traffic, but now he looked at her as if wondering why she'd stopped talking.

"I worked hard on the dress," she explained. "Both the design and the execution. I spent weeks on the embroidery on the bodice and even longer sewing the sequins on the skirt."

She scrutinized his reaction. Could he hear how much it meant to her? The hours hunched over her machine making sure each stitch was perfect?

But he was momentarily distracted by a car merging in front of him. "It sounds very detailed," he finally said.

Cordi looked out her window. They drove through Chinatown, passing templelike buildings with curved roofs and sharp corners reaching up to the gods, everything painted in red or gold to bring good fortune, watched over by shiny statues of cats or pigs or lions to ward off evil spirits. "It's so silly to be this passionate about a dress, isn't it? But it means a lot to me."

"It's not silly at all. Clothes are important, or so my sister tells me. Speaking of which, Cressida wanted me to invite you to a gala we're attending next month. Some sort of charity for schoolchildren in Chinatown, actually. Small world, huh? Maybe it will give you a chance to see what all the ladies are wearing to gala events. Give you more ideas."

A gala? Full of important people she would have no idea how to talk to?

"That sounds . . ." she said. "I wouldn't have anything to wear." She could make something, but it seemed too daunting—the guests probably wore expensive designer gowns. Nothing she could come up with would compare.

"Don't worry about that," Sam said. "What's your size? I'll send some things over."

Cordi opened and closed her mouth, shocked. She wasn't the type of girl to go to charity galas with a cute boy who knew exactly what she should wear. "You know, I'm not sure since I always make my clothes myself."

He glanced down the length of her body, sending shivers across her neck. "I'll have some dresses sent over and you can just wear the one that fits. How does that sound?"

"It sounds lovely, but . . ." Cordi couldn't stop making excuses, not used to this glamorous privilege. "I might not have the day off."

Sam grinned at her. "You'll be working for Sinclair by then. He'll consider it research."

"I don't have the job yet."

Sam laughed, as if her concern were no large matter. "You will. Cressida will make it happen. She really likes you, you know."

"I don't want Cressida to make it happen," she said, but her voice was small. "I want to make it happen myself."

He smiled. "And you will! I'm sure you're very talented."

Could it be this easy? She glanced at Sam. It was so unfair. How did people like him get to be where they were without trying, while people like her and Tessa and Audrey and Silly had to work extrahard just for a break? And all for what? A job? More work? It didn't make sense.

When they got to her parents' house, it seemed as if the streets had never been dirtier, the building small and run-down, the sidewalk overgrown with dying grass and littered with rotting leaves. She reached for the door. "You don't have to come in," she said, hoping he wouldn't insist. "I'll just grab my things and be right out."

Thankfully he nodded, flipping the radio on. "We can go to Schwab's after this and get ice cream, if you'd like."

Cordi paused in excited disbelief. She had read about Schwab's in a magazine but had never dared to venture there by herself, satisfied with daydreams of sitting at the counter with friends, perhaps running into a famous movie star, not that she would have known what to say.

"That sounds . . . bitchin'," she said, trying to act cool, then cringed at herself as she hurried inside to get the task over with.

Cordi went around to the back, where the bedroom window had a cut in the screen. She fumbled at the fake succulent she and Trina kept on the sill, feeling for the key hidden beneath the plastic spikes. She let herself through the back door at the kitchen, exhaling a deep breath. And then she took everything in.

The kitchen was clean but had a stained and old, run-down look. A pot sat on the stove, its side crusted with spilled broth. Glasses and bowls dried upside down in the sink. The walls were bare, the white paint peeling in spots.

She walked through the familiar, dark hallway to the room she used to share with her sister, trying hard to ignore the empty twin bed she'd slept in, now cluttered with Trina's books and belongings.

When she slid open the door to their shared closet, the half that was usually bursting with her things was empty. Instead, used paper bags filled with her clothes were stacked on the floor. Cordi grabbed them, grateful that Trina had folded the items neatly. She dug through the bags looking for her school dance dress, the one piece she knew would capture Mr. Sinclair's attention. It should have stood out, the skirt made of sequins, which she hadn't used on anything else she'd made, but she couldn't find it. She finally gave up and hurried out to Sam's car, carrying as much as she could in her arms.

"Are you sure you don't need my help?" Sam asked.

"No, I just need to make one more trip," she said, her mind still on the dress. What if she had just missed it?

She went back inside, and as she passed the kitchen, she caught the smell of sweet-and-sour soup, an easy dish Mother had taught her to make. Her breath hitched, and she sat down on her old bed, drained and exhausted. The hint of a headache blossomed behind her eyes. She hadn't eaten anything in hours, and a tremor started inside her, followed by a flood of memories—the way Mother had combed her hair before school, clipping her fringes so they wouldn't fall into her eyes, the way Mother showed affection in small ways, like always making sure she had rice, even if there was nothing else to eat, or taking the tougher jobs at the shop so Cordi didn't have to. Despite the pain associated with her home, a terrible longing wrenched through her.

Cordi forced herself to get up, to finish what she'd come to do. As she closed the closet door, she saw something sparkling from the shadows on Trina's side. She reached in, cursing the fact that with gloves on, she couldn't feel the textures of the fabric. But the clatter of sequins was evident, even if her fingers were numb, and she pulled the school dance dress out from where Trina had hidden it among her things.

Why had Trina kept it? It wasn't as if she cared about clothes. She never wore anything but ugly black trousers and plain buttoned shirts she thought made her look professional, when really the outfit made her look like she took herself annoyingly too seriously.

Trina had refused to work at the alterations shop after Cordi was old enough, convinced she was meant for bigger, more important things, as if Cordi weren't, as if Cordi's life were dispensable. Trina had scoffed when it turned out Cordi actually liked sewing, and then she had ridiculed every moment that Cordi enjoyed helping Mother fix the customers' clothes or making her own.

Yet here was the dress, Cordi's most prized possession, the master-piece she'd worked on for almost an entire year. What did Trina mean in keeping it? Did she resent Cordi so much that she didn't want Cordi to have it?

Sam's voice filtering in from outside startled her out of her rev-erie. He spoke to someone in the jovial, entitled tone of a man who had never been denied access anywhere, which sparked sharp irritation and exacerbated her already-growing headache. It wasn't fair to him, of course—he had been nothing but charming—yet she couldn't help seeing his confident manner as a result of the life of luxury and privilege she would never have.

Another person responded angrily. Trina.

Cordi rushed outside to find her sister, fists clenched, staring at Sam, who leaned casually against his car. Trina spun around, her face suddenly lax with surprise and guilt when her eyes fell on the dress in Cordi's arms.

Trina's mouth opened and closed.

"Thank you for packing all my things," Cordi said through clenched teeth. She didn't wait for her response. She swung the dress over her shoulder and got in the car.

And even though she had been somewhat annoyed with Sam for this very reason just a moment ago, she was grateful for his flashy car, his boyishly handsome face, and the way he made Trina's face go tomato red as he waved at her and drove away.

Schwab's was technically a pharmacy, but everyone went there for the ice cream, milkshakes, and fudge brownies from the lunch counter, or so Cordi had heard. Growing up, she hadn't understood the concept of enjoying a treat, so when her classmates talked about catching glimpses of the famous stars who liked to frequent the shop, the idea seemed unlikely, a dream far from her reality.

Yet as she and Sam stepped into the drugstore, she experienced a visceral shock, her senses heightened by the noise and crowd. The place was packed, every vinyl stool at the counter filled by men in business suits and women in bold-patterned dresses, legs crossed at their knees, kitten heels dangling from dainty feet. Some people stood, holding tall milkshake glasses or eating their ice cream as they crowded together. Conversation buzzed over the happy beat of a pop song on the jukebox. The smell of toasted bread and chicken mixed with the sweetness of chocolate cake.

Cordi felt everyone's eyes on her, probably wondering what she was doing in such a popular and fancy establishment. She resisted the urge to smooth down her hair, which must have looked a crumpled, sweaty mess after digging through her old closet, especially compared to the women on their lunch dates with their blow-dries and updos. She wanted to tap Sam on the shoulder and suggest they go somewhere else. Before she could, he waved at someone he recognized, took her hand, and pulled her toward the corner of the restaurant.

"Sam, what are you doing here?" a man said, clapping Sam on the shoulder as he stood. He threw his napkin over his half-eaten sandwich. "Here, I'm done, take my seat."

"No, really, we couldn't . . ." Sam protested halfheartedly, but he'd already pulled Cordi over to the stool and gently urged her to sit down.

"Consider this my treat," the man said as he pulled out his wallet and finally acknowledged her with a brief smile, gaze flickering back to Sam as if worried that doing so offended him somehow. "My date should be done soon as well." He nodded at the empty stool next to Cordi's. A full milkshake sat in front of it, the glass sweating with condensation, the whipped cream on top melting into a listless blob.

"Oh, no, please," Cordi said, though why she had no idea, considering she never allowed herself something as frivolous as ice cream, but Sam cut her off.

"Thanks, man," he said. He clapped his friend on his back, then leaned over Cordi to order. "They have the best fudge brownies and ice cream," he said to her. "I'm not sure if you're hungry, but the sandwiches are delicious."

"Th-thank you," she said, not knowing what else to say, nor did it matter because she practically had to shout to be heard. The music and the conversation grew louder, while a radio at the end of the counter announced the plays of a baseball game. A crowd gathered around it, cheering and clapping every now and then and shushing anyone within their vicinity.

"It's the World Series," Sam's friend said to him. "The Dodgers are in the lead, can you believe it?"

"You bet. I've got some money on the game myself," Sam said.

Cordi tried to follow along, smiling politely, but the truth was she couldn't muster interest in any sort of sport no matter how hard she tried. She was too distracted by her surroundings, watching the employees running around in their striped uniforms, pulling complicated knobs behind the counter to fill ice-cream cones or milkshake glasses, placing them on the counter in front of beaming faces. Everyone looked so beautiful, dressed to impress, so intent on themselves that she was free to observe with abandon.

That was until she caught the gaze of someone looking back at her. She blinked rapidly and almost looked away, but then she recognized the person, and he recognized her too. It was Mr. Sinclair, sitting by the door, his jacket unbuttoned, tie slightly loosened. The smallest trace of a smile curved his lips and he nodded at her, but when his gaze flickered to Sam, he frowned. Or perhaps that was just his default expression.

His blonde companion turned around with curiosity, then grinned and waved when she saw Cordi. It was Cressida—of course, who else.

"There she is," Sam's friend said as his date returned from the restroom. She was a pretty red-haired girl, and Cordi couldn't help staring. She looked so familiar but she couldn't place her, and the girl glared back.

"You're in our seat," she snapped. Her face was pale, almost a little green.

Sam's friend laughed. "We're done. We were just leaving."

Sam, being a gentleman, had remained standing behind Cordi, and gestured to the empty seat where the girl's milkshake remained untouched. "Please."

The girl covered her mouth, like she might be sick.

"Sweetheart," Sam's friend said, hands on her shoulders. "Let's get out of here, huh?"

She shook her head, thought better of it, then nodded. As they started toward the door, the announcer on the radio spoke rapidly and then shouted in excitement. Something momentous must have happened in the game. The crowd erupted into cheers, people jumping out of their seats, screaming happily. Men danced around, punching the air, ladies giggling and shrieking to cheer them on.

"Looks like the Dodgers won the World Series," Sam shouted over the noise at Cordi's confusion.

She nodded, but before she could think of anything else to say, a scream tore through the noise. A collective hush fell over the restaurant, all except for the radio commentator and the jukebox playing a familiar doo-wop number at odds with the sudden somberness in the air.

The crowd surrounding the radio had shifted slightly, gathering around something—someone—on the floor. Too many people blocked the view, but Cordi got out of her seat, fighting against the usual instinct to stay out of the way, drawn to whatever it was they stared at.

Mr. Sinclair was already there. He crouched over a fallen figure on the floor and held out an arm to keep everyone back. "Give her space," he said.

Cordi managed to push her way through the crowd. It was the red-haired girl, Sam's friend's date. She must have collapsed on her way out, her face taking on an even greener tinge than earlier. The veins underneath her pale skin were oddly dark, like someone had taken a marker to her face in a cruel joke. Cordi couldn't shake the sense that she knew the girl.

"Call an ambulance," Mr. Sinclair shouted to the staff behind the counter. "Miss Yin," he said when he saw her. "Please—where's Sam?"

Everyone in the crowd looked at her. Cordi glanced back in a panic, but Sam hadn't followed her into the fray.

"I think I know her," Cordi said.

Mr. Sinclair's face remained tense with concern. She knelt beside him and took the girl's hand. It was cold, though a small pulse beat at her wrist. Like on her face, veins showed prominently dark underneath the pale skin of her fingers and up her arms, reminding Cordi of something, but in the panic of the moment, she was incapable of thinking coherently.

"Her date was just here," Cordi said, but she didn't see the man in the crowd anywhere.

"Richard?" Mr. Sinclair asked. "He left before she collapsed. Let's not move her until the authorities get here."

Cordi placed the girl's hand down gently, embarrassed that she had acted rashly, but Mr. Sinclair nodded at her with reassurance.

"Why don't you go sit with Sam?" he suggested. "Don't let this spoil your date."

"Oh, but it's not . . ." Well, it was sort of a date, wasn't it? Except for some reason, she wasn't sure she wanted Mr. Sinclair to think there was anything more serious going on, and then she felt utterly foolish for caring at all, especially when a girl had fainted. It seemed a bit silly to pretend they could just go back to whatever they had been doing.

Except that was exactly what happened. People dispersed, returning to their seats and whispering to each other. Someone turned off the radio, but the jukebox continued playing in a joyful mockery, the sound of an ambulance drowning it out a few seconds later. Mr. Sinclair remained with the red-haired girl as the authorities came in.

When Cordi found Sam at their seats, Cressida had joined her brother.

"Well, isn't that an absolute gas," she said, pulling Cordi into a hug as if they had been involved in the trauma, though Cordi supposed it wasn't every day that they witnessed a girl collapsing at an ice-cream counter.

"Poor thing," Cordi said. "I could have sworn I've seen her before, but I can't remember where."

"That was Rachel Cunningham," Cressida said.

"Cressida knows everyone," Sam said.

"Her father works in city planning," Cressida explained, as if that were significant. "Perhaps your friend Silly knows her? Doesn't Silly work for the mayor?"

"Yes, but . . ." Then it hit Cordi. "I met her at our apartment. She was with Callum Domina." On the stairs, the girl had given Cordi the same annoyed look she'd worn today, right before Callum whisked her off downstairs.

"Oh, Callum," Cressida said with a bemused smile. She really did know everyone. "That's right. I saw them together at the club. I suppose it's over now. Not that Richard was much better for her. Did you see the way he just hightailed it out of here, like he couldn't be bothered? Now poor Gabe is stuck dealing with the mess."

Mr. Sinclair approached then. "I'm going to go with them," he said to Cressida. "In case there are any questions."

"Oh, Gabe, honestly, you can't be serious," Cressida whined. "You barely know her."

"I saw what happened—"

"So did everyone in here, and no one else is volunteering."

"Exactly." He buttoned his jacket.

"Stay, please," Cressida said. "You barely leave the office. You deserve an afternoon. And look who's here—Cordelia! You can talk all about your designs."

Mr. Sinclair smiled politely at Cordi. "We have a meeting on Monday. But please enjoy the rest of your afternoon." He glanced briefly at Sam, who was distracted by the sandwiches that had just arrived.

Cressida pouted and stole a french fry off Sam's plate.

Mr. Sinclair nodded at Cordi. "I'll see you soon, Miss Yin."

"Right, yes," she said awkwardly, and almost held out a hand to shake his but managed to stop herself by sitting on top of it. He respectfully ignored this.

Cressida gave a hard sigh as she watched him go.

Chapter Nineteen

When Tessa came home from work later that night, she wasn't wearing her customary Lacy's uniform of gray frock and pinned-back hair. Instead, she'd donned a rather becoming yellow floral hair scarf, twisted on the top of her head, the pattern coordinating with her fitted shift dress and strappy heels.

"I quit my job," she declared, starting to untie her headscarf, but apparently thinking better of it.

"You quit Lacy's?" Cordi asked. She had tried to keep working on the next dress for Cressida, but the pain in her fingers made her want to scream, so she'd given up and was perusing an article on zoo animal–inspired designs in the latest *LIFE* magazine.

"Yes." Tessa threw herself on the sofa next to Cordi. "Like Cressida said, why work at Petite when you can be the face of Petite?"

"Does that mean it's official? You'll model for them?"

"John has me booked for some photo shoots this week." Tessa sighed. "It's just about time too. I was getting jealous of all the luck you've had and what you've accomplished. All thanks to the spell you did."

"That we all did," Cordi corrected her.

"Ooh, I love that one," Tessa said, peering at the magazine in Cordi's lap, which was opened to a spread featuring Jackie Kennedy in a velvet cape-style coat.

"It looks like the one you bought at the alley." Cordi traced the outline of the silhouette.

"What happened to your fingers?" Tessa asked with a horrified gasp.

"Oh, it's . . ." She was about to brush it off, say it was nothing. She had wrapped all ten tips in gauze and it did look quite dramatic. "My fingernails have started to blacken. One fell off today."

Tessa's eyes widened. "Cordi, my God."

"I don't know if it's because I've been working so hard—those dresses, you know. But I don't think so." She paused, studying the floral design of Tessa's scarf. "Has anything strange happened to you?"

"Now that you mention it, my hair has been falling out more than usual. That's why I'm wearing this." Tessa gestured at her head. "I couldn't go to my first photo shoot with *limp hair*."

Cordi hesitated to ask, but she didn't know what else could have caused their troubles. "Do you think it has something to do with the magic? The lura?"

Tessa's lips pursed in concentration, the movement tightening the skin over her cheeks and revealing how thin she'd become. She looked gaunt, a bit skeletal. "I don't know."

"Have you felt this . . ." Cordi didn't know how to describe the shadowy presence that plagued her when the others weren't around without sounding insane. "Like you're not alone?"

Tessa's brows puckered. "Like what? A ghost?"

"Sort of?"

Tessa shook her head. A sick feeling rolled in Cordi's stomach, and she regretted bringing it up at all.

There was a knock at the door. Cordi set the magazine aside and went to answer it.

"Oh, hi, Mikhail," she said to their landlord.

The grumpy-faced man entered the apartment, hands on his hips as he studied the place, as if suspicious that they'd destroyed it since last month when he'd come to collect the rent.

Cordi offered him the envelope all the Mais had contributed their rent money to earlier in the week. "Here you go," she said.

Mikhail thumbed through the contents, then tucked it into his pocket.

"H-have you seen Callum around?" Cordi asked as he turned to leave without a word.

"What you want with him?" he demanded, voice gruff. "You should have nothing to do with him. He is not good man."

"It's nothing like that," Cordi said, shaking her head.

"I know men like him. He's all nice and charming, but you watch out. You are better off with someone who is good and loyal, who will provide."

"Someone like you?" Tessa purred from where she languished on the sofa.

Mikhail opened his mouth, then shut it. His tanned skin darkened.

"I just need to ask him something," Cordi explained. She twisted her fingers and winced when an ache pierced her index finger, and the nail gave a little beneath the gauze. "I saw a friend of his today. This red-haired girl named Rachel Cunningham—I think they were seeing each other. She fainted in the middle of Schwab's, and I thought he'd want to know."

"Seeing her? He's probably forgotten about her by now."

"Well, can you tell him anyway?"

"No."

Cordi sputtered, "I-I thought you were friends?"

"I rent him room sometimes. He never pays, but what do you expect. Acts like the building is his, all because he let me borrow money one time. And he said it was a gift!" Mikhail shouted. Cordi stepped back, but he didn't notice. "But never once does he forget."

Cordi glanced at Tessa, who raised her brows.

"If he rents a room here, then he must be around, right?" Tessa asked.

Mikhail waved a hand. "He uses it for dalliances. And we're not friends." He sucked in his cheeks like he was about to spit but must have remembered that he was indoors and it was his place.

"Well, do you have his number?" Cordi asked. "Or can you let him know we want to talk to him?"

Mikhail's face screwed up even more than normal. "I try. Sometimes he is around all the time, like little flea that is never satisfied. Sometimes he disappears for months." He yanked the door open, then spoke over his shoulder. "Better if you have nothing to do with him at all. I warn you."

After he left, Tessa raised her brows. "I really thought they were friends."

"Maybe they had a fight or something," Cordi said.

The door opened again, and she covered her mouth, thinking Mikhail had heard them, but it was only Silly. The girl looked exhausted, her frumpy dress suit wrinkled and sagging as if it too had had a long day. Her hair was a curly, frizzy mess, and the skin on her face drooped.

"I'm starving," she announced.

"Have you always worn glasses?" Tessa asked.

"Only for reading. But I've been getting a lot of headaches lately, and someone at work suggested it was my eyesight, so I'm giving them a try." She pushed the round frames up the bridge of her nose. "What's there to eat?"

"Nothing. We just gave Mikhail the rent, so we don't have much for groceries."

"I can buy us something," Cordi said, though it hurt her a bit to say it, so used to scrimping and scrounging, especially in the last few weeks. "I still have the money from Cressida for those dresses."

"But that's your money, darling," Tessa said. "You should save it or spend it on something wiser. We can scrounge up something. I'm sure we have oatmeal, at least."

Silly groaned. "If I have to eat oatmeal one more time, I'm going to gag."

"Let's . . . go out," Cordi insisted. "It'll be my treat." She felt bold all of a sudden. Usually she convinced herself she didn't need frivolous things like . . . friends . . . or having fun. But those days were behind her. She was a different person now. She was a designer! Well, almost. She had designed a dress that had been featured in a gossip column! And Cressida Thompson—famous, beautiful socialite Cressida—was going to wear her pieces, and possibly make her a design star. On Monday, she was going to meet with an actual buyer at an actual store, not just some warehouse in a slightly illegal marketplace. Things were looking up. As long as they didn't go horribly wrong.

She frowned at her hands.

"Where do you want to go?" Silly asked hopefully.

"How about the new restaurant on the corner?" Tessa suggested. "It's supposed to be an authentic Asian place."

"Let's go, then," Cordi said.

They ran into Audrey on their way downstairs. She must have been coming from the gallery because she wore her usual all-black outfit of loose blouse and pleated slacks.

"We're going to get some dinner. Want to come with us?" Cordi asked. "It's my treat."

Audrey's eyes flickered to Tessa's and Silly's faces. Cordi still got the sense that she didn't like either of them very much, so it came as a bit of a surprise when Audrey shrugged and turned around to walk down the stairs with them.

It was almost impossible to talk on the way to the restaurant— anything they tried to say drowned out by the whoosh of traffic and the loud thrum of machinery from the constant construction. Though Cordi didn't mind, using the opportunity to study the other pedestrians' clothes, Tessa huffed in annoyance, then smiled sweetly when people moved aside and stared in awe to let the girls pass. There was so much roadwork, they had to cross the pockmarked streets several times to avoid closed-off sections of the sidewalk.

The restaurant was tucked between two bars with music and loud conversation bursting through the doors. Once inside, the city noise muffled, and Cordi felt relieved to be in the new and clean place, so cozy it had enough space for only three tables. No one else was there despite the GRAND OPENING sign posted on the window. The old woman who greeted them ushered them to the front table and then brought out a metal pot of tea and four handleless blue porcelain cups.

"Dinner special?" she suggested, not bothering to hand them a menu. "Very good."

"Sure," Tessa answered for all of them.

After she left, an awkward silence settled over the table. Most of the time, they could count on Tessa to talk breezily about any subject, but today she fingered the edges of her headscarf almost self-consciously and wouldn't meet any of their eyes.

"So how are all your wishes or whatever going?" Audrey asked, picking up her cup of tea, which looked small and dainty and out of place in her rough hands.

Tessa sighed loudly, making clear that no matter what Audrey did, it would get on her nerves. But Audrey either didn't notice or didn't care.

"Have you all gotten what you wanted?" She slurped at the tea, almost deliberately too loud.

"Yes, I'm the new face of Petite Beauty, if you must know," Tessa said. "And Silly's been talking about her internship all month. Maybe you haven't been paying attention."

"I have been, I'm just asking how it's going," Audrey said.

"It's great," Silly said. "I love my work."

"Really?" Audrey peered at Silly, who sat across from her. Cordi could see why Audrey might be skeptical. Silly looked miserable, her wiry hair springing from her head in tangles, her eyes drooping, the bags underneath dark and deep.

"Oh yes. It's all very challenging. Which was exactly what I was hoping for." Silly took a sip of tea. "Though I am finding it hard to keep up. It seems to come so easily to the other interns, almost too easily. They don't really care about the internship, though. Their parents got them the position—either they knew the mayor or his son or their family paid the city a stipend to hire them."

No one said anything for a second. Usually Tessa would have fawned over Silly. Something about the youngest Mai brought out Tessa's protectiveness. She treated her like an overaffectionate auntie would, but today, Tessa barely acknowledged her.

"Being new is difficult," Cordi said finally, even though she felt impatient with Silly; she wished the girl wouldn't act so helpless. She really wasn't much younger than the rest of them. "I'm sure you just need some time to adjust."

Silly looked unconvinced, but then the woman brought out plates of dumplings, fried bread, and cubes of tofu swimming in soy sauce. She placed little bowls of rice in front of them before she disappeared back into the kitchen.

"How's the modeling going?" Cordi asked as they dug into their food.

Tessa sighed and placed her chopsticks on the ceramic rest next to her bowl. "It's fine. Honestly, it's not as glamorous as I thought it would be. Lots of sitting and standing and posing." Then she grinned good-naturedly. "I know, I know. That's what modeling is. But I thought there would be more . . . I don't know . . ."

"You want people to gush over you," Audrey said.

"Exactly!" Tessa slumped. "That's quite conceited, isn't it? I'm totally self-absorbed."

"We knew that about you," Audrey said. "You want to be famous."

"It takes time," Cordi told her. "But remember, you were in the newspaper the other day."

"Yeah, as a nobody. The journalist didn't even get my name. It was more about your dress than anything. And don't even get me started on my hair. I don't know why, but it's just been falling out so much."

"I had a classmate whose hair fell out," Audrey said. "Learned that it was because of stress. Had to get, like, five shots in her scalp."

Tessa gasped and clutched her head. "I'm scared of needles."

"Everyone's scared of needles," Audrey said flatly. "No one is ever not afraid of needles."

Tessa reached across the table and touched Cordi's hand. "What if we perform that spell again? The one Callum gave us. Maybe it will give us a little boost."

Cordi pulled back, the pain in her hands flaring.

"We should," Silly said, nodding vigorously. "It would totally help me at my job. I could catch up on all the work."

"I don't know . . ." Cordi flexed her fingers, still wrapped in bandages. "Don't you think all this is happening because of the spell? Like your hair, Tess, and your eyesight, Silly? And my fingernails? What if it's some weird side effect? We should talk to Callum before we do anything more."

"Nonsense." Tessa leaned back. "He gave us the spell. He would have warned us about any lasting damages."

"Would he, though?" Audrey asked. "I mean, we don't know anything about him."

And even Mikhail, who they'd thought was his friend, had said not to trust him.

"Oh, who cares!" Tessa exclaimed. "Hair grows back. Fingernails grow back. Eyesight . . . well, there's glasses." She smiled at Silly. "These are small prices to pay for all our dreams coming true. Look what we've all accomplished! And think about what else is waiting for us if we do just one more."

Cordi glanced at Audrey, the only one who seemed sensible about any of this.

"You know how I feel about lura," Audrey said. "Maybe if this is what's causing your troubles, you shouldn't do any more of it. It's just going to make things worse."

"No, it won't," Tessa snapped. "What do you know anyway? Silly's the one who did actual research on it. All you do is judge and complain."

"Tessa," Cordi said, shocked by her animosity.

Audrey wasn't. "They're your fingers," she said to Cordi.

"I'm just saying," Tessa said, sounding only slightly apologetic. "The last time we did a spell, it made things better."

Silly nodded eagerly. "Please, Cordi. It would really help right now." And she looked so miserable with her bloodshot eyes framed by her round glasses that Tessa wrapped an arm around her shoulder and gave Cordi a meaningful look. Cordi didn't know how to say no. She never knew how to say no.

"Okay," she said. "But we'll need to come up with another sacrifice."

Chapter Twenty

It was just a small spell: "Lura, take this gift and grant me my wish." There was nothing wrong with asking for a little bit more. Nothing nefarious about any of it. Cordi put in design sketches she didn't need anymore, Silly offered some old book, and Tessa dropped in a plain silver bracelet. It wasn't like they were hurting anyone. They weren't monsters.

Yet as they sat in a circle—Audrey watching from the sidelines like last time—chanting the words and holding hands, she felt that presence once again, like a small animal prowling the center of their group. This time it seemed larger, more solid and real.

The lights flickered on their third chant but didn't go out, and nothing momentous or disastrous happened by the time they finished. They opened their eyes as they let go of each other's hands, observing one another with cautious optimism.

Silly looked like she'd transformed the most, but only because she had looked the worse for wear. Her skin had a bright glow, her hair smooth and flowing in waves to frame her face. Her eyes no longer looked tired and swollen when she took off her glasses and blinked.

"I can see so much better again," she said with a delighted laugh. "Oh, thank you, Cordi!"

Tessa got up from the floor, unwinding the scarf from her hair as she ran to the bathroom. "My hair," she said with relief, running her fingers through her shiny black locks. She turned to Cordi. "What about you? Are your fingers all healed?"

Cordi had almost forgotten. She unwrapped the gauze carefully. Her nails looked normal, a healthy pink with white crescent tips. Even her thumbnail was back, perfect and intact, as if it had never fallen off in the first place.

"Well, that's . . ." Audrey said, looking for the first time like she wasn't horrified by what they'd done.

"Maybe you were wrong, Aud," Tessa said. "We should do the spell for you next time. Maybe you'll get an exhibit at your gallery instead of just working the front desk. Or . . . the other things you do there."

For a second, Audrey looked hopeful, as if behind her blank exterior ideas blossomed, aspirations growing lushly. But then she shook her head.

"No, I don't want to get involved with witchcraft."

"This isn't witchcraft, it's lura. It's totally different."

"No, it's not. You're just saying that so you can convince yourself it's not bad. Look, my aunt is delusional, but even she didn't mess with this stuff. She knew a bunch of people who dabbled in lura and all sorts of terrible things happened to them. And she refused to go into detail, but whatever happened to them, it made her turn away for good. And this is a lady who almost sold me to a man on the street because she thought he had a bag of dope. The only reason she didn't go through with it was because she had the sense to taste it first and turned out it was just sugar."

No one seemed to know how to respond to that horrifying story. Cordi almost reached out to hug Audrey, but she knew the other girl probably wouldn't appreciate the gesture.

"We're fine, Aud," Tessa said. "It's just a few little wishes—to give us a leg up. You don't think everyone else out there hasn't had some sort of help? People born into rich families or people who are well connected? This is just us helping ourselves."

"I don't care, it's your souls," Audrey said. "But just be careful."

"Stop saying stuff about souls," Tessa practically growled, clutching her headscarf tightly. "We all have to make sacrifices to get what we want, but we haven't sold those off yet."

Even though Tessa had quit her job at Lacy's, she took the Red Car with Cordi on Monday morning into the fancy finance district of downtown, where the department store dominated the center of the high-rise office buildings. Men in suits clutching briefcases and women dressed in pencil skirts and fitted jackets hurried down the sidewalks, and Cordi made mental notes of all the outfits.

Tessa would drop Cordi off at Lacy's before heading to John Lenore's office just a block away. Tessa wore a casual cotton dress and no makeup, making her look young and rather fresh-faced, and she attracted the stares of everyone in the car they'd boarded. They took two seats near the middle, bouncing and sliding along the vinyl cushions on the metal bench as the Red Car rattled down the rails.

"They'll do my makeup at the studio," Tessa explained, though Cordi hadn't asked. "So it would have been a waste to do it myself. The girls there are so critical—they said I was a bit heavy on the concealer and that I didn't know how to contour. So rude. Are you nervous about your meeting with Sinclair?"

"Yes," Cordi said. She hugged her weekend bag, filled with her best designs. What if Sinclair thought they were terrible? She'd already switched out a few pieces, doubting herself each time. What if she was a total failure, and her dream, the thing that she wanted more than anything, the thing she'd dabbled in lura for, was for nothing? What would she do?

Cordi spent the ride swallowing bile and trying not to throw up.

Lacy's was just as glittery and big and imposing as she remembered, but Tessa waltzed in like she couldn't care less, leading Cordi to an obscure door in the lobby that opened into a gray and narrow hallway, so different from the rest of the store that Cordi's pulse calmed, and she felt a little less nervous.

"This is the way to the staff lounge," Tessa said. "I used to take my lunch breaks in there." They passed a bright room furnished with a worn-out couch and a humming refrigerator and turned a corner to an elevator. "Sinclair is on the sixth floor." Tessa rolled her eyes, as if she found just the thought of him exasperating.

"Tessa?" a stern voice demanded. Cordi turned to see a lady in a gray dress suit, the skirt ending several inches below her knees, a length Cordi had never liked because it made everyone who wore it look a foot shorter and frumpier than they really were. This lady looked so scary and intimidating, though, that it didn't matter how tall she was. Cordi and Tessa cowered under her fierce gaze.

"Rosalie," Tessa said, the slightest warble in her voice. "Hi!"

"What are you doing here?" The woman approached, hands on her hips. Her hair was styled into a severe, wavy bob. It looked as if she held each strand meticulously in place by sheer willpower. Her red lipstick was reminiscent of a she-devil, her eyes blazing with fury. "You quit last week, if I must remind you. No notice, no warning." She glanced at Cordi. "And who are you?"

"I have a meeting with Mr. Sinclair," Cordi said. When Rosalie continued to glower, she started shaking. "My name is Cordelia Yin."

Rosalie's face untightened. "That's right, he did mention a new designer. Well, go on." The elevator had dinged open, but neither Cordi nor Tessa moved. "Not you, Tessa. This area is for staff only, and as you so kindly informed us last week, that no longer includes you."

Tessa gave Cordi a final, miserable look before Rosalie dragged her away by the elbow.

Cordi stepped onto the elevator, afraid to dawdle in case Rosalie came back. The interior wasn't as fancy as the gleaming mirrored gold ones for customers, but she felt more comfortable in the not-so-glamorous version.

On the sixth floor, she stepped onto a polished floor and had no idea where to go. The hallway was empty, lined with doors with employees' names engraved on plaques on the wall next to them. Cordi read each one, trying not to make eye contact with anyone, until she came across Gabe Sinclair's name. The door was closed, so she lingered, unsure what to do.

Then, feeling stupid for being so hesitant, she knocked gently.

"Come in," his familiar voice called out.

She fumbled at the door with her hands full, her palms sweaty, and when it finally popped open, Mr. Sinclair rushed over from his desk. Even in her nervousness, she admired his three-piece suit and his immaculate attention to every detail, even matching his gray tie to his socks—goodness. His office was extremely tidy, files stacked neatly on his desk, and a couch with cushions so plump and smooth, it looked like it had never been sat upon.

"Here, let me help you," he said.

"Oh, it's fine—"

"I'll take that." He grabbed her sketchbook and tossed it onto his desk, then took her weekend bag from her, their fingers brushing, the touch of his shockingly rough yet warm.

Cordi hid her hands in the pockets of her skirt. "How are you?" she asked. Then, blushing, she added quickly in case he thought that was too personal or informal, "I mean, after the incident at Schwab's. With the—with the girl, the red-haired—Rachel?" She pressed her lips together to stop talking.

His expression shuttered. He pressed a hand over his face, smoothing it down over his chin as he took a breath. "I'm afraid she didn't make it," he said quickly.

For a moment, Cordi thought she'd misheard. "What do you mean?"

"She died, Miss Yin." He coughed into his fist.

"But . . ." Cordi blinked. "She just fainted. It wasn't . . . What did they say? How?"

"I'm not sure. They wouldn't tell me much since I wasn't family—I just knew her through Cressida. And, well . . . I'm sure they'll get it sorted with her next of kin."

"Then . . . Callum must know. They would have called him, I'm sure."

"Right. You and Callum must be close."

"Well, no, I wouldn't say that."

"Did you know the girl?"

"No, not at all. I met her once when she was going out with Callum. I didn't even recognize her at first."

"It's horrible." They were both quiet. Cordi wasn't sure why the girl's death affected her so much. She had never known anyone who'd died before, and the girl was so close to her in age that it seemed an ominous reminder of her own fate in life.

Mr. Sinclair turned his focus to the clothes. "These are your designs, then?"

"Yes." Cordi tried to put the girl out of her mind, distracted as Mr. Sinclair motioned for her to open her bag. She took it from him and arranged the first pieces carefully on the couch.

"This skirt has pockets," she said, fingers shaking as she held up the pleated floral-print design. She'd sewn the pockets into the pleats so that they were hidden away. You couldn't tell they were there, even when they were full.

Mr. Sinclair nodded, but his face remained blank and serious. Cordi fumbled with a blouse next, then a color-blocked dress.

"Hmm."

Cordi started trembling. He hated her work. He barely looked at her, studying the garments with a frown.

After several excruciating seconds, he turned and stared right at her, and she was transfixed for a moment—perhaps he'd finally say something friendly rather than cutting straight to business. It took half a second for her to realize with an embarrassed flush that he was just waiting to hear about the next design.

"This blouse has a built-in boning," Cordi explained when he didn't seem at all moved by the color-blocked dress.

"You can barely see it," he said.

"Well, yes, that's the point." Oh no, that must have sounded rude. He gave no response.

Flushing hot and cold, Cordi fumbled for the last and most cherished design, her school dance dress. She trembled as she steeled herself for his reaction, or rather, lack thereof. If he remained blank-faced and stoic, she might hide forever and never look him in the eye again.

But when she revealed the dress, Mr. Sinclair jerked forward, as if someone had pinched him. His frozen expression finally cracked, settling into one of admiration. His hands reached out to touch the sequined skirt, but stopped as if he didn't feel worthy.

"You . . . made this?" he asked. "By yourself? By hand?"

She nodded, so overcome by his reaction that she couldn't speak for some seconds. "It took months. I worked on the skirt separately, and then . . ." She trailed off because Mr. Sinclair was no longer listening, running his fingers along the sequins and intricate embroidery.

"There's no way we can reproduce this," he said.

Her heart sank. "Oh."

"No, we'd have to sell this as one of a kind."

"Sell it?" She hugged the dress to herself. "No, I don't want to sell it."

Mr. Sinclair touched his jaw. "I suppose we could replicate it in a simpler design. Do you have others?" He glanced at her sketchbook on his desk. "May I?"

Cordi fought the instinct to take the sketchbook back, but she nodded. Mr. Sinclair seemed to sense her reticence, because he touched the cover carefully. Almost reverently, he opened it. He took his time with each design, even the simpler ones, but once again his serious expression returned. She had no idea what he thought, and she was embarrassed at how unskilled her drawings looked.

"These are all . . ." he started to say, flipping quickly through the rest of the notebook.

Crude. Ugly. Amateur. She braced herself for the rejection. It had been enough to show her work to someone, she tried to tell herself. Further than she had ever thought she'd get.

Mr. Sinclair looked up, meeting her eyes. "Cressida was right. Your talents are being wasted." He closed the sketchbook carefully. "How would you like to work here?"

"I . . . I'm sorry?"

He smiled knowingly. "I'm asking if you'd like to be a designer for Lacy's, Miss Yin. You'd work directly with me. And your first project would be figuring out how to get this"—he gestured at her treasured school dance gown—"onto our mannequins."

Chapter
Twenty-One

Cordi went home in dazed disbelief at the turn her life had taken. A designer. Her. She couldn't believe it, could barely comprehend all the logistics of employment that Mr. Sinclair had explained to her on her way out. She was so lost in thought, she didn't even care when her streetcar broke down and she had to walk three extra blocks to the apartment. When she got home, she didn't know what to do with herself, standing in the living room with no one to talk to. Her mind buzzed with excitement and accompanying worries.

Yes, her dream was coming true, but could she handle the work? Was she as talented as Mr. Sinclair and Cressida claimed, or was it just the lura? How long would it last? What else would she need to sacrifice?

Luckily, she had a busy schedule, having asked Ms. Ran for the day off to invite Cressida over to try on the dresses she'd made. Grateful for something distracting to do, she tidied up the apartment as best she could, folding the blankets usually strewn about the couches into a neat stack and shoving the magazines into a box. She would think about everything else later. She would worry over every step and minor detail when she didn't have to work on the rest of the elegant ball gowns Cressida had already half paid her to sew.

When Cressida stepped into their apartment, Cordi saw it with fresh eyes, the shabby rug that probably needed a good beating, the pillows that had seemed so vibrant to Cordi but now appeared thread-bare, the open kitchen with the peeling paint on the cupboards, and their mismatched mugs and scattered tea boxes on the bookcase-pantry.

"Why, it's so charming," Cressida said, but she held her purse up to her chest with her elbows tucked in like she was afraid she might touch something contaminated.

"I'm sorry it's such a mess," Cordi felt compelled to say, when in fact it was the cleanest it had been since they'd all moved in. "The dresses are over here."

Cordi led Cressida to her worktable by the window. With her fingers completely healed since the lura spell last night, Cordi had worked vigorously late into the evening, making up the time she'd lost when she'd been in excruciating pain. She'd been so determined, imbued with a sense of purpose and urgency she couldn't quite explain, she hadn't noticed how long she'd worked until the sky started to lighten. When she stepped back, she was shocked that two more dresses had material-ized as if out of the blue. She had only a vague recollection of cutting and assembling the pieces.

Now, the dresses hung from the wall brackets that usually held Tessa's plants. Cordi had moved them to the floor for the moment. It was a gloomy fall afternoon, and as the dresses waved gently against the backdrop of the window, they looked like ghosts, swaying back and forth. She stumbled and placed a hand on the back of the couch to steady herself.

Thankfully, Cressida didn't notice. She rushed to the dresses and gushed profusely over each one.

"Oh, how exquisite, they have pockets!" she exclaimed. "Gabe will love them. I talked with him before I came over—he's delighted with your work, you know."

Cordi smiled, but she tried not to read too much into it—of course Mr. Sinclair would like anything his fiancée wore on their honeymoon, or whatever it was a bride had a trousseau made for, though thinking about Mr. Sinclair and Cressida on their honeymoon didn't make her feel any better.

"Where can I try them on?" Cressida asked.

Cordi gestured to the bathroom, grateful for a moment of solitude as she took down the other dress and laid it across the chair by the sewing machine. When Cressida came out, Cordi moved as if in a trance, barely hearing anything the girl said. She pinched at the seams to see where they needed to be taken in, but the dress fit Cressida perfectly, and miraculously no alterations were needed.

The rest of Cressida's visit passed in a blur. Cordi got the vague impression that she smiled and nodded at the right moments, and made the appropriate responses, but her mind was hazy, her ears felt like they'd been stuffed with cotton, and when Cressida finally left, she sagged with relief against the back of the couch.

A terrible unease crawled over her skin, making the hairs on the back of her neck rise. She felt like someone was watching her. But no one was home.

It was a familiar presence that she sensed, the shadow thing that manifested when she'd performed the spells with Silly and Tessa. She couldn't see it, but she could feel it. She stepped back, clutching the sofa for balance, and something gave way on her finger. A nail—from her pinkie—ripped off, strings of skin or tissue or whatever still clinging to it, a few strands sticking to the puckered tip of her nubby finger.

Cordi opened her mouth, but she couldn't make a sound, as if her voice had been taken from her, all her will shriveled like the skin beneath her nails. Her knuckles resembled the leathery hide of an alligator—weathered and scabbed. She couldn't move, her breath stuck somewhere in her throat.

The worst part was that there was no pain. She couldn't feel a thing.

Luckily, Audrey stepped into the apartment at that moment, and though Cordi would have preferred Tessa or even Silly to Audrey's cold frankness, she was glad that someone was there.

"What?" Audrey asked at the sight of her. "Are you okay?"

Cordi shook her head.

Audrey approached the couch, concern pulling her brows tight. Then she looked down at Cordi's hand clutching the top edge of a sofa cushion.

"Oh fuck," she said.

"The spell worked," Cordi said. "I don't understand. My hands were fine this morning. Just a few minutes ago, even."

Audrey went to the bathroom and came back with a metal, square cookie box that they used as a first aid kit.

"My hands, Audrey. I can't feel them. How am I supposed to sew or design or do anything?"

Audrey carefully picked up Cordi's hand, the one with the bleeding, nubby pinkie finger, and started wrapping it in gauze. "Don't think about that right now."

"Don't think about it? It's all I ever think about—it's my life. How am I supposed to be a designer now? How am I supposed to fix this?" She burst into tears. There was still so much work to do on the rest of the dresses for Cressida, and her new job with Mr. Sinclair . . . Everything she'd wanted was coming true, but what if she couldn't even hold a needle and thread?

What if this was because of the lura? She needed to talk to Callum. She had to find him, but how?

Audrey's touch revived her, warmth started to spread along her skin, and with it came an unbearable sharp pain.

The other girl had stepped back as soon as Cordi started crying, looking very uncomfortable. "You know, you don't have to. Fix everything."

What a silly thing to say. Of course she did—it was in her nature to mend and patch and sew. She couldn't form an appropriate counterargument, so she wiped her face with the backs of her hands, then regretted it when the rough skin of her fingers scratched her inflamed cheeks. "I'm sorry—this isn't your problem. You warned us about the spell. You told us not to do it."

Audrey was quiet for a second. Her silence seemed uncaring. But then she reached out and patted Cordi's upper arm. "You're a good person, Cor. Almost too nice. You let Tessa walk all over you—"

"What? I do not," Cordi said indignantly, although despite her knee-jerk response, she knew it was true. "I just want to be a good friend. I like Tessa."

Audrey frowned. "Why?"

"What do you mean, why? She's nice and she's good to us. She shares everything she owns. We'd be eating with our fingers if it wasn't for her."

Audrey didn't argue, just stared blankly back at her.

"What?" Cordi said. "Why are you looking at me like that?"

"Your family was really shitty to you if that's all it takes to earn your trust."

Cordi let out a breath. She didn't want to talk about her family.

"A letter came for you," Audrey said, pulling a stack of mail from the back pocket of her black overalls.

Cordi took the envelope, recognizing Trina's careful cursive. She ripped it open, her eyes moving so fast in her eagerness to read the words, she had trouble absorbing the meaning. She forced herself to slow down as she sat at the kitchen table to study the letter more carefully while Audrey went to the fridge to get a snack.

Dear Cordi,

I am disappointed in you and don't know how else to tell you that you've disgraced our family, and you don't even have the decency to be sorry about it.

I hope you're having so much fun with your new friends, but just know that Mother and Father struggle every day at their shop, and the stress of having you as their daughter has been a huge strain. Their health declines each day, and I do not have enough time or energy to study *and* work *and* support them.

You should really consider fulfilling your filial duty and helping them with their bills and rent. After all, they raised you for free and you owe them.

You can send anything to me, but don't write your name on the return address or they'll just throw it out.

I hope you're doing well.

Trina

The letter started to shake, the words blurring, and Cordi looked up, wondering if they were experiencing an earthquake, then realized that it was her—she was the one who was shaking.

"Burn it," Audrey said, making Cordi jump. She hadn't realized she was still there, standing next to the counter with a glass of water.

"What? How did you—"

"Whatever that letter says, it's not good."

Cordi shrank into herself. When she didn't answer, Audrey snatched the letter from her hands and went to the stove. Only after the igniter clicked and the flame flared did Cordi lunge forward.

"No, don't—"

Audrey held a corner of the paper close to the flame. "Why? It's an evil letter that belongs in hell."

Cordi took it back anyway. Audrey was right, and there was no reason to keep the letter. But she couldn't bear to burn it. At least Trina had written. At least Cordi wasn't dead to her family. Her parents were angry, but maybe they'd take her back if she did right by them, if she showed them how sorry she was, sent them money, did what she could to help them.

"Seriously, if that letter is from your family, forget them," Audrey said as if she could read Cordi's thoughts. "Fuck 'em."

Cordi gasped. "Audrey!"

"They'll never accept you, not for who you are. You'll never be enough. If only you did this, if only you did that, if only you were more like whatever—it'll never stop." When Cordi remained silent, Audrey continued with a deep sigh, as if it were a task she didn't want to do but had no choice. "We've all been disowned at one time or another. Consider it a rite of passage for girls like us. My aunt used to beat the hell out of me. Cigarettes and booze and gambling, that's all she cared about."

"Audrey," Cordi whispered.

"I'm not telling you this so you'll feel sorry for me," Audrey said. "I'm telling you so you'll stop letting them control you. You're free now. You can choose to be free forever."

Cordi looked down at the letter. There was a truth to Audrey's words, but she couldn't bring herself to believe them, not completely. Mother and Father and Trina were her family, and she'd been raised to believe that meant everything. She was supposed to do everything for them, give up her life even, the way they had sacrificed so much in their lives for her. After all, that was what you did for someone you loved, even if you didn't show it through other ways. It was the least she could do when they'd brought her into the world, raised her, and worked so hard to support her. She would never be free, not when they were all still alive, not when she still had a debt to pay. Audrey had untethered herself from her own family, but Audrey was strong and brave and everything Cordi wasn't.

Cordi folded the letter, tucked it away, and tried to shove it out of her mind.

Chapter
Twenty-Two

When Silly and Tessa got home, Cordi practically pounced on them to show them her nails. Audrey had disappeared into her room.

Other than Cordi's pinkie, the rest were still intact, but they were blackened and bruised again.

"The spell worked, but it only lasted for a little bit," Cordi said. "What are we going to do?"

Tessa still looked as radiant as ever, her hair shiny, her face made up professionally from her photo shoot with Petite Beauty. But beneath the foundation and concealer, her bones looked more pronounced than usual. The effect lent her an ethereal, untouchable quality that made her even more appealing.

"Nothing has happened to you," Cordi said, turning to Silly instead. "What about you? Has your eyesight gotten worse?"

"Not really," Silly said.

"It's just me then?"

Tessa put an arm around Cordi's shoulders in a half hug. "I'm sorry, darling. Does it hurt?"

"Yes."

Tessa cooed affectionately. "It'll be okay. We'll figure something out."

"How?"

The phone rang. Silly went to her room while Cordi went to answer it, trying not to think about how stiff her fingers were as she wrapped them around the handle and brought it to her ear.

"Hello, Misses Mai residence," she said.

"Good, I was hoping you'd pick up." It was Sam. She hadn't heard from him after the day he had driven her to pick up her clothes and they had gone to Schwab's. Now she waited for her heart to skip or her belly to do an excited tumble, but all she felt was a bit of impatience. "What are your plans for the day?"

"Oh, just housework, I suppose." Then she wished she'd asked what he had in mind first.

"Well, I was wondering if you might like to join me at . . . the Café."

The way he said it, all dramatic, made it sound like he was asking her something much more important.

"It's a bit late to drink coffee, isn't it?" Cordi said. Even though her hands hurt, she couldn't stand still, especially when talking to someone on the phone, so she picked up a shirt she had wanted to fix because it was starting to fit all strange at the shoulders.

Sam's laugh made her feel like a child. "No, darling. The Café is a day club—a branch of the Society. It's quite exclusive. Bring a bathing suit. And your friends."

"I'm not sure if they've got something better to do."

"Oh, trust me, they won't want to turn this down."

Tessa raised her brows. *What?* she mouthed. She'd been watching Cordi on the phone with growing curiosity.

"Hold on, Sam, let me ask." Cordi placed the receiver against her chest. "Sam wants to know if we want to join him at the Café—"

"The Café?" Tessa screamed, cutting her off. "The Café!" Her eyes nearly popped out of her head. She bent at the waist as if her stomach pained her. "Yes! Tell him yes! Oh my Goddess, what to wear? Hat, cover-up, sandals. Silly! Get ready!" She banged on the other girl's door, then ran back to her room.

Cordi heard Sam laughing before she even put the phone back to her ear. "I guess the answer is yes," she said.

"I knew it. I'll have a car come pick you up in thirty minutes."

He hung up as Audrey and Silly came into the living room. Tessa dashed about her room in a whirlwind of clothes.

"What's going on?" Audrey asked.

"The Café!" Tessa shrieked, apparently unable to form any other coherent explanation.

Audrey raised her brows. "The Café?"

"Sam invited us to join him for the afternoon," Cordi explained.

"Oh my goodness," Silly said, covering her mouth. "I have nothing to wear." She went back to her room in a daze.

"What's the big deal?" Cordi asked.

"I . . . really don't care," Audrey said, and turned around.

"Are you kidding me?" Tessa shrieked, running back out to the living room. "The Café is even more exclusive than the Society. Only elite members get in. It's got a pool and a swim-up bar and . . . more bars. Massage rooms. Mud baths. Just think of the most pretentious rich-people amenities, and the Café will have it." She clenched her fists, her entire body tense like she might explode with excitement. "I'm getting a massage!" She ran back inside her room.

"There's also free food!" Silly shouted from her room.

"Why didn't you start with that?" Cordi said.

"What are you doing?" Tessa screamed from her room. "Go get ready!"

"I can't go," Cordi said. "Look at my fingers."

"Wear gloves," Tessa said. She'd emerged from her room in a sun hat.

"In the pool?"

"We won't actually swim. We'll be lounging outside."

"Then why is it such a big deal? We can lounge at home."

"Cordi." There was a dangerous edge to Tessa's voice. "Trust me. This is a chance you don't want to miss."

Tessa's eyes were sharp, focused, intense—and aimed at Cordi, who felt something wither inside her. "Okay," she said. "I guess I can wear gloves, but—"

"Great," Tessa replied. "Audrey?"

Audrey plopped onto the couch. "I'm not going."

Tessa stomped over, hands on hips, eyes blazing. Cordi cowered in her seat at the sewing machine, but Audrey simply looked up, unfazed.

"Good," Tessa said, her voice eerily calm. "I don't want you to go. You stay here, then, all by yourself, while we go eat fancy food and drink fancy drinks and have the time of our lives."

She walked away, and Audrey looked at Cordi, her eyes wide. Then she took a deep breath.

"Guess I'm coming along after all," she said.

The car ride didn't make the commute through downtown any more enjoyable, though at least they didn't have to breathe so much of the smog and they avoided the heat. Traffic grew more congested the farther they went down Grand Avenue, the driver navigating one-way streets made more complicated by the constant construction.

The Café was just on the other side of the Society nightclub at Sixth and Flower, and the car deposited them in front of a building that looked clean and businesslike but boring, nothing to make it stand out. It didn't even have a sign out front.

They entered a dimly lit lobby. A man sat at what looked like a concierge counter at a hotel.

"Welcome, ladies," he said as they approached, holding their bags over their shoulders, dressed in their pool clothes and floppy sun hats. "The Misses Mai?"

"Yes," Tessa said. "How did you know?"

"Mr. Thompson told me to expect you." He wrote something down in his appointment book and then smiled at them. "Come with me, please."

They followed him into a hallway. A waterfall built into the wall trickled nearby and echoed after them as the concierge escorted them into the elevator.

"Enjoy yourselves," he said with half a bow when a ding announced that they'd reached their floor.

The door opened onto a rooftop pool deck, and a blinding light pierced their retinas.

Cordi blinked as she took in the scene. A catchy doo-wop played, the smell of chlorine and suntan lotion and something fruity wafted in the air, and the sound of splashing water, laughter, and conversation surrounded them.

People lined up at a bar with a straw roof and tropical fruits decorating the counter, women dressed in two-pieces with halter straps, high-waisted bottoms cut in the trendy boyleg fashion, and men in vividly colorful, patterned swim trunks with matching unbuttoned shirts.

Comfortable-looking chaise longues surrounded the pool, decorated with bright and inviting throw pillows. Some people swam but most sat at the ledge, talking and sipping from glasses clinking with melting ice. Plants and palm trees bordered the deck, creating a private oasis and providing a bit of shade along with the tall umbrellas positioned next to the lounges.

"There you are," Sam said, interrupting their open-mouthed awe. "Finally. I've been dying for you to get here."

He was . . . shirtless. His skin was tanned, chest lightly sprinkled with hair and indented lines defining his abdomen. Was she supposed to look? It felt rude. But it also felt rude not to. *Where should she focus her eyes?* And then he grabbed her elbows and kissed both her cheeks, enveloping her for a moment in his expensive cologne, the bristle of his cheek scraping hers.

"Oh, hi," Cordi managed to blurt out, glad she'd worn her gloves, because they at least provided a barrier between her fingers and his skin as she braced her hands against his chest.

"Thank you for the invite," Tessa said breezily, scanning the crowd. She had the magical ability to look like she belonged anywhere, even an exclusive rooftop pool.

"Come this way, I've got a canopy waiting for us." Sam took Cordi's hand and led them across the pool deck.

On a raised platform, the edge of the rooftop was bordered by tall glass walls providing the perfect view of the city. Under each umbrella sat two large wicker sofas and several tables to set their drinks and things on.

A cabana boy in a white, collared shirt and salmon-pink swim shorts came by to take their order.

"A gin and tonic, please," Tessa said.

Cordi was at a loss, too overwhelmed. "Um, same."

"Me too," Audrey said.

"And me," Silly said.

Sam settled back on one of the beds, propped up by a number of pillows. "So what do you think?" he asked.

"It's lovely," Tessa said.

Cordi sat next to him because the other girls took up the second sofa and he seemed to expect her to stick close by. "Thanks so much, Sam."

"You deserve a day of relaxing," he said. "After all the work you've been doing for Cressida—and now I hear you're going to be Lacy's new designer. And I get to say I knew you first." He leaned his head so close, their cheeks touched.

"Oh, that . . . well." She still hadn't quite absorbed the fact that Mr. Sinclair had hired her. And being called a designer felt so surreal, part of her wondered whether Sam was really talking about someone else.

Sam grinned. He sat up and leaned toward Cordi. "Don't worry, you can thank me later."

What did that mean? Was she supposed to pay him back somehow? For what? Surely, Sam didn't think that he was the reason she'd gotten the job. Or perhaps he was. But that couldn't be true—Mr. Sinclair had noticed the gown she'd made for Cressida, and he had liked her other designs.

Before she could react, he'd turned to the others. "I've taken the liberty of booking you all massages. I hope that's okay."

Tessa beamed at him. "You're such a gentleman, Sam."

Silly touched her mouth. "I've never gotten a massage before."

"Well, obviously," Audrey said. "Why would you pay a stranger to touch you inappropriately?" She tugged on the colorful striped cover-up that Tessa had cajoled her into wearing instead of her usual black ensemble. It was the first time Cordi had seen her in anything that didn't remind her of death, and it had the strange effect of making her appear ashen, her skin pale in comparison to the bold print.

"You'll love it, trust me." Sam leaned back again and put on some sunglasses. Cordi was relieved she didn't have to meet his eyes.

Chapter
Twenty-Three

Cordi had no idea how long they spent at the Café, but after a long time languishing by the pool and the most relaxing massage ever and several drinks, she found herself lying on the daybed, waiting for the world to stop spinning. Sam was thankfully gone—he'd left for a work-related emergency—but the servers kept bringing whatever they asked for: appetizers and drinks and extra towels.

Tessa was busy exploring the rest of the club, which apparently had its own shopping center and restaurant, and Audrey was showing Silly how to swim, having found it a travesty that Silly had never learned.

Cordi flipped over onto her stomach, attempting to prop herself up on her elbows to read a magazine, when someone sat down on the daybed across from her. Expecting it to be Sam, she steeled herself, but when she looked up, she laughed in delight.

"Callum!"

"Why, look at you," he said. He wore a black, long-sleeved shirt that hugged the sharp lines of his body, paired with navy shorts. "I hardly recognized you, but then I saw your friends in the pool and knew it must be the Mais."

She sat up, thought about putting on her cover-up, but decided it would only draw attention to how self-conscious she felt. Callum's gaze moved over her body in an almost affectionate manner, like an artist admiring his finished project.

Cordi smiled. "I'm glad you're here. I wasn't sure Mikhail would give you my message."

"What message?"

"I asked him to tell you to get in touch with us—never mind, it doesn't matter. I'm so sorry about your girlfriend."

He tilted his head. "Girlfriend?"

"Rachel. That was her, wasn't it?" Oh no. What if Cordi had assumed wrongly?

But Callum's smile disappeared. "Oh, Rachel." He looked down. "I didn't know you knew her."

"I don't. I saw her faint at Schwab's. Right before."

His shoulders slumped. "It was so sudden."

Cordi wasn't sure what to do now or how to console him. She'd never lost anyone close to her.

But then Callum looked up. "That's so sweet of you to think of me. To be honest, we weren't dating for long."

"Well, I had actually wanted to see you for another reason."

"Oh?" He brightened again, looking so eager to come to her rescue.

"Something's wrong. You have to help." She looked around but no one paid them any attention, so she carefully took her gloves off and frantically explained what had happened to her hands, as well as Tessa's hair and Silly's headaches and how they'd performed the spell he'd given them again but it hadn't lasted very long, at least for her. "Look at my nails. What's wrong with me? Did I do something wrong? How can we fix it?"

Callum studied her fingers, but to her consternation, he only chuckled. Her panic grew.

"No, no," he said. "Like I said, all lura needs a sacrifice, and the stronger the spell, the more you have to give."

"I never sacrificed my *fingers*," Cordi said, her voice squeaky. She put her gloves back on quickly before anyone should pass by and spot them. "I would never . . . I need them to do what I'm wishing *for*. I love to sew. I can't give that up."

"Sweetheart, it's just a side effect. It sounds like your wishes are coming true stronger and faster than anyone else's. I heard you got a job as Lacy's new designer."

"I—how did you know?"

"Oh, news travels fast in our circles. And then you made those dresses for Cressida Thompson, who's been telling everyone that she discovered you. I swear, I've been hearing your name everywhere I go."

"Really?" Cordi was both delighted and horrified at the attention. "You know Cressida?"

"It's a small world. All the great families know each other. The ones that matter anyway—the Thompsons and the Tolouses and the Saladines." He nodded his chin at a girl at the bar, then looked around. "Even the Lacys. There's Desiree there —" He gestured to the elevator, but the doors closed before Cordi could get a good look at the matriarch who owned the department store. "They practically run this city."

"What about the Dominas? That's your last name, isn't it?"

Callum laughed. "Oh . . . well, that's a story for a different time. Listen, there's something you should know about the lura."

He sounded so serious that Cordi sat up straighter. "What is it?"

"The thing is . . ." He seemed uncharacteristically hesitant. "Lura doesn't last. It will fade. All of this." He gestured at her face, her body, then behind him to the pool and all around. "It will disappear. You will lose it all."

Her heart beat faster. "What do you mean?"

"It means you can't keep it forever. Your successes, your beauty."

"But you just said—"

"Yes, yes, nothing is wrong. Not really. But you need to keep . . . up with the spells. Do you understand?"

Cordi was starting to panic, her breathing erratic. "No. Why didn't you tell us this at the beginning? Why—"

"Sweetheart, sweetheart," he cut her off, his voice soothing, reaching out to gently take her hand. "Everything is fine. That's why I've been looking for you—I wanted to make sure you had everything you need. I'm here to help. You won't lose it all, trust me."

But Cordi was too distracted by the fact that everything she'd gained so far could simply be taken away. She couldn't let that happen, not when she'd worked so hard, not when she'd already been through so much.

"It's simple, really," Callum continued. "If you want it to last, you need to keep performing the magic. Offering gifts."

"But . . ." She tried to think ahead, to strategize as in a chess game—figuring out the consequences of her next move. Yet she found it impossible, and the more she tried to figure out her next step, the more she felt she was actually two steps behind.

"Not to worry, darling," he added, his charming, one-dimpled smile returning. "There is a way to make it more permanent. One last spell."

But Cordi hesitated.

"This one will make it all better," Callum said. When she still didn't say anything, he added, "The alternative is to lose everything you've already gained. But worse."

"Worse?"

"You won't just lose your new designer job, but you may not be able to sew again. Or design anything."

"What? No. That's—" That was the worst nightmare she could imagine. Things were finally happening—good things, for all of them. If she lost the ability to sew, where would she end up? What would she do? Where would she work? She didn't know how to do anything else. How would she pay rent? She'd have to beg her parents to take her back, and she doubted they would. She would be homeless, alone . . . useless.

"This spell will make it all better, I promise," Callum said. He was still holding her hand, his touch oddly soothing as his thumb gently massaged her wrist.

"What is it?" Cordi asked.

"You need to make sure, with this one, that you do exactly what I say."

"Wait, I want to write this down." Cordi grabbed a napkin off a side table and dug in her purse for a pen. She carefully wrote down his instructions, making him repeat himself several times.

"But listen. This spell is much stronger than the last. You must really want it and be willing to sacrifice more. Something bigger, something that means more to you. Do you understand?"

"Yes, I think so," Cordi said slowly, reading her notes, staring at the words *Lura, take this sacrifice and bring me to paradise.* "But why didn't you tell us about this before? You could have saved us a lot of worry."

"Because you would have been too scared to go through with it, and I knew that things would be all right. You can have everything you ever wanted, as long as you're willing to take the risk . . . do the work. And you are, aren't you? You have exactly what it takes. I can see that in you." He gave her hand one last gentle squeeze and let go. "You're very special, Cordi." She detected a strain in his voice, as if he wanted to say something else. But then it disappeared, and that dimple returned in his cheek. "I heard from Sam that you might be attending a charity gala next month."

"I don't know yet if I'm going," she said. She had bigger problems at the moment, and the thought of coming up with what to wear to something so out of her depth made her clench her fingers, and the skin on her knuckles cracked. A bead of blood soaked through her glove.

"You should go. Why not? When will you get the chance again? I'll be there myself."

"You will?"

"Of course. I was quite poor myself growing up, and I do what I can to help others in need."

"That's so sweet of you, Callum." The way he carried himself, not to mention the expensive clothes, the perfectly coiffed hair, and his general demeanor, gave her the impression he came from wealth.

"You have no idea." A sad dullness glazed over his eyes, as if he'd lost himself in his memories. "I'm an immigrant too, you know." She did know—he mentioned it often. This time she didn't hold back.

"Oh, I'm not an immigrant. I was born here."

"Hmm." He didn't look convinced. "Anyway, I know what it's like, to always be an outsider. I came from a rather small town in Europe—had to fight and crawl and claw my way here. And when I got here, I was alone and destitute, and no matter how hard I tried or worked, I never got anywhere. But I kept going. I never gave up. And that's all that matters. That's the difference between people like us and people who will never be successful." He leaned toward her.

Cordi couldn't help herself, moving close, eager to find out more about Callum.

"The difference is we want it, we want it so bad, and even if we have to work for it extrahard, all while watching everyone around us get everything they want so easily, we will do it."

She frowned. It was not an entirely new idea to her; in fact, it was something her parents had instilled in her as well, but lately, she was having a difficult time accepting it. She had worked hard for most of her life. So had her parents. But they'd never gotten very far, and neither had she, at least not until she and the Mais had started dabbling with lura.

"How did you get to where you are now, Callum? You came from such humble beginnings."

His eyes crinkled and that dimple appeared on his cheek. "I found the right opportunities. And made the right choices. Tough ones, but you can't get what you want by being weak. Do you understand what I'm saying?"

She nodded, although she was quite confused.

"I can see that you're like me, Cordelia. You're driven and talented, and you will be very successful. I'm glad I can give you a chance at your dreams. It's the least I can do."

"Thank you, Callum," Cordi said automatically.

"And the least you can do," he added, his grin chasing the somberness away, "is take all the opportunities you get! And go to the gala!"

"I'll . . . think about it."

"Don't worry, doll. This spell will fix everything, trust me. There are wonderful things waiting out there for you, Cordi." And then he leaned forward to place a breathtakingly cold hand on her knee. As usual, he wore thin cotton gloves, the stitching on them twisting and curving over his knuckles. "You just have to *want* it bad enough."

Chapter
Twenty-Four

Cordi was desperate to tell the Mais about her talk with Callum, but Tessa was so enthralled with the Café that she wouldn't stop chattering about it, and Cordi couldn't find a good break in the conversation. It was late and the Mais were exhausted by the time they got home, all collapsing on the couch, their bags falling to the ground at their feet. Cordi felt wrung out, the pain in her pinkie a gentle throb. She dreaded the climb up to her loft.

"That was such a ball," Silly said with a sigh. "I wish we had memberships there."

"Imagine going every weekend," Tessa said. "I'd love to have my birthday bash there. What do you think, Cordi? Could we make it happen?"

"There's something you should all know," Cordi said.

Tessa ran her fingers down the back of her head, her hair still wet from her dip in the pool. Her eyes widened in horror as she looked at her hand. Clumps of wet strands clung to it. Cordi sat up straight.

"Oh my God!" Tessa exclaimed. She looked like she might scream. She held up the dark, wet hair for them all to see.

"It could be the chlorine," Silly said. "From the pool. Everyone knows it's terrible for your hair and—"

In a panic, Tessa ran her fingers over her head, and more clumps broke off. Cordi covered her mouth. Tessa pulled out another clump, letting the wet strands slide off her fingers and fall to the floor with a slap. No one tried to stop her, all of them just as shocked. She reached up and grabbed another handful, her face contorted into fixed horror.

"Tessa," Cordi said.

But Tessa didn't hear, just continued pulling out more and more, until half her head was bald. Her eyes were bulbous in her thin face as she stared at the others. None of them knew what to say. Audrey stood up and stepped back, as if fearing she could contract whatever curse had afflicted Tessa.

"It's going to be fine," Cordi said finally, her voice calmer than she felt.

"H-how?" Tessa asked.

"Callum was at the Café—you all barely missed him, and he gave me another spell. We can fix it. He said that with the previous ones we've been doing, we'd have to keep doing more magic. But this spell is permanent."

Tessa stood up, fists at her sides. "Now." Towering over them with thin strands hanging loosely from her head, she looked like a ghost from one of Mother's frightening folktales.

Silly got up without hesitation and went to the kitchen to collect the metal bowl and candles.

"He told you this now?" Audrey asked. "Why didn't he tell us before?"

"Because he knew it would all work out, and he didn't want us to be scared about it," Cordi explained.

"You don't have to do it," Audrey said.

"Shut up, Audrey," Tessa said. "You're not losing your hair or eyesight or fingers."

"That's because I didn't ask for anything."

Tessa turned sharply, bending her head a bit so that her naked scalp was in full view, daring Audrey to keep speaking.

Cordi started curling her fists but stopped because it hurt. "We've already come this far." And then, when Audrey kept staring with her horrified, wide-eyed expression, Cordi looked down. "You don't have to stay."

Audrey inhaled sharply. She took a few steps back, and then slowly retreated to her room. Cordi regretted telling her to leave, but they all breathed easier with Audrey gone, free to perform the ritual without her judgment.

Silly had been busy preparing everything for the spell, lighting the candles so that a ring of little flames flickered on the rug. Kneeling on the floor, she smiled at Tessa reassuringly, resembling a worshipping acolyte in her desire to please.

"We need some sort of sacrifice," Cordi said. "Something that means a lot more to us than last time, Callum said."

"Oh, right."

They all went to their rooms to search. Cordi dug around her loft for something she could offer, but she didn't have much besides her clothes and a few books. She hadn't brought any sentimental objects other than the empty thread spool when she left home, and Trina hadn't packed anything other than Cordi's clothes.

Trina.

Anger and hurt flared whenever she thought of her sister. She took Trina's letter from underneath the mattress. It was a terrible, ghastly, painful letter, and yet she'd clung to it, practically cherished it in some morbid, self-destructive way. Why? Did she harbor some delusional hope that her parents would take her back if she did what Trina asked? If she helped support her parents, would she still have a place in her family? Would they love her again?

But had they ever loved her to begin with? Love was not blood and genes and a shared roof, as she always thought. No, love was coming home to a house of warmth, of being cared for and caring back, of kindness. Love was that swell in her chest every time she thought of the Mais.

She crumpled the letter and held it in her fist as she climbed down from her loft.

Tessa came back shortly with a cigarette case. "Another boyfriend gave me this," she said, her voice forcefully cheery. She'd wrapped her hair up in a towel and looked almost normal, except for the hollowness in her eyes. "But I'm renouncing my ways and shall no longer see him."

"How many boyfriends do you have?" Cordi asked, indulging her attempt to act like nothing was wrong.

Tessa thought for a while, taking quite a long time. "No idea."

Silly returned with a notebook. "I used to write down all my biggest fears," she explained. "And then I'd look them over once in a while. It helped me realize that nothing ever lasts, and everything I was afraid of usually worked itself out. But I'm done being scared. So." She tossed the notebook on top of Cordi's letter and Tessa's cigarette case.

The three of them sat down in a small circle and held hands. Tessa had taken Callum's written instructions from Cordi and placed them next to the bowl. The spell was quite simple.

"Lura, take this sacrifice and bring me to paradise," Tessa read out loud. She looked at the two of them.

The words stirred an unease inside Cordi, but then Tessa affectionately squeezed her hand, and a searing pain burst up her wrist and into her forearms. It was all she could do not to cry out, but she welcomed the pain because it reminded her of what was important. If she wanted to achieve her dreams, she needed to do the spell. She'd already worked so hard, and anyway, they'd come too far to go back now, even if they wanted to.

She nodded, and the three of them started reciting the words. Seven times, Callum had said.

At the first recitation, Cordi felt that thing enter the circle, emerging from the fire in a haze of smoke and solidifying into something real and sharp, an animalistic shape . . . almost like a coyote. With each recitation, it prowled the circle, lingering in front of her friends. When it reached Cordi, she met its eyes, or at least she looked where she thought eyes might be, and an intense sensation tightened around her lungs. The thing seemed to speak to her, but she couldn't understand what it said, and their chanting drowned out anything she might have heard.

Then it turned and slid into the bowl, curling among their sacrifices.

As they completed the seventh recitation, Cordi felt something give away deep inside, a terrible, wrenching sensation like someone had ripped out her lungs through her belly button. The flames flared and rose higher than the small candles were capable of. The lights went out, the apartment drowned in darkness, and a silence fell over them like a thick, suffocating blanket. The only sound was heavy breathing, although it sounded more like the gasping, desperate sound you made right before you started sobbing.

Cordi wondered who was crying, ready to reach out to comfort them, but then she realized it was her. It was all of them.

Then the lights flickered back on, and Tessa collapsed toward Cordi, pulling her into her arms. Cordi felt exhausted, drained of all energy. She wanted to lie down and sleep forever and ever. Silly joined them, wrapping her arms around Cordi and Tessa, and they continued to cry.

Audrey's door burst open. She stopped short when she saw the three of them in a heap on the floor, the metal bowl filled with black ashen lumps, the candles burned down to nothing. "What the fuck did you all do?" she asked.

———— ⦇⦈ ————

Just like after the last spell, Cordi's fingers were restored, her hands no longer in pain. On Tuesday, her nails remained intact and healthy well into her shift at Ms. Ran's fabric store, and she finally allowed herself to let out a breath of relief.

She'd been preparing mentally all day to tell Ms. Ran about her new job, and as the shop finally closed, her heart started beating in trepidation.

"I got a job at Lacy's," she explained quickly before losing her nerve. "So I can't work weekdays anymore. I can still come on the weekends, though." She added the last reluctantly because she truthfully didn't want to, nor did she need the extra money with her new salary. But she couldn't shake the habit of not disappointing her elders, nor did she want to leave Ms. Ran without help.

Ms. Ran punched numbers into a calculating machine at the front counter, which was slightly raised from the floor by a step so it looked like she was a judge presiding from on high. "I know."

"Oh. Okay."

"I knew it only a matter of time before you move on, something better. People with talent never last."

Though her words were complimentary, her tone was rather unkind, and she still hadn't looked Cordi in the eyes. Things had been slightly tense all day, as if they both felt something lingering in the air that neither wanted to address.

"I want to keep working for you," Cordi said apologetically. "I love it here."

"Love?" Ms. Ran paused in her calculations. "It only a job, silly girl. No love needed."

"But—"

"You will be very successful. I can tell. I have an eye for these things. That's why I didn't want to hire you at first. Because I knew it wouldn't be for long. But ayah, I have a soft spot. I don't know. Okay, fine. You go and make a life for yourself. A good name." She finally met Cordi's eyes and smiled. "You don't have to come back. Okay? I know this will be chump change compared to what you'll be making at the fancy store."

"But I—"

"It's okay, see." Ms. Ran dug around her things and then handed Cordi an envelope. "I knew it was coming. I prepare and everything. So don't worry. You're not the first and won't be the last." She smiled, the skin around her mouth and eyes stretching tight. "Now go. I don't want to talk about it anymore." She waved her hand and went back to punching numbers.

Cordi clutched the envelope and considered leaving it behind but knew that Ms. Ran would see it as a great insult, so she tucked it into her purse and left quietly, her heart aching all the more because she hadn't expected this goodbye to hurt so much.

Chapter Twenty-Five

The next morning, Cordi chose her outfit with care, a practical dress with her signature hidden pockets. She forced all thoughts from her mind as she made her way to her first day as Lacy's newest designer.

She followed the crowd of girls dressed in gray frocks as they headed into the department store with linked arms and in giggling conversations. She'd never felt so lonely. She wished that Tessa still worked there. They could have commuted together, shared lunch breaks, and shopped during their free time.

It didn't help that the other shopgirls stole quick glances at Cordi, then turned back to one another to whisper. If Tessa were there, she'd have glared back at the shopgirls, her beauty so intimidating that they wouldn't have dared to continue whispering about her.

Mr. Sinclair had told her to meet him at his office.

"There you are," he said when Cordi knocked at his partially open door. He got up as she stepped inside. "Come along, they should have your office ready by now."

"My office?"

Mr. Sinclair led her down the hall. "The view isn't very good, I'm afraid, but it's a good space to spread out your work."

Her office was a little smaller than his, and the window faced a brick building just a couple of feet away, but a large drafting table dominated the wall opposite the desk. A neat stack of thin tracing papers for patterns sat on top, a row of pens and markers lined the right edge of the desk, and an adjustable floor lamp cast a welcoming light over the whole room.

"I'll let you settle in," Mr. Sinclair said, glancing at his watch. "And let's meet in ten minutes to discuss your first project?"

Cordi couldn't believe that she had an office, a real office with a desk and a window and a door she could close. She could barely manage a nod. Mr. Sinclair smiled kindly, then left.

Cordi walked around the room. It only took about five steps to complete the tour, but they were five very bouncy steps. She put her purse on the desk, then tucked it away in a drawer before moving to sit at the drafting table. It was quite extravagant, with several knobs along the legs to adjust the height and angle. The wheels were locked, but she kicked the switch easily and rolled the table to the window where the lighting was perfect, even if the view was nonexistent. It could have been worse. It could have looked out onto a dirty alleyway or a dumpster.

She stood in the middle of the room, her chest swelling with a mixture of pride and guilt. Her parents had no idea that she was here, doing what she had always wanted. Not that it mattered. They'd probably think she was rising above her station, claiming a spot she had no right to.

She was going to prove them wrong. She was going to work so hard, be so successful that they'd regret not listening to her. Even Trina, who had never believed in her, who had always rooted for her to fail because her desire to be right was greater than her love for Cordi, if such a love existed at all.

After settling in, Cordi found a notebook and pen and walked back to Mr. Sinclair's office. He stood at the conference table in the corner of the room and had spread copies of the designs from her sketchbook in front of him.

"Thank you for letting me make use of that," he said by way of acknowledgment, gesturing to her notebook on the table. "I've copied the designs I'd like to start off with."

He hadn't chosen that many. Only six pages from an entire sketch-book of her ideas, and he hadn't picked her favorite ones.

"You have many great sketches in there," Mr. Sinclair said as if reading her thoughts, or maybe the disappointment showed on her face. "But we have to think in terms of commercial value. Can we mass-produce the design? Keep costs of production low so we can sell it at a reasonable price point? Your gown—the one you brought in, for example. How much would you say it cost to make?"

She thought about the time she'd poured into the work. The weekends scouring the flea market and garment district for the right materials. The days at the sewing machine.

"I'd say a hundred dollars," Mr. Sinclair said. "Considering the embroidery work and the sequins, not to mention the actual labor. But think objectively. If you hadn't made it yourself, if you saw the dress in the store, would you pay that much for it?"

"Well, not me," Cordi said. "I can barely afford rent."

Mr. Sinclair smiled, and she was distinctly aware of the subtle hint of his cologne mixing with another pleasantly masculine scent. Only now did she notice they stood rather close, her skin prickling with awareness. "But you are the exact demographic we hope to appeal to."

"But I thought only wealthy people shopped at Lacy's."

"We're hoping our next line will bring in the working class. Ladies like you who want to look good while at work or at home or for a night out on the town." He was genuine and direct, which she found both alarming and refreshing. "Which is why you're the best person for the job. You're designing for you. For girls like you. Start with simple but quality pieces. Basic but elevated designs. Can you do that?"

His intense gaze made her want to step back. She twisted her fingers together, and he glanced down at her hands. They'd been fine all weekend, and this morning when she woke up, she'd inspected them for any signs of deterioration. She felt no pain or numbness then. But now . . . a black tinge appeared just beneath the surface of the cuticles and spread over her nail beds like a drop of blood on a napkin.

Mr. Sinclair moved to sit at his desk. "Why don't you start working on some new designs to propose to me by the end of this week?"

"Sure!" Her heart thudded with nervousness. "How many? Are we thinking dresses? Skirts? Pants?"

He smiled. "Anything suited for fall."

She couldn't tell if he was being condescending or if he was just busy or if she was overanalyzing the situation, and anyway, he'd already turned away. She'd been dismissed.

Cordi walked backward out the door and rushed to her office. At the drafting table, she flipped her sketchbook to a blank page and poised her pencil over it. But nothing came to mind. Usually she had a reason to make something new. She'd needed the blouse with the boning for an awards ceremony at school, and each of her dresses had been designed for one event or another. All the sketches that Mr. Sinclair had chosen told a story, a moment in her life. She hadn't had many special days, so making a new outfit had been a way to amplify the joy of each occasion.

Now, sitting in the room with its bare walls and the blank pages in front of her, she had no idea where to start. She tried to imagine who she'd be designing the pieces for, but she couldn't picture exactly who these women were.

Her fingers tingled, a numbness now spreading to the rest of her hands. She stretched them, but nothing helped. They didn't *hurt*, but they definitely didn't look or feel normal, and now the nails looked blacker than they had seconds ago, the bruises ugly and prominent.

Cordi made half attempts at work, but even after a few hours, she'd sketched nothing more than a basic bodice shape. As soon as the chime announced the lunch break, she let out a deep breath.

A knock at the door made her jump, and she covered her sketchbook out of habit. Mr. Sinclair moved into her office. As he approached her desk, she realized how tall he was—which wasn't something Cordi normally noticed because most people were taller than her. But it felt different because he dominated the enclosed space and filled the corners of her awareness.

"I must apologize," he said. "I would have liked to take you out for lunch on your first day, but I have a previous engagement."

"Oh, that's okay," Cordi said, growing warm with inexplicable embarrassment. "Tessa wanted to meet me for lunch, actually."

"We'll have to go out a different day," he said, and added quickly, "I would have liked to celebrate you—your hire—" His cheeks grew red. "But it's been rather busy."

"That's all right," Cordi said, stepping back and bumping against her chair, which rolled across the floor dramatically.

Cordi was glad when Mr. Sinclair turned to go because the distracting thumping of her heart finally calmed, but she was dismayed that they couldn't move past their first awkward encounters. She realized she wanted him to like her, but only the same way she wanted everyone to like her, obviously, and because she would be working with him. That was all.

"By the way," he added, pausing midstep, and she faced him with renewed hope to somehow salvage the conversation. "Cressida mentioned that Sam invited you to the Pockets of Poverty gala for research."

"What? Oh." She hadn't heard from Sam since seeing him at the Café. She'd put the gala out of her mind. "I wasn't really planning on going."

"You should go. Though I wouldn't go for the purpose of research. Those ladies all live in fantasy worlds, bent on dressing up to impress one another. We—you and I—"

Her stomach did weird flippy-floppy things at his choice of words.

"—are designing for the real world," he continued. "But it would be fun, nonetheless. Perhaps a way to promote the line."

"Right."

He nodded and left.

Cordi dropped her head in her hands. She was exhausted even though she had no real reason to be. She hadn't done much all morning but sit at her desk and not design anything, worrying over the fact that she hadn't designed anything.

Going back to her sketching wouldn't do her any good, so she made her way to the elevator.

Tessa had arranged to meet her in front of Lacy's during her lunch break, but Cordi didn't see her anywhere. She waited ten minutes, inspecting her fingers. The pain was back, and she couldn't bear waiting any longer, too anxious to stand still. She started walking, panic increasing as she wove through the lunchtime crowd, circling the block, then returned to Lacy's. Where was Tessa? How could she just stand Cordi up like that? Was Cordi so unimportant that Tessa couldn't even bother to call and cancel lunch, or let her know she was running late? Tears of anger burned hot behind her eyes.

She had no appetite, but she bought a sandwich from the coffee cart in the lunchroom and ate it quickly by herself at the corner table.

Before Cordi went back to her work, she bought a bottle of dark nail polish from the beauty section using her employee discount, then stood at the windowsill in her new office to paint over the bruises.

Chapter
Twenty-Six

When Cordi got home, the apartment was empty. The light in the entrance cast long shadows over the furniture, making the plants at the window look like clawed monsters. She flicked on all the lights and lit some candles for good measure.

It felt like she had had a terribly long and busy day, though she'd actually worked much longer shifts at the fabric store. At that thought, a heaviness settled over her. She missed the busy atmosphere of the alley, running her fingers along yards of fabric, talking briefly with customers about the projects they planned to make with their purchases. As tiring as the job had been, she'd enjoyed the rush and productivity, the sense that she'd accomplished so much within a day, and being around people. Loneliness sank into her bones as she walked around the apartment, wishing she had someone to talk to.

A knock at the front door made her jump embarrassingly high. She chided herself as she answered it, but no one was there. A box sat on the floor instead. Her name was written on an envelope taped to the top, and it felt quite light when she carried it to the kitchen table.

The card inside read, "Cordelia, I hope you find these to your liking. Feel free to keep both and wear the one that fits." The card was monogrammed with the initials *ST*. Sam Thompson.

Cordi opened the box and pulled out a beautiful cream-pink evening gown that was much more revealing than anything she would have chosen for herself. The V-neck was way too deep, the straps probably too thin for her busty frame. The fabric itself was gorgeous, gossamer, sparkly chiffon layered over a silky lining, with the most intricate lace details on the trim.

The second dress was a replica in a different size, so Cordi went to the bathroom to try both on. One was too tight, the other too loose, so she would need to adjust them anyway. She draped the dresses over the sofa and debated whether she even wanted to go to the gala. She found something unsettling about the "Pockets of Poverty" name, even though she should have been grateful that it benefited needy kids growing up in Chinatown, kids like her.

When Tessa came home that evening, she climbed the rungs to Cordi's loft and poked her head over the ledge. She wore a black head-scarf tied in a thick knot at her crown, so Cordi, sitting on her mattress hunched over her breakfast tray table while she attempted to sketch, thought at first that she was some sort of animal. A solid manifestation of the presence she often felt when no one was around. She clutched her blanket to her chest, only mildly relieved when Tessa's face appeared.

"Oh, Cordi, please forgive me," Tessa said, her eyes shining with tears. "You're not mad, are you?"

Cordi swiped eraser shavings off her sketchbook. "About what?"

"I was supposed to meet you for lunch, but I completely forgot! Well, I didn't forget, but something happened and then it was too late and the darn streetcar stopped working—can you believe it?"

That happened to Cordi all the time and it was a huge inconvenience, but she refused to show any empathy.

Tessa went on. "Anyway, by the time I finally got to Lacy's, you were already gone and I'm so sorry. I didn't stand you up, I promise."

Cordi had been nursing a low-burning rage ever since she'd gotten home. She took a deep breath, wanting to cling to her anger, but on seeing Tessa's pleading pout, it died out. "It's all right. I didn't wait long."

Tessa grinned. "Can I come up?"

Cordi paused, not because she didn't want her to but because it was the first time anyone would join her in her isolated spot. It would be the first time a friend had come into her room, ever. She'd never invited any classmates over when she was a kid—not that anyone would have wanted to—and this felt so momentous that she grew instinctively still, worried she'd make it all go wrong.

"Sure," she said finally.

Tessa pulled herself up, and Cordi was delighted to see she wore the color-blocked dress Cordi had made for her last week when her hands had felt better. She'd been so relieved to be able to sew again, she'd made a dress for Silly too, and a new apron for Audrey covered in pockets to tuck her paintbrushes away.

When Tessa entered the loft, she had to stoop, her headscarf knot skimming the ceiling. "Goodness, how do you stand it up here? It's so cramped. You should just move into my room."

"What, share?" Cordi almost choked and started coughing.

Tessa thumped her a few times on the back. "Jeez, I'm not that terrible. I keep my room pretty tidy. Not like Silly's, you know. I think I saw a rotten apple core in there once."

"It's not that," Cordi said. It was the fact that Tessa, who was so charming and kind and could be friends with anyone, had chosen her. Was willing to share her comfortable room that she paid much more for with Cordi. But before she could explain herself, Tessa had already moved on, dropping down to sit gracefully next to Cordi on the mattress.

"You'll flip a lid when you hear what happened today. I was at the Petite headquarters—they wanted to redo some shots that didn't turn out so well—anyway, they share a building with a modeling agency. I was on my way to meet you for lunch when this woman stopped me. She was so glam—I thought she was going to snap an ankle, her heels were so high. Her hair was a bit old-fashioned, though—no one really does S-waves anymore, do they? But it turned out, she's a talent scout for the agency, and she *noticed* me, Cordi. I've been *discovered*."

"Wow," Cordi said. It was good news—great news—and yet she was so nervous she'd say something wrong that would push Tessa away. Tessa, who lounged next to her like they were good friends—no, *best* friends. Cordi had never had a best friend, and she wished for the right words that would seal the connection.

If Tessa noticed Cordi's careful reverence, she didn't show it. "And you know what caught her attention? It was this thing." She gestured down at her body, at the dress. "Your work, Cordi. She commented on it, said it looked like an original Pucci, which I told her was exactly what I said when I saw it. I told her all about how you love to sew and design and you're working at Lacy's now, and she invited me to her office, and then we spent most of the afternoon chatting, and the next thing I knew, she pulled up a contract right then and there. Said she had to snag me before someone else did." Tessa threw up her arms, falling back on the mattress with the silliest grin on her face.

Cordi turned while sitting cross-legged to smile down at her. "Tessa, that's amazing. I'm so happy for you."

"It's finally happening." Tessa sighed dreamily. "All of it, all our dreams, everything we deserve. Because we do deserve it." She touched Cordi's hand as if afraid Cordi might protest.

"Absolutely."

Tessa had a soft smile on her face, lost in her own thoughts. Her expression relaxed from the one she always kept carefully in place to something more real, more vulnerable, a slight pull bringing her eyebrows together and lines hugging her mouth in worry. It lasted for only half a second before she snapped out of it and contorted her face back into its usual carefree mask.

"We do, don't we?" she asked, her voice small and genuine, losing that dramatic stage quality it usually had.

"Of course we do," Cordi said. "All of this . . . it may be the lura that helped us get it, but it was always there all along. Our talent, your beauty—"

Tessa waved a hand demurely.

"No, really," Cordi said. "It's not as if we haven't worked hard for this."

"You're right." Tessa sat up and turned to face Cordi directly. "What is success, anyway, but privilege disguised as opportunity." Usually, Tessa bent down whenever she talked to Cordi, but seated, they were finally eye to eye. "God." She snorted with derision. "I can't believe I just said that. That's what my father used to tell me. He said I would never make it without his help. He wanted to keep me, and my mom, like we were prize cars or something. He always said that I would only become anything because of his background and money and influence."

As usual, Cordi didn't know what to say. She wished she had all the right words to comfort Tessa, to make her stay, to strengthen the bond between them. She reached out and patted her hand instead.

"My mom and I are his second family," Tessa continued. "As a child, I never thought anything was odd. He only came home for dinner some nights, but Mama told me he had a busy job. It made sense because we had nice things. We lived in a pretty bad neighborhood, but I was much better off than my friends, you know? I always had nice clothes and good food and stuff. Then one day, I was doing an assignment in school and reading the newspaper, and there he was. Perfect politician, family man—except the family wasn't us. It was this beautiful white lady and their two beautiful, blond-haired, blue-eyed kids."

She fidgeted with her hair scarf, not meeting Cordi's eyes.

"I thought Mama didn't know. I showed her the newspaper, thinking she'd be mad. But she knew all along. She was okay with it, as long as we had our house and our things. But I couldn't do it. I left as soon as I could, and he didn't care. Not at first. But then a year ago, he saw me, at a club. I was with my friends, minding my own business, and he was with another girl probably younger than me. It was so gross. But he wanted to reconnect after that, and when I told him I wanted nothing to do with him, he started sending me checks. I cashed some of them, and he wouldn't leave me alone after that—saying I owed him. Kept bothering me and coming to my house. That's why I had to move. And I haven't accepted anything else, but he keeps sending them, and my old roommates bring them to me."

Tessa finally looked at Cordi.

"What do you do with the money?" Cordi asked.

"Nothing. I wouldn't be able to live with myself. Because then he would be right, wouldn't he? But he's not. Because I'm going to *be* someone. I'm going to be on billboards and magazines, and he can never say that it was because of him."

"No," Cordi agreed. But she heard a hollow ring in Tessa's voice.

"I'm sorry I missed our lunch. I was really looking forward to hearing about your day."

"You can still hear about it," Cordi said, smiling brightly to show her all was forgiven.

Tessa reached out and hugged her, her bony shoulders stabbing Cordi's. Like all her hugs, it was over as quickly as it started. "I'm starving. I think it's Silly's turn to cook."

Silly wanted to go out instead.

"I got the promotion!" she squealed as Cordi and Tessa climbed down from the loft. "They picked me out of the other five interns!" Tessa and Silly started jumping and shrieking. Cordi joined in because she knew that after the moment she'd just shared with Tessa, there was no way Silly could steal her spot in Tessa's heart. Audrey came out of her room to see what all the fuss was about.

"Audrey, I got it, I got the job!" Silly shouted.

"I heard," Audrey said flatly, but the smallest smile cracked her sarcastic shield. "Congratulations. You've been working really hard."

"I know, but I really think it's your doing, Cordi," Silly said.

"What? What did I do?"

"It was your dress." Silly held out her arms. "Everyone kept looking at me, all impressed."

"They were probably doing that because they knew you'd get the job," Cordi said, but she was secretly pleased that people had noticed something she'd made, and that it had given Silly the confidence she needed. Already she stood taller, her shoulders pulled back, an excited gleam in her eyes.

"And I swear, I thought they were going to give it to my archnemesis, Gina Townsend," she continued. "She can't even spell 'cephalopod'!"

"Why do you need to spell that?" Audrey asked. "Are you writing about . . . octopi?"

"First of all, it's 'octopuses,' and second . . . no. We were just talking about sea creatures."

Audrey gave Cordi a helpless look, but for once, Cordi actually felt friendly toward Silly and she didn't want to ruin the moment, and besides, who cared! Silly was finally getting everything she deserved.

"I would have died if Gina got the internship, but the mayor pulled me into his office to tell me in person that they'd chosen me. I was so surprised since he's never actually talked to me or acknowledged my existence in any way, and I usually report to Mr. Applenine, but I suppose he wanted to meet me since I would stay on as an official new employee in his office." She squealed again.

Tessa had gone uncharacteristically quiet, but she perked up as Silly finished. "So? Are we going to celebrate?"

"Yes!" Silly bounced. "It'll be my treat!"

The air was humid when they stepped out of the building, the ground dotted with a light drizzle that released gaseous fumes from the asphalt.

"Must have rained," Silly said, and as usual when someone commented on the weather, everyone looked up. Neon advertisements glowed on the billboards above the buildings, and vertical lights cut white slices in the black sky some distance away.

"Look, you can see Hollywood," Tessa said. "They're probably having some glitzy movie premiere. God, I'd do anything to be a movie star. Imagine all the free cigarettes and booze."

"But you get free stuff now," Cordi pointed out, having witnessed men fighting to buy her drinks just for a few minutes of her attention at the Society.

"It's not free when you have to work this hard for it," Tessa teased, gesturing at the wiggle dress Cordi had made for her that fit so well that her hip bone jutted prominently against the thick fabric. She nudged Cordi playfully, then lit a cigarette as they walked.

They went to a fancy restaurant about a block away, and as the host led them to a table in the middle of the room, all the guests stopped to look at them. Cordi assumed it was Tessa who really attracted the attention, especially in her boldly colorful dress, but Cordi herself had chosen a pink piece with a fitted bodice and flared skirt, and Audrey had put on a perfectly pressed black jacket over her usual blouse and slacks, which immediately upscaled her look. Silly wore the gray dress suit Cordi had made for her, her skirt at a flattering length that didn't make her look frumpy for once. They were a rather becoming group.

"Champagne for the table," Silly ordered as soon as the server approached.

"Silly," Cordi protested. They could have bought a month's worth of groceries with that.

"I insist," Silly said, smiling at the server.

"I'll have the salad," Tessa said, tapping her lips with a finger so cleanly manicured that Cordi clenched her fist and tried not to obsess over her own bruised nails. "With chicken."

"Have the steak," Silly said. "We should all have the steak. Let's indulge tonight. I'm paying. We'll all have the steak," she told the server. He nodded graciously and retreated.

"Silly," Audrey said. "You haven't gotten paid for your new position yet."

"But I will," Silly said. Twin spots of pink appeared on the apples of her cheek. "Just let me do this. I'm so happy right now, I think I could die."

The server returned with their champagne and poured the bubbly liquid into their tall sparkling flutes. Silly picked up her glass and raised it. "To the Mais," she declared.

"To the Mais," Tessa and Cordi repeated. Audrey held up her glass.

Silly giggled. Cordi almost choked on the champagne, the bubbles clogging her throat like a large pill. Tessa shook her head, but she smiled.

It was Audrey who brought up Cordi's hesitance about the gala as they waited for their food. "Bet they'll have loads of this stuff at that fancy charity party you're going to," she said, swishing the champagne around in her glass. "Too bad you can't snag us a couple bottles."

"You don't want to go?" Tessa asked, reading Cordi's face. "Why not? It sounds amazing. Think of all the people you'll meet."

"I think Cressida's family knows the mayor's family," Silly said. "Maybe she could put in a good word with her parents to put in a good word with the mayor about me."

"Why do you need that? You're already hired," Cordi said.

"Yes, but it wouldn't hurt. Job security. A raise."

"You just got the job," Audrey said. "And you already want a raise?"

"Always reach for more," Tessa quipped. "Never settle for the status quo. Careers are like bodies of water. Once you're stagnant, you start to fester." She looked pointedly at Audrey, then turned abruptly to Cordi before Audrey could make an equally scathing remark. "Plus, you'll get to be with Sam Thompson. All the girls will be so jealous."

"Oh . . . well . . ." Cordi blushed.

Tessa squealed. "I knew it. You love him, don't you? You'd be an idiot not to. He's handsome and rich and from one of the great Los

Angeles families, you know. They run this town. And you could be part of that."

"Oh, but I don't think he has any real interest in me," Cordi said. "I mean, why would he?"

"Why would you say that? You're a lovely person, and he'd be lucky to have you."

"He hasn't called."

"He sent you two priceless ball gowns," Audrey said. "Isn't that proof he's interested?"

"And he invited us to the Café," Tessa said. When Cordi didn't answer, completely unconvinced, she added, "If you need a reason to like Sam, I can give you about ten million of them, all sitting in that lovely bank of theirs downtown."

Chapter Twenty-Seven

Cordi thought she'd love her job designing for Lacy's, and she really did, but the first week dragged, the tension mounting as more time passed and her pages remained blank. On Friday morning, Mr. Sinclair asked to see the designs that afternoon, which finally spurred her to just sketch something. The pressure seemed to work because she managed to cobble together two pairs of shorts, a skirt, and a long-sleeve collared shirt that would look best under a strappy dress, a design inspired by her own need to alter the gown Sam had sent.

As she brought the sketchbook to Mr. Sinclair's desk, she felt both relieved that she had something to show him and nervous that he'd hate everything she'd come up with.

He didn't look up right away, busy signing something on his desk. "Oh, good," he said at the sound of her footsteps. "Let's go to the pizza place around the corner. You like pizza, right? I meant to take you out earlier this week, but it's been so hectic." He capped his pen, got up, remembered his jacket, and buttoned it hurriedly as he passed her. "Bring your sketchbook—we can look through it while we eat. Come on." Usually so serious, his grin was quite shocking, the way it transformed and brightened his face. "We have to hurry if we want to beat the crowd."

"Oh." Cordi quickened her steps to follow him. "I need to get my purse."

"No need, it's my treat. Come on, come on." He pressed the elevator button repeatedly. She'd never seen him like that, so boyish and giddy. "They have a specialty green pepper pizza they *only* make on Fridays, but it sells out immediately, so we need to be the first in line—yes!" The elevator dinged open, and he rushed her inside, holding down the button for the lobby floor. "If you hold it down, it won't stop on any other floors."

"Is that true?"

"I don't know, but I can't risk it not being true."

Cordi laughed. "I'm really excited about this pizza now."

"You have good intuition." She caught a trace of a twinkle in his eye.

They passed the perfume counter on their way out of the store, and the salesgirls stared as they rushed past.

Outside, the tall buildings provided little shade from the sunblasted sky. The smell of car exhaust mixed with that of burgers and pasta sauce and every other sort of food as the restaurants roared to life for the lunch rush. People in business suits walked quickly down the sidewalks, and Cordi and Mr. Sinclair joined the throng. After they almost got separated, he held her elbow lightly, his fingers sending warm tingles up her arm, guiding her safely around a corner. It was easier for him to navigate the crowd because he was taller and broader, and she admired the ease at which people moved aside when they saw his serious, determined face.

"Yes," he whispered excitedly when they reached the pizza restaurant, and they found only one couple in front of them. As a large group of business associates approached from the opposite direction, he rushed forward, pulling Cordi through the door.

Cordi couldn't help smiling, and Mr. Sinclair's lips were pinched in a suppressed smile as well.

"You don't mind sharing a pie, do you?" he asked as they read the menu posted above the cashier.

"Oh no, anything is fine with me."

"They also have a pineapple malt," he added, waiting for her reaction.

"Oh, great. That sounds . . . interesting. I'll try it."

His lips tensed, like he was fighting back a smile, and he put in their order and led her to a seat by the window. "I like to eat outside in theory, but in practice, we're just bait for flies and mosquitoes. So a window seat is the next best thing." He wiped down his side of the table with a napkin before folding his hands neatly and looking at her, resuming his serious, professional demeanor.

"You must come here a lot."

"Like I said, the pizza is to die for."

She nodded and clutched her sketchbook, trying desperately to think of something to say to impress him.

"So what made you want to be a designer?" he asked.

Cordi was caught a bit off guard by the question, mostly because only recently had she dared to dream of such a job. "To remind people that we exist," she said without really thinking about it.

"Interesting. Explain."

"I mean . . . I didn't . . ." She fell quiet, regretting her words and wondering how much he really cared to know about her, but Mr. Sinclair only nodded and waited for her to continue. "It's as if . . . you know, in stores . . . clothes aren't really made for girls like me." Her words felt like ice cubes stuck in a tray that came tumbling out with a hard shake. "So I learned to sew because I had to—I mean, I love sewing and I can make my own clothes. But . . . what if I couldn't? It's like . . . I get reminded every day that I don't really exist. On TV or the radio or in magazines or anything, really, there are so few Asian people. Maybe they keep them in the back where they think they belong or something—it's just . . . Or like in school, I was yelled at any time I spoke Vietnamese, even to my own sister. And . . . even clothes are a constant reminder that I don't belong. They don't fit, because I don't fit. And . . ." She trailed off, feeling foolish for not being able to finish articulating how she felt, ashamed at realizing how much of it was true, and also worried about burdening Mr. Sinclair with these realizations. After all, she didn't know him very well.

"Clothes are very important," Mr. Sinclair said, not missing a beat, as if he didn't notice that Cordi was practically trembling from her outburst. "Clothing may seem frivolous, but appearances matter. We wear clothes every second of the day. It must be tough, not finding many options for yourself, especially when you were growing up."

Cordi could barely swallow past the lump in her throat, all her attention fixed on willing her tears not to fall. She blinked furiously. "Thank you," she whispered. After a few seconds, she managed to ask, "What about you? How did you get into fashion?"

"I'm more interested in the business side of it. But after a while, I developed an eye. My sisters are thrilled that I work in fashion. They get to use my discount and see what will be popular before their friends."

"How many sisters do you have?"

"Five."

Cordi raised her eyebrows in surprise and he let out a breath.

"I know. They're all married now, thank goodness. It's a lot of pressure being the oldest brother, you know."

Cordi smiled, easily picturing Mr. Sinclair as a protective and brooding sort of brother, scaring all prospective partners away.

"What about you?" he asked. "Any siblings?"

"An older sister," Cordi answered, and was saved from having to say anything about Trina when their food and drinks arrived. The pizza looked delectable, cheese melted around an assortment of toppings—chicken, green peppers, a sprinkling of vegetables.

She set her sketchbook aside as they both dug in.

"I'm a bit nervous to show you my designs," she found herself admitting as they ate.

"Why?"

"It was rather difficult to come up with anything . . . impressive."

"Your job isn't to impress me. I'm not your boss," he said. "I'm a buyer, you're a designer. If anything, you're higher than me in the hierarchy."

"But you're the one who hired me."

"Technically, you report to Rosalie. I make business decisions, but they're not based on your creativity." He wiped his fingers on a napkin. "If I could sell everything you made, I would, but we have to think reasonably for commercial purposes." He held out a hand. "We're on the same side, so there's nothing to be nervous about."

Still, Cordi had butterflies in her stomach as she handed over the sketchbook and waited for him to flip through it. What was he thinking? His expression was unreadable, brows furrowed, jawline tight. Every doubt she'd had all week resurfaced with a vengeance. She wasn't good enough, she was a fraud, she didn't deserve to sit there, eating pizza and drinking a malt, she should be back at work proving herself.

She gasped as something snapped against her finger, and a sharp pain wrenched through her hands. She'd twisted a napkin into a ball and clutched it so hard that the fingernail on her index finger broke. Even under the nail polish, she could see how fragile and brittle it had become.

"Hmm," Mr. Sinclair said.

Cordi looked up. "What do you think?"

"They all have pockets," he said, but that didn't answer her question, and he looked so serious.

"Do you hate them?" she asked, unable to stop wringing her fingers, wincing at the pain.

"We can work with them," he said.

Cordi's heart sank, and she looked down to see that the skin on her knuckles was dry and ashen and forming scabs. Was the lura magic wearing off again? Was that why Mr. Sinclair didn't like her designs? Or rather, was that why she hadn't come up with anything worthy?

And with that came an even more devastating question: Was the only reason her designs were any good, the only reason she had gotten this job, because of the spell? Was any of her work even that great? Did she deserve to be here? She had worked hard, she wanted it badly, and that was the secret to success—according to Callum anyway. Wanting it enough. Being willing to do the work. But the words were rather contradictory coming from a man who offered magic to make their dreams come true. And then there was what Tessa said, about how everyone who ever succeeded had some sort of help to begin with.

Her emotions warred. She had thought all this time that her designs were her own, that they were good, and that all lura had done was get them noticed. But what if the magic was behind everything? The dresses she had made for Cressida in a sort of feverish frenzy—were they really hers? Or did they belong to the lura? And did it matter if she was the one who had made them in the end?

"You're coming to the gala this weekend, aren't you?" Mr. Sinclair interrupted her spiraling thoughts.

Cordi had a tough time bringing her attention back to the conversation. Mr. Sinclair closed the sketchbook, and she stared at it, devastated. "I . . . I haven't decided yet."

"You know the theme is 'Pockets of Poverty.' Perhaps we could tie in your new line with the charity. It would mean mass production, if the founders agree to it."

"Mass . . ." she repeated. That meant hundreds, maybe thousands, of women wearing something she'd created. If the designs sold anyway.

"You should come this weekend," he said again. "We can pitch it to the board. I'll be there. And Cressida. She speaks very highly of you, so you'll have a friend. Friends." He smiled, once again transforming his face. Then he looked down and started tidying up their table. "It's a great networking opportunity."

Cordi got up to help him. "If you think so." A sense of dread stole over her, but she steeled herself. It wouldn't be the first time she had to do something she didn't want to, but at least she'd get to look at some pretty dresses while she did it.

Chapter
Twenty-Eight

In the morning, Cordi went to the bank by herself, so aware of the envelope in her pocket that it might as well have been on fire. It held her first paycheck for her job at Lacy's, and it was the most she'd ever been paid—apart from Cressida's lump sum, which had gone so quickly to the rent and bills, paying back Tessa for groceries, and fabric for new dresses she had to sew to fit her taller body, that she hadn't had a moment to enjoy it.

But this money was different. Because it signified something momentous . . . that her dream was now a reality, that she was doing what she loved, even if it was tougher than she'd envisioned. But she was determined to work hard and not rely solely on the magic, for while it had given her a head start, she still wanted to claim her successes as her own. Every time she thought about her position at Lacy's, she was also filled with a dread that she could lose it, that everything she'd worked so hard for could be taken away.

When she handed the check over to the bank teller, she half expected balloons to fall from the ceiling, for someone to jump out from behind the counter and congratulate her. But of course nothing like that happened. The teller didn't even blink at the amount.

"Here you are," he said, handing her a neat stack of twenty-dollar bills.

"Thank you," Cordi said, cradling the money in both her hands. The bills were so crisp and new, they felt almost fake.

She stepped away from the teller and counted it again. It was much more than she needed. She had enough for rent, for her share of the groceries and bills, and even some to set aside. Her heart practically stopped, so relieved from the pressure of scrounging just to get by.

She wasn't used to having so much left over. What should she do with it? Treat the Mais all to a nice dinner? They could go out for drinks. They could go shopping.

And then, because she usually associated her family with money and money problems, she thought of her parents.

She could give them the extra money. They needed it. And she was a good, filial daughter. Or at least, she had been at one time, and she could still be. This amount could earn them at least a month or two of freedom from worrying whether they could pay the bills or would have enough to eat. She could give them a relief similar to the sort she had just felt, but maybe even more so because they had borne the weight of poverty for years and years.

But why should she share her hard-won earnings? They had disowned her. They hardly cared about her.

Except she knew that wasn't true. How could they not love her? They were her parents. They'd sacrificed everything for her and Trina by leaving their country, and they'd worked so hard. If she could take away all their problems and save them from misery, she would. But since she couldn't, she could at least do a small thing now, and give them the extra money she didn't need.

She looked through her datebook, even though she knew without looking that Trina would be working at the store. It was her only chance to meet with her sister without her parents' knowledge for another week.

The streetcar ride went by in a blur as she tried to envision what would happen once she reached the shop, what she would say, how Trina would react. It could go a number of ways, but she hoped that

Trina would be grateful, would maybe even be happy to see her, though she knew that was a far-fetched wish.

At the stop, she hesitated before the open doors of the streetcar. She could still turn around and go back to the apartment. She could keep the money.

But she'd get another paycheck in two weeks. And again after that. She had more than enough, and it would only grow. She stepped off the streetcar determined to go through with it.

The walk to her parents' shop was short, but once she got to the plaza, she couldn't move another step. She took in several breaths. The storefront looked particularly decrepit, but she couldn't tell if that was because she was used to the fancy glitter of Lacy's Department Store now, or if it was because her parents hadn't made enough money to repair the blinking OPEN sign or have the windows cleaned recently.

She forced herself to move forward, across the parking lot, and then into the store.

The bell above the door dinged, announcing her presence. The counter stood empty, but Trina shouted, "Coming!" from the back.

Then her sister rushed to the front, dusting her hands on her pants, and stopped when she saw Cordi.

"Hi," Cordi said.

Trina's face was always tense, so Cordi wasn't sure if Trina was angry at seeing her. They hadn't spoken since the day Cordi had picked up her clothes and driven off with Sam—unless you counted Trina's letter— and she waited with bated breath to see what Trina would say.

Which was nothing.

"I came to, um . . ." Cordi couldn't finish. She didn't know how to say the words without Trina taking them as condescending. So she took the money she'd set aside and put it on the counter.

Trina stared at it. Then at Cordi. She still didn't say anything.

"I got a job. At Lacy's." Cordi felt the need to explain. "So I have a little more than I need right now. I thought . . . you might . . . Mother and Father might need it more than I do."

Trina remained frozen in place.

"Maybe just don't tell them it's from me," Cordi said needlessly, since Trina had made it clear in her letter that their parents didn't want to hear from her.

Finally, her sister moved, picking up the cash to count it. "This is a lot," she said.

Cordi nodded. "Hopefully enough for a month, at least."

"Where did you get it?"

"I told you, I got a job at Lacy's."

"Doing what?" Her tone was derisive.

Cordi felt as if Trina had injected poison straight into her heart. "Designing. Clothes. I'm a designer now." Saying it out loud felt bizarre and fake, like a lie.

"Designer? Who would hire a Vietnamese designer?"

"Lacy's," Cordi snapped. "Lacy's did. They hired me."

Trina made a sound of disappointment. "You don't have to lie. You made this money with your new friends. Those girls. Doing God knows what."

"What?" Cordi couldn't believe what she'd just heard.

"I don't know what you're up to—selling drugs or probably yourself— to make this much, but I don't care." Trina tucked the money into her pocket. "I'll use it to pay our bills."

Bile rose at what Trina's words implied, leaving a bitter taste in Cordi's mouth. "I made that money because my designs are worth that money," she snapped.

"Even if that's so, it wouldn't have been possible without Mother teaching you everything you know. This is the least you can do to pay her back."

Cordi's mouth opened and closed. Her brain refused to come up with a proper response.

Trina kept going, as if Cordi's silence were encouragement to air her complaints. "It must be nice to have all this freedom to go off and do whatever you want and follow your dreams. What a privilege it is. Wish

I had the same chance. But I didn't—I was too busy taking care of you, baby sister." There was nothing affectionate in the endearment, the flesh around her nose swelling into an expression of scorn and disgust. "And now I have to take care of them and the shop, since you abandoned us."

Cordi breathed fast, her chest heaving. She thought of a million things to say. She thought of all the hurt she'd carried all these years, all the ways that she had sacrificed herself just as much as Trina had. But then a memory came to her, of Trina leaning down to wipe Cordi's tears when Cordi hadn't wanted to go to first grade because the kids had been so mean. Trina had held her hand and sat with her for the first hour, missing her own class and ignoring the stares from the students. So when Cordi opened her mouth, she didn't know who was more shocked at what came out.

"I love you too," Cordi snapped.

And she walked out of the store as fast as she could before she burst into tears.

———— ⚜ ————

Cordi stopped in front of the grocery store next door, gasping in gulps of air to keep from sobbing outright. After a few minutes, she adjusted the strap of her purse more securely on her shoulder, inhaled deeply, and turned to go home.

She stopped as she caught sight of a couple walking across the parking lot. It was her parents, moving slowly, backs slightly bent, dressed in gray and fading khaki as if they themselves wished to disappear into the background. She'd been gone for only a few months, but it felt like years. They looked so old, so frail. Their hair was practically all white. Had it really been that long?

They hadn't noticed her, and she should have slipped away, but she was frozen. Ten more steps to the shop door, and they might not even notice her standing there.

But then Mother glanced up. Her face looked more wrinkled, her eyelids drooping, but her gaze showed recognition as it fixed on Cordi. She tapped Father on his arm and pointed, and when he saw Cordi as well, his face turned to stone.

Without a word, they lifted their chins and kept walking, disappearing into the store and leaving Cordi feeling like she had been turned inside out. She waited for the pain to subside, for her heart to stop wrenching, but it never did.

Chapter Twenty-Nine

Later that evening, Sam came to the door, but his face fell when he saw Cordi in one of the dresses that he had sent over.

"What did you do to it?" he asked.

Cordi held the skirt out, her hands hidden in fancy silk gloves that she'd been forced to buy to cover up the ashen scabs that had spread from her knuckles up to her wrists. "I fixed it to suit me." She'd added sleeves in a coordinating off-white fabric and adjusted the neckline into a sweetheart bodice more flattering to her body type than the original V-neck. "It was way too revealing before."

"That was the whole point." At the look on her face, he added quickly, "That's the fashion nowadays. You would have looked so chic."

"I love the alterations," Audrey said, coming up behind Cordi. "You look like a princess."

Coming from Audrey, Cordi wasn't sure it was a compliment, but she was grateful for the solidarity.

The car ride was tense at first. Sam kept glancing over at her.

"You do look lovely," he said, but at that point, Cordi wasn't sure if he was just trying to make up for earlier.

"Thank you. So do you." It was true. He looked very striking in his black-and-white attire, a silk bow tie defining the elegance of the evening. "Are you passionate about the charity this gala is for?"

"I believe in all charities," he said, which wasn't much of an answer.

Cordi tried to think of a different topic of conversation, but she had no idea what they had in common. She remembered Cressida mentioning that he worked in finance, something she had no interest in and wasn't in the mood to talk about.

"I was hoping to run into someone tonight," she said when Sam contributed nothing to fill the silence.

"Oh yeah?"

"His name is Callum Domina. Do you know him?"

Sam leaned forward over the steering wheel. "Callum . . . Yes, I believe so. Blond fella, a bit of a drinker. Not sure Cressida would approve of him."

"He's actually been rather nice to me—us, the girls. He helped us all get our apartment."

"Can't imagine that's very hard to do. There are loads of places available."

Cordi wanted to roll her eyes. Of course someone as rich as Sam Thompson would have no trouble finding a place.

"Why are you hoping to run into him tonight?"

"It's nothing like that," Cordi said, wondering if he was jealous. "I just have a question for him."

"Hmm. He'll probably be there. He likes to cozy up to the ladies." Traffic had slowed significantly, and Sam pulled up behind a line of elegant, polished cars. "Old, young, I've never seen him discriminate."

Cordi had no response to that, so she just looked out the window.

Once again, they lapsed into silence. Sam smiled at her and then turned on the radio. A catchy number filled the car, adding a light mood to the air that didn't quite touch her heart.

Inside the shiny ballroom, lit with glittery chandeliers and flickering candles on side tables and in small niches, elegantly dressed women in jeweled evening gowns hung on the arms of tuxedoed men. Whether it was understood or not, the guests adhered to an aesthetically pleasing color scheme of pale off-white for the ladies and black for the men. Only a few women had veered slightly, like Cordi in her pale-pink dress.

Cressida found them the moment they stepped through the entrance. She kissed the air around Cordi's cheeks, then held her at arm's length to admire her dress.

"Did you make this?" she asked.

"No," Cordi started to say.

"It's a Bella Sharpe," Mr. Sinclair said. He stood behind Cressida, though he looked less like a date and more like a disapproving bodyguard. She felt a pang in her heart at seeing them together, knowing it was silly—they'd been together when she first met Cressida, but she'd gotten so used to working with Mr. Sinclair alone that the sight of them as a couple felt a bit like being punched in the gut. "You altered it. I love it."

Cressida's eyes widened. "Love it? You never love anything." She leaned scandalously close to Cordi. "You're invoking quite the change in Gabe. He hasn't talked about anything but your designs." Cordi looked at Mr. Sinclair in surprise, since she hadn't gotten that impression from him at all, but he was frowning at Cressida, who kept talking without stopping to take a breath. "And they are genius. I've been telling everyone for years that women's clothing needs more pockets. Are you thirsty? I'm thirsty." She turned to her brother. "We're thirsty."

Sam nodded and left without a word, though Cordi suspected he must have been dying for an excuse to get away ever since the moment he'd seen Cordi's dress.

Everything about the gala was extravagant. Cordi was awed by all the guests who knew exactly what to do, what to wear, and how to act. She'd only read about such events in magazines, yet here she was, just like Cinderella at the ball, and the Fairy Godmother had cast a spell so no one would guess who she really was.

Sam had dashed to the other side of the ballroom, stopping to embrace a pretty girl, who turned her face up for a kiss. Cordi tried to stir up a bit of indignation. Jealousy. Rage. Hurt. She felt nothing.

Cressida seemed to sense this, because she leaned close and said in a loud whisper, "If you don't fancy my brother, don't worry, there are tons more men I can introduce you to." She linked their arms and began walking slowly at a saunter through the room with Gabe close behind. They drew the attention of the guests they passed, both men and women, but Cressida pretended indifference. "Why, I believe Gabe here is single."

Mr. Sinclair coughed. "Cressida."

"But I thought the two of you were together," Cordi said. She had thought they were engaged, actually, ever since they'd come to Ms. Ran's shop looking for fabric for Cressida's trousseau. Had she been wrong this whole time?

"Gabe? Oh gosh. We're cousins, darling. But I don't know if he's right for you—he's much too serious. Women only want him for the clothes, and I bet they're bored out of their minds when they realize that's all he talks about."

"Cress," Mr. Sinclair said, voice tense like he was stifling a groan.

"We need to find you someone cultured and interesting."

"But . . . then who are you marrying?" Cordi asked. And more importantly, did that mean that Mr. Sinclair was unattached . . . to anyone else? But even if he was, he'd done nothing to indicate he would be interested in Cordi. So she tried not to look at him, and that only made her more aware of him than ever.

"Marrying?"

"The wedding dress and the gowns . . ."

"Oh, I thought those would be nice to have, once the occasion arises."

Cordi frowned, then met Mr. Sinclair's gaze. He didn't look away, his expression signaling that he understood exactly how she felt. How nice it must feel, being rich enough to have fancy ball gowns and a wedding dress made just because. His attitude that day at the fabric shop made sense now. He hadn't been snobbish; he had just seen it for the unnecessary extravagance that it was.

Sam came back then with their drinks, smiling and giving Cordi the impression of a puppy, eager to please, but also dying to run off and play.

"Do you think you can track down Callum Domina?" Cordi asked him, hoping he'd take the request as an excuse to leave her and actually enjoy the party.

"Certainly," he said, and disappeared again.

"What do you want with Callum Domina?" Mr. Sinclair asked, his voice agitated.

"I just want to ask him something," Cordi said. He'd assured her that the last spell would be permanent, so why had her nails grown dark again?

"You shouldn't get involved with him. He's not a nice man."

"You're the second person to tell me that," Cordi said.

"A strong indication that it's true."

"Oh, Callum isn't that bad," Cressida said. "He just needs a push in the right direction now and then."

Cordi was starting to realize that Cressida felt that way about everyone. They all just needed the right guidance, and she was the one to provide it. The way she led Cordi through the ballroom now, like she had Cordi on a short, expensive, fancy leash, though Cordi was actually grateful. She would have had no idea what to do or who to talk to, and with Cressida next to her, everyone was dying to shake her hand and shower her with flattering compliments. Cordi had never smiled so much in her life, her head feeling fuzzy and light as they wove their way through the crowd.

They spent most of the evening like that, with Cressida introducing Cordi to her friends as they mingled with the rich people of the Society. Cordi even recognized some of them from her brief foray into the Café.

Everyone was fixated on Cordi, asking her so many questions. Where was she from? Who were her parents?

"You'll really want to meet these ladies," Cressida said, pulling Cordi along excitedly as they approached two older women.

One had the whitest hair that looked more like fluff, cut close to her head. The other had wavy gray hair to her waist, and though they must have been Cordi's mother's age or older, they had a preserved beauty that only money could buy. Dressed in their elegant white ball gowns, they resembled statuesque queens, their faces unchanging as Cordi and Cressida approached them.

"Ladies," Cressida said. "You'll be ecstatic to meet my new friend, the groundbreakingly talented Cordelia Yin. Cordelia is from Chinatown, and she's *the* new designer at Lacy's."

"Really?" the white-haired woman said. "You're my new girl?"

"Cordelia, this is Desiree Lacy. Of Lacy's Department Store."

"Mrs. Lacy—you've—you—I—" Cordi sputtered. This was the owner, her boss's boss's boss's boss.

"It's *Miss* Lacy, dear. I never married," the woman said with a smile. "And please call me Desiree. Gabe showed me your work, and I must say, it's quite revolutionary. And get this, Ramona," she added to her companion. "They all have *pockets*. Women's clothes, with pockets. Can you imagine?"

"Revolutionary indeed," the gray-haired woman said. She held out a hand, and as Cordi took it, she wondered if she was supposed to kiss it or something. Luckily the woman pulled it back before she did anything to embarrass herself. "Ramona Rickens."

"Ramona is the head of the charity," Cressida said. "She's responsible for this beautiful gala we have the honor of attending tonight."

"I . . . am . . . so honored," Cordi said, and inwardly flinched. "Thank you for having me."

Mr. Sinclair, who they had lost in the crowd, found them at that moment, and stood next to Cordi. "Isn't it a coincidence," he said, "that the charity is called Pockets and each piece in Cordelia's line features pockets?" He smiled briefly at Cordi, who grew uncomfortable with being talked about so much, though hope sparked in her heart at what it could mean, having the attention of these two influential women.

Ramona turned to Desiree. "It *is* a wonderful coincidence! Perhaps we could partner! A percentage of the profits from the line could go to charity. We'll raise the price to make up for it, of course."

"Naturally," Desiree said, but she focused her steel gaze on Cordi. "Wouldn't that be something? Emerging on the scene with a bang. An overnight success. Our first Chinese designer, beautiful to boot. What would you be willing to do for that, huh?"

"I'm actually Vietnamese," Cordi said, but Ramona had moved on.

"Come, Des, my mind is now reeling," she said, pulling Desiree Lacy away. "We must discuss."

"Ta-ta, Cressida. It was lovely to meet you, Cordelia. We will be in touch!"

"I—yes—thank you—" Cordi waved. *Why?* What was *wrong* with her?

"That's wonderful!" Cressida said. "Great work, Gabe." Cressida leaned close to Cordi. "Do you know what this means? You've made it. You're going to be absolutely famous."

Cordi met Mr. Sinclair's eyes, and he smiled at her, a genuine smile that brightened his face and made Cordi smile too. She had no way of thanking him, so she just let their gazes rest comfortably on each other until Cressida pulled her away to enjoy the rest of the party.

Chapter Thirty

The following Saturday morning, the phone rang, and Cordi happened to be in the living room altering one of her dresses, which, like many others, now didn't fit at the shoulders. It was the only thing she could manage with her fingers hurting so much. She'd attempted to sew on her machine, but she could barely hold the fabric down to securely feed it under the needle. She didn't want to make a mistake, despite the anxiety that grew each day that she still hadn't started on the bridal gown for Cressida, which she was less motivated to make now that she knew Cressida wasn't even engaged.

"Misses Mai residence," she said, studying the shoulder seams of the dress. How had it gotten so tight?

"Gosh, you make me wish I had roommates so we could have some quirky little opening line."

"Cressida, hi!"

Tessa came out of her bedroom and gave Cordi a quizzical look.

"I was wondering if you'd like to come back to the Café today?" Cressida asked. "And perhaps bring over the dresses you're working on? I'd love to show them off to all my friends. It will certainly help promote your new line—everyone's been dying to hear more about it."

"Oh! I-I don't know. I still have so much more work to do."

Tessa shook her head vigorously. "Is she asking you to the Café?" she hissed. "Tell her yes!"

"Is that Tessa?" Cressida asked. Her voice had changed—it no longer sounded light and soft, but almost a bit unfriendly.

"Yes. Well, you see, I promised Tessa I'd spend the day with her,"
Cordi said. Tessa started gesturing wildly, and Cordi waved at her to
stop. "But you know, she'd love to come to the Café. Perhaps I can
convince her?"

Cressida seemed to chew this over. "Of course," she said warmly,
as if she hadn't hesitated for so long. "I love Tessa. You can bring all
your—what did you call yourselves?—the Mais along if you want. Shall
I send a car?"

"That would be lovely." Cordi thanked her and hung up the phone.

"Well?" Tessa demanded.

"You all should go without me," Cordi said. "Cressida will send a car."

"I can't go without you. Cressida invited you. I'll look like such a
hanger-on."

As usual, Silly had her bedroom door open, and she must have been
listening to their conversation the whole time, because she came and
stood in the doorway. "We're going to the Café?"

"Only if Miss Yin lets us," Tessa said with a pout.

Silly twisted her fingers together. "You and I can go together if she
doesn't want to go."

"Oh, all right." Cordi got up from the sofa. It seemed like lately her
life was about making other people happy, which was, admittedly, not
much different from her life with her parents except for the fact that she
was more aware of it now, and therefore angry about it.

When they got to the rooftop of the Café, Cordi wasn't sure where to
go, clutching Cressida's gown to her chest. She'd folded it into a paper
bag to protect it, and it stuck to her skin, already sweaty just from
standing a few minutes in the heat of the pool deck. Sam wasn't there

to welcome them this time, and they stood in the open like lost lambs waiting to be sacrificed.

"There you are," Cressida said, bounding up from a lounge chair to rescue them. She wore an open silk robe over a black one-piece bathing suit. "Is this it?" She took the gown from the bag and held it up, smiling with approval. She kissed Cordi's cheeks, waved at Tessa and Silly, and led them to a cluster of comfy seats with a large umbrella in the center to shade them from the sun. A group of men and women lounged around, and Cressida motioned to them to make room.

"This is my friend Cordelia Yin," she said to the group. "She's the designer for Pockets. And *I* discovered her." She waved the gown at the group, then tossed it casually on the lounge chair behind her.

"Oh my," a woman said, sitting up and pulling her sunglasses down her nose. "Cress has shown me what you've made. I can't wait for the line to launch." She held out a hand. "Emily Saladine."

Cordi shook it, self-consciously aware of how tender her fingers felt.

"I love your gloves," Emily added.

A man snapped his fingers at Tessa. "I knew you looked familiar. You're on a billboard, aren't you?"

Tessa beamed.

"That's right," another man chimed in. "For some makeup brand."

"Some makeup brand?" Emily rolled her eyes good-naturedly. "Please excuse Patrick, he has no idea about anything important. Tessa is the new face of Petite Beauty."

"Yes," Tessa said. "Cressida introduced me to John Lenore herself."

Another girl joined their group, shrieking as she pulled Tessa into a hug. "You're here! Oh my, I missed you!"

Cordi studied the new girl, wondering if they were close friends. They must have been, because Tessa squealed back as she pulled the girl onto the seat next to her. They started whispering and giggling obnoxiously to each other, so Cordi directed her focus on the glistening surface of the pool.

A man swam a graceful lap in the water, and his sun-soaked back and black curly hair looked so much like Mr. Sinclair's that she almost waved when he resurfaced. But then he turned around, and she realized it wasn't him. Disappointment twisted inside her, replaced instantly by embarrassment for feeling so. Even if he were there, it wasn't as if he'd be excited to see her outside the office, so why was she being so foolish?

"I normally wouldn't ask," Cordi heard Tessa's friend say, "but it belonged to my mother, you know."

"Oh no, I didn't—I have no idea what happened to it," Tessa said, a slight edge to her voice.

"I mean, they don't make those anymore," the girl whined.

"What is it?" Cressida asked, holding a glass daintily in her hand.

"It's this jade hairbrush my mom gave me. It went missing—I lost it when I moved." The girl pouted. She must have been one of Tessa's former roommates. "I just thought, you used to borrow it sometimes, so maybe you had it," she said to Tessa.

"No, I said I didn't."

Tension hung in the air at Tessa's clipped response. Cordi frowned, unable to put her finger on the unease that she felt, as if she had forgotten something but couldn't remember what.

Cressida smiled. "I'm sure it will turn up."

A man plopped down next to Cordi and threw an arm around her shoulder. Cordi almost pushed him off before she realized that it was Cressida's brother, Sam.

"I thought I heard your voice," he said.

"Hi," she said.

"Haven't you got a drink? That won't do." He snapped his fingers at a passing server and ordered for her and the Mais without asking what they wanted.

"I say, you do look lovely today, Cordelia," he said. "Did you make this dress?"

She wore a loose cover-up cinched at the waist. Perfect for the pool, but Cordi really wore it because everything else fit awkwardly lately.

"Yes," she said. "I—"

"Would you like to swim?" Sam asked.

"Not particularly—"

"Come on, let's go. It's blazing hot out." He pulled her to her feet despite her protests, tugging at the sleeve of her cover-up. "Take this off, you won't need it."

She pushed his hands away, stopping short of slapping them. If they hadn't been out in public, she would have slapped more than his hands. She could feel everyone watching them but pretended not to as she pulled off her loose cover-up.

Sam grinned, oblivious to her annoyance, and pulled her toward the water.

"Oh, what about your gloves?" He started to take them off for her.

"No!" She yanked her hands back. At his look of shock, she added, "They go with my outfit." She gestured toward her simple black high-waisted two-piece that didn't match the gloves at all.

But Sam shrugged. "You're the designer." His devilishly handsome face was marked by shadows in the harsh sunlight. He pulled her into the water. It was pleasantly warm, but that didn't do anything to ease her discomfort.

"I don't know how to swim," she warned him. It wasn't as if her parents could afford lessons.

"It doesn't get deeper than five feet," he said. "Come on, I'll teach you. The first step is learning how to float."

Cordi gasped as he swept her off her feet, one hand between her shoulder blades and one right above her butt.

"Stop wiggling," he said. "Relax."

Relax? How could she relax when he was practically groping her in broad daylight?

"I don't want to do this," she pleaded, hoping the fear in her voice would appeal to his better senses.

He smiled. "It's scary at first, but it will be fun."

"I don't want to do this," she repeated, unable to think of any other words to convey how miserable she felt.

He frowned. His hand moved across her shoulder blades. "What's wrong with your back?" His fingers stopped at something, a bump in her flesh that Cordi hadn't realized was there until he found it. Was that why her clothes had been fitting strangely? "It feels like a spike—"

"I don't want to do this!" she shouted, and thrashed until he let her go.

He held up his hands dramatically, as if she'd threatened him with a weapon.

She jerked her way out of the water and back to her friends, but they were gone. Cressida and her group too. She stood there feeling abandoned and exposed, as if everyone on the pool deck were watching her, seeing her alone and miserable and loving it. She pulled her cover-up back on hastily, glad for some semblance of protection.

Cordi looked around the deck and was relieved to see that no one paid her any attention. Still, loneliness settled in—how could the girls just leave her? Where had they gone?

She sat there for what felt like an eternity, on the verge of tears, before she grabbed her bag and got up. She hadn't wanted to come here in the first place. If Tessa and Silly didn't have the decency to wait for her, then she'd leave without them. See how they liked it.

In the lobby, as she rushed down the dim hallway, she almost bumped into a man.

"Oh, I'm sorry," she said, then stopped short. "Mr. Sinclair?"

It was him, though he looked different. His casual T-shirt and swimming shorts made him appear ten years younger, but he still had the worried expression of someone much older.

"Miss Yin," he said, his fingers fumbling at the spot where a suit jacket button might have been. "I didn't know you were a member here."

"I'm not. Cressida invited me. I didn't know you were a member." It made sense—Cressida was his cousin, after all—but even though she had thought she'd seen him earlier, she couldn't imagine Mr. Sinclair splashing about in a swimming pool or knowing how to relax. He seemed to thrive on work and stress. That's probably why they got on so well.

"I'm not, technically," he said. "I'm here because of Cressida. I don't like it, or rather, it's awkward, but she asked—she insists that I use the club now and then." He sounded absolutely miserable.

"Cheer up," Cordi said, even though she understood completely how he felt. "There's a pool and a bar—it can't be that bad."

"It's not that—I know what people will say." He stopped speaking abruptly and looked at her as if just seeing her for the first time. "I'm sorry. You're on your way out, aren't you? I should go up. I think they're waiting for me." He took a breath. "I'll see you at work."

Cordi wanted to reach out, to ask what was bothering him and encourage him to keep talking and offer words of comfort. But he rushed to the elevator in a few long strides, then rocked back and forth on his heels while he waited for it to open. As Cordi walked away, she fought her instinct to turn back and take him with her.

Chapter
Thirty-One

On Monday, Cordi was in the workroom at Lacy's, a separate space from her office, filled with piles of fabric and samples and a larger drafting table, when a knock came at the door.

It was Mr. Sinclair, looking like himself again in his work suit, his expression serious but confident, so unlike the nervous, unsure man she had run into at the Café over the weekend. He gave no sign that he remembered the encounter, as if the people they were outside the office didn't exist.

He carried a giant binder with him. "The pattern pieces are here."

"Oh, wonderful." She'd drawn the pieces herself, worked with a patternmaker to create multiple sizes, and had waited eagerly all last week to see how they'd turned out.

She cleared some space on the drafting table so Mr. Sinclair could place the binder between them. They bent over the pieces, shoulders pressing close as he flipped the pages. The scent of his cologne teased her every time he moved, just barely there, mixing with another fragrance that she couldn't describe but that reminded her of autumn, of leaves and golden light and—

"Miss Yin?" he said.

"What?" She shook herself inwardly.

"I was asking when you think the boning on the shirt will arrive."

"Oh, maybe in the next week or two." *Pay attention,* she scolded herself.

As she and Mr. Sinclair went over the designs together, they fell into their natural rhythm of conversation, debating constructively over what worked and what didn't.

After a while, Mr. Sinclair checked his watch. "We've worked through the lunch break. I didn't even hear the chime."

"Me neither." Cordi's stomach growled in protest.

"Well, we can't have that," he said, almost smiling. "Can I treat you to a meal?"

She tried not to sound too eager. "Are you sure? Your favorite place isn't serving the special today."

"I have another favorite place. They have soup."

It was a hot day, but the office was always freezing, so a warm meal sounded incredibly comforting.

She was tempted to say something teasing, but then remembered that they were at work and she didn't want to embarrass herself. So she just nodded, and they left the office together.

Mr. Sinclair led her to a small, obscure restaurant with only five tables, all empty. An old woman stood behind the counter, tallying up a stack of receipts, while Cordi could see an old man through the window opening into the kitchen.

"I always get the number five, the spicy beef soup," he said. "But they're all delicious."

Cordi perused the rest of the menu. "I think I'll have the number seven." The ribeye.

"Good choice," he said, frowning like he might change his mind.

After they ordered, they sat at the table by the door.

Cordi tried to resist asking about running into him at the Café, she really did, but she couldn't stand the awkward tension. It felt like all day something had lingered between them.

"Did you end up enjoying your time at the Café?" she asked.

He leaned back in his seat, resigned, as if he'd been expecting her to ask the question. "It went exactly how I expected, to tell you the truth. Which was . . . complicated."

She nodded. She didn't understand what he meant at all, but she didn't want to push him to talk about it if he didn't want to. She toyed with her disposable chopsticks instead.

"Cressida's family and mine are estranged," he said. He paused as if not sure whether she cared to listen, but she looked at him encouragingly. "Her mom and my mom are sisters. Twins, as a matter of fact. But something happened. Years before we were even born, and they haven't talked since. Her mother married Lloyd Thompson and, as you can see, did very well for herself. My mother . . . did not."

Cordi put the chopsticks down and leaned in close.

"I grew up very poor," he continued. "I know it's in bad taste to mention it, but with five younger sisters and no father—he died when I was seven—things became rather dire. Before working at Lacy's, I was a courier, delivering packages for businesses. It's not exactly the worst job, but it wasn't going to win me any awards or get me anywhere. But I learned a lot about different businesses. The pay was never enough, so I waited tables at weddings if I could find a gig over the weekends. That's how I ran into Cressida. At one of her friends' wedding. She recognized me, wanted to reconcile, and got me a job at Lacy's. A low-paying, bottom-of-the-rung position, and while I worked there, Cressida funded my schooling. A few years later I earned a degree and qualified for a higher position."

He took a swallow of water.

"My mother was against it from the start," he said. "She didn't want anything to do with Cressida's family. It's put something of a strain on our relationship, but she has no choice but to accept the money I give her. Our families still don't acknowledge each other. Except Cressida and me. And Sam, but he's always done what Cressida tells him. So it's somewhat awkward when Cressida insists I join her at their clubs and places of business. I have to talk to my aunt and uncle as if they haven't ignored my mother or left her to suffer all these years. Not that she'd accept their help, but they're more than happy to pretend that she doesn't exist—that our family hasn't . . ." He trailed off.

Cordi sat quietly, absorbing his words, imagining the way he must have grown up. No wonder he was so serious and worried all the time. "It must have been so tough for you," she said. "To have so much responsibility when you were—are—still so young." It was easy to forget, what with his maturity and seriousness, that he couldn't be more than a few years older than Cordi.

He straightened and looked slightly uncomfortable, perhaps not used to discussing his background.

"Have you ever talked with Cressida about the situation?"

He smiled tightly. "You've met her. You can imagine how well something like that would turn out."

"Not well, I would guess."

"I'm grateful for what she's done for me. If I have to put up with a few awkward social interactions, it's a small price to pay. We all have to give up something for what we want, don't we?"

It was a familiar refrain, one that she seemed to hear a lot lately, as if the universe were reminding her that she would never have enough, never be able to pay the price for success.

"I grew up poor too," Cordi said. "It's hard not to think about money all the time when the difference between starving one day or living the next is a matter of whether you'll make five dollars before the night is over."

"Yes, exactly," he said.

"You don't want the Thompsons to think you're just using Cressida for . . . easy money. Or as a way to get ahead. Or even to get rich, really. You need the income, for your mom and family, and also just for yourself."

He nodded, looking down at his hands. They were rough and calloused, which she had always found strange for someone working an office job.

"They can't possibly think that you're . . . you're greedy," Cordi said. "You work so hard. I heard you tripled the perfume sales in your first year." She'd overheard the girls talking about it in the lunchroom one day. "And you're changing things for the better. You've certainly changed *my* life."

If she didn't know any better, she could have sworn she saw him blush, but it was more likely because the old woman set two steaming bowls of soup in front of them at that moment, before leaving them to their conversation.

"It will never be enough," Mr. Sinclair said. "I'll always have to work harder than others. To prove myself." He picked up his chopsticks. "And that's why I'm so excited for your line, Miss Yin. It's the first business decision I've made on my own. Of course, Cressida is the one who discovered your talents, but . . ."

Guilt flooded her. Yes, she had worked hard on the designs, but she had also had the lura's help, imbuing her with the energy and skills that she couldn't have managed without.

"You've contributed just as much as I have," she said.

He leaned over to blow on his food, and she became hyperaware of the purse of his lips, the curve at the corners as he smiled. Her breath caught at how different it made him look. Boyish and playful, like someone who might have laughed a lot in a different life.

"It's something we can both be proud of," he said.

Chapter Thirty-Two

Over the next few weeks, she avoided the Mais as much as you could avoid people you lived with. She woke up earlier and left the apartment before Silly was up. She stayed at work longer to skip dinner at home. Tessa's modeling gigs thankfully ran late, and Audrey often worked in her studio at night. By the time Cordi got home, Silly was the only one in the apartment, but she usually went to bed early because of her headaches.

It wasn't just what had happened at the Café—how they had abandoned her—and in all honesty, she wasn't even angry about it. Tessa had explained that Cressida had invited them to the restaurant inside, and it wasn't like they knew Cordi was going to be back from the pool so soon. She and Silly had thought Cordi would want to spend more time with Sam. She was just tired of worrying and talking about spells, with Tessa not budging on her stance and Silly agreeing with her on everything while Audrey judged them all in brutal silence.

"Cressida says she's going to talk to her parents about getting us *elite* memberships at the Society!" Tessa had exclaimed. "She's going to make it happen. And after that, things will be so easy for us. We'll have everything we ever wanted."

Cordi didn't understand Tessa's obsession with the club. She was happy with what the spells had done for her. Except for the fact that she sometimes longed for her old face back. When she looked in the mirror, she no longer saw herself but instead some tired stranger. She wasn't sleeping well. She had no appetite but was always hungry and weak. Her body felt heavy and slow, and her clothes no longer fit right, the seams tight on her shoulders and back.

Her nails were growing back, but the texture was rough and porous and the edges sharp no matter how often she filed them. They'd taken on a dark-green fungal color. The skin on her fingers was rough and leathery, and she'd gotten into the habit of wearing gloves all the time, similar to the ones Callum always wore. They made her feel safer, and truth be told, she didn't like to look at the damage on her hands.

Cressida had phoned a few times since that day at the Café to check in on her wedding dress.

"Perhaps you can find a different designer," Cordi said. She couldn't muster up inspiration for the dress now that it was obvious that Cressida didn't even need it. "I'll forgo the rest of the payment."

A painful silence followed.

"No," Cressida said simply.

"Cressida," Cordi started, ready to launch into a spiel about how wild it was. Why did she want a dress for a wedding that wasn't happening?

"You said you would design the dress, and you owe it to me to finish what you started. Once you start something, you have to see it through, Cordelia."

Cordi sucked in a breath, not knowing why those words felt like a punch to her gut. "You're right. I'll keep working on it."

"Lovely."

The days went by quickly. Mr. Sinclair and Cordi settled on five designs for the store to produce—all with pockets. The collection would simply be called "Pockets by Cordelia Yin," the logo a simple triangle with the cream and black color scheme used by Pockets of Poverty, which would officially sponsor the launch.

The whole experience felt very surreal, as if it were all happening to someone else. It didn't help that her fingers and arms were numb, giving her an overall sensation of being one step removed from everything. Her biggest dream was coming true, and yet she had to view it through a hazy lens, feeling nothing.

"We have an official date for the launch," Mr. Sinclair declared one morning, walking into the workroom with two cups of coffee. She loved how easily they'd fallen into the rhythm of small considerations, nice favors, little luxuries that she'd never shared with anyone else. Except, perhaps, the Mais.

"A real, concrete date?" she asked, turning to Mr. Sinclair. The sales team kept changing the launch for some reason or other.

"Yes, in just three weeks."

Cordi flipped through her datebook. "I think that's perfect."

"Are you excited?" he asked, smiling gently.

She sipped her coffee. "I'm . . . nervous. It doesn't feel real."

She wondered if perhaps it wasn't real. Perhaps it was all happening only because of the lura, not because of any talent she had.

No, she scolded herself. She had designed everything. She had worked hard to get here. The lura had just helped her get in the door. Hadn't it? Did she really deserve to be here? She was so confused.

Mr. Sinclair touched her shoulder lightly, as if he could read the turmoil of her thoughts. All her awareness focused on the spot like she'd been stung there. The way he looked at her made her wonder whether he could see beyond the glamour of the lura spell, like he saw what she really looked like, used to look like. The real her.

"It *is* real," he said. "And it's going to be everything you dreamed of."

She wanted to place her hand over his, but then she remembered the grotesqueness of her fingers, so she curled her brittle nails against her palms and simply smiled and nodded.

"So we'll go to the doctor," Tessa said when Cordi brought up the problem with her fingers later that night, unable to ignore the deterioration any longer. The last spell hadn't resolved anything, not completely, and she had no idea how to get hold of Callum to ask him what had gone wrong.

"Today?" Cordi said. "Right now?"

Tessa sighed. "I'm exhausted, Cordi."

But Cordi wouldn't let it drop until Tessa and Silly relented, so later that week, the three of them walked to the clinic around the corner from the apartment.

They sat in the waiting room, surrounded by crying children and tired-looking parents. No one made eye contact, and the nurse barely smiled when she led Cordi to a freezing room, where she waited some more.

When the doctor finally examined her, he turned her fingers over and over in his latex-gloved hands in confusion.

"I don't understand the problem," he said.

"My fingernails look like rotting claws," Cordi said, careful to remain calm, even as panic rose inside her like steam in a boiling kettle.

"Is this some sort of joke? A prank?"

"What? No."

"There's nothing wrong with your fingers." He turned away with a huff. "Unless you have a real problem, please don't waste my time. I have a hundred other patients to see."

"But—"

"Please take care of the bill on your way out."

Bill? For what?

The other girls ran into similar problems.

"He said there's nothing wrong with my hair," Tessa said, even though her scalp showed through in spots. The spell hadn't lasted long for any of them. "And he told me to stop being so vain about my looks."

"According to the doctor, my vision is twenty-twenty," Silly said. "I couldn't see anything on the board, but he made me guess so I just spouted out different letters at random. Apparently they all turned out to be right."

They met Audrey at a local deli to pick up some groceries, and she seemed unsurprised.

"It's the lura," she said with certainty. "I'm sure of it."

"Does that mean no one else can see our . . . deformities?" Tessa asked.

"It looks that way," Silly said.

Audrey pushed a grocery cart down the aisle while Silly and Tessa grabbed things off the shelves. Cordi was too distraught to think about what they would eat that week. Why weren't the girls more worried about what was happening to them? What if her fingers got so bad she could never sew again?

"Just because no one else can see doesn't mean it's not happening," Cordi said, her voice wavering. How could the girls act so calm about this? "It doesn't mean it doesn't hurt."

"It's not so bad," Tessa said. "I was thinking of changing my hair-style anyway. Short hair is radioactive these days. Maybe I'll get a pixie cut. Or start a wig collection."

"Yeah, and honestly, I've always wanted glasses," Silly said. "They make me look more sophisticated. People take me more seriously at work. The mayor actually read a report I prepared last week, and I can't help but wonder if it's all because of these babies." She tapped her black frames, then walked into a pole. "Ow! Oh my gosh, ow, that really hurt."

"You okay?" Cordi patted her arm.

"Where did that pole come from?" Silly whined, rubbing her fore-head, where a red spot had formed.

Cordi didn't want to state the obvious—that it had been there all along and Silly's eyesight was growing worse.

"We'll be okay," Tessa said, and she smiled, but it didn't quite hide the worry in her eyes.

Chapter Thirty-Three

If no one else could see their deformities, it meant that it was all in their minds. So Cordi downed several aspirin, wrapped her fingers in gauze, and spent Friday night and all of Saturday working feverishly on Cressida's wedding dress despite the pain, her mind in a fuzzy haze. At the end of the second day, she seemed to wake from a walking dream. She stood in the dark by the window framed by Tessa's vines, the plants cascading and multiplying in the dark reflection of the glass. She felt like some creature emerging from the forest. She didn't look like herself in the reflection, and her heart skipped a beat at the idea of a stranger in her home, until she remembered that with the luracal spell, she looked . . . enhanced.

And hanging in front of her—though she had no recollection of finishing—was the wedding dress. It was gorgeous, the long sleeves made of lace, the fitted bodice structured by boning, and the skirt flaring out with yards of fabric.

Quickly, she packed the dress into the biggest box she could find. For reasons she couldn't explain, she wanted it out of the apartment. Something about it frightened her, and her fingers trembled as she looked in the phone book to find a courier willing to deliver it to the Thompsons'.

Tessa wanted to go out that night, no longer caring what they looked like since it was clear that despite their deformities, they appeared as beautiful and radiant as ever to the rest of the world. Even though Cordi didn't really want to go, she didn't want to stay home by herself either. The apartment felt eerie lately. Her skin prickled even when she was alone and no one could possibly be watching her. She couldn't shake the feeling that something lay in wait in the shadows. So she forced herself to get dressed and was relieved when Audrey agreed to come along. Audrey's grounded, no-nonsense air helped stabilize Cordi when she felt like things were spinning out of control, which was quite often lately.

Audrey couldn't see their deformities, which added to Cordi's paranoia that it wasn't real.

"But my hands really hurt," she insisted.

"I believe you," Audrey said.

"How come you can't see it now?" Tessa asked Audrey with a suspicious narrowing of her eyes. "You were able to before."

Audrey seemed like she might ignore her completely, but breathed out heavily through her nostrils. "Not that I'm an expert, but maybe it's that I didn't dabble in the last spell. You know how I felt about lura. I tried to warn you—"

"Oh, stop it, let's just have fun tonight," Tessa interrupted. "Can we just enjoy ourselves? What use is all this worrying going to do anyway?"

Cordi supposed she was right, though no matter how hard she tried to push the thoughts away, a looming cloud of stress followed her around.

"I've never been to the Society," Audrey explained on their way out. "Rich people will be great inspiration for this satirical sculpture I'm working on." Her outfit had passed Tessa's inspection—an all-black jumpsuit just fancy enough for a night out.

The line to get into the Society was even longer than the last time they'd been there, but Cordi, Silly, and Audrey followed Tessa to the front as admiring eyes watched them. The bouncer let them through without a moment's hesitation, and once again, Cordi found herself at the center of attention. Everyone on the dance floor turned to stare as the club manager, Mr. Lavender, showed them to a table. The music played without pausing, but the singer quieted briefly as if showing respect for royalty.

Cordi hated every second of it, every eye on her adding to the heavy weight on her shoulders. She tried not to stoop, her muscles tense and stiff, following after Tessa, who raised her head and cast her gaze upon the crowd like a queen. Even though no one else could see Tessa's baldness, she'd chosen a wig of shiny waves for the night and looked more radiant than ever.

Cordi let out a sigh of relief once they made it to their canopied table, the curtains shielding them from the crowd. But as soon as they sat down, Tessa got up to pull back the curtains.

"We need to be seen tonight," she said. No one else protested, so Cordi sat stiffly on the luxurious sofa, wishing she were at home, wishing she could hide away not just her fingers but her whole body, to cease existing for just one night, to stop having to worry about everything all on her own.

Had life been simpler before the lura spells? Or had it just been different?

As Mr. Lavender poured wine into their fancy glasses, she tried to appreciate everything she had. She was here with friends, something she'd wished for all her life. Not only was she a designer, but she'd quickly become one of the most sought-after names that season. Soon, Pockets by Cordelia Yin would be in stock at Lacy's, sold to and worn by thousands of women just like her. All her dreams would come true.

But for some reason, her sister Trina's face flashed in her mind. Ads for the new line had gone out, the catalog already mailed. Trina couldn't afford to shop at Lacy's, but they received the catalog at the shop every month. Cordi had loved to copy the designs and make outfits for herself, and Trina often flipped through the glossy pages, perhaps imagining a life in which she could afford those items. Had her sister seen her new designs in the most recent catalog?

Even if she had, Trina would never give Cordi the satisfaction of admitting it. She would never be proud of Cordi, if only out of spite.

A numbness came over her. The hurt that usually came every time she thought of Trina and her parents wasn't as painful, more like a twinge than the excruciating twist she normally felt when she remembered that they had disowned her.

"You look exquisite!" Sam shouted to be heard above the music. She hadn't even noticed him joining their group, and he leaned down to kiss her. Cordi was so surprised that she turned and almost caught the kiss on her mouth. Sam grinned and held her face with both hands as if he were about to kiss her again, properly.

Cordi pulled back and stood up. Luckily, Cressida appeared right behind him, so she used her as an excuse to escape.

"Cressida, hi!" She put more enthusiasm into the greeting than she really felt.

"Cordelia!" Cressida squealed. They kissed the air near each other's cheeks—who *was* she? When had she become the sort of person who kissed other girls' cheeks like they'd been friends all their lives?

"I was hoping you'd be here," Cressida said, holding Cordi at arm's length. "The dress, it's gorgeous. I love it so, so much. I've been telling everyone about you, and soon you'll be so famous, you'll barely be able to see straight."

Cordi laughed nervously. "But that's not what I want at all."

"Of course it is!" Cressida laughed, but then she really looked at Cordi's face. "Isn't it? I mean, you've worked so hard and . . . you did all that . . ." The music swelled and drowned out her words.

"Darling, sit," Tessa said, pulling Cressida down next to her, looking around for some way to please her. "Here, have some wine."

Sam took a spot next to Cordi and couldn't seem to stop touching her, his arm wrapped around her shoulder, his hand on her knee.

"We should sneak away," he whispered in her ear.

She resisted the urge to duck out from beneath his arm. "I'm enjoying my time with my friends."

He pouted—actually *pouted*—but sipped his drink and didn't insist.

Across the dance floor, Cordi saw Gabe Sinclair climb the steps to the table he usually sat at with Cressida and Sam. He caught her eye and nodded, but didn't join them, instead sitting at his usual seat with an icy drink. She envied him, alone and away from everyone's watch, appraising or not.

"If you'll excuse me a moment," Cordi said, "I have something I need to talk to Mr. Sinclair about."

"But you see him all the time," Tessa said. "Can't it wait 'til Monday?"

"Oh, let her go," Cressida said. "Gabe is all alone over there."

Mr. Sinclair smiled when she approached his table, which had been crowded the last time Cordi had seen him here. Now he sat by himself, enjoying the music. The singer had a soft croon, guiding couples into a swaying, slow dance on the floor.

"Aren't you lonely by yourself?" Cordi asked, sitting next to him.

"I'm not by myself anymore," he pointed out.

She tried to think of something clever to say, her mind going blank. But Mr. Sinclair didn't seem eager to talk. He leaned back in his seat and watched the singer and the band playing a rhythmic but slow tune. His foot tapped to the beat, which Cordi found both odd and endearing because the rest of him remained perfectly, professionally still.

"Do you—" she started to ask at the same time that he also spoke.

"Would you like to dance?"

"Oh yes," she responded without thinking.

He looked surprised, both by his own question and that she'd accepted, but it was too late to take it back now, for both of them. So he stood and held out a hand.

For the first time that night, Cordi didn't care if anyone watched as she took Mr. Sinclair's hand and walked with him to the dance floor. The song was still a slow one, so he hesitated a second. Cordi closed the gap between them, resting her forearms casually on his shoulders while his hands went naturally to her waist. It struck her that before the lura spell, before she'd been changed, she wouldn't have reached his shoulders so easily, and he probably would have had to lean down a little. He had no idea what she really looked like. All he saw was a beautiful face the spell made people see.

But she didn't have to think about that now. She brushed the thought aside and swayed with him along to the music.

They didn't speak at all. The beat defined their movements. Their gazes locked.

She worked with Mr. Sinclair almost every day, knew what expressions he made when he was upset, the way his brows pulled together in concentration, the way the muscles around his mouth relaxed when he was pleased. She could practically predict what he would wear or eat on any given day. But as they danced, she realized she didn't really know him at all, not the way he held her gaze, the gentle pressure of his hand, supportive but not controlling, the sway of his body.

With anyone else, she might have felt shy and self-conscious. But her hand rested gently on the hard curve of his shoulder, her body moving along to the swaying of his. He was a strong dancer, his arm around her as he led her through the steps. This close, the slight scent of his aftershave mixed with something so heavenly and elusive that she found herself leaning closer.

The song ended much too quickly. The crowd applauded. He stepped back. She took a breath.

For a second, Cordi let the most wonderful fantasy play out in her head—of Mr. Sinclair and her, together, falling in love, doing things couples do, like . . . walking in the park, cuddling on benches, sharing dessert. Her heart swelled with emotion she felt only when she was with him.

But then the numbness replaced it. And she realized it could never happen. They couldn't be together, not when who she was, who he knew her to be, was a complete lie. A luracal spell, a deception. She could never be with *anyone*, so long as she looked like this. He would thankfully never see the deformed version of her, the monster, yet he would never know what she actually looked like either. Perhaps that was the real sacrifice. She could have all the beauty and success she wanted, if only she gave up on ever really loving someone or being loved back.

Her heart cracked.

And then Callum appeared behind him.

Cordi almost missed him, so lost in Mr. Sinclair's gaze, but then Callum turned and noticed her. Fear flashed in his eyes, gone instantly, but she had seen it.

It was the moment that Callum turned and fled that Cordi knew without a doubt that something wasn't right.

Something had definitely gone wrong with his spell.

That explained everything, the girls' deformities, how nothing lasted. He must have made a mistake. Why else would he avoid her?

She couldn't let him get away.

"I'm sorry," Cordi said to Mr. Sinclair as she moved past him to rush after Callum.

"Miss Yin," Mr. Sinclair said, taking her hand.

She paused, meeting his eyes. Confusion played with something else in his gaze, begging her for something she couldn't give him.

"I need . . ." she said.

She had to catch Callum and get to the bottom of what he'd done.

"Something *is* going on between the two of you," Mr. Sinclair said.

"No," Cordi protested. "There isn't. I just . . . need to talk to him about something important."

Mr. Sinclair's breath hitched. He clearly didn't believe her, but he stepped back and let her go without another word. She fought the urge to stay and explain exactly what was going on, but there was no time.

She locked her sight on Callum's shiny blond hair as he moved through the crowd, and she raced after him, bumping into people as she did.

Soon, Tessa appeared next to her. "We saw you from the table," she explained, gesturing behind at Audrey and Silly. "Come on, he's leaving the club."

Cordi didn't care who was in her way. She ran after Callum and followed him through a side exit. The cold air of the night washed over her face, flushed and hot from the wine and the dancing. In the alleyway Callum broke into a run when he realized they'd found him.

"Stop, we just want to talk!" Cordi shouted, chasing after him and almost toppling him when she grabbed the back of his shirt.

"Whoa whoa whoa," he gasped, trying to wrench free.

But her fingers . . .

The deformity was now much worse than before. Her nails looked like claws, and she couldn't control them—she could barely feel her fingers, and the numbness had returned and spread like a rash.

"All right, easy now, easy." He spoke to her like she was some sort of wild animal.

"Why did you run?" she asked, and her voice came out gravelly and hoarse, as if she'd been screaming all night. "We just want to talk."

"You chased me. I was frightened."

Tessa caught up to them, her wig lopsided. "Frightened? We're a bunch of girls, you wimp."

"Okay—" Callum's eyes darted back and forth, and if Cordi hadn't been clinging to his shirt, he might have bolted again. "Come on, ladies." He tried to inject the cheerful tone he always used, but it came out forced. "What's going on?"

"What kind of spell did you give us?" Cordi asked. "Things are happening. Strange . . . physical things."

"Yeah." Tessa pulled off her wig to reveal her bald head. "Like this."

Audrey and Silly caught up to them, except Silly ran into a fire hydrant, yowled, and hopped on one foot. She blinked owlishly and patted her dress, searching for something—her glasses—but then must have remembered that she'd left them at home since her vision had improved.

Cordi gave Callum a horrified look. "What exactly did you do to us?"

He held up his palms. "I gave you what you wanted. Beauty and success, that's what you asked for."

"Stop lying!" She shook him and found she was stronger than she felt, because he thrashed and fell to the ground.

Cordi stared at her hands. They were black and scaly, the skin rough and dry, and thick talons extended from the tips of her fingers, sharp and curled.

"What's happening to me?" she gasped, only it came out more like a growl.

Audrey approached and grabbed Cordi's hands. "What's wrong? I don't see anything."

"You can't see it?" Cordi hoped it was just in her head, but Tessa erased all doubt with her pitying look.

"Oh, Cordi," Tessa said.

They all turned on Callum. He braced himself on his hands.

"Tell us the truth," Tessa said. "What did you do to us? What do these spells mean?"

"All lura needs a sacrifice," he said, as if reciting some sort of rule he'd been forced to memorize.

"We did offer sacrifices. The tokens," Silly said desperately. "You said we needed an object of sentimentality. Every time we performed a spell, we sacrificed something to the lura. We always provided a gift."

"Those were just symbols. But something as big as what you asked for needs a bigger payment. I mean, you can't expect beauty and riches in exchange for, what, a compact mirror and a bookmark?"

"You said that's all we needed!" Tessa looked as if she might hit him. Cordi wished she would.

Callum flinched. "I'm sorry! I needed you to go along with the spell. I-I—"

"Why?" Cordi growled. "Why did you need us to go along with it?"

"Lura needs sacrifice, you see. To do the spell, but also to keep your power."

It took a moment for that to sink in.

"So you sacrificed us to keep your power?" Tessa shrieked.

"You sacrificed yourselves!" he shouted back. "You said the words: 'Lura, take this sacrifice and bring me to paradise.' I didn't perform that spell—you did. You wanted it. It wouldn't have worked if you didn't want it to. It wouldn't be this powerful either. Look at yourselves. The more beautiful you are, the more successful you are, the stronger the magic is. The stronger the sacrifice needs to be. So . . . the more you must sacrifice yourselves."

Tessa raised her fists and he cowered.

"I'm sorry!" he pleaded. "I should have been more up front."

Cordi tried to figure out what it all meant. Did it mean the physical ailments wouldn't be the end? What would happen to her? What would happen to all of them?

"But you said it has to be something you love," Audrey said. They all waited for Callum's answer. "You don't love them."

"It's stronger if the sacrifice is loved," Callum said. "The spell still works if it's not, but . . . there are repercussions."

"What sort of repercussions?" Audrey asked.

"Well . . ." Callum nodded at Cordi, alluding perhaps to her monstrous form. "You can never tell . . . how bad it will be. It's complicated—depending on the wishes, and the lurast."

"How do we stop it?" Tessa asked.

"Do we have to give up everything?" Silly asked, her eyes out of focus, blinking in their general direction. "Renounce our wishes, that sort of thing?"

"You can't," Callum said. "Once a spell is cast, it can't be reversed. Payment must be made. Your bodies will continue to . . . deteriorate until the spell is complete, and the lura claims your souls."

"Our souls," Cordi said, still not believing that was what they'd given up. If she had known . . . if Callum had told them the truth . . . she never would have agreed to it.

"But it doesn't have to be *their* souls," Audrey said. "Does it?"

They all looked at her, trying to understand what she implied.

"What do you mean?" Tessa asked.

"Lura needs *a* sacrifice," Audrey said. "But it doesn't matter who, does it?" She turned to Callum. "I mean, you used us. So why can't they . . . use someone else?"

He gave her an appraising look. "You mean could they give up another person in their place?"

Cordi shook her head, repulsed by the idea.

"Is that possible?" Silly asked.

"It must be," Tessa said. "I mean . . ." Her throat throbbed as she gulped, not meeting anyone's eyes. "The things I offered . . . they weren't mine. One was my mother's mirror."

"But she gave it to you," Cordi said.

"No . . . I took it. When I left."

Then something clicked. Cordi understood why she had felt so uneasy at the Café the other day when Tessa ran into her former roommate. "Your hairbrush wasn't yours either. You stole it from your friend."

Tessa looked away. "She barely used it. And she was always leaving me her dishes to wash and was always a mess. Silly gave me the idea, after we learned about it in that book from the library. As long as the object was valuable, the spell should still work. We both did it."

Cordi turned to Silly. She'd always found her annoying, and now she had the satisfaction of finally having a reason.

"I was trying to help Tessa," Silly protested. "She didn't know why the spells worked so well for you but not for her."

"Oh, who cares?" Tessa cried. "This is more important." She towered over Callum. "How do we do it?"

Cordi scoffed. "We can't *sacrifice someone else.*"

"Sweetie . . . look at you," Tessa said. She pulled out her compact mirror, the same one she'd given Callum as a token in the ritual, the one she'd apparently stolen from her mother, only now it was tarnished and rusted, a startling contrast to how shiny it had been right after the ritual.

Cordi didn't want to see her reflection, but she couldn't resist either. She took the mirror from Tessa with her claws. Her face looked blanched, like the blood had been drained from her body. Her shoulders stooped. Her back refused to straighten when she tried, a tightness in her muscles sending shooting pains down her spine. Her dress fit her all wrong, and she felt spikes poke against its fabric when she ran her fingers over her shoulder blades. Her arms also looked strange, elongated disproportionately, like spider legs.

She was changing into some sort of monster.

"Why am I like this?" She heard the panicked wail in her own voice. "What's happening to me?" she demanded.

Callum cowered. "I told you, the more successful and beautiful you become, the faster the spell works. The faster your . . ." He waved a hand at their faces, but looked away as if he couldn't face what he'd done. "Disfigurement will be."

"Will I become a monster like Cordi?" Tessa asked, her hands clutching the sides of her face. Cordi wilted a little inside—of course Tessa would only worry about herself—and wanted to shout back defensively that Tessa barely looked any better with her flaking, naked scalp, sunken eyes, and pale lips.

"Eventually, perhaps, if you can withstand the change."

For a second, Tessa only stared at him. Then she threw her wig at his face, the long strands fanning themselves over his head and sliding down into his lap. "What the *fuck* does that mean?"

"It means we'll die," Silly said with a sob. "If our bodies aren't strong enough, we'll just . . ."

"No, no, no," Tessa moaned, covering her face with her arms and walking away. Then she dropped her hands and turned a deathly glare on Callum.

"Cordi is different, though," he stammered and looked her way. "It seems you must . . . you might be . . . you're powerful enough to survive. I've never seen a spell work so well on anyone. Because of your great successes . . . you must be forced to give up more, faster."

"How do I stop it?" Cordi asked. "There must be a counterspell."

Callum shook his head. "Lura is permanent. Once a spell is in motion, there's nothing you can do. Except complete the payment."

"So . . ." Cordi couldn't stop staring at her fingers. "I'll become a monster. And then . . . what?"

"You'll still lose your soul," Callum said. "So you might survive, but no one who isn't a lurast will be able to see you. You'll wander around a monster, invisible to the world, but without your soul, eventually you'll forget who you are . . ."

Cordi gasped but couldn't seem to get enough air. "What use is being alive if that happens?"

"*We* can see you," Tessa said.

"But you're all going to die," Audrey said, not sounding particularly sad, simply making a logistic argument.

Silly sobbed behind them.

Tessa glared at Audrey and pulled Silly into her arms. "No, we won't. We'll fix this. We'll offer someone in our place. That will work, right?"

Callum sat cross-legged on the sidewalk, looking slightly less terrified. No cars had passed down the dark street, which was good because it would have been an odd sight. Then again, they were in downtown LA late on a Saturday night. People would just assume they were drunk.

Callum considered the question. "Yes . . . I believe it is possible. We'd have to combine two different spells. You'd have to sacrifice someone you love. Someone who means something." He glanced up at them. "It needs to be soon. Especially for you, Cordelia. The others might have a few weeks, but at the rate you're progressing, you may only have a few days left before you turn into a monster forever. It will be too late then."

"Days?" Cordi choked. But it made sense. She'd been so eager for success, had worked so hard—on Cressida's dresses and the designs for Mr. Sinclair. She'd racked up quite the debt, in lura terms.

"We'll find someone," Tessa said, taking Cordi's hands—which were more like a monster's talons—in her own. "Just give us the instructions."

"It's too complicated," he said. "Much more than repeating the words. I'll need to be there."

The girls looked at each other. Cordi started to step back, not wanting any part of it, but Silly nodded eagerly.

"Can you meet us back at our apartment tomorrow night?" Tessa asked.

"Yes." Callum got to his feet, seemingly confident that they wouldn't hurt him now, though Cordi was still considering it. He'd lied to them, tricked them. "Have the new sacrifice ready. I'll gather what I need and meet you there."

"How do we know we can trust you?" Cordi asked.

"Can you afford not to?"

"I can just kill you instead," Cordi growled. "Perhaps we should use *you* as the sacrifice." She was tempted to. Some instinct reared up to attack, and she probably would have if only they didn't need his help to fix things.

He held up his hands and backed away.

"I'll go with him," Audrey said. "We'll get what he needs, and I'll make sure he comes back to perform the spell."

"Audrey," Cordi started to protest, but Tessa cut her off.

"Good idea," Tessa said. "We'll find our sacrifices and meet at the apartment."

"But—" Cordi said. There were so many things wrong with the plan, she didn't know where to start.

"It's fine, Cordi," Audrey said. "I want to help. I should have tried harder to stop you all, but . . . honestly I didn't care that much when none of you listened at first. It's my fault too. No one deserves what will happen to you. I'll be fine. I can protect myself."

Callum held a hand to his chest. "Please, I would never hurt an innocent girl like Audrey."

Cordi exhaled in exasperation and it came out as a growl.

"Look, in my defense, I thought you knew," Callum said. "Everyone knows lura is dangerous and comes with a price. That's why people are so frightened of it."

"What do you mean, 'everyone'?" Cordi growled.

"I mean, everyone import—" He cut himself off. "Anyone who has ever dabbled in it knows what they're doing."

"Well, we obviously didn't."

"You wanted it. Everything you asked for—the beauty and success. You wanted it. Remember? Or it wouldn't have worked."

"You still should have told us the truth." It was getting harder for Cordi to speak normally, her throat making hard clicking noises.

"I'll make it up to you." He pressed his hands together in supplication. "I promise."

Chapter
Thirty-Four

"You can't seriously be thinking of sacrificing someone else in our place," Cordi said when they got home, stooping to get through the door. The apartment felt too small and cramped for her monstrous form. It was one in the morning, but everyone was wide awake. "What are you doing?" she asked Silly, who had grabbed the address book by the phone and started flipping through it.

"I'm deciding who I want to sacrifice," she said, squinting at the names.

"I *know* who I'm going to sacrifice," Tessa said, taking off her wig, flakes of skin from her scalp falling off with it. "My dad."

"You don't love him, though," Silly said. "Callum said it has to be someone you love."

"I do, kind of. I mean, he's my father. It's a complicated love. Anyway, I have no problem sacrificing him if I need to. What about you?"

"I think," Silly said timidly, "I might want to sacrifice my grandmother. I mean, I love her but she's not like a nice grandmother. She's always wasting our money, and she beat me all the time. Plus, she's old. She'll die of lung cancer soon anyway."

Tessa nodded.

"This is unbelievable!" Cordi burst out. "You guys are talking about killing people. Murder. For what—so we can all stay pretty and have good jobs?"

"It's not *just a job*," Tessa said, with conviction.

In a way, Cordi understood. She'd never thought she'd achieve her dream of being a designer, and now that her dream had come true, she didn't want to give it up.

"I don't know why you're getting so bent out of shape about this," Tessa said. "Yours is the easiest."

"What?"

"Your sacrifice," Tessa said in a voice that indicated it should be obvious.

"How? Who?"

"Your sister," Tessa said. Cordi had mentioned her troubled relationship with Trina when she'd sacrificed her letter in their last spell, but she didn't think Tessa had read much into it or understood her situation the way Audrey had.

Cordi gave her a horrified look.

"What?" Tessa said. "She deserves whatever's coming to her."

"*Nothing* is coming to her," Cordi snapped. Trina? She couldn't sacrifice Trina. She loved her sister. Didn't she?

The words from Trina's letter flashed in her mind. *Disappointed. Shame.* Burning, on fire, disappearing word by word, but remaining forever branded in her mind and heart.

"The fact that you're thinking about it means you should do it," Tessa said.

"No," Cordi said reflexively, her voice flat.

"Cordi, you look like a gargoyle," Tessa said. "Cute, but a gargoyle. You're all hunched and your hands are like—" She made clawing motions in the air. "You just need to sprout wings. Callum said you have *days*. It's not even about keeping your beauty and success at this point. It's about keeping your soul." Tessa folded her arms, like she knew everything, like she knew what Cordi would decide, like she knew Cordi better than Cordi knew herself.

But Cordi had already made her decision. She and Trina were . . . complicated. But she loved her sister even if things were fraught, even if Trina might not love her back. And besides, there was no way she would sacrifice anyone in her own family, even if it meant whatever fate awaited her.

"No," Cordi said. "I won't do it."

"Cor," Tessa pleaded.

"You'll be lost forever, Cordi," Silly said.

"I know. I won't do it. I can't."

"Please," Tessa said. "I can't lose you. You're like a sister to me—all of you are like sisters. I'd do anything—I'd sacrifice everyone for you. Please, Cordi, just . . . let's just go through with this. It's just one thing, one simple act."

"One simple act of *murder*?" Cordi hissed.

"Yes. And then we'll never have to think about it again! We'll never speak of it."

Cordi shook her head. Tears came to her eyes at Tessa's words, but she wouldn't change her mind.

"Cordi," Tessa said again.

Cordi climbed the ladder to her loft and yanked the curtains closed. She threw herself on the mattress, bone tired. But she didn't sleep at all that night. She kept listening for the door, wondering when Audrey would return, hoping Callum hadn't put her in danger and that she was safe.

The phone rang early the next day. The girls' bedroom doors remained closed. Cordi was glad to be alone, answering quietly so they wouldn't hear her, struggling to growl out the words as coherently as possible. She had a hard time believing that she sounded normal to others.

"There's a problem with one of the designs." Mr. Sinclair's voice sounded hoarse through the phone.

Cordi remembered guiltily how she had left him on the dance floor last night, and winced. Was his voice colder than usual? Was he angry at her?

"Can you come into the office today?" he asked. "I know it's Sunday, but it will put us behind if we wait until tomorrow."

"I can come in," Cordi said.

"Great, thank you, Miss Yin." So formal, as if they hadn't danced closely and seen into each other's souls last night.

It was just as well. She couldn't be with him in her beautiful, changed state anyway. And she was about to lose her soul.

The weight of her decision pressed down on her stooped shoulders as she got ready. The heavy silence of the apartment gave the impression that the others wouldn't be awake anytime soon. She studied herself in the mirror, knowing people wouldn't be able to see her deformities, unless of course they were lurasts, but she couldn't help feeling self-conscious. She applied more makeup than she normally would have, and everything else she covered strategically with gloves, a loose dress, and a cardigan.

As she made the commute to Lacy's, she huddled in the corner of the streetcar, but other passengers only smiled at her the way they had since the first lura spell, as if they didn't notice anything wrong with her, as if she were still the beautiful version of herself the magic had created. She wondered why she didn't feel sadder about the news that she would soon fade away. It felt unreal, impossible, something that couldn't happen to her. And yet, she'd made the choice, and maybe today, maybe tomorrow, the lura would claim her soul.

Mr. Sinclair met her in the lobby of the department store with two cups of coffee. He handed one to her as he studied her face closely.

"Is everything all right?" he asked.

Cordi looked up. A dark bristle covered his jawline, shadows heavy beneath his eyes, which were slightly bloodshot.

"I just didn't sleep well," she admitted.

He nodded. "Neither did I."

They didn't mention their dance last night, an added weight on Cordi's shoulders.

The store was technically open, but not many customers shopped this early on Sunday—most were at church or spending time with their families. The rush would start in the late morning, when everyone would be full and content and happy after a late, heavy breakfast.

"What's wrong with one of the designs?" she asked. "Which one is it?"

They stepped onto the elevator, the metal gears turning. There was always a hitch between the fourth and fifth floors that made Cordi nervous.

"It's the short skirt," he said, referring to a skirt she'd designed with hidden built-in shorts. "The pockets are too bulky, so they're visible, not to mention lumpy in the prototype. We need to make them smaller."

"But that defeats the purpose," she said. "Small pockets are worse than no pockets."

"Exactly."

They fell into silence, and she debated the problem as they made their way to the workroom. Not a tidy area, it was a mess of draped fabrics, prototypes, sample pieces, half-finished garments, and swatches of different colors. The skirt in question lay on the large table in the middle of the room.

Cordi picked it up, turning it this way and that. Because it was twirly and floaty, they'd opted for fabric in a simple, solid green that she'd named Bitter Apple.

"We can't go with thinner fabric for the pockets," Mr. Sinclair said. "Or else they won't be able to hold much weight, and they'd droop."

"That's worse than small pockets," she agreed. "What if we choose a thicker fabric for the actual skirt?"

"It won't be as flowy then."

"We could add pleats. Then it will still twirl."

"Is that too tennis uniform?"

She held the skirt up. "Not if we keep the pleats to a minimum."

He considered it. "Perhaps more of a circle skirt with an elastic waist?"

They debated it for some time. Cordi sketched out a few possible solutions. Then he turned to her and asked, "Can you whip up a few samples for us to make sure it works?"

Cordi's claws curled. "I would but . . . I've been having a bit of trouble with my . . ." Gripping a pen had been a manageable struggle, and she'd been able to handle her other tasks, but for some reason as soon as she started sewing anything, her fingers burned with excruciating pain.

"It's fine." He collected her sketches. "I'm sure we can have one of our seamstresses work on this tomorrow."

"I'm so sorry," she said, feeling like a complete failure.

"Don't be. You've already gone above and beyond by coming in today. I wanted to show you something else." He dug through a pile of fabric scraps and pulled out a binder. "The proofs of the new catalog arrived. We'll have to replace the skirt, of course, but . . ." He trailed off as he handed it to her.

Cordi held the binder in both hands, then set it down on the worktable to flip through the laminated pages with glossy photographs of models wearing her clothes. It felt incredibly surreal—seeing the blouse with the boning on a real woman sitting behind a desk, the scene set so that shoppers could easily picture themselves in the model's place. The Lacy logo at the top corner of each page—it all looked so professional, so smooth and bright and well done. There was the coat she'd designed, and the dress. They were all beautiful and . . . and real.

It hit her that this was her dream coming to life. These were her own creations. Sure, the lura spell had set it in motion, but she had made it happen. It had all been her own work. Perhaps she hadn't needed the magic after all. Perhaps the spells hadn't even been necessary. She set the binder on the table, her fingers trembling as regret saturated every ounce of blood in her body.

"Congratulations," Mr. Sinclair said, interrupting the downward slope of her thoughts. She let out a shaky breath and looked up at him. He smiled.

Cordi felt warm all over, an immediate relief after the numbness that had taken over her body. She resisted the urge to move closer to Mr. Sinclair.

He was looking at her differently. Something had shifted in his gaze, a familiarity he didn't usually allow when they worked together. He cleared his throat and turned away. The light she'd felt from him dissipated, and her body numbed and turned to stone again.

"Thank you for coming on such short notice," Mr. Sinclair said, formal and businesslike. "And for your efficient work. We'll still lose some money—some orders had already been filled when we discovered the mistake—but we would have lost much more without your help."

"I'm sorry I wasn't able to do more."

"Nonsense."

As Cordi gathered her things to leave, she realized that at the rate her body was deteriorating, it might be the last time she saw Mr. Sinclair. Her back ached from forcing it to straighten as much as she could, and her claws had started to poke holes through her gloves. "Mr. Sinclair."

"You know, it's strange that we've worked together all this time and we still don't use our first names. You're welcome to call me Gabriel. Gabe, for short."

"Gabriel. I—you can call me Cordi too, if you'd like."

He smiled.

"Listen, I'm sorry about last night," she said. "I didn't mean to leave so abruptly—there was an emergency. And then . . . things got out of hand. It's complicated, but I had a really nice time with you. It was . . . one of the best dances I've ever had. Well, it was really only half a dance. I suppose we'll have to make up for it . . . one day." She laughed nervously, forcing herself to *stop talking now.*

He looked away. Was he angry? It had been pretty rude, running out on him like that. But when he turned back, she could see his color had risen. He wasn't angry. He was just shy.

"It's fine. I know you and Callum have some sort of . . . of thing going on."

"What? No, we don't."

The elevator dinged, but they both ignored it.

"You look for him at every social event," Mr. Sinclair—Gabriel— said. "You drop everything to run after him."

"I—no—that's—there—I told you." She couldn't tell if she was having difficulty talking because her body was further deteriorating, or if it was just her usual nervous incoherence. "I had something to ask him. But that's it."

"There's nothing going on between the two of you?"

"Definitely not."

"Well." He looked down. Hands in his pockets. Feet shuffling. He pressed the elevator button again. "Sam will be happy."

"There's even less between Sam and me."

He finally met her eyes. The same intensity from last night's dance lit up between them. The warmth returned to her fingers, spreading with relief over her body and aching back.

"Really?" Gabriel said.

Cordi nodded, not trusting herself to speak. He moved closer. His gaze dropped a bit, to the vicinity of her lips.

Then the elevator dinged again, and they sprang apart.

When the doors opened, no one was inside, but Cordi couldn't help but feel guilty, and once again the tingly numbness returned. She desperately wanted to do something, anything. She'd always been a mender, a tendency born out of pure necessity. Her family couldn't afford new things, so she had learned to patch rips and fix broken tools. She'd stitched hems and altered dresses to fit because she had no choice—it was impossible to fit herself into the mold the world had made for everyone else.

But there was nothing left to fix now. This life—with its beauty and riches and success—wasn't made for her, and she could rip apart the seams as often as she wanted, but no matter what, she could never alter the pieces to fit.

They stood quietly side by side as they rode the elevator down. Outside the building, Gabriel paused, like he might say something, but thought better of it. Then he gave a simple nod goodbye and left.

Cordi wandered around a nearby park, not wanting to return to the apartment yet. The full reality of what would happen to her had finally hit home. She was going to die.

Or the spell would take her soul. Would she suffer? Who would tell her parents and Trina? They had disowned her, but they still had a right to know if she was dead.

Most people would have had affairs to settle, wills to write, but Cordi had very little to pass on. She had a total of $500 in her bank account, more money than she'd ever had before. Trina wouldn't turn down $500, but it was hardly enough to bother writing up a will.

She wished she could see her parents, wished they would talk to her. Did they love her? Did they know that she loved them, even though they had treated her terribly? What would life have been like if she and Trina had had a better relationship?

Tempted to take the bus to Chinatown to stop by the store, if only to get a glimpse of her parents through the window of their shop, she forced herself to take a different line back home so she couldn't detour to her parents' house.

She got back to the apartment in the evening. She heard lively conversation as she walked down the hallway, something she hadn't expected after the somber few hours she'd spent on her own. Her steps slowed as she opened the door with caution.

Tessa and Silly sat on the sofa with their backs to her, laughing about something. Audrey faced Callum, who sat on the love seat, his hair perfectly pomaded, his outfit of black slacks and dark-blue jacket pristine.

But there was another person with them.

She sat opposite Callum, sipping a steaming cup of tea. The familiar square of her shoulders under a boring gray cardigan sent a bolt of nostalgia through Cordi. Trina turned to the door as Cordi walked in, a rare smile brightening her face.

"Hi, Cordi," Trina said.

Chapter Thirty-Five

It took Cordi a moment to process everything. Trina, her sister, was there, smiling at her. Smiling. What was Trina doing in the apartment? Why was she smiling?

Tessa propped an elbow over the back of the sofa and turned to Cordi. "Come in. Join us for tea."

Cordi approached slowly, and everyone watched her like *she* was a frightened, wild animal. She sat in the only available seat left, next to Callum, who grinned at her as if it were the most natural thing that he was there along with her sister.

The last time she'd seen Trina, they'd had that terrible argument after Cordi offered her money to help pay their parents' endless bills. And yet here Trina sat, smiling like they were best friends. Like she was happy to see Cordi, which Cordi could not remember ever being true before.

Something seemed off about her, though. A glaze over her eyes as if she were incredibly drunk. Or drugged.

The cup of tea in her hands remained full and steaming.

"I invited Trina over," Tessa said, elbow still propped over the back of the sofa. At least Silly had the decency to look sheepish over what they'd done. Audrey gave Cordi an expression that said everything would be explained later, but nothing about this made sense.

Cordi's fists clenched. She'd *told* them she had no intention of sacrificing anyone, and yet they'd still invited her sister over.

"Have some tea," Tessa said, not acknowledging the anger with which Cordi held herself.

"I'm okay," Cordi said.

"Are you sure?" Trina asked, her voice unusually sweet. "It's delicious."

"Callum made it," Tessa said.

Callum smiled. "We were discussing your success, Cordelia. Funny how your sister knew nothing about it."

"We haven't talked much," Cordi said. "I need to talk to you." She stood, but she didn't know who that was directed to. All of them, actually, except Trina, who gazed adoringly up at her in the most disconcerting way.

"Why don't you take a nap, darling?" Callum said to Trina, and she closed her eyes, her cup and saucer teetering on her lap.

Cordi took the tea to the kitchen to dump in the sink. "What did you do to her?" she demanded.

"Nothing," Callum said. "It's just chamomile. It relaxes you."

"Relaxes," Cordi scoffed. "She's drugged out of her mind."

"It won't matter soon," Tessa said.

"And you," Cordi said, turning on Audrey. "I thought you wanted nothing to do with this. I thought you were the reasonable one."

"I didn't agree to this," Audrey snapped. "I spent the whole day following that idiot around." She jabbed a thumb at Callum. "He had to gather a million supplies from three different places."

"But I'm here," Callum said.

"When we came back, those idiots"—Audrey jerked her head at Tessa, whose mouth dropped open in protest—"had already dragged your sister here. I tried to get your sister to go home, but she didn't listen—she wanted to wait to talk to you. They told her that you had more money to give her."

Cordi wanted to block everything out, but then she stared at her hands. The claws had torn through the gloves, her fingers rough, now covered completely in obsidian scales. Her talons curled, the sharp points reflecting a gleam of light. She caught a flash of her reflection in the dark windows behind Tessa's plants, looking like some creature in the forest. "What . . ."

"See, we have to do this," Tessa said.

"No." Cordi couldn't stop inspecting her fingers as well as her reflection. Even her face had turned scaly. Her arms elongated, her legs bent at odd angles. She was still so numb, she hadn't felt any of the changes. She was a monster.

"Here." Tessa guided Cordi back to her seat and gave her a mug of tea. "Trust me," she said when Cordi sniffed it suspiciously. "We'll figure this out together."

Cordi wrapped her numb hands around the cup, feeling the warmth distantly, as if through thick leather gloves.

"Drink it. I promise I would never do anything to hurt you," Tessa said. She rubbed Cordi's arms. "You're my best friend."

Cordi's heart swelled at those words. She'd always longed to be someone's best friend. Now she had three close friends who looked out for her. And Tessa, dear sweet Tessa, had shown her what family could be.

But what Tessa and Silly wanted was impossible. She couldn't go through with it.

She sipped the tea, and it tasted just like the jasmine tea she'd bought at the grocery store. It was soothing in a way she desperately needed.

Trina's head lolled on the back of the armchair. In rest, her brows remained pulled together, the lines around her mouth tight. She was only ten years older than Cordi, but she could have passed for their mother. Despite how mean and resentful Trina had been, Cordi would always appreciate that Trina had made her own sacrifices to take care of her while their parents worked constantly.

"I can't do it," Cordi said. "I'm not going to sacrifice her in my place."

"Shh." Tessa sat on the arm of Cordi's chair and leaned over to hug her. "You don't have to."

Cordi leaned against her friend. Tessa had been so kind to her, so warm and loving and accepting in every way. Her arms, though bony, felt strong and comforting as she held Cordi, and rocked and patted her like a baby.

Cordi's eyelids grew heavy. She stared down at the tea. "I'm not going to do it," she repeated, but her tongue and lips were swollen, the words coming out slurred.

"Don't worry," Tessa said. "You won't have to." She cupped the side of Cordi's face with one hand, pressing her head down to rest on her shoulder. Cordi let her eyes close, too exhausted to fight even as Tessa spoke the next words. "We'll do it for you."

There was smoke everywhere. In her nose and eyes, filling the whole apartment. Cordi lay on the cold floor of the living room. The furniture was gone—no, it was pushed against the walls.

She blinked and tried to get up, but her entire body felt like she'd been dunked in the grimy LA River, clothes and all. Her muscles refused to respond.

Her vision cleared as she fought to stay awake. The shapes of bodies moved all around her, but the only person Cordi recognized was Trina, who lay on her back next to Cordi. Her eyes were closed, her face tense even in rest, the skin puckered between her eyebrows.

"Trina?" Cordi said, but it came out in a monstrous grunt. She looked down at her misshapen, ugly body, limbs distorted, back curved.

Callum stepped between her and Trina, speaking in a foreign language.

Cordi lifted her head enough to see Tessa and Silly standing with Callum in a circle. Candlelight cast the room in flickering shadows, little pinpricks of flames surrounding Cordi and Trina. Instead of a metal bowl at the center of the circle, it was her and Trina. Because they were the sacrifices.

Where was Audrey? She tried to turn but the smoke grew thicker, and she didn't see her anywhere. She heard a thump, like the distant sound of a fist on the door, but no one else paid it any attention. Audrey must be trapped in her room—Cordi was sure she wouldn't have simply let this happen.

Callum's voice rose as he chanted, raising his arms and spreading red powder into the air. Cordi turned to the floor to keep it out of her eyes. Some of the powder fell onto Trina's face, and it started glowing hot and bright like the embers of a fire, singeing her skin. Smoke rose from where the powder touched her.

Pinpricks dotted Cordi's own skin, a searing sensation spreading all over her body. Her eyes burned, her vision clouded. She blinked, and it grew smokier, and all she could see was Trina's face in front of her. Groaning, her sister woke, and she looked around the room in confusion. Neither of them moved, and Cordi wasn't sure that they could have if they tried.

"Cordi?" Trina whispered.

"Trina," Cordi said. "I'm sorry. I'll get us out of here. Don't worry."

Trina's throat throbbed, and Cordi saw a sharpness in her eyes that wasn't there before. The drugged haziness from earlier was gone. "Cordi, I'm sorry too," she said.

"What? Why? This isn't your fault—it's mine."

"Something's wrong. And I need to tell you . . ." Trina swallowed. "I was so cruel to you. I don't know . . ." She squeezed her eyes shut. "Don't know why."

"It's okay," Cordi said. She tried to block out Callum's voice through the fog. He spoke words she didn't understand to a rhythm that reminded her very much of a clock's chime. "We'll talk about it later. I need to——"

"Cordi, look at me," Trina said. Her words came faster, no longer slurred. "I'm sorry. I was a terrible sister. I should have been kinder to you. But . . . my life hasn't been easy either, you know. I wasn't born here like you—I came with Mother and Father, and they relied on me so much, to do everything, to translate for them when I barely knew English myself, to understand all that was going on, and I was just a kid! And then you came along, and they were so kind to you, their perfect child."

If Trina didn't look so desperate, Cordi might have protested. She'd never been their parents' favorite. She'd always been the wrongdoer, the one who didn't understand their traditions, the one constantly getting disowned. Trina was the one they put on a pedestal, often comparing Cordi to her older sister and asking why she couldn't be more like her.

Trina continued. "They did everything for you—everything they didn't do for me. They gave you all the right things, taught you so much. All the things they didn't do for me. And I was jealous. I know you're my little sister and I should take care of you, but I was a kid too. I deserved love and care too." Tears filled her eyes, the first time Cordi had ever seen her exhibit any emotion other than bitterness.

"You do," Cordi said. "You are loved. I care about you."

Trina squeezed her eyes shut, tears spilling from them. "I don't hate you. I don't hate you, Cordi."

Cordi realized she had never understood her sister, had never considered what she'd been through. She'd always viewed Trina within the context of her own pain, which was exactly how Trina must have viewed her. They both had so much to learn from each other, so much to apologize for and forgive.

"It's okay," Cordi said. "I don't hate you either."

Trina smiled. A tear fell from her eye, pooling at the corner by her nose. Cordi wished she could brush it away.

Callum's voice grew louder. Behind Trina, his shape appeared through the thick fog, his face tense with anticipation. He leaned down, his movements quick and urgent.

"No," Cordi growled, but she still couldn't move.

Then, before her eyes, with nothing she could do to stop it, Callum reached over Trina's body with a short knife and slid the blade across Trina's throat.

"Noooo!" Cordi roared.

Trina's face went still. Her body twitched as blood poured from the gaping wound. She jerked several more times, then stopped.

Cordi couldn't breathe, couldn't think, couldn't believe the horror, even as it replayed itself in her mind. Trina's throat was slit. She wasn't breathing. She wasn't even frowning anymore. She was dead.

"No," Cordi gasped, and finally managed to wrench herself upright. She crawled to Trina but couldn't bring herself to touch her.

"Did it work?" Tessa asked.

Cordi whirled on her. Smoke filled the room, but she spotted Tessa's tall figure in the haze. "You did this." Her words came out in growls.

Tessa flinched. "Why is she still like that? We sacrificed her sister. Shouldn't she turn back to her normal self?"

Callum didn't answer. He wasn't paying attention, an expression of bliss on his face. He spread his arms, and the red embers that covered Trina's face floated to him, covering his body in bright sparks. His skin glowed like a hot ember.

He opened his eyes. They were the deepest shade of red, though as the seconds passed, they darkened, and Cordi couldn't remember what color they had been before.

Then he smiled. "Thank you," he said.

Her insides turned to ice. Something was very wrong. Not just the fact that her sister was dead, but there was something else, something changing inside her.

"What did you do?" Tessa asked. She sounded angry when she should have been scared.

Callum laughed, sending shivers down Cordi's curved spine. "You idiots. You really thought you could have whatever you wanted for free? No payment whatsoever?"

"What happened?" Tessa demanded. "Why isn't Cordi changing back? You said if we sacrificed her sister, she'd return to normal."

"Oh, you really are so precious," Callum said.

Tessa ran at him, nails extended.

He shoved her aside easily. She crumpled to the floor like a rag doll.

"I took your souls," he said. "You greedy, stupid girls wanted everything so badly, you didn't even think for one second of the consequences. So I took your sister's soul too." He laughed at Cordi, who still crouched over Trina's limp body. "It's what you deserved."

Cordi dragged herself to her full monstrous height, towering over him, and she reached out with her knifelike claws. Callum ducked, but not before she caught him in the shoulder. He cried out, clutching his arm.

Silly was sobbing in the corner, covering her face.

Callum grimaced at all of them. "You deserve to die," he said. And then he ran for the door.

Cordi scrambled after him, but her monstrous form made her move awkwardly, her limbs still stiff from the drugged tea. When he slammed the door shut behind him, she couldn't wrap her claws around the knob.

"No," Tessa breathed. "No, no, this was supposed to work. He said he would fix everything." Tears streamed down her face. In the flickering light of the candles, she looked ghoulish, shadows elongating her nose and cheekbones.

"How could you?" Cordi growled.

Even though her words were incoherent, Tessa seemed to understand. "I'm sorry, Cor. I couldn't let you die or turn into . . . into this." Tessa gestured at Cordi. "And she was so horrid to you. And when I called her and told her to come over for tea, all she cared about was if you had more money to give her."

It sounded horrible, yes, but Cordi understood why Trina couldn't think about anything else. Growing up, it had been difficult for Cordi to *not* think about money because they lived under constant threat of hunger and eviction. Trina wasn't being greedy; she was just trying to survive.

And now she was dead.

"I thought it would work," Tessa said, "that we could change you back."

Cordi wanted to be angry—she *was* angry. But her heart was so full of grief, she had no room left for anything else.

She leaned down and scooped Trina easily into her spindly, muscular arms. Her sister's body felt light and thin, almost insubstantial. She'd always been a small person. It was only in Cordi's mind that she'd seemed so big, so invincible.

Cordi didn't know what to do, but she knew she couldn't stay there, in the apartment, with the people who had killed her sister. Callum had wielded the knife, but Tessa and Silly had lured Trina there, had drugged Cordi, had assisted in the murder.

Mother and Father would be devastated. And who would tell them? Even if she could go to them, how could she possibly explain what had happened?

But she could bring Trina home to them.

She carried her sister to the door.

"Where are you going?" Tessa asked. "You can't go, Cordi. Please stay, we'll figure this out."

Cordi turned and roared. She had no more words, just anger and frustration and despair, and her scream filled the apartment, rattled the windows.

Tessa covered her head with her arms. Clumps of ashen skin fell from her scalp. Silly wailed louder.

Cordi had never seen them so frightened of her. Of what they had done.

She turned and carried her sister away.

Chapter Thirty-Six

Cordi was distantly aware of the streets, the buildings with their bright lights, the cars rushing past. She couldn't process anything beyond her suffocating grief, and all she could focus on was Trina's body in her arms as she carried her back to their parents.

She didn't mind the walk through the quiet, dark streets of downtown LA. It was so late, even the clubs and bars had closed, and not a soul was around. In her monstrous form, she was much taller, her longer limbs carrying her quickly through the districts, reaching Chinatown as the sky began to lighten. Soon, Mother and Father would open the shop, probably panicked over Trina, who had never once come home past curfew.

What to do? Should she take Trina to their house? Leave her body for them to find? But then they would worry all day. Better for them to find out sooner rather than later.

The store was closer than the house anyway, so Cordi headed there. Thankfully it wasn't open yet. She didn't know what time it was, but she knew she didn't have long.

The parking lot of the small shopping center was empty. Cordi placed her sister's body gently down on the sidewalk in front of the store. Slumped over, she looked like she could have just been sleeping.

Cordi wanted to smooth Trina's hair from her face but couldn't because of her claws. She didn't know how long she sat next to her sister's body, thinking of all the things she'd meant to say, both the good and the bad, the apologies and the accusations, but mostly she thought about the love they could have shared if only they had known how. If only they had been taught.

She was about to get up and leave when someone screamed. It was Mother. She shouted and sobbed as she ran to her daughter's body.

"No!" Mother wailed as Cordi slinked away. "Na-Na. Na-Na." Mother shook Trina's shoulders, then screamed again at the sight of her blood and the gash in her neck when Trina's head rolled back.

Cordi couldn't watch. She ran. It was easier to move on all fours now. Mother's wails followed her down the street, and Cordi slipped down an alleyway and hid behind a dumpster, even though it seemed like no one could see her, her heart pounding. A stray cat hissed at her as it darted over the wall.

She had no idea what to do next. No clue where to go. She could go back to the apartment, but she couldn't deal with the Mais, not now, not yet.

She had no other ideas. No one else cared about her, and the realization was a stab to the heart. She had thought she'd found her new family in the Mais. They'd been like sisters to her, and she had wanted so badly to fit into their little group, to belong in a way that she never had before, that she'd let them change her. She'd wanted them to be her new family. She'd forgotten that she had her own family, and that her sister cared about her even if she didn't know how to show it.

Now, she had no one. Not her sister. Not her parents. Not the Mais, who had betrayed her. She was all alone, and it was just as well that she was a monster, doomed to lose her soul.

Cordi was restless, so she moved aimlessly, ending up at Elysian Park, its fields wide and dotted with picnic benches. She headed up a dusty trail searching for solitude and ended up close to a water reservoir, where she sat on a tree stump and let tears flow freely down her face. No one seemed to notice her, the ugly creature skulking along the grass. Their eyes glided past her monstrous body. She still wore the huge cardigan and boxy dress she'd thrown on to go to the office yesterday, spikes and knobby limbs poking at the fabric at odd angles. Her time with Gabriel Sinclair felt so far away, a distant memory.

She had no idea how long she sat in the park, watching children chase after the ducks. The squirrels and other critters had no regard for her, just like the people.

This must be what it meant to give up your soul. To become invisible to everyone. Callum had said she would have days, but he must have lied about that too.

"Cordelia?"

Cordi gave a start. She turned and almost ran off into the lake.

Cressida Thompson stood on the grass, looking like the perfect society girl in her yellow, belted A-line dress with matching gloves and pillbox hat. The exact same outfit that Cordi always pictured she would wear one day when she was famous and rich, when she had *made* it.

"Cordelia, that *is* you."

Cordi wondered if she could dart past Cressida. How had the girl found her? How could Cressida even see her when everyone else looked past her, everyone but the Mais and Callum? And what must she think of Cordi the monster?

Why didn't she run away?

"It's okay," Cressida said. "I'm here to help."

"How?" Cordelia grunted.

To her surprise, Cressida understood her. "Gabe came to me. He asked me to help."

"Gabe?" Cordi frowned. "Mr. Sinclair?" *How did he know? When?*

"I'll take you home first and then explain," Cressida said. "About what Callum did."

"You . . . know about that?"

"Yes. But come with me, Cordelia. You need to rest. You look exhausted."

Rest. It sounded amazing, a place to lie down. But could she trust Cressida? Everyone else had betrayed her.

"You don't have anywhere else to go," Cressida said, as if she could read her thoughts. "So come with me. Let me help you."

Cordi debated it. Cressida had no reason to betray her. Cordi didn't have anything that she wanted. And she was lost and alone and had no one else.

She got up and followed her home.

Cressida lived in a towering mansion in the heights just a mile outside downtown proper. She didn't say much on their way there, sitting in the back seat with Cordi while a chauffeur navigated the traffic.

Once home, she led Cordi to a room on the second floor. The place was huge, shiny with sharp angles, like a museum, with sculptures on white pillars and canvas paintings on the walls. Cressida took Cordi straight to a sun-drenched bedroom, decorated with heavy, cream-colored furniture and an inviting, plush bed.

"I'll check up on you later," she said, and left Cordi to herself.

Exhausted from walking all night and not sleeping much the previous day, Cordi collapsed on the bed, still dressed in her ill-fitting clothes, and passed out.

When she woke up, it was still daylight, or perhaps an entire day had passed, Cordi wasn't sure. A glare on the floor beamed straight into her eyes. She went to the windows to pull the drapes closed and passed a mirror. She barely recognized the tall, hunched creature staring back. Her dress looked like a baggy pillowcase covering the angular body underneath, nothing like what she normally wore or designed. If Mr. Sinclair saw her now, he'd be repulsed, but she'd probably never see him again. Her heart ached.

She took off her cardigan and studied her scaly skin. She looked like she'd been burned alive.

There was a knock at the door.

"Come in," she said in an animallike grunt.

Cressida came in with a fancy mirrored tray. "Thought you might like some food."

Cordi's stomach growled as if on cue. The tray held a whole rotisserie chicken and some bread. Cordi began scarfing it down without a thought as to how she looked. She hadn't eaten at all yesterday, and she was still hungry even after she'd cleaned all the meat off the bone. She felt like she could devour the whole carcass.

"Tell me what happened," Cressida said. She sat on the tufted bench at the end of the bed.

"I thought you said you knew. About Callum. About what he did."

"I have a close idea. It isn't the first time he, or other lurasts, have tricked an innocent into giving up their soul to gain power."

Cordi sucked in a breath. Cressida knew more about lura than her bright-eyed, cheery debutante persona let on, and she talked about the taboo subject as if she were talking about the newest dress at Lacy's. Her expression revealed a rawness Cordi had never seen before.

So Cordi told her everything: how she'd met Callum, how he'd stopped by with a bottle of wine, how they hadn't believed him when he promised them everything they'd ever wanted. Shame and embarrassment bore down on her when she admitted that she and the Mais had wanted desperately to be successful and rich, to be, essentially, like Cressida, and to have a chance to join the coveted society Cressida belonged to.

"I didn't want to do it," Cordi said when she got to the part about sacrificing Trina. "But they tricked me. They're willing to kill just to keep this—this—" She held out her hands, though of course she no longer resembled the image that she had given up her soul for. As Cressida listened to Cordi's story, nothing on her face showed surprise, or even horror at the knowledge of Trina's death. Cordi looked at Cressida. "You're a lurast too, aren't you?" How else could she see Cordi's monstrousness?

"Yes," Cressida said, but then shook her head. "I mean, no, it's complicated. I come from a family of lurasts. I don't practice it myself, necessarily, not if I can help it. But the thing about lura is that once you've cast a spell, made a deal, it never ends. It's passed down through the generations. It's a permanent, ongoing sacrifice, and the debt will never be repaid. Except with death."

"But why don't you look like this?" Cordi asked.

"My great-great-great-aunt, or something like that, made the ultimate sacrifice," Cressida said. "She gave up her soul and life so that her children and their descendants could have it all. So that we can be what you see. There's a whole group, a Society . . . an Order. In fact, all the elite members of the Society are part of the Order. People think we're so exclusive because we're all snobs, but the truth is, you can only be one of us if you have your own pact with the lura."

Cordi blinked, not sure that she had heard right. "You're saying that all the rich families are lurasts?"

"In some way or another. They've either sacrificed themselves so their descendants can have all the privilege and success that lura promises. Or . . . they sacrificed someone else. More than likely the latter. Our Society doesn't have the best history, since we're being completely honest. Everyone in it has a dark past. You don't get to be this"—she gestured at herself—"or have all of this"—she waved at the room, the house, the clothes, the furniture, the . . . everything—"by being a good person."

Cordi tried to absorb the new information. Part of her was relieved that she wasn't the only person to have been so selfish and greedy, to want what she wanted so badly that she'd given up her soul to have it. Other people had done the same. Had done worse.

And yet, another part of her was horrified. It sickened her that people would knowingly kill and sacrifice others just for success. Or good looks. Things that really didn't amount to anything at the end of the day.

"The dresses," Cordi said. "Did you know . . . when you commissioned me for the designs?"

Cressida smiled, her expression a bit dreamy. "No. I really did want a trousseau." She laughed. "We're just drawn to each other. Lurasts, I mean. It's the power, we can't resist. And you have a magnetic pull about you. The magic likes you."

"How do we stop it?" Cordi asked. "How do we prevent this from ever happening again?"

Cressida took a deep breath. "People have always tried to destroy lurasts. That's why it's all so secretive and exclusive. We can't trust just anyone, and not everyone has what it takes to join us."

"That's not what I mean. Can we somehow stop the whole thing from happening? So people won't be sacrificed just because of other people's greed?"

"We try to prevent that. That's why the Order was formed, so we can keep strict watch on members who abuse their power. It's certainly okay to sacrifice yourself and whatever offerings you wish, as long as you don't trick others or use them for your personal gain. That's why we're stepping in to punish Callum. A case like this is the only time it's acceptable to sacrifice someone else in your stead."

"So it's true. You *can* sacrifice someone else in your place. Callum didn't lie about that."

"No, he didn't lie. You could have chosen to sacrifice your sister's soul to the lura, and you would have permanently kept what the spell gave you. But he betrayed you. Instead of using your sister's sacrifice to complete your spell and make your transformation permanent, he tricked you and made a separate pact with the lura to keep the power for himself."

"Why?" Cordi was aware of the whine in her voice, but she simply didn't understand. "We've never done anything to him."

"Callum isn't part of a lurast family," Cressida said. "Someone must have taken pity on him and given him his first spell, and now he needs to continue making sacrifices because neither he nor anyone in his family has paid the ultimate sacrifice to keep the power. The thing about a luracal spell is that it's only as strong as the sacrifice you make. It's only as powerful as the love you have for what you give up. So if you try to cheat, if you offer something you don't love, it backfires. It may work for a time, but these things have a way of evening out."

"So he still needs to sacrifice someone he loves? Was he planning to make us the ultimate sacrifice?"

"He has to love you for it to work. Or you have to love him and sacrifice yourself willingly. That's why his power is only temporary, which means he has to continue finding ways to . . . refuel, so to speak. What he did—it goes against our Society's rules. He should have told you the consequences of the spell to begin with. It's why I—we—are going to help you. As restitution for what one of our own did to you."

"How?"

"We'll use Callum as your sacrifice. He has to pay for what he's done."

Callum deserved it, but she wasn't a murderer. The image of blood gushing from Trina's throat replayed in her mind.

"The others have already agreed to it," Cressida said.

"The others? You mean the Mais? You spoke to them?"

"Yes. Well, Audrey called Gabe because she knew he'd have my number. They're both very concerned about you. *Gabe* was very concerned . . . you should have seen him. He's never . . . he refuses to come near here, but he did for you."

Her heart leaped. But it didn't matter. Not when she was a monster.

"So I came to your apartment earlier today, but you were gone," Cressida continued. "If it's any consolation, my parents were going to offer you a place among us. An elite membership."

Cordi wanted to laugh, a hysterical, nonsensical laugh, but she managed to bite it back. It was all so stupid. All their dreams had been so superficial, so pretentious and dumb. What did it matter? What was the point of having access to a pool and bar and pampering when she was going to lose her soul?

"We went to your apartment, and I saw the girls in . . . a bad state," Cressida continued. "And that's when I knew. I suspected, of course.

When your friends showed up at the Society looking so . . . Without a clue as to your background, I knew that something suspicious, something luracal, was going on. I sent Gabe away—he doesn't want anything to do with this business. I asked someone from our Order to help find you. Like I said, we're drawn to each other, so it wasn't hard. And you, especially, Cordelia, you have an energy about you. I could tell right away that you had a gift. The lura likes some people more than others. It's why you've been so successful—with lura added to your natural talents, it was only a matter of time before you became even more famous and prosperous."

"It's also why I've changed into this so quickly," Cordi said, holding out her claws. "Isn't it? The other girls didn't deteriorate so fast."

"That's true."

"If we sacrifice Callum, all of this will go away? I'll change back into myself?"

"You'll be a lurast, through and through. It is a great honor, Cordelia. I mean, think about what you can do with your beauty and riches. What you can accomplish with your . . . privilege. You could help other girls like you. Our Society very rarely accepts anyone new, but my parents both agreed that you're special."

Cordi remained silent, unwilling to entertain what Cressida suggested.

"Cordelia," Cressida said kindly, leaning forward. She had the patient air of a mother reasoning with a five-year-old. "It's either this or death. There's no way to reverse it. You offered up the sacrifice the moment you said the words *take this gift*. Otherwise, it wouldn't have worked." She averted her gaze. "I didn't ask for this, you know. At least you had a choice. Mine was made for me."

Cordi wanted to point out that whether Cressida had made the decision or not, she still reaped the benefits. Just looking at her beautiful face, her slender, elegantly dressed body sitting on expensive furniture that cost more than Cordi's parents' house, in a mansion that was bigger than the Mais' entire apartment building. She was rich and successful, afforded a position in life above others simply because she was born into the right family.

"If I make the sacrifice and go along with it," Cordi said, "it would be permanent. I'll look different forever."

Cressida nodded. "We've all had to make sacrifices at one point or another—to become who we are."

Chapter Thirty-Seven

Cordi was so unbelievably tired that she slept for most of the day, and when she woke, the room was cast in the amber glow of sunlight. A knock came at the door, and she forced herself out of bed to open it.

There stood Sam Thompson, dressed somberly in a suit appropriate for a funeral, his face revealing nothing when he looked upon her grotesque form.

"Sam," she growled. "Hi."

"Good evening," he said, not greeting her by name or indicating in any way that he knew her, had danced with her at the Society, and escorted her to the gala. "It's time." Usually chatty, Sam was silent as he led her downstairs, through the hallway to a door that led into the basement.

Her joints protested as she took the steps slowly, finally giving up and dropping to all fours. The rest of the house had been kept dim, but underground, the lights were almost blindingly bright.

It wasn't like any basement Cordi had seen before. The floor was finished in shiny, pink-glazed marble, the ceilings high, and it was outfitted like a modern ballroom with a full bar in the corner, though no one staffed it.

Cressida stood in the center of the room, in front of a group of ten people. They all looked very serious, dressed in the style of people with no natural sense of fashion but who could afford quality. Cordi was shocked to see Ms. Lacy among them, but the woman gave no sign of recognizing Cordi, nor did Ramona Rickens from the Pockets of Poverty charity.

"Welcome to the Society," Cressida said. "The real Society. These men and women are the heads of their clans. They've come here to punish Callum for disobeying the order."

The people's expressions remained neutral at being introduced, and they didn't seem shocked to see Cordi in her monstrous state.

"Can they cure me?" Cordi asked.

Cressida looked at her sympathetically. "I'm afraid not. A deal is a deal. You gave up your soul for success, and you must pay for it. Or make a different deal, like I mentioned before. Callum tricked you, so we as the Order will punish him for his crimes. We'll sacrifice him in your place . . ." She paused, pressing her lips together. "There is one catch, however. The nature of the spell he used requires the sacrifice of someone you love."

Cordi shook her head. "I can't do that."

"I know."

"And I definitely don't love Callum."

"We've come up with a compromise. Instead of sacrificing someone you love to complete the spell, you can have Callum's power instead. Then you can make your own deal with the lura, buy yourself some time to figure out what to do."

"I don't want to be a lurast."

"Whether you want to or not, you already are."

Cordi had an overwhelming urge to lie down, to throw herself to the floor.

Cressida patted her on her spiky shoulder. "If you want my advice, Cordelia, do it. Take this offer. We don't give it lightly. We're planning to punish Callum anyway. You might as well benefit from his death after what he did to you and your friends. After what he did to your sister."

"But I don't want revenge."

"If not for yourself, think about all the girls he could hurt in the future. This isn't the first time he's taken advantage of someone innocent, and it probably won't be the last. Except this time he made the mistake of taking advantage of someone who can do something about it, who has the power to stop him. You."

Cressida was right. Callum preyed on young, hopeful dreamers, full of wants and passions. How many other souls had he stolen? How many more would he take if no one stopped him?

"Where is he now?" Cordi asked.

"He's on his way here," Cressida said. "He knows he can't ignore a summons from the Order. If he does, he'll get kicked out and sever his connection to the lura. He'll have to continue sacrificing without receiving any power in return just to stay alive. And eventually he'll die anyway. So you may as well use his death to your benefit."

A chime rang. One of the Society members left the room.

"That must be Callum at the door," Cressida said.

But when the man came back, he didn't have Callum with him. He had the three Mais—Tessa, Silly, and Audrey. Silly and Tessa looked . . . terrible. Tessa's bald scalp was scabbed and bleeding, and her face looked oddly raw. It took Cordi a moment to realize that she'd lost her eyebrows and eyelashes. Her lips were cracked, her body bone-thin, her dress hanging off her skeleton.

Silly didn't look any better, hunched over. She no longer wore glasses, presumably because she had no reason to—her eyes were clouded over as if she were blind.

Audrey grabbed Cordi's hands. "I tried to stop them. They locked me in my room—I heard Callum doing the spell, and what happened after . . . I couldn't do anything." Her face tensed in rage. "I'm so sorry, Cordi."

Out of habit, Cordi wanted to reply that it was okay, but she shook her head because she knew it wasn't, and because nothing ever would be okay again.

"You can see me," Cordi blurted out instead. She had been invisible to everyone else.

"I think the magic gets stronger every time I'm around a luracal spell," Audrey said. "And I was so close to that last one with Callum . . . and your sister . . ." Her voice trailed off.

Cordi swallowed a knot in her throat.

"Cordi," Tessa said, rushing up to her. "I'm so sorry. We thought it would work. We—"

Cordi pulled away, because it was either that or smack her friend— no, Tessa wasn't a friend. She was manipulative and selfish, and Cordi had simply been another sucker who fell for her charms.

Audrey grabbed Cordi's elbow and pulled her aside.

"There's an alternative," she hissed.

"What?"

"Cressida," Audrey said, and Cressida walked over, not looking pleased at being summoned. "Callum betrayed us, but he wasn't wrong. Cordi can still sacrifice someone she loves and complete the first spell, right?"

Cordi was already shaking her head, but then Cressida's answer made her stop.

"Yes."

Cordi huffed, making an unflattering grunt. "That's preposterous."

"I know it sounds insane," Audrey said, and turned to Cressida. "But it's an option. Right? You told me, on the phone, you said . . ."

Cressida nodded. "Callum's death will buy you time, but in the end, you will still have to make a sacrifice."

"Stop—I won't do it," Cordi interjected. "Who would I even sac- rifice? My parents?"

Audrey's eyes flickered to Tessa and Silly, but she remained tight-lipped.

Cordi almost burst into laughter. "Them? I don't love them."

"I think you do a little."

"After what they did to my sister?"

"They're dying anyway," Audrey snapped. "And if you have to sacrifice someone eventually, then you might as well just get it over with now."

Cressida also met Cordi's eyes with intense sincerity. "It's true. Look at them. They're even worse off than you. We've agreed to punish Callum, but we're not going to murder other family members so that these girls can become one of us. This is a gift, one they're extending to you, and only you. You should take it, Cordelia."

Cordi sucked in a breath. She could never do something so horrible to her only friends. And yet . . . after what they'd done . . . after they had tricked Trina and murdered her . . . Maybe it wasn't so out of the question. And Audrey had a point—if they were going to die anyway, their deaths could at least be for something.

She shook her head, more out of confusion than refusal.

"Damn it, Cordi," Audrey whispered.

Tessa had crept closer as the three of them whispered furiously to each other, and her face showed a deep sadness mixed with resignation.

"Do it, Cordi," Tessa said.

Anger flared every time Cordi looked at Tessa, picturing her sister's slit throat all over again. A small sense of satisfaction filled her at how ugly Tessa had become, though it was nothing compared to what she deserved.

"Cordi, I'm so sorry," Tessa said. "Everything is so messed up. It was terrible what we did . . . your sister . . ." Tessa bit back a sob. "I thought I was doing the right thing. I thought that it would cure you, make you beautiful again." She couldn't hold back the tears now, and it wasn't the pretty crying that she'd done in the past, but a full, sobbing ugly cry, snot dripping from her nose.

Cordi found her heart hardening even though it hurt to see Tessa like that. But Tessa had done it. She was responsible. Silly always did what Tessa wanted, and together, they had killed Trina. Cordi had told them again and again it wasn't what she wanted, and they had done it anyway.

"I don't expect you to forgive us," Tessa added. "So just take me as the sacrifice. At least . . . at least we can save you."

Cordi felt numb all over, unable to make a decision.

"We're all fading away," Silly said, her voice faint, as if she were already gone. "It'll all be over soon."

Cordi was furious with them, but she didn't want them to *die*. And yet, what could she do? What should she do?

Cordi turned to Cressida and the somber faces of the members of the Order. "Is there anything you can do for them?" she asked. "Can't I buy all of us time? Why does it have to be just me?"

"You're the one who would benefit the most," Cressida said. "Your transformation indicates that the lura works best with you." As she talked, Society members prepared for the ritual. A woman poured powder into a bowl, mixing in droplets from a tincture. Another lit candles and placed them on the floor in a circle, the flames casting long shadows on the wall. It looked like a much more complex version of the rituals they performed in the apartment, like the one Callum had done on—

Cordi cut off the thought. She didn't want to replay Trina's death in her mind, repeating like a broken television set stuck on the same static-lined scene.

A man handed Cressida a cloth, and she began wiping her fingers with it, revealing markings that looked eerily familiar. It took Cordi a moment to realize that she'd seen them before—on Callum's hands when he'd taken off his gloves before performing the first ritual on the Mais. The markings were black, crisscrossing over each other just beneath the skin, like darkened veins.

Cordi turned to the other girls. "But I don't want to be a lurast. One of you should take the power. Figure out how to save the others."

"It has to be you, Cordelia," Cressida said. "It only works with someone who's shown signs that they can endure such power. From the way your body has transformed instead of deteriorating like theirs, you're the only one who could possibly withstand it."

It was true. Tessa and Silly looked like they were decaying, whereas Cordi had morphed into some sort of monster.

"Oh." Someone had appeared at the door. It was Callum. No one had heard him enter. "Shit." He took one look at Cordi and then bolted.

Cordi acted on instinct and lunged. She pinned him to the floor, her sharp claws digging into his shoulder, where a bandage covered the wound she'd inflicted on him earlier. She was tempted to tear him to pieces, rip out his throat with her jaws. Her lips pulled back, and she bared her teeth. Only a small part of her remained in control, aware that everyone watched her, aware that she was still human and not entirely a monster.

"Argh! Get off! Please—I'm sorry—I'll fix everything," Callum begged.

"Why did you do it, Callum?" Cordi asked, easing back, ready to pounce on him if he tried to escape.

Callum wouldn't meet her eyes, his gaze sliding over her spindly legs and sharp claws. His avoidance reminded her of something.

"Rachel Cunningham," Cordi said. His head snapped up. "That girl you were dating. You used her too, didn't you? That's why she died in the end."

"I didn't mean for her to die," he said. "She wanted it, just like you, and she was so close. She could have had it all, but she couldn't do it in the end. She wasn't willing to kill her little sister. We had a fight. I tried to warn her, I swear I did, but she wouldn't listen to me."

"But why us?" Cordi asked. "We've never done anything to you. We didn't even know you."

Callum sputtered something unintelligible, his lips quivering.

"What?" Cordi demanded, annoyed. Callum had been so charming and confident when he had tricked them. Now he had actual tears in his eyes, his body trembling as he curled into himself. She found his manner pathetic, not even worthy of sympathy. "Speak up."

"You w-were . . ." he stammered. "You were easy."

"Easy?"

"No one would have missed you," he continued. "Your family abandoned you. And no one important cares about girls like you. No one notices. With girls like you it's always been . . . easy."

Cordi couldn't breathe. *Easy.* That's what it came down to. They were small, insignificant prey.

"Please, Cordelia," Callum begged. He crawled toward her and clasped his hands. "Please. I'll fix this. I always find a way. I always find the next sacrifice. I can buy us time—"

"Stop your sniveling," Cressida said, standing over him. Two men grabbed Callum and pulled him across the floor. "You know that won't work for much longer. You've been living on borrowed time, Callum. Stealing other girls' sacrifices only works temporarily. You'll have to make the ultimate sacrifice in the end."

"I would do it—" Callum sobbed brokenly. "I just . . . I don't have anyone."

"You mean you don't love anyone," Cressida said. "You never have. That's why you'll never be a true lurast. You'll never be one of us."

"Please . . ." He collapsed onto his elbows, crouched like a shriveled insect.

Behind them the men and women of the Order drew a circle in salt on the ground around the lit candles, big enough to encompass several people.

"We know what you did to these girls, Callum. And possibly other victims. Your lies and trickery. You deliberately went against the Societal Pact. You abused your luracal gifts, and now you'll be punished."

"Don't take away my lura." His eyes shifted all around the circle, where the other members had moved to surround him. He clambered up onto his knees, still held down by the two men who'd dragged him to the center of the circle. "Please. I'll change. I'll help these girls. I'll reverse the spell."

"You know you can't reverse a luracal spell," Cressida said.

"I'll do anything, please." His eyes fell on Cordi in fear. "Don't take my power away."

"Don't worry." Cressida moved out of the circle and nodded at the men, who strapped Callum to chains anchored on the floor. "We're not going to take your power away. We're planning to take your life. A sacrifice for the one you stole."

Callum's eyes widened, mouth stretched in terror. "No—please—"

Cressida turned to Cordi. "Will you accept it, in restitution for the wrong done to you?"

Cordi hesitated. Callum writhed on the floor, trying to free himself. The men moved out of the circle and joined the other Order members, who mixed powders in small marble bowls.

"Yes," Tessa said, taking Cordi's hand. Cordi tried to pull away, but her claws left a red line across Tessa's palm, making the other girl cry out, so she stopped. Tessa looked up at her. "What we did to your sister was wrong. We had no right. You should take the power. Learn from our mistakes. Help others like us who don't know any better. It's too late for us, but . . . let me make things right."

Cordi didn't know what to do. Her friends were literally dying in front of her, and she was a hideous beast now. Was there any way to come back from this? Did she even want to try?

It seemed so much easier to give up. To let the spell claim what it had set out to, to let others clean up the mess.

"You could help your parents," Silly said. "They already lost one daughter. They shouldn't have to lose another."

And those words slammed into Cordi's gut, knocking the breath out of her. Her parents would never know the truth behind Trina's death. And even though they had disowned her months ago, she couldn't bear the thought of them alone, abandoned completely, both daughters gone.

"Okay," Cordi said. "I'll do it."

Cressida held out her hand and led Cordi into the circle. Not letting go, Tessa joined her, looking serenely blank and calm for someone who was about to be sacrificed.

Chapter Thirty-Eight

Cordi stood over Callum's prone body and stared down at his terrified face. His forehead was clammy with beads of sweat. His legs jerked as he tried to move away from her, even though she had no intention to do him harm. The Order would punish him.

The ritual began. Smoke filled the air, mixing with the powders the Order members threw into the ring, until she couldn't see anything but Callum. She was aware of Tessa next to her, but she tried her hardest not to think about her. Her feelings were too raw and unsettled, a wound that she couldn't help picking at. She was outraged at what Tessa had done, but Cordi knew she should be grateful for what Tessa was doing now, and yet she was unable to believe Tessa didn't have an ulterior motive.

The cloud of smoke obscured everything around them. She couldn't hear the chants of the Society members anymore, as if they had been transported somewhere else altogether.

Tessa breathed quickly, her fingers clutching Cordi's claws, not caring that they left scratches in her skin.

Despite herself, Cordi whispered, "It's okay." Even though she had no idea whether it would be.

Callum continued writhing on the floor, whimpering as he turned his face this way and that. Occasionally, he looked at her and wailed and tried to break free, but the chains held.

"Cordelia," he begged. "Please, Cordelia, you must understand. I had to do it. You don't know what I've been through, the sacrifices I had to make. I can't go back. I can't give this up. I've come too far."

"What do you want me to do about it?" she asked genuinely.

His eyes watered and his lower lip trembled.

And then a shadow rose within the smoke and moved around them. At first Cordi thought it was a trick of the light, but the shape solidified. It had no face, nothing to indicate whether it was a person or animal, but Cordi knew it was alive. Felt something throbbing within its depths, like a heartbeat.

Tessa began trembling.

It was the same presence Cordi felt when she sat in the circle and did the spells with the Mais. But this time, the presence seemed much bigger, much more powerful. A gravitational pull drew her toward it. She couldn't stop, even when Tessa tried to tug her back, and then Tessa's hands slipped away.

The presence loomed close, and then it consumed her.

Her world became nothing but heavy darkness as she entered a thick fog. It filled her lungs and eyes. She tried to cough but couldn't breathe. Blink, but she had no eyes. She couldn't feel her monster form or her human one. She simply existed.

Something watched her in the stillness. Something breathed all around her and waited.

"Hello," Cordi said, or tried to say, but she no longer had a voice or mouth or body.

"You have made a sacrifice," the thing said, its voice loud and gravelly, coming from all directions. Cordi realized that this, whatever it was, was Lura. And she was here to make a new pact.

"Yes," she said, though she wasn't sure which sacrifice it referred to—the first one she'd made in exchange for beauty and success, the death of Trina to complete that first spell, or this one, with Callum's punishment and Tessa's atonement.

"You sought to replace your soul with your sister's, Katrina Yin."

"No. I didn't want that. It wasn't my choice."

A quietness.

"I would have died instead," she added. "Once I realized what the original . . . sacrifice entailed. I was willing to pay the price."

The Lura remained quiet. It reminded Cordi of a wild cat, waiting, biding its time, ready to attack at any second.

"But my friends tricked me," she continued, "and then Callum tricked them. He took my sister as a sacrifice to make himself stronger. I don't know how—she was supposed to be sacrificed for *my* pact, only he did something and he took the sacrifice for his own gain instead."

The Lura throbbed and shifted, considering her words. "But you will take his life so that you may have his power."

Cordi wasn't sure how to answer. "If that isn't the only option, then I would rather Callum be otherwise punished for his crimes."

"He has already been punished. He is gone now. His soul is mine."

Cordi sucked in a breath. She knew that was what the Society planned to do, but knowing yet another murder had been committed was a shock. How much death would be enough to pay for their greed?

"Do you accept his power?" the Lura asked. "If you choose to do so, I will make a new pact with you. But you will need to make another sacrifice to complete this arrangement. You will have time, but not long." Cordi thought about Callum's frightened eyes. The terror when he'd begged them not to take away his gifts. She didn't care about power. She'd never cared about beauty much either, though of course she'd enjoyed both when she'd had them. She could have it all again—she was being given a second chance, with Tessa's soul.

But all she'd ever cared about, all she truly wanted, was to be accepted. Before they'd killed her sister, before things had spiraled out of control, her friendship with the Mais had been the best thing that had ever happened to her. It had never been about the job or the fame or riches. It had always been about finally having friends, being loved, being part of a family.

She just wanted to go back to that. Coming home to her friends, having dinner, talking, simply *being* with each other. It had always been enough for her. She just hadn't realized it before it was too late. None of them had.

"I *will* make a new pact," she said. "But I don't want Callum's power. I don't want any gifts."

"Then perhaps you accept your friend's life. Tessa. She will die so you can keep what you've already achieved."

Cordi hesitated, thinking through what that would mean. She wouldn't see her parents again, would never have a chance to ask for their forgiveness. But at least Silly and Audrey would be safe. Even though Cordi didn't know if she could possibly forgive Silly for what she'd done, she couldn't let her suffer. And Audrey had tried to stop them—Cordi had to do what she could to wipe her slate clean.

"I don't want to take Tessa's sacrifice either," she said. "I want to save my friends. Tessa Hong, Silly Trinidad, and Audrey Wo. They made their own pact with lura, but they were tricked, as I was. Is there any way that Callum's death, Trina's, and . . ." She swallowed. "And my own . . . can erase their deals? Turn them back to how they were? Spare their lives?"

The Lura was silent, but a faint light permeated the stillness. "You wish to sacrifice yourself and eschew the gifts presented to you?"

"I have no need for any gifts."

"You would reject powers beyond your wildest dreams?" Images played out in the shadows, of Cordi, beautiful and radiant, famous, successful, everyone loving her, wanting her in their lives, accepting her as she'd always wanted.

It wasn't real, though. It was just an illusion. She could tell because she didn't look like that—it wasn't her, and that wasn't her life.

"All I want," Cordi said, "I already have. The love and acceptance of my friends. And now, I wish for them to be safe. They've learned their lesson, we all have. Please give them a chance to live their lives."

The Lura seemed to breathe, the stillness throbbing. And then it sighed. "You have made the ultimate sacrifice. You've willingly offered your soul for the sake of your loved ones. And for that, I will make a new deal with you."

"My life for theirs," Cordi whispered.

"No." Someone else's voice broke through, and a new presence emerged in the fog. "No, don't do it, Cordi." It sounded like Tessa.

"A sacrifice must be made," the Lura hissed.

"And I'll make it." Tessa—where was she? Cordi wanted to shove her out of the circle. This was Cordi's spell, *her* new pact. Why did Tessa have to have everything, even now?

"*I* will," Cordi said. "Take me."

The Lura inhaled deeply. And then it collapsed, the stillness imploded, and Cordi felt no more.

Chapter
Thirty-Nine

The afterlife was terribly painful and felt very much like the world's worst hangover. Her body ached. Her head spun, her mouth was all dry, and when she opened her eyes, everything looked blurry. And Tessa, Silly, and Audrey all stood to the side, watching her. It took her a moment to realize she was lying in bed, in the bedroom in Cressida's house.

Cordi groaned. "Are we dead?" she asked. But if she was dead, why were the Mais with her? "What happened? I thought I made a deal to save you girls."

It took them all a moment to react.

Tessa said, "We could hear you—like you were crying, saying you wanted to die. I couldn't take it."

"So you interrupted the spell?"

"I wanted to save you."

"I was trying to save *you*," Cordi said.

Tessa burst into tears. "Why, Cordi? We deserved what was coming to us. We did a terrible thing."

Cordi didn't know how to respond. As her vision began to clear, she finally took in the sight of them. They all looked . . . normal. As in, themselves. How they'd looked when they first met, before the spells. Audrey smiled, a strange sight in itself, and Silly looked at Cordi through clear, bright eyes. The only one who wasn't back to normal was Tessa. Her hair was gone, and her glow and natural charm were diminished, dulled.

And Cordi . . . She looked at her hands. Her nails were back, peach-colored, and her fingers were human.

"We're ourselves again," she said. It was exactly what she had wanted. For all the trouble to go away. For their mistakes to be reversed.

Silly was the only one who had a clear understanding of what had happened, apparently having interrogated one of the Society members at length about the technicalities of the magic. "The only way to break a spell is the ultimate self-sacrifice, which you can only do if you don't know that's how you break a spell. So no one who is a lurast, by choice anyway, would ever be able to break a spell. And that's why they couldn't tell one of us to do it, because then it wouldn't be a self-sacrifice, by definition. So by sacrificing yourself, you saved all of us. You made a new pact with the Lura by giving up your own soul to save ours. The Lura would have accepted your death as payment. But then . . ." Silly glanced at Tessa.

"I couldn't let you die," Tessa said.

"I was willing to," Cordi said. She couldn't believe that Tessa, who had always cherished her looks, had given up the one thing she most valued.

Tessa didn't meet her eyes. "I didn't want you to do it alone." And though her words were earnest, irritation flared in Cordi's chest, at Tessa's self-centeredness. Even now, Tessa couldn't resist stealing whatever small amount of attention she could. "I would have followed you. If you'd died. I . . . would have too." She finally looked at Cordi, but Cordi wasn't going to fall for that. She'd let Tessa talk her into so many wrong choices—she wasn't going to make the mistake of forgiving her now.

"That must be why Tessa's hair is . . ." Silly let her voice drift away, and then added quietly, "I can't believe you were willing to die for us."

"Yeah, even after what they did," Audrey said.

Trina's death hung in the air, like the lingering smell of blood.

"We thought we were doing it for you," Silly said.

"I didn't ask you to. I begged you not to." Cordi stared up at the ceiling. "Now she's gone. Forever. And it was all for nothing." She closed her eyes.

"I'm so sorry, Cordi," Tessa said. "I wish there was something we could do. Please. Just tell us what to do. Anything. We'll . . . we'll buy your entire line. It's launching soon. You still have that. You'll still have your dream."

Cordi clenched her fists. "Just . . . go. Please."

At first, they didn't listen. But then the sounds of their footsteps moved away, followed by the closing of a door. Cordi was finally alone.

When Cordi felt well enough to emerge from the room, the Order members had left. No one mentioned Callum or what they had done with his body, for which Cordi was grateful.

Tessa and Silly had gone home as well. Only Audrey stayed behind, waiting on the white leather sofa in the living room when Cordi came downstairs.

"I just wanted to make sure you were okay," Audrey said.

Cordi nodded. "Thank you, Audrey. You tried to talk us out of it. Every time. We should have listened."

"It's all right." Audrey folded her arms and looked down. "It's hard to want something and never be able to have it, no matter how hard you work, especially when you have to watch others who don't deserve it get exactly what they want. So of course lura would have been a tempting shortcut."

"I don't think I ever want to hear that word ever again."

Audrey made a sound of amusement. "What are you going to do now?"

"I'm not going back," Cordi said. She couldn't fathom the idea of returning to their apartment, where Trina had been killed and where she would be confronted with the loss of their friendships and the lives they could have had if they hadn't been so greedy and foolish and selfish.

"Maybe . . ." Audrey said, then stopped.

"What?"

"We could . . . look for a pad . . . together." Audrey's knuckles were white, her hands gripping her own elbows. "You don't have to be alone."

Cordi considered it. Audrey wasn't Tessa. She didn't greet Cordi with a drink after a long day of work, didn't invite her out shopping, didn't invite her out at all. But she hadn't killed Trina, and she had tried to stop Cordi from making mistakes, and in the end, she had let Cordi decide for herself, and even now, she didn't judge her for it.

"That would be nice," Cordi said, and Audrey smiled.

After Audrey went home, Cordi told Cressida their plans. She didn't want to impose any more on the Thompsons.

"You're welcome to stay as long as you like," Cressida said generously.

"I promise I'll leave as soon as we find a new place to stay," Cordi said, sitting at the foot of her bed while Cressida stayed by the door.

"Nonsense." She paused on her way out. "I think I know someone who might have a spare—"

"Thank you," Cordi interrupted her. "But I can manage on my own." She smiled to show that she was grateful. It would have been easy to let Cressida help, to use her influence and connections to find Cordi an affordable place. But she was done with favors and unfair advantages.

"By the way," Cressida added. "You should probably give Gabe a call. He was very worried about you, you know."

Cordi nodded but couldn't bring herself to do so. Not yet. She doubted that Gabe would even want to speak to her again after the last time they saw each other. She wasn't even sure if she still had her job at Lacy's after she'd missed the last two days of work without calling in, and she couldn't stomach doing so now.

She spent most of the week recovering, her strength returning more with each day. She tried to stay in her bedroom, unwilling to be a burden to Cressida's family, who in turn did their best to respect her privacy. Every day, despite Cordi's protests, Cressida had a breakfast tray sent up, and Cordi would peruse the daily paper for apartments, circling each one that she could afford, though with what salary, she didn't know. On Friday, Cordi borrowed a simple dress from Cressida that fit too snugly and visited a few rentals. She was pretty sure the Mais would all be gone in the afternoon, so she decided to stop by their apartment to pick up some of her clothes. She walked up the stairs with trepidation, filled with memories of coming home after a long day of work, eager to see her friends. The apartment felt both familiar and foreign, and she resisted the urge to knock like a visitor as she inserted her key into the knob.

The apartment was, thankfully, empty, as she'd hoped.

The girls had cleaned—the furniture was back in place, the throw pillows all fluffed, and the floor was covered with a new rug. The image of Trina's body flashed in Cordi's mind, and she clenched her eyes shut to ward it off.

She climbed up to her loft and grabbed a bag to stuff as many things as she could inside, once again flooded with sadness that it wasn't the first time she'd made a hasty exit to start a different life.

The bag was full and she'd packed only half of her wardrobe—she'd made so many more outfits since she'd moved here. As much as she dreaded it, she knew she'd have to return to pick up the rest of her things.

Cordi should have left after that, but for some reason, when she got back downstairs, she stood behind the couch, surveying the area. Tears filled her eyes as she realized things would never be the same. She would never find a place like this, beautiful and cozy and filled with friends she had longed for all her life, though she understand it had been a deception, just like all the other things the Lura had promised.

Her gaze fell on the notepad by the phone, and she had to wipe her eyes to make sure she wasn't seeing things. Her name was scribbled on a notepad in Tessa's handwriting, with Gabriel Sinclair's phone number. Other than the time he had asked her to come in to fix the skirt, Mr.

Sinclair had never phoned the apartment. This call must have been recent.

Cordi dreaded calling him back, pretty sure that he would be angry at her disappearance so close to the launch of their line. Most likely, he had tried to reach her only to fire her, or perhaps scold her. But she didn't want to leave him wondering what had happened. And if she was being completely honest, she wanted to hear his voice, hoped that perhaps he wouldn't be angry. She dialed his number, breathing fast. No one answered and the machine clicked on.

"Hi," she said. "Mr. S—Gabriel—Gabe. It's me. Um, Cordi. I—" She squeezed her eyes shut. "If you need to call me back, I'm actually staying at Cressida's house. But I . . ." She realized she didn't know Cressida's number, so instead of making a further fool of herself, she slammed the phone down.

As soon as she did, it rang, making her jump. Her hand was still on the receiver, so she picked up.

"Hello? The Misses . . . Mai residence." She stumbled over their usual greeting.

"Li-Ah?" a familiar voice asked. "Is this Li-Ah? It's your mother. I found your phone number in Trina's room."

Cordi clutched the phone. "Mother?"

She heard a sharp intake of breath. "Come home, Li-Ah. We have to talk."

Come home. Cordi never thought she'd hear those words. She had longed for them, daydreamed about them from the moment she had been forced out of her house.

Her parents were waiting for her in the kitchen when she let herself in through the back entrance. At first, she stood awkwardly, letting them study her. She studied them in return. They looked like they'd aged five years in the last months. Hair grayer, wrinkles deeper, backs more stooped.

No one said anything. She closed the door behind her quietly, then stood in the middle of the kitchen, hands folded in front of her like a little girl caught in the act of sneaking back in. Her parents remained somber at the table.

"Hi," Cordi said finally, because she couldn't stand the silence any longer.

"Your sister is gone," Mother said in Vietnamese. She had already told Cordi the news—what she thought was news to Cordi anyway—over the phone, but she seemed to need to say it again, as if she still didn't believe it. "She was . . . killed. She was working late at the shop. Told me she wanted to get as much work done as possible before we opened. They must have wanted to rob us, whoever killed her. They slit her throat. I got there too late. If I had gotten there sooner—" Mother's lower lip quivered.

"It wasn't your fault," Cordi said, sitting down at the table and taking her hand. "It wasn't." She was two breaths away from admitting the truth—that it was *her* fault, hers and her friends'. For their greed, for their selfishness, they had taken an innocent woman's life.

"Yes," Mother said. "It was. All my fault. I made her work so hard. She wouldn't have been there if I hadn't lectured her about making money. She would have been at home. Safe. I was too hard on her." Then Mother looked up, straight at Cordi. "On both of you."

Cordi wasn't sure what she meant. Mother and Father had never even come close to apologizing for anything, so she didn't think that was where this was going.

But Mother grasped her hands in turn. "Come home, Li-Ah," she said.

Cordi looked at her mother's fingers, the skin papery, riddled with spots, not sure she'd heard right.

"We want you to come home," Father said, his voice hoarse.

"We . . . we are sorry," Mother added. This time, she spoke in English, and Cordi realized that there was no word for *sorry* in their language. She racked her brain for it—maybe she was just rusty, she hadn't spoken Vietnamese much since she'd moved out—but she simply didn't know. The only thing that came close was "xin lỗi," meaning, "give me the blame." *Forgive me.* Not *I'm sorry.* The phrase was simply unfair—it put pressure on the victim to forgive instead of on the wrongdoer to admit that they were wrong.

Maybe that was why her parents had never said it. It just wasn't in their vocabulary. And it felt weird to hear them say it now.

"The funeral was yesterday," Mother continued, switching back to their native tongue as if she hadn't uttered the first apology Cordi had ever heard from them in her life. "And you weren't there . . . it was so wrong. So . . . empty without you." She gripped Cordi's hands tighter. "Please, Li-Ah. Come back. We are family. We should stay together."

Then they did something she never would have expected. They got up and pulled her into a hug.

Cordi sat stiffly as both Mother and Father bent down and wrapped their arms around her. She couldn't remember the last time they'd hugged her. It would have been when she was a child. Nothing fit right, all joints and elbows, chins bumping against her head.

"We're so sorry, Li-Ah," Mother said again.

Father patted Cordi's shoulder to indicate that he agreed. He had never been one for many words, letting Mother speak for both of them.

"The house . . . it's not the same without you," he said.

Cordi was so surprised to see tears on his cheeks—on Mother's too. Everything she resented them for rose to the surface in a boiling fury, threatening to burn through her throat.

"You never loved me," she said, pulling back.

Their faces were etched with pain.

"Of course we love you," Mother said. "How can we not? You are our flesh and blood. I carried you here." She touched her belly. "And here." She placed a hand over her heart. "Always here."

Tears welled in Cordi's eyes. "You never showed it."

"In our country," Father said, "it is not good to show."

"But this isn't your country," Cordi snapped. "You moved here. You chose this place. You chose this life. And you made Trina and me live it, and then you blamed us for everything that made you unhappy."

Mother buried her face in her hands. "We know. We know." She touched Cordi's hands pleadingly. "We have made so many mistakes. But never say that we didn't love you. Maybe . . . we did not know how to love you the way that you needed to be loved. We could only love you the way we have always been taught. By teaching you hard work, by showing you how to survive in a cruel world, by giving you the skills that we learned."

Cordi's anger flashed. Skills like toiling for hours, bent over a sewing machine until her back ached? Working and working and working with nothing to show for it? Heat flared in her chest, burned its way up her throat.

But just when it reached new heights, when the flame touched dangerous levels, she saw their pain written in the deep lines on their faces. And she knew that Mother spoke the truth. She had loved her daughters. And so had Father, in the only way they knew how.

She tried to cling to her anger, to the hot fury, but like water splashed onto coals, it hissed and smoked and dissipated. Her hurt became a numb throbbing, a fatigued muscle. Overworked. Perhaps it was time to put it to rest.

Because at the end of the day, she knew that they loved her. That they were only trying their best. And in her own way, Trina had tried her best too.

"It's okay," she said. And it really was. At least for now. Maybe tomorrow she would think about everything they had or hadn't done for her, and the resentment would return. And the next day, she might be angrier than ever. And the following day, she would question every decision they'd ever made. But for now, she forgave them. For now, she could accept that they thought they were doing what was best. "I understand." She would try anyway.

"We miss you," Mother said, words Cordi never thought she would hear. "Come home, hah? You have room to yourself now."

Cordi glanced at the door to her bedroom. It was so tempting, now that she knew she couldn't stay with the Mais. The idea of returning somewhere safe and familiar was so comforting. It had been the only place she'd known up until recently.

But she hadn't missed it. She'd missed her family, but she didn't miss living with them, and while she was glad her parents wanted her back, she was ready to be on her own. She was ready to move on to the next part of her life. She thought briefly of Gabe Sinclair with a pang in her heart because she wasn't sure if that included him. She wasn't sure if he'd speak to her again—but she dearly hoped that he would.

"I lived with these girls," she said. "They were like sisters to me." She wished she could take the words back, because in the end, they hadn't been like sisters, except for Audrey.

Mother understood what she was really saying. Her face remained blank, the permanent frown a discouraging reminder that Cordi would always disappoint. But if that was true, if nothing she did was ever good enough, then Cordi would at least do what made herself happy.

"I'll come home to visit as much as I can," she said. "If you want me to."

"Yes," Mother said quickly, taking her hand. "Yes."

"The shop," Father said.

Of course. Now that Trina was gone, they needed her to work at the shop. Cordi thought about the evenings and weekends spent behind the counter. She hadn't hated the work, but the idea of returning there, toiling away at the machines for what little allowance her parents gave her, brought her no joy.

Then again, she wasn't sure if she had any other options. She didn't know if she still had a job at Lacy's.

"It's yours," Father said.

"What?" Cordi asked, not sure she'd heard him right.

"We give to you," Mother said, patting Cordi's hand. "We retire. You have it."

"How?"

"We have some money saved," Father said. "Not a lot. But enough."

"I can take care of you," Cordi said without thinking. It wasn't even a question—they were her parents.

"Just for a little bit," Father said, clearly pained at having to admit they needed help. "But first, you take care of yourself."

"Do what you planned," Mother said. "Sell dresses. Design new things. It was a good idea. We just didn't know. We were scared. We wanted to hang on to the past, keep you our little girl, and it was frightening to see you had plans for the future that didn't include us."

"But it did," she said. "I wanted you to help me."

Mother patted her hands. "I know. I was wrong. You had a good idea. You can save the shop, I see that now."

Cordi's ears filled with ringing. They were admitting she was right. The argument that had started all this, that had escalated to an explosion disrupting all their lives—she had won in the end.

"Or sell it," Father said. "Buy something better. Up to you."

They both looked at her and did the third surprising thing. Smiled.

Cordi almost burst into tears. "Let's talk about that later," she said, unable to wrap her mind around everything that was happening. "But . . . I'm hungry. Can we . . . can we eat?"

Chapter Forty

She went back to Cressida's, feeling like she might burst, eager to share her good news, but when she got to the door, her excitement fizzled. She wasn't really friends with Cressida or her family, so it didn't feel right to rush in and tell them everything, not the way she would have done several weeks ago with the Mais.

She was surprised to see Sam Thompson in the living room as she let herself in. For all she knew, he lived there, but she hadn't seen him during her entire stay.

"Sam," she said.

He sat on the tufted leather sofa, reading a newspaper with one foot propped on his other knee, and he looked up at her with a cheerful yet confused expression. It took him a moment to recognize her. "Cordi," he said. He set his paper down. "How are you? You look . . . rested."

She smiled, clasping her hands in front of herself awkwardly. "I'm okay. I think. The good news is, I'll be out of your way soon. Not you, specifically. Cressida, your family—I'll be leaving."

She hadn't liked any of the apartments she'd gone to look at in the past week, and she'd decided to stay with her parents while she continued her search. She wouldn't stay with them long—she simply couldn't. But it would make them happy, and it knocked one problem off her list, for now.

"So soon?" He got up and walked closer to her, putting his hands casually in his pockets.

Cordi nodded, tucking a strand of hair behind her ear nervously.

"So this is the real you, huh?" he said.

The living room was decorated with gilt-framed mirrors, and Cordi caught a glimpse of her reflection. Her features had returned to normal, and she was glad to see her tan skin and familiar face again.

"This is me," Cordi said. She smiled at him.

He grinned, his boyish face endearingly sweet. She imagined that if she had a little brother, he'd be like Sam.

The phone rang, sitting on a mahogany accent table by the sofa. Sam frowned at it. "That must be Sinclair again. He's been calling non-stop for the last hour."

"Gabe?" Cordi asked.

"You better pick up," Sam said. "I've never heard him so distraught. I think he likes you."

Cordi didn't know how to respond, and the phone continued ringing. Sam finally reached over to pick it up.

"Thompson residence," he said. He listened a moment and then held the receiver out to her. "I knew it."

Cordi held the phone against her chest as she tried to figure out what to do or say. Sam winked at her, dipped his head, and left her alone.

"Miss Yin?" She heard Gabriel Sinclair's voice through the phone when she finally brought it to her ear.

All sorts of thoughts went through her mind in a matter of seconds. Was he angry? He'd regressed to calling her Miss Yin again—why? Was she fired? Had he called to lecture her?

"Mr. Sinclair," she croaked.

A brief silence. "It's good to finally speak with you," he said, though from the way he said it, it didn't sound like he thought anything was good about it. She couldn't read much in his tone, actually, and she started sweating, picturing his unhappy, angry face.

"Yes, I'm sorry, I've been . . . missing. I'm . . . there was . . ."

He waited for her to finish, but when it was clear she had no idea how to explain the past week, he let her off the hook. "I heard about your sister." His voice was soft now, and full of sympathy.

"Yes," Cordi said, although the last thing she wanted was to use Trina's death as an excuse to avoid her problems. "But it's not just that. It's more complicated."

A pause. Then: "Would you mind—I would love—that is . . . do you have time? To meet? In person? To discuss it?"

"I—yes." And it was as if his nervousness rubbed off on her because she found herself stumbling over her words as well. "Of course. If that—if *you* have time."

"I do," he said quickly.

"Me too."

Another moment of awkwardness.

"Right now?" he added.

"S-sure!"

"Great."

"Where?" Cordi asked.

"Would it be weird . . . if we went to that pizza place again?"

"Not weird at all."

"They're having their special, you see," he said.

"The green pepper."

"Yes," he said, sounding pleasantly surprised. "You remember."

Cordi grinned. A bit of apprehension lingered in her belly at the thought of having to answer for her disappearance, and the fact that she looked entirely different from when he'd last seen her. But the sound of his voice was soothing. Whatever it was he wanted to talk about couldn't be so bad, could it? Not if he wanted to discuss it over pizza.

"I'll see you soon," she said, and hung up first in her excitement. "Oh, oops." She picked up the phone again, but there was only a dial tone. Still, she smiled as she hurried up the stairs to change.

Gabriel Sinclair was sitting by the window at the same table they'd eaten at last time. She almost didn't recognize him without his suit. He wore a cerulean-blue sweater that hugged the curves of his shoulders and biceps, his casual khaki slacks giving him the air of someone more relaxed than she knew him to be.

Cordi had chosen a simple sleeveless dress that could have passed as either professional or casual. She hadn't been sure if this was supposed to be a business meeting and spent far too much time debating between the sensible but cute Kedettes or the uncomfortable but professional Mary Jane heels. She was glad she'd gone for the flats.

Gabriel stood up, sat down, then stood again as she approached. His fingers fidgeted awkwardly at his stomach, as if buttoning a suit jacket, until he remembered he wasn't wearing one.

"Miss Yin—Cordelia—I . . . hi." He studied her face closely.

"Hi."

"You look . . ."

"Different, I know," she said. Her heart pounded as she waited for his reaction. Her skin had returned to its darker complexion, she was shorter, and he had to bend his neck to meet her eyes. There was no reasonable way to explain any of it, so she didn't bother trying.

"I was about to say 'wonderful,'" he said.

Cordi wasn't sure how to react. *Did he really mean it?* She sat across from him because she had no idea what else to do. He sat too. They stared at each other.

"I'm sorry about the past week," she said.

"I've missed you," he blurted at the same time. And then put his forehead in his hands, visibly distraught.

Cordi tried really hard not to laugh. By all accounts, she should have been just as distraught as he was. She was the one who had missed a whole week of work without saying a word. But after what she'd gone through, nights as a literal monster, losing her sister, being accepted by her parents again, she just felt happy to be sitting in a cheerful restaurant across the table from a man with whom, she realized, she might be falling in love.

"I've missed you too," she said quietly.

He finally looked back up, putting his hands in his lap. Emotions warred for dominance on his face—surprise and delight and then back to his usual stoicism. "How are you?" he asked.

She smiled. "All things considered, I'm doing quite well."

"Good." He was tense, his back straight, shoulders taut.

"How are you?" she asked.

He sighed. "The truth is, this week has been awful."

"Has it? Was it because of me? How is the launch going? Did the skirt pass the inspection? I'm so sorry, I should have called. I abandoned you to deal with everything on your own."

"No. I mean, yes. The skirt is fine. The launch is going smoothly—no other hiccups. I was worried about you. But mostly, I thought . . ." He wrung his hands on the table. "When we saw each other last, I . . . I completely overstepped, and I thought perhaps that was why you didn't come back. I—it was a mistake—well, not a mistake, but I shouldn't have—I—"

She placed a hand over his to stop his nervous fidgeting. "You didn't overstep."

He met her eyes. "I didn't?"

"No. In fact, I wish you would have . . . stepped further."

He considered what she said. A hint of a smile twitched at the corner of his lips.

Their food arrived then, putting a pause to the conversation. But neither of them moved when the server left.

"Aren't you going to eat?" she asked. "It's your favorite."

"I just . . . I'm . . ." He smiled fully at her. "What happened?"

She had a sense that he already knew. Of course he did. He was the one who'd asked Cressida to intervene. "I have so much to tell you," she said. And then, despite every instinct in her body warning her against it, she did. Once she began, she couldn't stop herself. She told him everything that had happened in the past few months, starting from when she'd moved in with the Mais to meeting Callum to discovering that Cressida and everyone in the Order had been involved.

"I know it sounds far-fetched," she said. "All this business with the lura. I thought it wasn't real, but it turns out it is, and it's everywhere and—"

He reached over the pizza and touched her hand. "I believe you. Cressida is my cousin, after all."

"But you're not a lurast," she said. Was he involved somehow? Doubt and apprehension coursed through her veins. If he turned out to be part of the Order, she didn't know what she would do, whether she would walk away or stay.

"No," he said. "It was the reason Cressida's mother and mine fell out, you see. When my mother discovered that her family were lurasts, that everything they'd achieved was because of their willingness to sacrifice someone else in their stead, she wanted nothing to do with it. So the rest of her family banished her. Like an excommunication. When I reconnected with Cressida, my mom was unhappy but said it wasn't her place to dictate whether I got to see my family or not. But she made me promise to never dabble in lura. And I haven't, for her sake. And after seeing the effects it has on certain people, I never would, even if I hadn't promised her."

"I wish I had known," Cordi said, looking at her hands. She still had moments of panic when she thought they were bruised and blackened, only to breathe a deep sigh of relief to find that there was nothing wrong with them. "I would have never agreed to it."

"Don't be too hard on yourself. You were tricked. You were a victim. And so were your friends."

She tried not to scoff. "They were willing to murder to keep what lura gave them."

"But they didn't," he pointed out.

"Except Trina."

He gripped her hand tighter. "I'm sorry, Cordi," he said.

Something in her chest, which had remained numb and cold, started to melt. All day, a tension had kept her bones and muscles bound together like a puppet strung with intricate threads that threatened to snap. Now, the threads loosened enough for her to breathe easier.

"It was all a mistake," Cordi whispered. "For all of us, I mean. We all made the decision together." She had been there when Callum cast the first spell. She had agreed to it, and she had wanted it so much, had given it power. And every spell after that, she had kept sacrificing more and more to keep what she'd been given, to ask for more. She wasn't innocent. None of them were.

"But it's over now," Gabe said. "And you can move on."

She smiled. And finally, the grip that had been tightening around her heart for days released, and she took in a deep breath.

Their fingers still laced together, and Cordi looked down at their hands.

"My parents are retiring and giving me their shop," she blurted out.

He smoothed his thumb back and forth over her palm, sending ticklish tingles over her skin. "Does that mean we won't work together anymore?"

She laughed in disbelief. "You mean I'm not fired?"

"Of course not. You're the best designer we've ever had. Your name is all over the launch—it wouldn't be the same without you. We'd have to change everything, and that would put us behind production for months. And you had a perfectly good reason for missing work."

She sat up straighter, a lightness filling her body for the first time in a long time. "That's great news. Because I have so many ideas. I mean, for the shop, for the designs, for everything."

Gabriel grinned, brightening his entire face and sending an electric thrill through her body. "I can't wait to hear them."

Later that month, Cordi took the Red Car to the garment district on Olympic Boulevard, excited to see the familiar canopy of tents covering the alley between the wholesale shops. The rattle of the metal gate brought back memories as Ms. Ran opened her shop. When she saw Cordi, the older woman's face showed her surprise.

"What took you so long?" she nearly shrieked. Several heads turned their way.

Cordi breathed in the scent of unwashed fabric. "Hi, Ms. Ran." She hesitated before leaning in to give her a hug, not realizing how much she'd missed her. Ms. Ran held her in a surprisingly strong grip, as if she too couldn't believe how much she had missed Cordi.

"When you say you quit, I say okay, but I didn't say stay away forever." Ms. Ran held Cordi's shoulders, studying her face. "Hmm. You should start using night cream. I have one you should try. Come back and I'll give you next time."

Cordi tried not to laugh. "How have you been?"

Ms. Ran shrugged and went to the counter. "The same. What? You think the place fall apart without you?"

"Is business all right?"

"It's the same. Everything same."

"And you're happy?"

Ms. Ran narrowed her eyes. "Why?" she asked slowly.

"It's just . . ." Cordi leaned closer. "My parents are giving me their alterations shop, but I'm going to make some changes, and I'm going to need lots of fabric."

"So you buy wholesale?" Ms. Ran asked, flipping open a ledger. "What type you need?"

"I was thinking of an arrangement that's a little different."

"Like what?"

"Well, more like business partners."

Ms. Ran looked Cordi up and down. For a moment, Cordi wondered if she'd been foolish to come. But then Ms. Ran placed her pencil between the pages of her ledger. "Tell me more."

Cordi taped up the final box with all her things and stacked it on top of the ones Audrey had already placed by the door. Gabe was coming over to help them move to their new place in Chinatown. The apartment was close enough to easily visit her parents and was near the shop, which she now owned and was in the middle of renovating.

Tessa stood in the center of the living room. An air of caution lingered in the apartment like thick fog. Audrey went in and out, practically skipping, carrying boxes to the car she'd bought with the money she'd saved. If she was sad about moving out, she didn't show it, even whistling to herself as she took a box from Cordi.

Cordi had tried to find a time when Tessa and Silly wouldn't be home, but it had been no use. They'd both been fired from their jobs, so they were always around. The only good thing about their predicament was that Mikhail felt so sorry for them that he had lowered the rent with the promise that they would get jobs soon. He had been shockingly sad to hear Cordi and Audrey would be moving out.

"But loft is so charming," he'd said, taking the envelope full of cash. Cordi had paid for the next month even though she didn't have to, if only because she felt guilty for leaving on such short notice. "You sure?"

She smiled. "I'm grateful you let me stay here even though you didn't want to at first."

"Well, you were very convincing," he muttered.

"I wasn't, actually. It was Callum." It occurred to her that Callum must have had some hold on Mikhail, must have tricked him into renting to girls like the Mais so he could prey on their dreams. She wanted to apologize to the landlord. He had been a victim in Callum's schemes as well.

But Mikhail was distracted by Tessa when she came up behind Cordi. He didn't seem to care that Tessa looked quite different, especially today, when she'd had no reason to get dressed or make herself pretty, and she walked around the apartment in a ratty bathrobe, her face unwashed and tired. Cordi left the two of them alone and went to pack the rest of her things.

Now Tessa stood by the door, her fingers twisting together. "Cordi . . ." she started, her tone strained and apologetic, full of unsaid things.

Audrey pulled out a long strip of packing tape, the loud rip of the adhesive painfully sharp. She slapped it onto a box as if purposefully filling the silence.

Cordi didn't say anything. How did you say goodbye to the girl you once considered your best friend but who also murdered your sister? Ever since the day they'd met, Cordi had thought Tessa was the friend she'd always wanted, but after what happened, Cordi never wanted to see her again.

"I'm going to miss you, Cordi," Tessa said. "And I'm sorry again . . . for . . . you know."

Cordi nodded. "Well, I mean . . . you should be."

Tessa wiped her eyes. She was about to say something, but a knock at the door interrupted them. "I guess this is it," she said instead with a hiccup.

Cordi opened the door. Gabe stood in the hallway, his face brightening when he saw her.

"Are you ready?" he asked.

"Hi, yes," she said, letting him in.

The girls greeted him politely, and then after an awkward pause, they grabbed boxes of Cordi's things to carry outside to a truck he'd borrowed from a friend. Cordi didn't have much—other than her clothes, of course—and then they stood on the sidewalk, not meeting each other's eyes.

Audrey raised her hand in farewell to Tessa and Silly, then got into her new car, a maroon compact with plenty of trunk space for her large art pieces, the back now filled with boxes. As her engine hummed to life, Cordi turned toward Gabe's truck.

Tessa watched Gabe get in the driver's seat and turn on the engine. She peered through the passenger window. "You better take care of her, Sinclair."

"I'm pretty sure she can take care of herself," he shot back.

Tessa straightened. Then she smiled sadly at Cordi. "You're really sure about this?"

Cordi only stared back at her.

Tessa wrung her fingers together. "This isn't goodbye, you know."

"Tess," Cordi said with exasperation.

"Friendships like ours don't come around often," Tessa said. "You are my one and only. My soulmate."

Cordi's eyes filled with tears. "Tessa," she choked. "I hate you." But even as she said the words, she knew they weren't completely true. Memories of their time together flitted through her mind—their first night out, when Tessa had worn the blue gown; Tessa riding the streetcar with Cordi on her first day at her new job. If only Tessa were someone different, though the thought made her feel both hopeful and forlorn. There would never be another Tessa.

Maybe one day . . . that would be okay.

Tessa smiled tightly. "Okay, well." She hugged Cordi, once again so briefly that Cordi didn't have time to react. "I still love you, I'm sorry, goodbye." She dabbed at her eyes as she jogged up the steps to stand next to Silly. The two clung to each other. The sight of them together like that no longer made Cordi feel anything. Why had she ever cared so much?

Cordi gave the Mais one last wave and was annoyed at herself for it, having made up her mind to never forgive them, but she couldn't stop herself. Then she got in the truck with Gabe. As he pulled away from the curb, she resisted the urge to turn around and look at the girls, to see Tessa's face one last time.

Gabe reached over and took her hand. She inhaled the scent of his cologne.

"Everything all right?" he asked.

"Yeah," she said, "or at least, everything will be." She curled her fingers over his, admiring the way they were both calloused and tanned. Working hands. Unremarkable in any way.

Acknowledgments

My greatest heartfelt thanks to my unicorn-witch-agent Mary C. Moore for always being so supportive and unflappable, even when I surprise you with a manuscript-size mess of an idea out of the blue that has nothing to do with anything we've ever talked about. This book wouldn't be what it is without you, or half as magical. Thank you for not letting me get away with anything.

Thank you so much to Adrienne Procaccini for believing in me and this story and introducing me to the Witches of Eastwick, and huge thanks to Jodi Warshaw for your craftsmanship and edits and kind words and making this book infinitely better. Thank you as well to all the staff at 47North for making my dreams into reality.

I'm incredibly grateful to my beta readers: Kylie Lee Baker, for letting me text you anxiety-induced messages at all hours of the day and for introducing me to the Forest app; Yume Kitasei, who tried really hard to convince me not to [redacted]; and Amber Reed, for inspiring that description of the coffee percolator. Thanks also to Waka T. Brown for the tips on historical research and general commiserating over writing woes.

To Cat-Anh and Vy Hoang for sticking with me even when I write stories about mean older sisters—I promise none of them are based on you. To my parents for never letting me forget how to speak Vietnamese, and especially to my mom, Tan Nguyen, for teaching me how to sew pockets into everything—I miss you so much. Con viết một cuốn sách nữa!

Thanks to my book friends for being the sounding board to my ideas: Susie Tae and your expert knowledge on the Los Angeles Red Car, Asia Evans for the mochi egg tart, Adrian Garza for questioning everything we read, Taona Haderlein for the companionable misery of developing carpal tunnel syndrome, Lauren for the sticker tips, and Valerie for being endearingly enthusiastic about our never-ending TBR list.

This story owes a lot of its magic to the librarians and staff at Huntington Beach Public Library, who continue to feed me books inside and out of my comfort zone. Thank you to Jessica Framson for the incredible support and leadership, April Lammers for recommending traumatizing horror novels so that I have to keep writing stories to help me heal, and Amy Crepeau for meeting my demand for fake Devonshire cream (and scones!). Thanks also to Laura Jenkins for our Wednesday night therapy sessions, Steven Park for the massive tomes of Asian mythology, Marissa Chamberlain for being our resident historian, Nick Auricchio for showing me how to find myself on the Authorities, and to everyone else who makes this world a better-read place.

Thank you to all the book clubs I've had the fortune to run and to all the members whose discussions remind me why I continue doing what I do—Alyse Hendrick, Sharolyn and Jennifer Pendleton, Diane Pavesic, Maggie Ratanapratum, Melanie Bergeland, Laura Steingard, Melissa Koller Nielsen, Kitty Rozenstraten, Claudia Bennett, Naomi Abeywickrama, Marie Murphy, Gloria, and Marcela Curtiss. Thanks a ton to the young readers of the Wise Owl Tween Book Club, whose silliness, smarts, and curiosity continue to foster my imagination in amazing ways. I look forward to our walks and talks and shenanigans every month.

A super-huge thank-you to Leticia Aceves for watching my baby monster so I can write and do all the things—none of this would be possible without you. And last, the biggest, hugest, heart-warmest thanks to my husband for helping me build such a creative life and encouraging me in all my endeavors. As usual, words will not be enough, so I offer you the devil horns emoji, kissy-winky face, jazz hands, cartwheel, cartwheel, cartwheel, brain exploding, heart, heart, heart.

About the Author

Photo © 2022 Francisco J. Zuñiga

Van Hoang's first name is pronounced like the "van" in "minivan." Her last name is pronounced "hah-wawng." Van earned her bachelor's in English at the University of New Mexico and her master's in library information science at San José State University. She was born in Vietnam; grew up in Orange County, California; and now resides in Los Angeles with her husband, kid, and two dogs. For more information, visit www.authorvanhoang.com.